NATIONAL ENDEAVOUR

By

Chris French

MAPLE
PUBLISHERS

NATIONAL ENDEAVOUR

Author: Chris French

Copyright © 2025 Chris French

The right of Chris French to be identified as author of this work has been asserted by the author in accordance with section 77 and 78 of the Copyright, Designs and Patents Act 1988.

ISBN 978-1-83538-601-9 (Paperback)
      978-1-83538-603-3 (E-Book)

Book Layout and Cover Design by:
    Maple Publishers
    www.maplepublishers.com

Published by:
    Maple Publishers
    Fairbourne Drive, Atterbury,
    Milton Keynes,
    MK10 9RG, UK
    www.maplepublishers.com

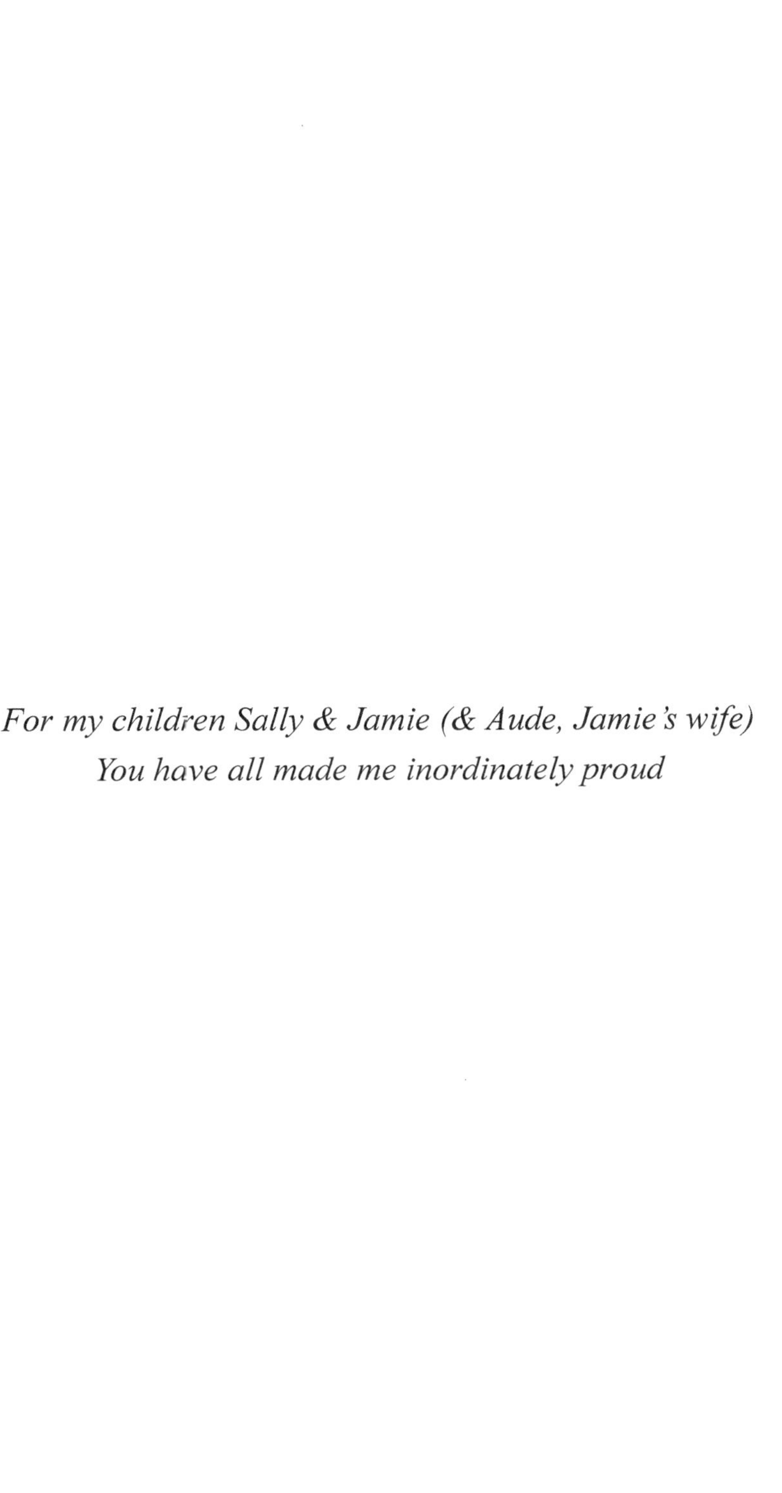

For my children Sally & Jamie (& Aude, Jamie's wife)
You have all made me inordinately proud

Contents

Preface

This is a novel written from a great frustration that UK politics has become all talk and little action. Everything that goes wrong at a policy level in the country is a failure of its management, which is the ruling party, nationally or locally. There is no difference between the political parties, they are all as inept as each other.

The government will blame the laws, but they don't pass better laws. They allow regulators to oversee chaos and ineptitude without any sanctions. Britain is in a mess. Nothing works as it should and the government is paralysed by inaction.

We, the public, know what's wrong and we cannot understand how the problems and solutions are so plain to see but are in the politicians' blind spot. If governing is too difficult, stand aside for others who can make changes happen.

This novel tries to show how a benevolent dictator with charisma can make the necessary changes. The solutions stand being accused of being simplistic and that matters are much more complicated. But it is not difficult to pass laws when you have a big majority. Pass the laws, take the initiative and put things right. Cabinets have far too many people sitting around the table. A small executive team can be the decision makers delegating to ministers to carry out the strategies and plans.

The UK has been in a spiral of decline since being victorious in the Second World War but never enjoying the fruits of that victory. The permissive society that came along with the later part of the 20th century brought freedom to many, particularly the ability to choose. Choices of marriage or not, sexual preferences, no children or as many as is wanted, career or flexible working, rent or buy a home and retire when a person felt that work was too tedious. All of these choices were encouraged by a state that provided "cradle to grave" protections and a National Health Service "free at the point of delivery".

The story opens in 2031 with Julie Carter, a single mother of a son, who, faced with an impossible life, decided to put herself forward in a by-election and against all the odds was elected as an independent MP. She formed a new political party called National Endeavour to bring back a communal ideology in the belief that by all working together, the problems could be solved.

This is a story of a rebirth of a nation.

Chapter 1

Epiphany

23ʳᵈ March 2031

Just when Julie Carter thought that life couldn't get more difficult for herself and her 9 year-old son Jamie, it did. It was eight o'clock in the evening and Jamie, a lively and funny lad, had just gone to bed when, with a smile on her lips, she opened an envelope with a postmark of six days previously. "Pretty much the standard time for a first class letter these days," she thought. She unfolded the letter and gasped in shock at the contents. "Dear Ms Julie Carter. This letter gives you formal notice that you will be required to vacate the premises described in the heading above on or before 15 September 2031. The owner of the premises has entered a care home and the premises are required to be sold." There then followed the legal jargon which confirmed that this was an allowable termination of the tenancy.

Julie's mind was now racing. "How quickly could I find an alternative home for us?" Jamie was settled in at the local junior school with his friends and he was playing well in the school football team. "How do I stay in the school catchment area?" They lived in Elm Park near Reading just a short bus ride from her office and the station. "Are there any other flats nearby and where could I find one?" She sat at the table with her head in her hands and then the old Julie quickly came back. "I can sort this", she said out loud. "I may be only five-foot four-inches but I have determination and a self-belief. I refuse to be beaten. I can do this."

She was a single parent working full time as a wages clerk and bookkeeper in a doors and floors installation company at its corporate office opposite Reading Station. She was constantly juggling her job with being a mother and keeping house. Jamie's father, Dave (may he rot in hell), didn't hang around long after his son's birth and had become a more distant father over the years. He had contributed almost nothing financially and even less emotionally, so Julie had had to do it all. She was fortunate to have the support of her parents, who lived ten miles away in Didcot in South Oxfordshire. Her father Tom had recently been in hospital to have a knee replacement operation and it had not gone well. He had been in pain for months as the surgery was cancelled at least three times for a variety of excuses. Nobody complained about the dire state of the NHS anymore. It was now accepted by everybody, that it couldn't be fixed, as the medical professions and the government would never agree on anything.

Her boss, John Wainwright, was a good man. She had persuaded him that she could be in the office after dropping Jamie off at school for 9.30am and work until 3.30pm giving her enough time to pick him up from school. She had a computer at home and could log in to the office to clear up any outstanding work between 8 and 9 o'clock in the evening. Julie never could work out why she was able to talk people round to her view, but she knew that mostly, she could. At school her A-levels were outstanding and she could have applied to an Oxford College, but she wanted to study further from home. She chose Exeter University and had a great time leaving with a First Class Degree in Politics and Economics. By the common consent of her tutors and fellow students, she was smart. She saw solutions and after her course she continued to take an interest in politics. When BBC's 'Question Time' was on, she regularly shouted at the TV giving her view. She was an avid reader of historical novels and political biographies. She had been offered an opportunity to do a Doctorate at Exeter, but she wanted a break from academia. She was also contacted by her local MP to enquire whether she fancied being a researcher, but that meant travelling to London every day. Instead, she had a gap year and went with her friend Doris backpacking around Thailand, Cambodia & Vietnam. She loved the trip and it was in Vietnam where she had met Dave, backpacking his way with his mate Simon. They stayed as a foursome for the remainder of the trip and she and Dave became an item. When she returned home, she discovered that she was pregnant and Jamie was born on 28th February 2022.

Julie was 32, having been born on Christmas Day 1998. Jamie was a bright happy boy, not great at sports but he enjoyed football. He enjoyed school, especially writing and reading. He always had his nose stuck in a book.

In the kitchen were 20 large bottles of water, delivered the day before by Thames Water. All the local residents had been told by a leaflet through their door that the water from the taps was not safe to drink, although it could be used to flush the toilet. That flush was not always possible as the water was regularly cut off for necessary repairs. Her mother, Margaret, would often get the train from Didcot Parkway to Reading to help out with Jamie and Julie made that return journey at weekends. The trains, when they ran at all due to "ongoing industrial action", were never on time and Margaret rarely got a seat, standing in a crowded part of the compartment by the poorly functioning toilet. Even though Julie worked full time she still received a small amount of Universal Credit and Child Benefit. In Jamie's early years she could barely afford child minding costs and there were occasions when going to work was just economically unviable. Last year, she did manage a week long break with a friend from work to Vienna, when her parents Tom & Margaret, not only paid for the trip, but also were able to look after Jamie while she was away. She had had a great time and for the first time since breaking up with Jamie's father, she had a short but meaningful dalliance with Gael, an Australian man from far away Melbourne. Nothing physically happened because he had recently ended a long term relationship, but he was funny and they became firm friends, albeit for such a short time. Back home she had wished that they had made love, if only just the once, because it just felt her trip and time with him had something missing. It had also been a long time since she had had this type of friendship with another person and wanted it to be more fulfilled.

She was jolted back from her thoughts to the present. If she were unable to find somewhere to live close by in Reading then she would have no alternative but to move back to her family home with her parents in Didcot and commute to work by train. But what about Jamie's school and his friends?

Julie spent the next three months in a fruitless search for a flat that she could afford. How had rents gone up by so much over the last year? She suspected that her eviction was because the family of the landlord could let out the flat on a rent higher than they knew she could afford.

In May, before she had even decided where to live, her father Tom died. His knee operation left him almost disabled and he lost a good deal of mobility. He enjoyed getting out and about but he could no longer play bowls, which he greatly enjoyed. He developed an infection and had to attend the Accident & Emergency Department at the John Radcliffe (JR) Hospital in Oxford as getting to see his GP was impossible. In late April he was admitted into the JR but developed pneumonia and died early the following month. Tom was a healthy man, admittedly 70 years of age, "but that's not old," Julie thought. She helped her mother with the funeral arrangements and in July she got Jamie into a junior school in Didcot for September. There was a school bus from the bottom of the road and she was able to keep her job going. The family of the landlord were overjoyed at getting the flat back sooner than they expected and had a new tenant in on a higher rent after a quick clean and paint job. They never explained to Julie the change of mind on selling, because they didn't need to. By the beginning of August she and Jamie were back living with her mother.

Since moving back to Didcot to live with mum, she had tried to register with a NHS dentist for Jamie, but all of the dentists that she tried were only taking private patients. She had a bit of better luck with a GP surgery, but that was mainly due to her mother being already registered with them. Julie regularly thought "Why doesn't anything work in Britain anymore? Everything was broken and the politicians seemed paralysed by the immensity of what was needed. If the country was a business, all of the Members of Parliament would probably be sacked."

Julie had started listing in an exercise book everything that she thought was in need of sorting out. Quickly the list started to grow and she seemed to add to it daily.

It was pretty much agreed by all commentators that the National Health Service (NHS) problems could not be solved without throwing more money at them, but that had been tried and it was still not functioning for the patients. Julie's dad should not have died but the staff caring for him had been overwhelmed. Why did it seem easier to win the lottery than get an appointment with her GP? Perhaps the appointments should be the lottery prizes. If they were they would sell more tickets.

Now that she lived in Didcot, her journey every morning to work was on the train. The best service for her was regularly cancelled due to driver sickness or a strike. "Why was it so expensive compared with transport across Europe?" Last year on a holiday in Sorrento, her parents had travelled to Pompeii by train and the 45 minute journey cost less than £10 for both of them each way, a quarter of the cost of 15 minutes from Didcot Parkway to Reading. She rarely got a seat on the train, yet the First Class compartment was half empty.

Her biggest problem was housing. Living in her parents' family home with her mother and Jamie wasn't ideal. Jamie was bursting with energy like all 9 year-olds. He was untidy, boisterous and made a lot of noise. Margaret loved her grandson, who called her 'Grannyma', and was very tolerant of him, but Julie knew that they would all be happier if Julie had her own place. "Still", she thought. "You do your best with the cards that life deals you."

At least she had somewhere to stay. The homeless figure of 1.5m was growing and yet she noticed empty properties all over the place. In a village close by, two properties had been empty for more than 20 years. "That can't be right," she thought. Julie's friend, Doris, from school and the backpacking trip, had moved down to Dorset into a village near the coast that she had admitted was like a ghost town in the winter. So many empty holiday lets and second home owners but the locals couldn't afford the house prices or rents. A development in Didcot had recently announced new houses for sale. Half of the houses had five bedrooms so they clearly were not for first time buyers. The others, even the cheapest was fourteen times average annual earnings. Without a huge deposit, and who could save that much while paying ever increasing rents, there was no chance of getting on that first step of the housing ladder. It was just so depressing to see the farmer down the road making such a large profit selling agricultural land at development land prices.

Julie went to the fridge to make a sandwich. The cucumber was from the Netherlands. "Why are we importing salad crops from a country that has the same weather as we do?" she thought. "We grow cucumbers." She then looked at the tomatoes. Britain was in the peak season for growing tomatoes, yet these came from Spain. She looked through the rest of the fresh fruit. Apples from New Zealand, pears from South Africa, bananas from Ecuador, "fair enough", she thought on the last one. Strawberries. Julie loved strawberries. The taste of Wimbledon from Germany? "You must be kidding", she thought. She took out two ice cubes for a glass of water.

Her mind went back to her flat in Reading and the regular supply of bottled water when it was unsafe to drink what was coming out of the tap. Thames Water had only two jobs, supplying clean water and taking the waste water away. For years it hadn't done either of them well. The supply of drinking water to Didcot was currently halted because an E.coli bug had got into the system. Despite recent very public apologies from the company, waste sewage water was still being pumped into the rivers and water courses. Julie used to enjoy wild water swimming in the Thames at Abingdon. She hadn't risked that for 10 years since the last time she had an infection from the river water.

"What do our politicians do all day? Why don't the regulators like OFWAT and the Environment Agency hold water companies to a greater account? Why does everything work better in other countries? Who is going to come forward and make it better? Nobody, because in the end any person of quality and acumen will be crushed by the system. The media, party political interests and big business always gang together to defeat somebody wanting to make things better. If a government cannot make the trains work for the public, what chance is there of the big decisions being taken through by anyone else? What we need is a national endeavour," Julie thought. "A single purpose of everybody working together and doing the right things. Making people follow a joint purpose would surely be labelled right-wing yet the benefits that flowed would be mainly used to help the poor and homeless, so producing a left wing socialist outcome. How could it be of the right and the left politically at the same time? We need somebody to persuade the rich to give up a little and everyone to work to make the pie bigger, grow the economy, so there is enough pie for everyone. Where is there a person in Britain in any walk of life who could do that?"

She started to develop her thinking along these lines using her degree course for reference. "The person to rise up and sort out the country would have no existing political alignments because the political parties would not embrace it. So an independent thinker, but how does one person make the changes? It can't be one person so it has to be a movement. In the past one might have said 'Crusade' but that word for little good reason was now deemed toxic. This one person would draw others into the fold, a new party with new ideas. The public, fed up with the political failures could go for a new party, other countries have managed it. But where is that person? How does anyone manage UK plc, when the job is so large? Perhaps, the skill is not in managing the processes but managing the people who manage the processes. The right person would have a really good team but who would join someone with such a mad idea?"

Julie suddenly felt exhausted by all of this thinking and got ready for bed. In the night at precisely 3.20am, she awoke and saw the time on the clock by the side of the bed. That was her moment of Epiphany. She had dreamt that someone had shouted "Julie, it must be you".

She sat upright in the bed. She was not a religious person but was really startled at the clarity of the message in the dream. Was this how a calling happens? Was this how faith was born? History was littered with instances of people who thought that a God had appeared to them in a dream. Was this what had happened. As an atheist, Julie was not ready to accept the message other than it was a dream. She reasoned that it was a sub-conscious dredging up of what she had thought about during the evening.

Should she accept the message or was it just a one-off occurrence? Would there be another message? "Of course not, this is ridiculous", she thought. The message should be ignored, because wasn't it only a fantasy? Julie had had one spiritual experience in her life. It was when she visited Basilique du Sacré-Cœur de Montmartre in Paris. She had entered the church as a tourist and as she looked up, she felt a hand on her shoulder. She turned to see who it was and there was nobody there, but her eyes were immediately fixed to a scene of the crucifixion in a side chapel. She shivered and a tear had rolled down from her left eye on to her cheek. On her return to the UK she went to her local church and she explained to the vicar what had happened. She expected him to give some explanation, but instead he shouted for her to leave his church and as she left, he screamed out, "We don't want fantasists in here." She thought that this was a strange response from a man asking others to join him in softly spoken words every Sunday.

Julie lay back down on the bed, wide awake and thought about what she should do. There were only two choices, ignore it, and get on with her life, challenging as it mostly was, or she could think about taking the message seriously and following its direction. She thought "Sometimes in life you're the grease and sometimes you're the glue. What will she be?"

But what could it mean if she were to follow the message? "What does 'It must be you, mean'?" The country had over 70 million people so what difference could one single parent make? She had no experience of managing anything so how could she make anything work better? On the plus side, she was good with people and had a knack of getting people over to her point of view. She knew a lot about politics, enough to know that political parties took at least 100 years to get a taste of government and would not accept a new lone voice crying in the wilderness. A low profile person could stay under the radar for quite some time. She thought of the old proverb, 'Mighty oaks from little acorns grow.' Perhaps it was best to start small, take time to learn and persuade others to join up and build on solid foundations. Perhaps the best idea would be to go back to sleep so that she could be ready for the day ahead. She decided to do nothing because it was after all only a dream. Good plan.

Chapter 2

Who Disturbs Morpheus?

On 9th June 2031, Guy Clifton, the local MP for the South Oxfordshire constituency, was declared bankrupt after he had made some unwise investments the previous year. As a bankrupt he was not able to sit or vote in the House of Commons. This situation continued for six months, and because he was not discharged from bankruptcy on 9th December 2031 his seat was declared vacant. A by-election was called for 19th February 2032 and everybody expected the well turned out successor Conservative candidate to romp home. South Oxfordshire had been a loyal Conservative constituency since the 1970's.

Julie had read about the woes of her disgraced constituency MP and had some sympathy for him. He had a good reputation as a loyal husband and father of two girls but he had been the victim of falling for a get rich quick scheme. Julie's interest in politics had always been on a national or international scale. Part of her degree was the studying of the elections since 1970. Recently she had started to take an interest in local politics and had read a good book about Jo Cox, a much admired Labour Party MP who was killed in 2016. The local TV news station on the BBC every night was speculating about who would be standing for which party in the forthcoming by-election. The Monster Raving Loony Party would be fielding a candidate and Julie wondered how this person could afford the costs of standing with no chance of retaining their deposit. She opened up her laptop and Googled for the relevant information. She was surprised to see that it would only cost £500 in fees to get your name on the ballot for a by-election and if a candidate got 5% or more of the vote, the whole fee was refunded.

After the Christmas and New Year festivities were over, Julie and her mother Margaret had taken down all of the decorations and stowed the artificial Christmas tree in the loft. 6th January, twelfth night, was adhered to still by most people because it was considered bad luck to have tinsel around the day after. "What a suspicious quasi-religious country we still are," Julie mused.

That night she finished her evening job work, played a game with Jamie then later, with her mother she had a cup of hot chocolate and turned in for the night. At precisely 3.20am, she awoke and saw the time on the clock by the side of the bed getting a distinct feeling of déjà vu. She had again dreamt that someone had shouted "Julie, it must be you".

Julie didn't believe in ghosts or the paranormal so what was happening was clearly in her sub conscious mind. If that were true, she reasoned, then subconsciously the message was that she should put her name forward as an independent candidate at the by-election. She wouldn't win but she would get the opportunity to get a few things off of her chest.

Over breakfast the next day she discussed the matter with her mother. "I could only do it with your support, as it would mean being away many evenings and weekends. Would that be an issue for you to look after Jamie," Julie asked her mother.

"Of course it wouldn't. We're getting along famously now that he's shown me a few things on his mini-computer. You go for it." She took an hour off work and called in at the Council Offices and got all of the paperwork.

The next evening she completed the papers and wrote a cheque for £500, money she had saved from living with her mother and not paying rent, although she made a household contribution. The next day she again called at the Council offices and lodged the papers. After a few days she received an e-mail telling her that everything was in order and she would appear on the ballot paper."

"So that's it", she thought. "But what do I do next?" It was six weeks to Polling Day and she had nothing prepared, no party machinery to produce leaflets and no team to knock on doors. On reading in the election pack supplied, that she could not spend more than £200,000 on her campaign, she laughed out loud. The next night, she sat down and drew up a plan of action with the purpose of keeping costs to a minimum, but with having maximum impact. She would concentrate on meetings in the local town and village halls and hope to attract crowds by word of mouth. Getting people out on a cold February evening would be a challenge, but she was up for it. She would get a small number of A4 leaflets printed in colour with her photograph, thinking that 1,000 would be enough. Her best hope was to get interviewed on Radio Oxford. She was quite adept, like all people of her age, with social media and as the elections in 2029 had shown, they had been crucial in getting the message across. Her friend at work, Lula, had offered to help. Lula was an 'influencer' and had over 1,000 followers. Julie was one of them and so she knew that Lula was pretty able with the social media stuff.

Julie collected her 1,000 leaflets from a printers in Didcot, not realising how heavy the two boxes would be. She wrestled them into the boot of her car and later set off for her first village hall meeting. Lula had put the message out locally and the editor of the village newsletter had also agreed to round up a few of his villager friends to attend.

❉ ❉ ❉

East Botney is a small village in Oxfordshire, one of over 90 villages in the county. It is not a remarkable place in any sense, but it is a pleasant place to live. There is a main line station eight miles away with trains to London every hour for a fifty-five minutes journey. There is an hourly bus service into Oxford but the last one returned to the village at 7pm and there was no Sunday service.

The oldest house in the village was built in the mid-fifteenth century as a farmhouse for a large area of agricultural land. Up until 1990, the village had been a very quiet rural community. Since the millennium, much of this land, owned by an Oxford University college had been sold for housing and rather too many executive 5-bedroomed properties had been built. The location's popularity was primarily for its ease for commuters to travel into London and for doctors, physicists and university professors who needed to get to the Oxford colleges, Harwell or one of the prestigious hospitals.

The village up until recently had a pub, and although the premises were still there, there was a suspicion that the pub company would like to convert it into a large house and develop the car park with another couple of properties. A closed village pub is a sorry sight and the locals would have like it re-opened, but the pub company deemed it commercially unviable.

East Botney, with no functioning pub, was a sleepy dormitory village with just short of 1,000 houses and a few apartments in an old mill. There are some allotments, not all in use, a small village pond and a village hall. It was in this village hall in 2032 that a revolution began that would not only change the United Kingdom, but also the continent of Europe forever. And this is what happened.

Alongside the names from all the known political parties, including the very well-known Monster Raving Looney candidate, appeared the name of Julie Carter. As an independent candidate, she had no interest from the media and little money to support her campaign. This was her first foray into the political arena and the beneficiaries were a small number of residents of East Botney in their village hall.

The meeting was advertised for 7.30pm and surprisingly twelve villagers showed up, illustrating the paucity of decent programmes on the television and that it was cold outside. It didn't help that it was dark in arguably the worst month of winter, but at least it wasn't frosty or snowing. A plus was that the hall was on the way by footpath across the field to the next village that did have a pub. At 7.30pm precisely, Julie Carter came from the side, onto the stage and said loudly "Good evening". At 5 feet 4 inches and medium build and in her early thirties, she was not physically imposing. She wore a warm jacket and low heel shoes. She placed her handbag on the small table at the rear of the stage. There was no lectern on which to place a written speech and no microphone. Nobody asked for the hearing loop to be switched on. The small audience leaned back in their seats.

"Thank you for coming out tonight on such a cold evening. This is my first presentation in my journey to become your next Member of Parliament. I have no experience of politics except at the receiving end. At that end, all I have seen is chaos, obfuscation and misery for ordinary people. I have a nine year-old son who does not go to the school closest to where we live because there were no places left for him. There are children at that popular and rated outstanding school that travel up to five miles to get there, but there was no place for my son even though he lives around the corner. He has to get a bus to a school with an inadequate designation from the schools inspectorate. Recently he had to wait six months for a tonsillectomy procedure even though it was deemed urgent and he was in constant pain and discomfort. We live with my mother in Didcot because, although I work full time, we cannot afford the rent on the most basic studio flat. Without help from my mother, I could not afford the astronomical child care costs that enable me to work. I receive no support from my son's father, even though I have supplied his details to the Child Support Agency."

The audience stirred in their seats. This was all a little uncomfortable and some were looking longingly at the door at the far side of the room. Then a change in mood occurred and they, as one, sat bolt upright when Julie started to articulate what all of them knew to be true.

"Everything in this country is broken. Nothing works for the ordinary person. My son and I are ordinary people. You, in this room, are also I suspect ordinary people. We, and you I am guessing, have been failed by every department of government. A political system that is more concerned with its own party and status than the needs of the citizens. My son has no future unless things change. Some of you here will have grandchildren, just like my son, and they will have no future either. My son will work hard at a failing school and may go to a university.

He will leave that place with a mountain of debt that he will carry for most of the rest of his life. His degree will not guarantee him a prestigious job so perhaps he should have taken an apprenticeship after all and learned a trade. There will be no debt, but the way that society is structured, he will always be made to feel second class, both academically and in advancement at job interviews. He will be in his twenties and still living at home because he will never be able to afford a sufficient deposit to purchase his own home. He might make it if he has a working partner, but any thoughts of raising his own family will be in the distant future." At this point the audience, most of whom were grandparents themselves, nodded in agreement.

"If my son is unwell again, he will join a waiting list for treatment until he is incapacitated, because it is only this condition that will propel him up the queue. He will watch his mother in her senior years get wholly failed by the care system, which is inadequate on every level. I suspect that all of you in this room fear the advancing years and even now, some of you will see assisted suicide as the ultimate way out of an appalling old age. We have all allowed this to happen and now we must reverse it. It is not enough to have policies because all political parties have those. What I need is your belief in me that for you I can achieve something. When I was a young girl I sat on my father's knee and he told me that in the United Kingdom anybody can be Prime Minister. When you see the people who have held this office in my lifetime, you know that he was right. We have had the liars, those who have been economic with the truth. We have been given wild impossible promises on how things would be better if their party was in power. Instead we have witnessed a relentless decline with the richest enriching themselves above what their talent and endeavours deserve and the poor, mostly ordinarily working class families facing the terrible grind and just getting by. I say that the tide must be turned and the ordinary people like you and me must be able to see some equality of outcomes."

The audience were now leaning forward in their chairs and one man audibly said "Yeah". Then something strange happened, which no person in that room was ever able to explain. Julie walked to the front of the stage, spread her arms wide and said "I can fix all of this, just give me that chance." And they believed her. Spontaneously, they all stood and cheered. After the meeting ended, there was a stunned silence and the twelve drifted out, but not to the pub. They went home.

The news of the meeting went through the village like a wild fire. The next day in West Botney Village Hall, the second advertised husting of the independent candidate was packed. All of the seats were taken and those willing to stand were pressed around the walls on three sides. Her message was the same as the day before. "We have a housing crisis to fix, we need to look after our elderly friends and relatives better and we have to give a purpose to the young people. Stability, security, opportunity."

Someone at the back shouted, "You'll never get any change because the establishment and the judiciary will thwart you at every turn."

Her answer was "You are right, so we will have to put in place those changes to procedures and laws that mean that all of our plans will go through."

"But how does one person do that when the main political parties will stop you?"

Julie smiled and said "But I won't be alone. My message will give me a large victory in this constituency and when it is heard, others will join to this cause, because the message cannot be denied."

A hand was raised and a woman rose to her feet. "You will not have the support of the political press, whose job it will be to tear your message apart and you with it." The hall was filled with a murmur of agreement.

Julie spread her arms wide and the audience became silent. "I will win this election and other Members of Parliament will join with me. By the time of the General Election, whenever that is, I will be the leader of a significant party. We will grow and at the election following we will have such a large majority that everything will be possible. How do I know this? It is because of the fundamental truth that the voter, the ordinary citizen, you, have been so badly failed by all political parties, that a clear message will gain traction. That clear message is "We are all equal and entitled to be treated as equals. We should all share in the prosperity of the country and we can only do so by setting all the vested interests aside and cleaning up the political establishment." The seated audience jumped to their feet and the applause and cheering shook the prefabricated hall.

Gail Dunstone had attended the meeting, but her husband Ben had stayed at home. Politics was not really his thing. When Gail arrived home, her face was flushed and Ben noticed a sparkle in her eyes, something that he hadn't seen in years. "So what was it like," Ben asked?

Gail tried to explain what she had seen and heard. "She was just a smallish woman, but she had presence. Whatever she said, we all immediately understood because she spoke in terms of our fears and hopes. She was not like any other politician or presenter that I had ever seen. She seemed to emit a glow of confidence and addressed each of us individually and collectively at the same time. Her basic message was that all of the political structures were broken and nothing was working like it should. She spoke about the wealth of the country, the waste, the failed projects and the lack of trickle down to the ordinary working class person. Strangely, she did not come across as a socialist, explaining that only capitalism would make her programme of change work. Yet she also had a strong left-wing message of equality, particularly of opportunity. Her central and defining messages were that change had to come about and there was no will for the changes necessary in any of the current political parties. The changes that she was offering were breathtaking in their scope. Everyone in the hall was stunned and as we left, I just had this feeling that something big had happened, but I can't tell you what it was. I am sure, that I will vote for her."

Ben was sceptical. "We have been married for over 40 years and in that time, we have seen about 10 General Elections. We have seen political parties with large majorities, small majorities and even a couple of coalitions. Long periods of Conservative rule have been followed by slightly less long Labour administrations. Nothing has changed really. We have been on a long trajectory of accumulated failures. We may all get slightly better off if we work, but fundamentally, we have an underclass of working poor, drug taking and rising crime. She won't change that."

Gail shrugged her shoulders and said "I want to see her again, so why not come with me and you will see what we all saw tonight. Her next meeting is in Abingdon tomorrow in the Abbey Hall. We'd better get there early as it will be packed." And it was.

Julie's diminutive figure seemed so small in the large space, which often served as a venue for a craft fayre. She spread her arms out wide and said, "Thank you all for coming. I see some familiar faces and that is always comforting. Over the last week, every evening, I have been at meetings in village halls in support of my candidacy for the forthcoming by-election. I am independent so I have no affiliations to a political party. I make no excuses on their behalf and I blame them for their continuing abysmal performance. In those village halls I have told the audiences, I see some of you here in the room, things that they and you already know. The country is financially a basket case, bankrupt, skint, almost a third world economy. There is no growth and no money to fix anything. Most of what masquerades as services cannot be accessed by us and we have not a single politician with vision and determination to put it right. Tonight I am going to share with you a different message. I'm going to tell you what is possible and if I win this by-election with your support and votes, then this will be a very large step to the next phase, which is to persuade any politician with any degree of honour, to join with me. I will of course devote my energies to the particular problems that we face in South Oxfordshire, because it is unlikely that these issues will be recognised by any other politician, let alone get fixed.

The largest issue for the constituency by far is the South East Strategic Reservoir which is being built by Thames Water. This project is larger than Gatwick Airport on our doorsteps and when finished in 2040, it will take 10 years to fill. There is no benefit for us, as its purpose is to supply London with drinking water. We are in the middle of millions of lorry movements and we can start to see the banks rising up to 30 metres high. We have a long diversion in place of a major commuting road between Grove and Didcot Parkway Station, which has added 20 minutes to journey times. All of this and we will see no benefit from it. I assure you all here, that I am on the case and I will minimise the difficulties for you." Spontaneous applause broke out in the hall.

"I will also be pressing for the new railway station at Wantage Road in Grove, a project that has been promised for years and nothing is happening any time soon.

Before I take questions from you I want to share a conversation that I had last week at Silverstone, the home of British motor racing. I was lucky to be invited to an Open Day and there I met a current Formula 1 driver, who races for a team based in Britain. He was proud to be British and he drapes himself in the Union Jack when on the podium. He likes to hear the British National Anthem when he or his team win a race. So I said to him, "You are very proud to be British aren't you?"

He said, "Of course, yes, very much so."

So I said, "Why do you live in Monaco then?"

"He said with a great smile, "It's the tax isn't it. I earn loads of money and in Monaco I pay hardly any tax on it."

"He may well pay a little tax in some other jurisdictions. It's no secret that this driver earns £25m per year. If he paid UK tax, he would still have £12.5m in the bank every year. He has a four years deal. That is £50m after tax. How much money does an individual need? I then asked him about when he visits England and if he had a car."

"No," he replied. "The racing team lets me use one of the pool cars."

I asked him, "Do you own a house?"

"Oh yeah," he proudly said. "I own two houses and a flat. The house is empty for when I need it and the other house and flat are let out."

"OK. Let's understand this. We have an individual who pays no income tax in UK, pays no road tax but uses our roads, pays some

Council Tax but not the full amount on the empty house and earns money from properties that he has sent to his bank in Monaco, where he pays little tax. If he needs help abroad from the British Consulate it is there for him, but even though he will earn £100m over four years, just four years of his racing career, he pays nothing for this protection. Why do we allow this? If we all paid what is due, we would all pay a little less and our public services could be properly funded."

Julie took questions and gave this closing statement. "Please vote for me on polling day. Please ask your friends to do the same. You are all with me on the beginning of a fantastic journey with which there is no downside. We will make our lives, our children's lives and our grandchildren's lives better."

After Abingdon, word of mouth about her messages and how she delivered them spread far and wide. Everywhere in the constituency Julie packed the halls with standing room only. Inevitably, the invitation for an interview on Radio Oxford arrived. The radio station was devoting time to all of the candidates in the by-election and Julie's time was well publicised.

The interview started with an introduction from the station's Chief Political Correspondent, Daniel Buckingham. "Welcome to the show Julie. Why do you think that you will command any voice for the constituency when independent candidates don't have the support of a party? Even if elected, you won't be able to make any changes will you?"

Julie's main persuasive quality was her physical presence so that was not going to work on a radio audience, although over the course of the interview it did start to work on the presenter. Julie started slowly and gently but greatly increased her volume and tone as she made this statement.

"In the main the voters in the constituency of South Oxfordshire are just like me. We struggle to get by, we worry about the health of the members of our family and we want our children to have happy and prosperous lives. I have no vested interests, either commercially or personally. I just can't get past the commonly held view that we would all do better if the government, centrally and locally, were more competent at getting decisions right first time and acting upon them quickly. I am promising that I will make changes. No weasel words about pledges and best efforts."

Daniel interrupted her "How can you make such a promise?" At that moment he looked into Julie's eyes and he believed that she could make the changes. What had had this effect on him? Later, he explained to his partner that it was a moment of enlightenment. A moment that made him want to shout "Hell, yeah", but he didn't.

Julie was calm when she said, "I have the ability to persuade people to my point of view. It is not magic or alchemy, it is just that I understand their fears and hopes and I persuade them, that through me, their problems can be solved or at least their situation improved." Daniel got a message through his headphones that the station's telephone switchboard had lit up with people wanting to ask questions and to agree with Julie's comments.

Daniel went to the callers and Julia answered each question with clarity and passion. At the end of each answer, she asked every caller "Would you give a little more at work, pay a little more tax and support a government that was obviously putting everything right and succeeding?" They all said that they would, but invariably with the caveat that they would want to see some progress first.

After the short interview, the content was picked up by BBC News and started to be used in news programmes. A video feed of the interview went viral and Julie was inundated with requests for interviews from the printed media. In no time, she became the most talked about politician in the county. She committed herself to doing everything to improve her chances of being elected and so she agreed to just about every request to be on radio and television interviews. The weekend papers ran special features on her because she was news.

Her campaign slogan was simple, "If the system isn't working for you, vote for me and I will get it changed for you."

And the voters of South Oxfordshire did vote for her. She got the message out in all of the wards and parishes. She had more leaflets printed and soon she had a volunteer team to knock on doors to deliver them. She left the leaflets in public places and at the venues that she gave a presentation. She had limited campaign funds, all supplied from her own savings as she refused the offer of donations. Word of mouth of her messages and what she had said at meetings were passed amongst staff in their workplaces and by members in social clubs. When she turned out for a meeting in every village hall, town hall, market place and company canteen there were no spare seats and crowds formed six deep. She had meetings in the market towns of Didcot, Abingdon & Wantage even though some of the venues were not fully in the constituency, but the workers in those towns were. At the end of each of her presentations, a hush was followed by ecstatic applause and standing ovations. She had the mood of the voter from the beginning of every speech. She told them what they already knew and that was that the system was against them and could not be changed. Unless they voted for her.

She promised changes and everyone that she came into contact with believed her. The other candidates in the election were having to toe their party line and they came across as disconnected from the real issues, locally and nationally. No other candidate could match her basic integrity and they all spoke from failed policies. They had no vision or plans to offer that countered her simple solutions.

The day of the by-election arrived and it was a massacre. Julie obtained a record share of the votes cast of 75% on a record turnout of 78%. At the start of the campaign it was expected to be an easy government win even though the by-election was called over the disgraced sitting member. After the event, some commentators put Julie's success to the complacency in the other candidates, particularly the Conservative one.

The Returning Officer read out the results with a gleam in his eye. Even at three o'clock in the morning Julie looked radiant. She stood at the lectern and gave the customary victory speech. She did the thanking of the Returning Officer and his staff, complimented the other candidates on having a clean contest and then said this, "Thank you to the voters for coming out in large numbers on such a wintry day. You will not be aware of this but you have lit a spark that will over time cause an inferno in the politics of these islands. Today I am privileged to represent the constituency of South Oxfordshire in Parliament. Over the last few weeks you have heard my messages, my promises and my solutions. I now take these to the seat of power and you must believe that change is coming."

As she got down from the stage a man came up to her and handed her a brown paper envelope.

❖

Chapter 3

How Not To Do It

After her election as the Member of Parliament for South Oxfordshire, Julie had to decide how her future should be organised. She resigned her job in Reading with the great goodwill of John the manager, who thought it likely that she would want to return after failing to hold on to her seat at the next general election. Independent MPs didn't last long and there was no doubt that the Conservative Party's formidable political machinery would not take her so lightly next time.

She was in no rush to take up her seat in Parliament thinking that one week to sort out her affairs was wise, as time might be in short supply, once she had attended. She was aware that soon after taking her seat in the House of Commons she would be expected to give a Maiden Speech. Her political knowledge was a little out of date from her degree course and so she set about studying in detail the past two general elections of 2024 & 2029. These elections were remarkable for the same reason. The Conservatives went into 2024 with a large majority and were crushed at the ballot box. The Labour Party emerged with a large majority, yet in 2029 they lost most of it and ended up in the opposition group in a coalition. The results of course came about for the same reason. Both parties had taken the electorate for granted by over promising to fix all of the problems, then under delivering on the job, so entering the election with a very poor record in government.

Fortunately for her there were lots of documents, reports, recorded podcasts and TV programmes on the subject for her to study. At the time of the 2024 election Julie was in her mid-twenties and had other matters on her mind like bringing up a lively two-year old boy. She remembered little about the campaign except that she had just returned from a holiday in Spain with her parents, the day before Polling Day on 4th July. Jamie was a handful on the plane and the other passengers irritated looks had lived with her for a while.

She looked up the announcement of the election on You Tube. "Oh dear," she thought when seeing Prime Minister Rishi Sunak on 22nd May standing at a lectern outside 10 Downing Street in the pouring rain. The reports in the papers on the Conservative campaign were not kind, recording that it went from crisis to crisis. Sunak had made a major blunder by returning home early from D-Day Commemorations and had to make an unreserved apology. "Ouch," she thought. Julie then looked up the critiques of the Conservative Manifesto. All the reports were that it was a document of hope over substance. Certain tax giveaways would be funded by very uncertain savings on welfare and tax avoidance. "What were they thinking," she said almost audibly. "A Manifesto is the document that must tell the truth about where a party in government will go and any lies will come to light sooner or later." She read that two weeks into the four weeks campaign it looked a possibility that the Conservatives would face an electoral drubbing, the likes of which they had never had. From the notes, it was plain to see that what had really hurt the party's fortunes were the emerging stories of members of his party and government laying bets not only the date of the election, but in some cases against themselves winning their constituency.

Julie now looked at the election campaign from the Labour Party's perspective. The Party led by Sir Keir Starmer adopted a strategy of not messing up their lead in the polls and turning a certain victory in to defeat. He had schooled his team to avoid falling out amongst themselves and saying anything that might put off the undecided voter. A critique in The Times reported that the Manifesto was dependent on its finances for growth and would only appeal to people who disliked the Conservatives and were ready to roll their sleeves up and get the economy going.

From the coverage in the press a person might have thought that there were no other parties involved. Were these others worth considering or was it always a two horse race? She scrolled down and found a reference to the Liberal Democrats, the perennial third placed party. She smiled as she saw their leader having some fun falling in the water more than once, playing tennis, unconvincingly doing an assault course (he should be careful at his age) and all the top people enjoying (or not) a roller coaster. Julie was a bit perplexed. "I thought that a General Election was a serious business. Had the Lib Dems taken it a bit less casually they might have spotted a real opportunity to garner even more disaffected Conservatives, who under no circumstances would ever have voted Labour." They targeted some marginal seats and did really well with a big increase in their numbers of MPs, but Julie had the feeling that they had missed an opportunity.

She carried on reading the election review and noticed that four weeks from polling day, the mood changed when the Reform UK Party President Nigel Farage entered the stage. He put himself forward as a candidate and quickly increased the party's profile and voter acceptance in the polls. Disaffected Conservative voters seemed to be ready to vote for Reform UK and the party started to get some real traction. Nigel had charisma, a quality that you can't define, but you know it when it comes through the door with a pint of beer in its hand.

Julie recalled that from the time she left school, single issue protesting, often with criminal damage, got steadily worse as the police seemed to ignore it. By the time of the 2024 election, violent protests in the UK were now seen as an accepted way of behaving. Old women and young people were vandalising works of art, buildings with historic status and even attempting to damage one of the four copies of Magna Carta. One of Julie's friends had missed a job interview as a result of people lying down in the road. Other friends had missed hospital appointments and she recalled reading in the paper about one pair of siblings missing their parents' joint funeral.

She wondered whether the nationalist parties gave any further insight to the 2024 election, or should she concentrate on the bigger picture. The independence aspirations of Scotland and Wales were important and should not be brushed aside. Had nobody ever thought of a Federal system and would that appeal to the Scots and the Welsh? The situation in Northern Ireland was complicated and best left to the experts she reasoned.

From all of this research, Julie concluded that at the time of the 2024 election the country was in a mess with zero growth, public services in meltdown, the NHS going from hero to zero and with politicians so meek that they were unable to make the clarion call needed to stir up a national endeavour.

"That was catchy," she thought. "If I ever have more than me then I will have a party and I will call it National Endeavour."

In 2024, the country was looking for leadership, vision and some harder times as long as there was some progress towards a better life. The Conservatives were desperate to move the dial by stressing that the electorate should look to the future with them and forget the party's miserable last seven years out of fourteen. The Labour Party's simple message was that the country needed a change and by the look of the dismal economic numbers, they were right. Despite all of the government's efforts, they started the month of May twenty points behind Labour and never made it a single point less.

Julie sat back in her chair and thought, "What have I learned? Charisma is the quality to have if you want to lead. Nigel Farage had it and the others didn't, so from a point of zero, in less than two weeks, he galvanised a dreary election and influenced the result. All of the party's manifestos were cautious and showed the fear of putting voters off. A manifesto should set out clearly the problems and how they could be resolved. Both parties showed a lack of bravery and confidence.

Labour romped home and the Conservatives suffered a terrible defeat. In five years of government that massive Labour majority would disappear. She was keen to understand how by 2029 the Labour Party could lose its dominant majority and end up in opposition to a coalition led by the Conservative & Reform UK parties. How could they have squandered such an advantageous position?

"Time for a break," she thought. All of this reading and analysis was making her head ache and she felt tired. I need to learn all of this so that I can make a meaningful contribution. In bed that night Julie had her first doubt. "Why must it be me? I am not the brightest tool in the box. I didn't go to Oxford or Cambridge but my degree from Exeter was a good one. I'm just a mum who wants to make life better for her child. I pay my taxes and I don't break the law, but is that enough?" She drifted off to sleep thinking, "It should be enough."

The next day she was back studying politics, but this time the election and campaigns for 2029. In that year, the pendulum of politics had swung again. The Labour Party, elected by a large majority in 2024 under Sir Keir Starmer and his novice Cabinet had good intentions but were worn down and defeated by events and in-fighting. The five years of the Labour Government from 2024 just didn't get a chance to put their many ideas into laws and make progress. It was a government of reaction, just responding to events. Fire-fighting.

Julie noted that right from the beginning, the different factions in the party, so skilfully managed by Sir Keir up to the election, came out of the woodwork once the election was done. Sir Keir thought that he was leading a centre-left government but others on the left had different ideas. The trade unions demanded and got payback for their financial support. The left wing unions put into place all sorts of laws that restricted their ability to strike for more pay for their members to be repealed. The public sector wage bill ballooned and inflation started to rise. The country was financially broke before the election so the additional borrowing to settle the public sector wage demands sent the cost of interest and inflation both soaring. The value of the pound started a steady decline.

"This is madness," thought Julie. "Couldn't those Labour members see that by pursuing their narrow interests, they were damaging the economy irrevocably and making the achievement of their plans more difficult?"

All of the clever and necessary initiatives in the Labour Manifesto of 2024 were challenged in the courts as soon as they saw the light of day. There were so many environmental, European Union and obscure laws to navigate that any individual or group with small financial resources could hold up government plans for months, years or forever. The judiciary was unhelpful preferring to agree to any lunatic argument and pedantic case. Julie thought, "There can be no progress without having clear laws and sorting out the judges."

Unsurprisingly, the Holy Grail of growth so frequently trumpeted during the election campaign didn't materialise as the levers that generated it couldn't be made to operate. The planning system, slow to be reformed, meant no new nuclear power stations for twenty years so fossil fuel burning continued. All the government MPs were in favour of on-shore wind farms as long as the turbines were nowhere near their constituents. Any progress towards achieving the country's climate change goals was missed. Julie sat back and took some moments to think this passage in the political critique through. "It's just like the dying days of the Conservatives in 2024. No leadership, everybody pulling in different directions. No vision, no determination, no new good ideas. Just paralysis."

By 2025, the government, so bold in its Manifesto in stating what it would do, suddenly lost the determination to make the difficult decisions that would have got large numbers of economically inactive people back to work. Net immigration continued at pre-2024 levels because all the solutions that seemed so plausible in opposition, didn't work in government. Left wing members of the party lobbied continuously to increase taxes on companies and rich individuals and when the weak government couldn't resist them, investment in business declined. Quite a few rich people, seeing the writing on the wall, left and went to live in one of the low tax territories. The left wing, buoyed by an increase in the NI and tax take, moderate though it was, then demanded higher than inflation increases to welfare benefits and disability benefits. In 2025, expenditure again rose faster than income and borrowing increased and interest liabilities rose sharply. There were no new infrastructure projects approved and social care remained unresolved. Julie sucked noisily through her teeth. "The government had lots of clever people so why couldn't they see all of this coming and get ahead of events? Was it because there were no managers of calibre in place? Did the special advisors straight out of college, know nothing but having bright woke persuasive ideas? Where were the civil servants in all of this? Perhaps they were hoping that the government failed while they stood aside knowing better?"

While reading, Julie remembered the crisis of 2026, when the financial markets suddenly woke up and saw a government in trouble with zero growth, rising unemployment and wage inflation, increases in the cost of living and tax revenues being not enough to support the spending programme. Government borrowing increased, the National Debt rose every month and interest payments, the cost of servicing the debt, rose also. The Chancellor had no choice but to raise income tax and VAT so breaking the key manifesto pledges of 2024. The Chancellor also introduced new windfall taxes on the banks, which increased their mortgage and borrowing rates to counter the losses. Mortgage rates for over 2 million borrowers not on fixed rate terms, immediately saw their monthly payments increase. Julie recalled that this was the first time that she was pleased not to have a mortgage. Predictably the government's popularity as shown in regular polling was now in free fall. Sir Keir did what all leaders do in these circumstances, he reshuffled his Cabinet. As some commentators cruelly noted "it was like shuffling the deck chairs on the Titanic." Right at the end of 2026, it was reported that there were ominous signs that raising borrowing on a monthly basis might not be available. The main credit referencing agencies downgraded government debt to A+, a long way from AAA that it needed to be to benefit from supply of funds at a good rate of interest.

Julie didn't know what the ramifications of this were. She took a moment to think. "What would happen if the borrowing tap was suddenly turned off? Could the Bank of England metaphorically print some money and give it to the Treasury? If the government didn't have the money, would it stop making payments to the poorest and disabled? Would the public sector wage bill not be made? Would it, could it, default on contractual payments? This is serious stuff yet I don't remember it being something that we worried about," she thought.

January 2027 came and nothing that the new Cabinet members could do had made any difference. Government borrowing had noticeably tightened so the interest charged by the lenders increased as the perceived risk of holding UK debt also rose. Julie read in one article that the UK economy was looking a bit more like a banana republic and for the historians, a bit like when in 1976 Dennis Healey had to approach the International Monetary Fund for an emergency loan. The Economist, a respected newspaper, declared the country "bust".

In the summer of 2027, one of the old favourites came back to haunt the country and the government. The train drivers made large pay demands and when they could not be met, strikes were called. The government had taken into public ownership most of the franchises and was in a stronger position to protect the commuters. On the Statute Book there were powers available to demand a minimum service level but the government was fearful of applying it. The drivers on the London Underground, not wishing to be left out, joined their "brothers" so bringing the capital to a grinding halt in the peak of the tourist season. Some tube lines didn't require drivers as they were computer controlled, but the government didn't want to upset the drivers by deploying the trains.

The National Health Service with increased funding was still stuck with 7 million people waiting for treatment, only a little less than in 2024. The promised additional doctors and nurses took longer to train than when they were needed, which of course everybody knew. It was probably just as well because the country's finances could not have sustained the increased wage bill. Similarly, the additional police promised also failed to be recruited and all crime, particularly knife crime, increased. The boats kept arriving across the Channel in record numbers. Labour's reasoned softly, softly, approach had made no difference to the desire of people in Calais to come to England.

2028 dawned and it would be the fourth year of a Labour Government and only one year from the next general election. Julie at that moment realised how short the time frame was. Some plans, particularly large infrastructure projects could span many governments. The large reservoir in her county had been in the planning for decades and although it had been started, its completion date was a long time away. She had pledged at election meetings for her constituents that she would try to ensure that construction works would be done with the minimum amount of disruption.

She supposed the lesson for any new government was to 'hit the ground running' as time was short. There was a limited honeymoon period where the new government was given some leeway. She recalled a school project looking at the first hundred days of the US government that brought an end to the Great Depression in the 1930's. "President, F.D. Roosevelt," she recalled, "had been bold, but he had vision too."

The Labour Party in 2028 with a huge majority in Parliament found itself in exactly the same position as the Conservative Party in early 2024. Limping along from crisis to crisis and the election a year away. Julie wondered how the party would put a case to the electorate, certainly not based on any measurement of success. Perhaps they will adopt the Rishi Sunak approach of 2024 and try to put their record aside and talk about the future. The problem for them was that they had been the future.

Her research had brought her to the beginning of 2029, election year and well within her living memory. There was no New Year cheer for Sir Keir. He reshuffled his Cabinet again in an attempt to find some new talent, new ideas and new solutions. The problems of the previous years had worsened. Interest rates were at a decade high, mortgage arrears were at an unsustainable level and repossessions were on the increase. The promised housebuilding of 320,000 units per year had fallen woefully short at an average of 210,000. Government borrowing was below record monthly levels because of an austerity programme and tax raising from every conceivable source. "The country was in recession again," thought Julie. "The endless cycle of boom and bust.

Every government had at its disposal all of the brightest economic and organisational brains on the planet and yet the same old mistakes get made and the same old excuses follow," she screamed internally. "Why is it so difficult to get everyone pulling in the same direction? Why don't people understand that self-interested groups cause chaos?"

At school she remembered the lesson on 'The Dunkirk Spirit'. The Second World War, which had finished nearly 90 years previously might have been the last time that the public 'were all in it together'. "How difficult would it be to foster that spirit once again? Perhaps the freedoms that everyone jealously guarded would prevent some people giving up a little for the public good. How would people respond to being told what they should or should not do? Everything in this direction did smell heavily of right wing politics and all of the historic prejudices that a dictatorship might bring out. But what if by following a right wing agenda the main beneficiaries were not the well-to-do but the poor, wasn't that left wing politics? Is it that the only way to get everyone on to the same level is by levelling down rather than levelling up? "Economic growth is the only answer," Julie thought. "If you can make the cake bigger then everyone gets a bigger slice. The winning strategy is to ensure that the largest slices are not disproportionately larger than all of the other slices. Prime Minister Liz Truss might have had the right strategy in the autumn of 2022 but she lasted only 49 days in power, because she implemented it very badly. The Labour Party also got it right in 2024 with their central message, only they lacked the determination to see it through and got diverted by too many people with their own agenda."

With these thoughts circulating in her mind and a fresh cup of coffee, Julie settled down to the last year run-up to the 2029 election. The country was then officially in recession, two consecutive quarters of negative growth. Taxes were higher, unemployment was higher, NHS waiting lists were going up and net migration into the UK was at 580,000. With an election, now the latest at 6 months away, the mood at No. 10 Downing Street was funereal. The only good news for the Prime Minister was that the polls were showing a three way tie. Keir's nightmare of Reform UK & Conservatives getting together looked improbable as the parties had a deep dislike for each other, but they managed a reconciliation for polling purposes and did not contest some seats. The Liberal Democrats were polling well and looked like again they would be taking votes from all the other parties. "Why don't we give them a chance was widely heard?"

In the same way that some managers in business are only able to do the congratulating and giving out bonuses and pay rises, but were unable to do the reprimanding and firing, so it was that Sir Keir, a kind and honourable man didn't seem over the length of the Parliament to have the ruthlessness to replace poor performing ministers quickly enough and to change failing policies sooner. In the end, all the old problems became the same problems, unresolved.

The government's in-tray mostly contained the "too difficult to fix" stuff and so the political cans were kicked down the road. Trains didn't need overpaid drivers when technology was there to take over, but the Transport Minister avoided this confrontation but refused the unions' wage demands and the strikes continued.

On a cold day, 27th February 2029, King Charles III died age 80 and was succeeded by his son the Prince of Wales as King William V. After waiting nearly 75 years to succeed, Charles quickly became a much admired monarch. The funeral at Westminster Abbey and later a small committal service at St. George's Chapel in Windsor followed the same programme of events for his mother in 2022. Camilla, now the Dowager Queen, as always maintained a dignified presence supported by members of the Royal Family. The Duke and Duchess of Sussex and their children travelled from their home in USA for the state events. Arrangements immediately commenced for the coronation of William & Catherine, agreed to be a low key affair in May.

The 2029 election came on 21st June, close to the last possible date. The party leaders, worn out by the constant barracking in the media about their lacklustre performances wanted to get it over and done. The polls predicted a hung parliament with no party having an overall majority and that's how it turned out. So history repeated itself. The

Conservatives blew a large majority at the 2024 election and Labour did the same in 2029.

A couple of weeks later and after a good deal of haggling a coalition government of Conservatives, Reform UK & the Liberal Democrats was formed. A strange concoction of two competing hard right parties and a centre-left bunch of liberals. One commentator likened the Lib Dems to the person who would sleep with anybody no matter how coarse or grizzly and afterwards complain about the quality of the sex.

The coalition was made in hell and the people involved eventually got what they deserved. There was no pretence about brotherly love. Their first act, possibly their most heinous, was to reintroduce the two child benefit rule. The only believable excuse was that the country was in crisis and it needed money and a functioning government. From the start, ministers briefed against each other, derided their own policies off the record to journalists and consequently chaos ensued. The Whips Office of each party had the impossible job of keeping their charges in line and some crucial votes were lost. The crucial vote that they did win was the first vote of no confidence.

The end of 2029 was a sombre time. Everybody wanted a rest from each daily crisis and to look forward to a chance for celebrations at Christmas. Parliament went into recess much to all of the MP's delight. The constant failures, bickering and humiliations were taking a toll on the coalition government. When Parliament reconvened it was much more of the same, as though the Christmas break had not fostered any goodwill to anyone else.

Julie put away the books. Now she understood what had to be done, it was all so clear. 2032 was her year, but every year from now was also going to be her year. Where did this inner belief come from? Did she have a Guardian Angel sitting with her? She was now ready for her Maiden Speech in Parliament. It would not take long to write and she was sure that it wouldn't be appreciated inside those hallowed walls. She was going to tell all of the MPs what the public wanted her to say.

⸎

Chapter 4

The Maiden Speech

Wednesday, 3rd March 2032

A parliamentary civil servant was at the South Oxfordshire by-election count and immediately after Julie gave her victory speech she was presented with a brown paper envelope. Inside was a sheaf of notes on what to do as a Member of Parliament and what to expect. "That's very efficient and welcome," she thought.

There was an offer to arrange travel to London and accommodation, but as the journey to the capital from Didcot was a short distance and she could easily return home, she declined the offer of a hotel. She also decided to arrange her own travel. She was given details of the New Members' Reception Area in Portcullis House and asked to bring proof of identity, P45, Bank Account details and National Insurance number. On her first day she wouldn't be able to bring anybody with her as other security passes couldn't be issued until a later date.

On her first morning as a Member of Parliament, Julie got the 8.15 train from Didcot to Paddington and the London Underground to Westminster. The journey from Paddington took less than thirty minutes. The journey from Julie's home station Didcot Parkway to Paddington should have taken forty-five minutes, but it took one hour and twenty three minutes. The planned train had no driver (gone sick?) so it was cancelled and the next one delayed her journey by being held up by a freight train outside Slough. A freight train on the main Great Western rail line during the peak rush hour? Who thought of that? The commuters pay for the trains to run but they get no consideration from the train company.

As a Member of Parliament Julie could claim a first class fare on her expenses and when any staff member accompanied her, the cost of a similar ticket would come from her office expenses allowance. On the train, Julie had to be careful what pages on her I-Pad she was viewing as you never knew nowadays who could be listening or even recording you on their smart phone. The first class carriage was half empty but she noticed that the standard class carriages were full with people crammed into the aisles and between the carriage spaces. Although all of the platforms on route could have taken a twelve carriage train, this one had only six. "Why not have a longer train to ease the congestion," she thought?

Julie arrived in Westminster and went directly to the New Members' Reception Area via the main entrance in Portcullis House. She showed her proofs of identity to secure admittance. Julie then had her photo taken and shortly after received her official House of Commons security pass, which had to be worn at all times. The Independent Parliamentary Standards Authority (IPSA) had sent her an email to her parliamentary account, which had to be kept very separate from her personal accounts. She was then given a rucksack, a laptop and was supplied with a parliamentary email address and telephone number. The email contained a link to a form that had to be completed to set up her salary and expenses claims and payments.

Julie then had a short discussion with a staff member concerning any personal and office security concerns. The subject had never crossed her mind. Everyone in her part of Didcot knew where she lived. She suspected that anyone in her constituency of South Oxfordshire could find out her address with little trouble. Were Jamie and her mother Margaret in any danger? She hadn't given them a thought, which made her feel a bit guilty. Julie was then shown her locker and had the arrangements explained. As she wasn't a member of an established political party, there was no party whip to show her the location of a shared desk pending the allocation of an office. She was introduced to Delia Harris, her "buddy", an employee of the House of Commons Service who was available during office hours to give her any assistance she might need. Delia gave her information on services available like office cleaning and parliamentary procedures. For the first few weeks, Delia would also make her aware of different induction and training events and provide her with a small amount of office stationery. She was notified that she had to take the oath of affirmation at an early date and Delia would arrange it for her and give the details.

Delia explained that the Customer Services Hub in Portcullis House was the place to go for any query and information. Specific help was available on Procedural, Library and Digital facilities. Once any staff member requiring access to Parliament had been cleared by IPSA, this was where they would collect their passes.

Delia took Julie under her wing more than she would other new Members because Julie had no party members to help her. She arranged a meeting with an office member of the Parliamentary Commissioner for Standards to register her interests. This was a very short meeting as she had nothing to register. She had received no hospitality, no fees for anything and didn't have another job outside Parliament. She was also taken to the Members' Human Resources (HR) Advice Service to discuss HR issues including the recruitment of up to six members of staff.

Julie quickly realised that she needed some office support. She later hired Harry Armstrong, a recently unemployed senior manager from an accountants firm in Didcot to be her constituency manager and agent. He had been highly recommended by John, her boss in Reading. Harry had voted for her and was not a member of any political party so that was quickly done. In a short time Harry had a constituency office set up in a long time empty shop in Didcot and was dealing with correspondence and buying furniture. Julie decided, along with nearly all MPs that Friday of each week would be "Constituents Day", a day in the office to listen to problems and attend local events.

Next she needed a personal assistant to accompany her at all times and to keep her diary. Guy Clifton, the outgoing Conservative member had this role filled by a very competent woman called Iris Murphy.

Fortunately, she had taken some time off after Guy and was now ready to come back to work. She knew the ropes and she immediately took to Julie, as everybody quickly did. Iris was meticulous at keeping receipts and making notes about everything.

As an independent MP, Julie was shown to a small office that she would share with Simon Greenslade, another independent MP, who had been elected in Scotland on an 'anti-wind farm on land' issue. He wasn't in the office and anyway she would have had no time to get acquainted with him as she was whisked away for a tour of essential offices and services.

Delia advised her that she would be emailed by a staff member from the House of Commons Library offering to provide advice and background on her Maiden Speech. "So much to do on this busy first day. Thank goodness for Delia," Julie thought. She was given a copy of 'Behaviour Code for Parliament', which set out clear guidelines on personal behaviour towards others on the premises. After a sandwich lunch, she met Delia again and was shown to her IPSA account manager and received training on the online system, which was mainly used to claim and reconcile her office and personal expenses. "I hope that I can remember how to train Iris & Harry on this lot," she thought.

At the end of this first day, her head swimming with information and procedures, she decided to go home early in the afternoon and spend some time with Jamie and to prepare her maiden speech.

The next day she formally took up her seat as a Member of Parliament in the House of Commons. All MPs & peers took an oath of allegiance to the Crown, commonly known as 'swearing in'. Julie took the oath, the only person that day to do so. She was given a friendly welcome as she took her seat on the non-government benches. The Speaker came in to start the session which commenced with him reading out the Orders of the Day. This was quite lengthy as it comprised Government legislation at various stages of completion and some motions that required debate and voting.

Julie sat and listened to all of the procedures and still found it hard to believe that she was there, an ordinary person, but a person who had come to shake things up and get things done.

She was ready to deliver her first parliamentary speech, her Maiden Speech. She felt that this was an important personal moment and would define her parliamentary career. She had received some information on what was expected. In the main it was not supposed to be controversial. Julie thought, "They are in for a shock because good riddance to that idea."

The Speaker looked towards Julie, who was directly in his sight line, and announced "I call the newly elected Member for South Oxfordshire". These first speeches were commonly between 6 and 10 minutes long. Little did the Speaker or the House of Commons know what was about to happen, an event that was later described as historical. It was Wednesday, morning 11.45am, a little less than an hour before Prime Minister's Questions (PMQ's), so the Commons was already three quarters full. The Public Gallery, ready for the appearance of the Prime Minister, was also full. Journalists sat in the Chamber with their pens and pencils at the ready. The Members of all parties sat back relaxing on the benches and some exchanging pleasantries to colleagues. A normal Wednesday morning in the House of Commons. "She's a comely wench," said the portly red-faced Conservative sporting a wine stained MCC tie. The recipient of this misogynistic slur, his female colleague sitting next to him said, "They all are to you but sadly the gun might be cocked and loaded but there's only a blank in the chamber." Julie Carter, the new Member was independent and unaligned to a political party, so there was no expectation that she would say anything worth listening to.

Julie rose to her feet, a substantial script in her hand and said in a loud voice, "Thank you Mr. Speaker. I will start my first speech in this House with the customary thanks to my predecessor and give tribute to his work in my constituency. By any reckoning, he was a fine MP who had given good and faithful service to his constituents. South Oxfordshire is a semi-rural constituency, which is having a reservoir built the size of Gatwick Airport, which will supply London with its clean water. In order to provide this facility to the capital's residents, my constituents are in the middle of suffering at least two decades of great disruption, but that is the nature of infrastructure projects. We should all expect to sacrifice something for the public good.

"I am clearly not old enough to remember that it was in the 1970's under the Conservatives when the voters were reduced to living their lives in candlelight due to power cuts. A clear failure of management and government. Or in 1979 under Labour when the dead couldn't be buried, rubbish piled up in the streets, hospitals were barricaded by striking workers and a haulier's strike led to shortages in the shops in 'The Winter of Discontent'. It was a government paralysed by the events. I bring to the older Members' minds the year 1992 when Black Wednesday forced the Conservative Government to withdraw our currency from the European Exchange Rate Mechanism, following a failed attempt to manipulate the exchange rate of sterling. A clear case of financial ineptitude.

"For my constituents and those across this nation, the rot set in over 70 years ago and like all pernicious infections, it has progressed mostly under the consciousness until we get to 2031 when the present coalition government saw a breakdown in all of society's components. If you are sick without money, you can't get treated so you die on a trolley in the hospital corridor. If you want to buy your own home or even rent a property, the supply of accommodation is totally overwhelmed by demand, so only the rich, or those with rich parents, can afford the basic housing unit. The poor have no quick access to dentistry, chiropody or physio therapy. The old rot away in their own filth in inadequately staffed care homes at a cost of £100,000 a year. You can't get to work because the trains don't run due to incessant strikes. The rivers are full of sewage and if you go swimming in the sea from one of our beaches, you are likely to end up in hospital….on a trolley.

"Over the last 40 years, since the digital age and 24 hours broadcast news demanded new content, we have seen the intrusive scrutiny of every competent figure in business and society. The best people, who might have been attracted to serve in public life and in this House, have been put off by the media's demands for perfect people. Yet these media people are often deeply flawed individuals. We have in this Chamber, not the brightest and the best, but the mediocre. You have surrendered your integrity to your party's machine. You vote how you are told, you say what you are taught to say and you believe what the party tells you. I stand here as an independent member, beholden to no-one so in this speech I'm going to tell you about your inadequacies."

A Conservative member stood up to interrupt and protest. "Sit down sir", Julie said. "The convention of this House is that you will not interrupt my Maiden Speech." He sat down.

Julie continued, "These failed governments, including this one and the opposition parties, all staffed by second or mostly third rate individuals, have raced themselves to the bottom of the barrel of quality. They, you, have presided over a breakdown of the family, the social unit and the result is seen in the young people all around you. The young have no future because in the pursuit for votes their present is being drained away by you for the older generation. The post-war boom baby generation have had it all and continue to have it all. The young people have been disenfranchised from life's building blocks of owning their own house, having a family, financial and job security and being able to avoid crime, often violent crime. Truancy is at epidemic levels and you have allowed the situation to deteriorate. The unauthorised absence rate is now 5%, which means that there is a persistent truant in every class in the land. And what do many of these truants do? The carry out petty crime, often against their neighbours. Anti-social behaviour is rife and you do not have a clue how to stop it or even control it. On average, the wealth of the citizens in their sixties is 10 times greater than those citizens in their early thirties. How is this fair?

"We have a mental health and sick note culture. People are proud to have developed a physical or mental problem. As a country we cannot afford malingerers or narcissists who claim to be suffering from the latest fashionable illness. The NHS has collapsed under having to provide treatment for unidentifiable complaints. If you are genuinely unwell you cannot get a GP appointment. A&E departments at hospitals are overwhelmed. Voters are dying in their homes waiting for an ambulance to turn up that is currently waiting in a queue outside a hospital. The paramedics are unable to discharge the occupants to the wards as bed space is clogged up with old people who are not sick enough to be there. You have allowed all of this because you have no shame, you are utterly shameless."

At this point there was spontaneous applause from the public gallery and a shout of "Go girl, you tell them like it is." The Speaker should have admonished the public gallery occupants but did not. He squirmed uncomfortably in his chair like a pupil in a headmaster's office getting a right good telling off.

Julie continued "We have workers striking for no better reason than they fancy a day off. The train drivers were on strike yesterday although they are in the top 10% of earners in the country and have a four day week won in their previous campaign in 2025. The House must regret the deplorable incident of a train driver being dragged from his cab and being beaten nearly to death by frustrated commuters even though he was one of the few not on strike. We should not need train drivers at all. We have railway and underground lines that do not need drivers so where is the progress to get technology to solve that problem. Nowhere but the fear of addressing the challenge.

"The doctors are at it again despite being in the top 5% of earners in the country. Every time the doctors get a raise in their salary, it seems that they reduce their hours for the NHS and do more private work. We need full time doctors. When the NHS was set up after the Second World War the doctors were not interested until money was thrown in their direction. Nothing has changed. When will we train enough NHS doctors who want to work full time for our health service? We train up our nurses then when they are qualified they leave for Australia to be replaced by nurses from the Philippines.

"Over the last 10 years, the number of acts of terrorism have increased. Only last week, ten people were killed in an explosion on a bus in Newcastle. The suicide bomber was known to the security services as a potential risk. Well that worked out well for them in Newcastle, didn't it? A failed asylum seeker and a known terrorist risk is allowed to roam free to kill ordinary citizens going to work on a bus. Why was he not in detention or removed from the country? It is because we have become feeble and scared to do the right thing unless we upset somebody or infringe their human rights. You have allowed extremism to proliferate. You have not barred preachers of hate, you have allowed proscribed organisations to flourish and hate to be spread. We were once a harmonious multi-racial and tolerant multi-faith religious society. What have you done to stop that breaking up? Nothing.

"University campuses used to be places of learning and study. Now every University has a protest ongoing about something that has nothing to do with gaining a degree. University Chancellors could have nipped this in the bud years ago by cancelling or sending down students, but no, that was not considered a liberal act. Free speech must be above everything, except my neighbours' free speech against me reduces my freedoms. Universities must take back their premises and reputations as places of learning and enlightenment.

"The Justice system is ruined. How did you let this happen? You have passed laws that judges have ignored or chosen to interpret in the wrong way and the privileged judiciary have themselves been above criticism or the law. Parliament must reign in the judges and ensure that the laws are respected. Every judgement can be appealed several times. Why is this good for justice? Judicial Reviews have brought major infrastructure projects to a grinding halt at massive expense to the public purse and you have allowed it to happen with the excuse that the judiciary is independent. Independent of who? Independent of public opinion and common sense? It takes three years for some criminal cases to come to trial and if acquitted, the defendant has been badly wronged. There are too many prisoners for the prisons to cope with, so we let the prisoners out early. An elderly constituent of mine was robbed in her home and beaten badly by a person, who later was found guilty at trial. The sentence of 8 years was reduced on appeal to

6 years. The thug was told that he would only serve half the sentence, so 3 years. By deducting the time spent on remand, he served 87 days. What justice is this that you are presiding over?

"In 2021 at the Cop26 Climate Change Conference in Glasgow, much was made of the success of getting countries to sign up to reducing their climate harming emissions. You gave a commitment to reduce greenhouse gas emissions to 43% below 2005 levels by 2030 and you failed to do it. You agreed to have net zero by 2050. We are now 2032, just 18 years away and we are far from getting there. Every government since 2021 has watered down the targets and slowed the progress so you will be leaving our children and grandchildren with severe climate and weather conditions. You have failed to engage with other countries and we are all now waiting a cataclysmic event that will bring home the reality of this failure. We have had regular floods, but not like what is coming."

The two Members of the Green Party clapped loudly and received an admonishment glance from the Speaker. Members squirmed in their seats and looked at their watches. One of them even raised his left arm and with his right hand made a performance of pointing his watch to the Speaker's gaze. The Speaker was not about to bring this to an end as he sensed the hand of history in the chamber.

Julie Carter continued "The UK is a leading country in renewable energy, one of the few things that you have got right. This success though is in spite of you. The companies that have installed the wind turbines and solar panels have done it by exploiting the profit that you have allowed them to extract. The price of energy for the voters is tied to the fossil fuel generation and not the much lower price of renewables. So you have made your constituents pay more than they need. At the same time, you have given local authorities the powers, which has made it almost impossible to get any new renewable projects even started, due to the Kafkaesque and labyrinthine planning regulations. We have had regular power cuts as the National Grid gets overloaded at peak times. Another of your failures is that you did not invest quickly or early enough in nuclear energy. A failure of management and leadership."

Another spontaneous bout of applause broke out in the public gallery. The BBC Parliament Channel was now mainstream viewing the speech on BBC1. Other news channels that could get the live feed had locked in to it. Julie Carter's Maiden Speech had pushed all the other news programming off the TV and the usual 150,000 viewers for Prime Ministers' Questions was increasing exponentially, towards four million.

Julie continued "You have lost the war on drugs. More Class A drugs were seized last year than any year before, which of course, probably means that more drugs entered the country. Last week, sixteen people died from contaminated heroin in Bristol. The numbers in rehab have increased annually and there is a generation of addicts with no hope. Drug gangs operate with impunity. They drive expensive cars and flaunt their wealth without the authorities enquiring about the source of that wealth. Children are used by criminal gangs, who operate only slightly below the police's radar. You have tolerated Albanian sex trafficking, Russian extortion and money laundering. Gangs are in every major city and conurbation, flooding the streets with drugs and meting out their own deadly punishments.

"Young people are involved in these crimes because that is where some of the truants from school are. You have presided over a huge increase in shoplifting despite having facial recognition and other tools to identify the criminals. You have decriminalised all those crimes that don't affect you in this place. The police don't bother to arrest shoplifters, burglars or muggers anymore. You live in your posh houses in nice areas that rarely experience crime. You should try living in an inner city deprived area where muggings, sexual assault and knife crime are a daily occurrence. Less than 6% of crimes are solved. We have 46 police forces in the UK and 160 police officers solving one crime for every 16 committed. You should find these statistics embarrassing but you don't.

"Everywhere we look we see a failure of regulators. We have dirty rivers, planning and housebuilding in crisis, gambling out of control, policing failures, prisons overcrowded and violent, the scamming of the elderly by telephone at an all-time high, social housing in crisis and many more failures. These are your failures because you allowed weak regulators not to be held to account.

"Since 1963 all governments have failed to build sufficient housing to cope with the demographic population growth. As a result, demand for accommodation has massively outstripped supply and prices have risen to unsustainable levels. Governments of all parties have overseen the catastrophe that means that young people cannot buy their own most basic home. Rents have risen as the shortage of accommodation has bitten and now even renting has become unaffordable. Your response in this place has been to allow Nimbys to defeat sensible housebuilding plans, to increase the cost of a house by loading on climate change costs and to oversee the rise in slum landlords. You can't even agree how to refurbish this building, looking to choose the most expensive solution because it makes life a little easier for you. Delays cost the taxpayer money, but there is no evidence that you care. Next to Tower Bridge there is a high-rise development of luxury flats, initially sold for over £1m each. They were completed in 2023 and have all lain empty for 8 years. They are owned by people in Malaysia, China, Russia, Indonesia and other countries. The owners will never set foot in the UK and when the flats have sufficiently increased in value, they will be marketed for sale.

"You have allowed London, commonly known around the world as The Laundromat, to be the centre for the laundering of dirty money and a lot of it is tied up in property. This money hides behind companies and low tax havens, avoiding tax in many jurisdictions. You all parade your credentials as politicians against fraud and the non-payment of tax. The UK has more tax havens than any other country. You are all a disgrace.

Cecil Rhodes, a man rightly much maligned, did have something important to say on being British. He said "The greatest prize in life's lottery is being born English or British" if I may paraphrase. If he were alive now, his view would be changed.

"This speech contains a litany of your failures and this was not an exhaustive list. There are more and you know it. I am the wind of change blowing through this House and it is my pledge to sweep you all away unless you are prepared to join with me to improve matters for our constituents. My party, the National Endeavour Party, will put up a candidate in every constituency at every by-election and General Election."

Julie Carter sat down to rapturous applause in the Public Gallery. The Green Party and Nationalist Party Members all stood and applauded loudly. The Prime Minister & the Leader of the Opposition entered the Chamber with grim expressions. They had been watching the news coverage of the speech in the Members' lounge. There was not the usual rapturous applause from the sycophants on the back benches. The speaker called "The Prime Minister" as the opener for Questions.

The PM rose to her feet. "I would like to commend the Member for South Oxfordshire on her speech. A lot longer speech than is usual and not in the accustomed format." Booing was heard from the Public Gallery. The Speaker quickly called for that to cease. The PM continued, "It can be easy to select those issues that are in the process of resolution. This government has improved life for all citizens." "Rubbish" sounded in the Chamber. The Speaker called on the Leader of the Opposition to put his first question. "Isn't the Member for South Oxfordshire right?" There then followed 30 minutes of Party Politics that were so tedious that the news channels switched away to other news stories.

At the end of Prime Minister's Questions, when just about everybody had left the Chamber, Julie was still sitting there drinking in the atmosphere. She was collecting her papers together and getting ready to go when she was approached by another Member. "Hello"," he said. "My name is Edward Grey. I just wanted to say to you 'Well done'. It's about time we were told about our failures in open session, although most of us are not as dim as you portrayed. On the backbenches the whips make sure that we toe the party line and we are discouraged from having opinions at variance to the Government and Opposition Cabinets. If you want to get a more senior position in the government and party, you do the ministers' bidding. After that speech, you won't be popular amongst the hierarchies but there will be many backbenchers who will want to buy you a drink in the bar or a cup of tea. Including me on another day when you have time."

Julie thanked Edward and left Parliament to get a train home. Already her phone was collecting messages from all sections of the press and television.

※ ※ ※

Hastily convened meetings of senior editors were taking place in all of the main news companies. All had the same Agenda item. How quickly can we get Julie Carter on the programme for an interview?

Eight weeks after the Maiden Speech, the elected Members of Sinn Fein, who had never taken up their Commons seats because they refused to take the oath to the King, announced their intention to sit in the House of Commons. Sinn Fein, with great prescience, had decided that there was a massive change on the way and they wanted to be a part of it as it looked like there would be a convulsion in the UK Parliament and devolved countries. They were right as later events proved.

The day after the speech Julie was contacted on her Parliamentary phone by Jeremy Perry, the senior partner of 'Search and Select', a firm specialising in senior management recruitment. "Ms Carter, I am Jeremy Perry. I loved what you said in your Maiden Speech yesterday and I think that my firm can help you to recruit your future constituency candidates."

"I don't have any money at the moment but can I come and see you?"

They met the following day, two days after the speech, in Jeremy's plush offices in Belgravia.

After the introductions and the grateful receipt of coffee, Jeremy said, "If you are serious about recruiting close on 650 candidates, then you need help. Our normal fees are 30% of the first year's salary and bonuses, so that would be about £30,000 for every successful candidate.

After viewing your speech again with my partners, we think that you have a great potential for change and we would like to be a part of it. We will search and select all potential candidates and charge a minimal fee to cover expenses for those candidates not elected. For those that do get elected, we would agree a 50% fee reduction."

"We would need to owe you money until our fund raising picks up," said Julie. "Also I have some firm ideas of the sort of candidates that we want."

"No problem. My people will sit with you and establish the personal and job profiles. I counsel you that we must get started soon, if you want to proceed. It is a big job covering the whole country and an election could be called at short notice."

"Can I meet some of your researchers today?"

"They are in the next room waiting. I have a small agreement of our Business Terms for you to sign and then we are off and running."

Within a week of the meeting with Jeremy Perry, two by-elections were called for 15th July, one in the solid red wall constituency of Peterlee, County Durham and the other in the very blue constituency of West Byfleet in Surrey. In both places, the National Endeavour Party, with candidates specially chosen after interview by a nationally respected headhunting firm, were victorious with massive majorities. Change had started and it had a relentless progress. Brian Strong in West Byfleet and Peter Burrow in Peterlee joined Julie Carter in the House of Commons. National Endeavour now had three MPs and the numbers would soon grow further.

Chapter 5

Get Carter & Spread the Word

March 2032

After her maiden speech, Julie Carter was the talk of the Westminster bubble. In the tea rooms of the Houses of Parliament there was no other subject. The responses ranged from 'jumped up girl', 'know nothing stupid woman', 'not one of us' (whatever that meant in 2032) and 'a show-off, who wanted her 15 minutes of fame'. In the pubs and wine bars, journalists and media types boasted over their drinks that they would be 'the first to secure an interview', 'the writer of the piece that exposed her shallowness' or even 'the person who exposed her private life in all of its tawdriness'. One of them having had a little too much wine even suggested that he might seduce her!

The mainstream political parties had advisers of all sorts, called Special Advisors (SPADS). Their backgrounds and profiles were similar, irrespective of which party leader or minister that they advised. These bright young things had read Politics, Philosophy & Economics at Oxford or Cambridge and if they got a First Class Honours Degree, then they were on their way. There would be no manual labour involved for the rest of their lives. Because it is tiresome to have a career in business, where you have to learn to manage people and resources, they opt for politics. It matters little that they haven't done an honest day's work amongst ordinary people, because their boss never did either. No, the future is clearly mapped out. After the top degree, the establishment comes calling. If you prefer politics to diplomacy or spying, then a political party will take you on board and soon you are a SPAD.

Of course you are much too young and lacking experience to know anything about real life, but that won't stop you advising politicians and ministers on what the majority of normal people want. You have probably never met or spoken in depth with a normal person but you can read up on what they are like. You have been cossetted by professional middle class parents so you don't know what living in poverty or in a city housing estate might mean, but that's not a problem. A Member of Parliament (MP) might recruit you for his constituency office and get you to do some research. All the time you are building your network of people who are much like yourself. You write speeches, become expert in something obscure but useful for a short time, write an opinion paper, a conference speech that goes down well and before you know it, you are rubbing shoulders with more senior members of your party in Parliament. You are on an upward trajectory so the next step is that you are persuaded to work for a more prominent MP or even a Cabinet Minister. After a few years of this, the party thinks that you will be an ideal Member of Parliament and a safe seat is found for you. You are catapulted into a constituency somewhere in the midlands or north. No matter that you've never been there and don't have any idea what the people are like, you just have to smile a lot and pretend that you will be living in the constituency soon. After you win the seat, you are advised to adopt a fashionable cause and get noticed in the House of Commons tea room. If you have kept your nose clean, avoided a scandal, persuaded your wife or partner to play the game and followed the party line by agreeing to its policies, even when you don't, you will eventually be approached by a government minister to be a Parliamentary Private Secretary (PPS). This means that you act as the unpaid assistant to a government minister. As a backbench MP, you are the 'eyes and ears' of the minister in the House of Commons.

Julie Carter as an independent MP didn't have to worry about any of this. She had no party affiliation, did not seek a ministerial job and had no historical baggage in the past disasters.

The most watched political programme of the week was the Sunday politics programme with the BBC's Political Editor. The weekly viewing figures of 1.5 million was hardly huge but it was watched by people interested in politics. Julie had just returned to her temporary Parliamentary office, a cubicle really, when the phone started ringing with offers from all media sources to appear or give face-to-face interviews. The Sunday politics show people were very persistent, but she didn't choose them. Instead she chose to appear on BBC Breakfast with daily viewing figures of 6 million. These viewers were normal people and not those solely interested in politics. Julie needed to get her message across to the man and woman on the Clapham Omnibus, to quote an old phrase. Her choice of this programme caused major ructions inside the BBC. The political editors demanded to have a big hitting political interviewer to conduct the conversation, whereas the normal team on BBC Breakfast thought that they were perfectly capable of handling it. The contretemps went all the way to the top and the Director-General was given the role of peacemaker and decision taker.

"Why did Julie Carter choose BBC Breakfast above the overtly political Sunday show?" he asked. "Because she wanted to get to a wider audience of non-political people. Voters in fact. I'm sure that BBC Breakfast can handle this," was his decision.

The interview was scheduled for Monday, less than a week after her Maiden Speech to the Commons. Richard Robins, a veteran presenter and a person with a long career in interviewing people from all backgrounds was the natural choice, but instead Hazel Sharif was chosen as it was felt that she would better draw out from Julie Carter facts about where she had come from and where she was heading now. The stage and settees were ready and straight after the 8am news headlines Julie was introduced by Hazel.

"Good morning, you are watching BBC Breakfast and today we have the pleasure of introducing to you Julie Carter, Independent Member of Parliament for South Oxfordshire and the only member of the National Endeavour Party, a new name in politics. This is the first television interview that Julie has given since her explosive maiden speech last

Wednesday. A speech that has the whole political class seething with resentment and the public cheering to the rafters. Welcome Julie."

"Thank you Hazel, I'm delighted to be here."

"What is it like being the most unpopular Member of Parliament by your fellow MPs?"

"I said what had to be said. There is a fear among politicians of saying just how difficult living in Britain has become. It is not enough to say that it is the same in other developed countries, because all that means is that they are suffering the same malaise. In short, in Britain nothing works like it should. We have greed and vested interests getting the upper hand over ordinary working class people."

Hazel quickly asked "Are you a socialist or communist even?"

"I am an ordinary person struggling to get by like most of my constituents. I have a son Jamie who waited six months to have his tonsils out. Doctors agreed that he was an extreme case and in pain but it was not considered urgent enough. I didn't have £3,000 to pay for it to be done privately so instead my child suffers. I cannot accept a poor service for my son, so I can't accept it for my constituents either. To answer your question, I think that everyone should be treated equally irrespective of race, colour, religion, sex or personal orientation. I have right wing solutions to solve left wing problems."

"You announced that your new party would put up candidates in forthcoming elections. Will you be fielding candidates in the Metropolitan District elections in May? Also there were two by-elections announced yesterday, so will you be fielding candidates at both of these? How do you choose your candidates?"

"We will not be putting up candidates in local elections. We are a national party involved in national issues. We will be fielding candidates in both Parliamentary constituencies. We have commissioned a well-known recruitment firm to find our candidates, all 632 of them. If anyone out there thinks that they would like to come with me on this journey, then please contact my constituency office. We have strict criteria. We are looking for individuals who have achieved things and can build and manage teams. We are interested in attracting clever, successful business people who will bring their management expertise to our party and senior roles. We are not interested in career politicians, typically those straight from university into political parties as they don't have the work experience at a middle or senior level that we seek."

"What party machinery do you have to support you?"

"I am a single parent so I rely on family and friends to make sure that my son's needs are met. After my election I completed the formalities for a new MP. There is a department in Westminster that advises on recruitment for my various roles. I recently met a wonderful woman called Grace Kilbey, who has just stepped down from running a FTSE 100 company and she has brought with her a competent personal assistant. I am hopeful that she will be my Chief of Staff and she will manage the party and prospective candidates. I will be the face of the party and give interviews just like this one. I'm hopeful that through this interview with you today I will attract more prospective candidates."

"How have you raised money to fund your office and staff?"

"After my maiden speech, I was approached by prospective donors and my Chief of Staff will be ensuring that we abide by all of the rules before taking their cash. We will publish a list of all donors and their amounts in real time as we encourage transparency in all matters. Small donations from members of the public are welcome."

"Going back to your maiden speech, have you received any contacts from people who were upset by its content? Are you concerned over any personal safety issues?"

"Some MPs passed me in a corridor and were most rude about what I'd said. All of the emails and other social media posts have been almost universally supportive. Everything I said was true."

"You won't be in a position of power any time soon, but if there were three policies that you would like enacted, what would they be?"

Julie didn't have to think for a moment before replying, "Have only 10% of any village, parish or town available for second homes &

holiday lets. Bring all empty homes into occupation and the third would be to fine harshly all those avoiding paying the right amount of tax."

"Do we have only second and third rate politicians? Don't you respect any of them?"

"The evidence is there for all to see. Last night we had a march through Central London that ended in violence and three police officers needed hospital treatment. Forty arrests we made. This morning we learn that it is not expected that charges will be brought. Why no charges? We have given a licence to protesters to beat up the police, smash shop and bank windows, disrupt the lives of citizens wanting a pleasant night out in London and nothing happens to them. It is inevitable that there will be more of this on future nights."

Hazel asked, "Don't you believe in the right to protest? Aren't we a country that prides itself in having Free Speech?"

"Free Speech does not mean assaulting the police, who should be allowed to act with more force. If I exercise a freedom that reduces your right to free movement, is that right? I believe that all citizens should act within the law. I believe in prosecuting people who break laws and I think that the police and the Crown Prosecution Service are failing us by not doing so.

"Today, we have yet another rail strike so my constituents can't get to work. We have laws that can demand a minimum service requirement but the government is afraid to use them. We have anarchy and politicians of all parties paralysed into inaction."

"What does National Endeavour mean?"

"The country has fallen into a deep malaise. So many people don't want to work and prefer to get paid to sit at home. Children don't go to school and some willingly take part in drugs and knife crimes. Criminals do not fear being caught because they don't pay the fines or do the community service. We have car accidents where a driver has no licence, tax or insurance. There is no respect for the law because the people believe that the country has failed them. National Endeavour will ask those that have, to give up a bit to those who have not. We will ask everyone to pay their taxes, don't break the law and contribute in some way to a national endeavour to get the country back working again."

Hazel quickly picked up on a point in Julie's last answer. "You sound very right wing and left wing at the same time."

"I am no wing. I know what is right and what isn't. Some people don't know what is right so we must help them understand. We will need money to get our plans going, so the tax dodgers, companies that make excess profits and executives that take too much for themselves will have to pay some more. There is no free lunch ticket and everyone on benefits will need also to contribute something."

"Will you be locking a lot more people up in our overcrowded prisons?"

"We should be locking up hardened criminals. We will not be locking up people for short terms but they must be made to pay fines and carry out community service sentences. We need to bring back respect for the law and that includes barristers and judges."

Hazel decided to challenge Julie by asking "You have pointed out quite forcefully what you think is not going well but you haven't said how you are going to get into a position where you can help to put things right. How are you going to get some influence with those now in power?"

Julie looked straight at the camera and said, "I am one person, the first but not the last sitting MP for National Endeavour. I have no power, but as time passes that will change because that will be the will of the voter. I have many ideas that will make things better for you out there watching this programme."

In one of the millions of households watching, Robert Johnson said to his wife Norma, "Look, she is talking directly to us. Isn't she great?" Norma replied, "She has got something about her, hasn't she?"

Back in the studio Julie continued, "I will be joined by people of quality and competence whose primary purpose will be to improve the lives of everybody. They will be chosen because they are prepared to put the people above everything else. I know that I can join with others to resolve the country's problems and make life better for the vast majority. The privileged minority have had their way for far too long. It is inevitable that the moment will arrive when I will be given that trust."

Hazel said, "It's easy though to carp and criticise from the sidelines without having to put your ideas into practice. You, alone, will never improve matters. The main parties will keep you in the background and the establishment, just like in the TV programme 'Yes, Minister', will make you ineffective."

Julie again looked directly into the camera, "I have lots of ideas, all practical, all doable and I will be publishing them. Some of my party's ideas will be picked up by the government because they are sensible and that is a good thing. These ideas will be common sense solutions, but I predict that most will be ignored. As a country we need to take harsh measures and ask everyone to be very disciplined and focused if we are to overcome the problems."

Hazel said to Julie, who turned to face her, "Thank you for coming in. We wish you luck on your one person campaign."

Julie replied, "One person today, but many more in the future."

And of course there were, starting with two wins in the next two by-elections.

The interview on BBC Breakfast was picked up by all the news media. Julie spent the next few days doing interviews and a personal profile for The Sunday Times Magazine. After a week of responding to most of the media requests, she felt that it was time to get the politics side moving again. Attending Parliament was low on her priorities but she wanted to do her constituency work every Friday. This also meant that she had her weekends with Jamie.

The upcoming by-election in West Byfleet had been a solid Conservative seat since 1924, over 100 years. The sitting MP had died and had been deeply respected by the community. This was a part of

Surrey that was deep blue and nobody expected anything other than the Conservative candidate to romp home. The Labour Party had low expectations for the seat and devoted little time and resource to it. If a party were to do well with a protest vote against the Conservatives in this constituency then it would be the Liberal Democrats. The National Endeavour candidate was Brian Strong. Strong by name and strong with effectiveness.

Julie's strategy with Brian was the same that she had employed in South Oxfordshire. Get out and meet the people. With Julie standing beside him, Brian was guaranteed a good turnout in all of the local meetings. Julie had quickly become a national celebrity and people came out to see her. At every meeting, those attending had agreed that Julie had a real presence and just by being there, Brian Strong's profile had been lifted. The format was simple. Julie introduced Brian to the gathering, Brian kept to the prepared script and they both answered questions. Julie gave a final five minutes rallying call to finish the meeting. Brian was a good candidate and he had been one of the first to pass through the rigorous recruitment process. He was intelligent, well dressed but not too formally or ostentatiously and a quick thinker on his feet. He had left school at age sixteen and carried out an apprenticeship in an engineering company. He rose through management and became the Chief Executive at the relatively young age of forty-one. The company was bought by a German firm and he was let go. Now at the age of forty-eight he was still at the height of his managerial powers. He had quickly understood the need to be 'on message'. There was no room in National Endeavour for mavericks pursuing their own agendas. Discipline and loyalty were everything.

By-elections are not for the faint-hearted and lazy, as Brian discovered. Centrally, the office would set up the venues for the meetings and instruct Julie & Brian where and when to attend. They travelled light carrying leaflets to hand out in the village and town halls. There was no knocking on doors as they didn't have the teams to do it. The meetings were publicised on social media and on local billboards and each was crammed full, often with a good many left outside. The day of the by-election came and South Oxfordshire was repeated with Brian Strong being elected as the Member of Parliament for West Byfleet.

On the same day a by-election was held in Peterlee, County Durham and Peter Burrow was elected for National Endeavour. The very left-wing sitting MP had had the Whip withdrawn by his party for some unsavoury remarks about the problems in the Middle East. As he had passed seventy, he decided to pay his party back and in a fit of pique resigned his seat. Peter Burrow's background was in transport and had been the Senior Logistics Manager for a haulage firm. He was a young fit-looking man of fifty-six, married with two grown up daughters. He had seen Julie's maiden speech and was immediately taken with the idea that he wanted to join her. She had that effect on people. He had passed the recruitment process and was a local man from the north-east.

For these by-elections Julie had divided her time between Surrey and County Durham which exhausted her. These by-elections proved to Julie that she couldn't operate in a general election in this way as she would be spread too thinly. Also the distances from home meant that she had spent almost a month away from her son Jamie and constituency affairs.

Grace, her newly appointed Chief of Staff, came up with the idea of a video presentation. At each meeting of potential voters there would be a mixture of candidate and videos of Julie. A number of formats were tried and those settled on were a personal presentation by Julie, a question and answer session with a nationally recognisable political interviewer and a closing speech that could be changed for each candidate. Julie realised that she had to depend on the selection process of the candidates because it should produce self-motivated people to do the hard miles in the constituency and people of intelligence with presentation skills able to keep to the core messages. All the early signs were that this would work well.

Chapter 6

The Hapless Coalition & the End of Cheap Money

2032

When Julie Carter took her seat in the House of Commons in 2032, the country was one year into a second consecutive coalition. This time it was the Labour, Lib Dems, SNP & Greens and already the cracks between the parties were widening. Earlier in the year, in February, a Labour proposal to repeal some trade union legislation did not get the support of the Liberal Democrats and without their support it could not pass into law. In May, a severely watered down version was passed but it was so feeble that it had no effect at all, much to the unhappiness of the Trades Union Congress (TUC).

In the same February, a strike brought the docks to a standstill so the car manufacturers (actually they were only assemblers of parts imported) had those parts delayed and the workers were laid off. Just in Time production meant that if the parts didn't arrive "just in time" to be assembled, then the production line had to stop. A delegation from the Confederation of British Industry and The Institute of Directors met with ministers but no promises on an early resolution were forthcoming. "The dockworkers are not employed by us," said the minister with embarrassment and the business chiefs just shook their heads in resignation. In April, a South Korean white goods manufacturing company announced that it was shutting down its UK operation before the end of the year and it would be transferring the work to its plants in Spain and the Czech Republic with the loss of 850 jobs. A further 200 job losses in allied trades, shops etc. would also be lost. With some irony, the largest transport union responsible for the dock strike complained that its members in the doomed manufacturing company were losing their jobs.

The British Medical Association, representing resident doctors, had ended their series of strikes in 2024, having negotiated a pay offer that partly restored their historic pay levels of 2010. Since 2025 the doctors pay had been subject to pay commission recommendations, which all governments had accepted and paid in full, but apparently this was no longer sufficient. The doctors argued that their pay had fallen relative to inflation since 2024 and they were still short on that settlement. Buoyed by the success of their last campaigns in 2023 & 2024, another strike mandate was obtained, with a very large majority, and a series of strikes were announced for July. There would be no messing around this time as the BMA went straight for a five days walkout. Over 400,000 hospital appointments were cancelled and waiting lists rose after a few years of reducing.

It was into this turmoil that Julie Carter took her seat in the House of Commons and watched the political edifice crumble like a house of cards. In the summer, the coalition descended into open warfare as the arguing between the parties broke out for all to see. The four members of the Green Party were incensed by a report from the water industry regulator (OFWAT). The report described how all the main rivers in England were running with untreated sewage and worse of all, that OFWAT was powerless to do anything about it. To make matters worse, the Green Party's political reason to be in Parliament was to promote a zero emissions policy for 2035 and to date there had been glacial progress towards reducing carbon emissions.

The Green Party had an emergency meeting, not just the four members in Parliament, but their National Executive Committee as well. The meeting concluded that they had insufficient influence in the Chamber to make any difference at all. This realisation, was the right deduction and led to some serious soul-searching. The obvious conclusion reached was that they should seek an alliance with a party or two to help them win some arguments. One of the Green Party

MPs suggested talking with Julie Carter, who seemed to be getting some traction with her solutions in interviews in the media and in the opinion polls. The Green Party held off because they concluded that this Coalition was doomed and they would soon be one of the parties in a third coalition.

Julie spoke with the Greens, "I have formed the National Endeavour Party and soon I will have a number of MPs from all parties coming over to me. I have some solutions on the environment and green issues that will be just what will interest you. I will send over a document on our future policies. If you like what you see, then I suggest that you all leave your party and come and be full members of mine. I'm not looking for alliances, I am looking to increase the size of my party in Parliament. The four Green Party MPs went away and later studied the document sent over. Along with it were the rules of membership of Julie's party. The first rule was discretion and not leaking to the media. This rule was a deal breaker and anyone who did leak could no longer be a party member. Separately the four came to the conclusion that being part of something larger was more exciting but their Executive Committee decided to wait for the coalition to collapse.

As the year went on, the coalition seemed paralysed by inaction and the crises kept on coming. In August, a computer glitch stopped welfare payments to severely disabled people and their carers. In the confusion and in despair, a mother killed her disabled daughter then herself. The message left by the mother was truly damning and accused the government, the local authority and the NHS of abandoning them. As a result of the subsequent media coverage, respect for politicians dropped to a historic low and violence was not far away. It was evident that the social fabric was fraying. The rusty wire that kept civilisation in check broke on the morning of 7th September in a deprived area in southern Manchester.

The local Labour Party MP was attacked by four masked youths and she ended up in intensive care. It was clearly a targeted attack as on the same day in a separate incident her constituency office was burned to the ground. The Speaker in the Commons vented his frustration and reminded the politicians of the need to tone down the rhetoric and insults. When able, from her hospital bed, the South Manchester MP announced that she would resign her seat as she couldn't justify putting her family through a trauma like that again.

The ministers in the Coalition Cabinet had almost given up amongst themselves when in the late summer of 2032, just six months after Julie had been elected, a second vote of confidence was put in the House of Commons. It was defeated by a small majority, doubtless due to the fear of all MPs that a General Election would result in a lot of them seeking a new job.

A Think Tank produced a report showing that nothing economically or in all other measurable respects, had materially improved since 2024. Over 8 years had been lost and everybody's living standards had declined relative to the economies of the other G20 nations. The country was also closer to its emissions deadlines of 2050 without any evident changes.

The determination needed to make difficult political choices left the room with Margaret Thatcher in 1990. Since then all the leaders had been dominated by events and not the other way around. Small protest groups had hi-jacked the judiciary all the way to the Supreme Court. Governments had made one step forward then one dippy judge had pulled them two steps backwards. One person, or a small group with a sympathetic barrister working for free, could delay government policy for months or much longer. The judiciary revelled in the fact that they could use an obscure point to push their own agendas without anyone reigning them in. There were so many urgent and important issues needing resolution for the public good, yet they were constantly derailed for little purpose other than to massage someone's ego. This was when tough government was needed, but there wasn't any to be had. Any delay to an important change meant that it got shuffled to the bottom of the pile. There could be no progress until the judiciary applied the law and not be swayed by their own foibles or interests. The point was missed, that if the government was hindered due to a poorly drafted law, then the law should be re-legislated in a clearer form to reduce any doubts. However, Parliament's arcane procedures made this very difficult and in coalition impossible. For a sole political party to pull in 100% behind an issue would be a miracle, for a coalition it was not feasible.

An ordinary person might believe that when more than one political party joins with others in a coalition, it might mean that all those involved in this serious subject of law making, that all parties would pull in the same direction. History shows us that this is never the case. Each party to a coalition is eyeing up the next election and so party advantage must be pursued. When the coalition fractures or comes to an end, every party in it would wish to emerge stronger than the others. It can do this by either being successful in pushing through its own agenda or by scuppering, often making it look unintentional or bad fortune, the agenda of its coalition partners.

In every coalition there is the issue of the best jobs. The leader will come from the party with most seats in Parliament but the other big jobs are by negotiation. The Green Party, for instance, might like the Environment portfolio, because for them the position carried great significance. The Prime Minister will want the Chancellor of the Exchequer to be from his or her party as the nation's funding can make or break the leader.

The Home Secretary is often the difficult department in government so it's best to give that to your main rival. The recipient will be seen as incompetent when it all goes wrong on immigration, police and crime. In a coalition of equals (can there ever be one?) these jobs would be spread around and that's what happened in 2031. A Labour Party Prime Minister, their first ever female to hold the role, a Liberal Democrat Foreign Secretary & a Home Secretary from the SNP. What could possibly go wrong with that appointment, other than everything? The Greens got their reward by getting the environment portfolio, which made them happy. They hadn't figured out until it was too late for them that they would now be held responsible for the dreadful state of the rivers, the coastal beaches, the loss of Green Belt land and reducing food quality.

One step down from the Cabinet jobs were the Chairs of the Select Committees. In 2031 it was done on an almost equal basis to keep everyone happy, but it ignored the lack of experience and ability, which did not bode well. The sages on the political scene would point to the Select Committees as the real motors of power so the Chairs held real political sway. The Commons Select Committees were responsible for overseeing the work of government departments and agencies.

This house of cards, or some said political Jenga, was put in place and tasked with problems that had defeated two governments with large majorities (2019 & 2024) and one coalition (2029-31). Julie Carter was elected earlier in 2032 into this quagmire of indecision and watched the annus horibilis of 2033 gestate during 2032.

The economy had not improved since 2024. There was still little growth, often recessions, and increased government borrowing. It wasn't borrowing for infrastructure to generate growth and hand something on to the next generations, it was borrowing to pay for everyday expenditure. The welfare bill had gone out of control with claimants coming for every known, and some unknown malady. The recent favourites were the difficult ones to diagnose. After the present King and his brother had confessed to mental health issues in their lives after the death of their mother, it had become increasingly fashionable and not a disadvantage, to self-diagnose with the same problems. Attention Deficit Hyperactivity Disorder (ADHD), acknowledged as a medical condition for some, was adopted by anybody with a lack social skills to explain why they couldn't go to work or school. Bad behaviour or "I just can't be arsed to conform" were seen as a good path for a state handout. Covid lockdowns had shown people the attractiveness of staying at home and now so many were being paid by the taxpayer to do so.

As expenditure on welfare increased so did the money required by the NHS to prop up its failing service. A big chance to sort out social care for the elderly was missed, so they continued to stay in hospital, not ill, but not dischargeable either. More money, poorer service, longer waiting lists and resident doctors once again out on strike. "Let's just give it more money and it will get sorted" hadn't worked for a decade but it was tried again every year and in 2032.

As always when things are going badly, everybody is looking around for a minority to blame. In 2032 it was the immigrants who were blamed for the continuing housing crisis, the increased demand for NHS services, crime (although very few broke the law) and the cost of putting them up in hotels.

The Labour Government of 2024 had such bold ideas for housebuilding, One and a half million new homes in five years. They only did as well as previous administrations achieving one million in that time. Net migration in the same period was two million, so there was a shortfall of one million, or perhaps less if some migrants came in family units. Nevertheless, the under supply didn't catch up with the over demand so rents and house prices went inexorably higher. Labour tinkered around with the planning system, the Green Belt, brownfield, greyfield and every other colourfield sites; and anything they could think of without dealing with the reality that there were nearly enough houses, only too many were lying empty and others were the second homes of the privileged or holiday lets.

The right wing First Coalition of Conservatives, Reform UK & Lib Dems did not have a priority to help the homeless so nothing changed. In 2032, the left of centre Second Coalition had a real opportunity to get to grips with it but failed to do so. Commentators screamed out that the problems were the complex and unnecessary environment issues, climate change targets, glacially slow planning procedures and a shortage of labour and materials. There was a suspicion (more than a suspicion actually) that housebuilding companies were holding back land from development so that they could manipulate the price of houses for when they did bring them to market.

What did the members of the Second Coalition do? They argued between themselves about priorities that meant that in the end, nothing was done. The SNP wanted another independence referendum as a price for being part of the coalition and nobody would blame them for that. Previously the government in Westminster was the problem standing in their way, but now they were part of the government. The Liberal Democrats, supported by the Greens and SNP wanted to rejoin the EU but Labour, sixteen years after the Brexit vote could see this as a stick to beat them senseless for the next general election in 2034 so were having none of it. The Greens wanted every new home to have a heat pump, triple glazing and solar panels that increased the cost of every house. They also wanted every existing house to be given free insulation to enable less energy to be used. The cost of the insulation of twenty-five million homes was put at £20 billion of which only a tiny fraction was affordable. The planning for new small nuclear power stations was bogged down by too many regulations and MPs not wanting them anywhere near their houses or in their constituency.

What did the Second Coalition achieve from 2031? It showed the public how the current constitution and make-up of government could not serve the people. Into this void entered National Endeavour. Julie Carter had charisma, vision and determination and she was building a party of quality individuals who were used to getting things done.

Christmas 2032 was a bleak time for the government and the country. Unemployment had increased to 2 million and because of the continuing docks strike, there were fewer goods in the shops than normal A very wet summer and autumn saw crops rotting in the fields so expensive supplies from Spain and the Netherlands increased the cost of the weekly food shop. Everybody was looking for an uplift from the Second Coalition but it never came. The stealth taxes contained in the Autumn Budget Statement reduced household incomes and inflation climbed above 6%. Public sector workers were looking for a matching pay settlement, but the Treasury restricted the increases to 1%. The resident doctors, now striking every three months, came out on strike in December just as the high winter rate of admissions to hospitals began.

In 2032 there had been 6 by-elections, all won by National Endeavour. The first two in West Byfleet and Peterlee heralded that change was in the air. Later in the year four more had the same result. Additionally, there were 12 defections to National Endeavour from

SNP (1), The Greens (2), Labour Party (4), Liberal Democrats (2) and Conservatives (3).

By the end of 2032, the National Endeavour Party had grown to nineteen Members of Parliament and they spent most of their time holding ministers to account. On the last Prime Minister's Question Time before Christmas, the Speaker called on Julie Carter to pose a question. Julie stood up and said, "Could I please ask the Prime Minister and leader of the Second Coalition if she could explain why everything in the country is as bad under her government as it was under the First Coalition that it replaced?" The Prime Minister rose to speak amongst jeering from all sides and said pathetically "We are trying our best." Three days later she resigned and was replaced by her deputy.

Just before Christmas 2032 the Second Coalition government effectively ran out of money. The country had been living on borrowed cash for decades and it was inevitable that one day the lenders would increase interest rates to an unsustainable level or turn off the supply. Since the fiscal year of 1970/1, the government of the day managed to balance the budget on only five occasions, the last being in 2000/1. So for 30 years every government borrowed more to pay for its day to day spending.

The British government's debt was owned by a wide variety of investors, most notably pension funds. The budget deficit was financed by the government selling bonds. These bonds paid interest to the holder. Other purchasers of government bonds included insurance companies and overseas investors (28%). The bonds made up most of the government's debt.

The cost of servicing this debt fluctuated with interest rates nationally and internationally. In 2029, the annual cost of servicing the public debt amounted to around £130bn, about £400m per day. More was spent on interest payments than on Defence and Transport combined and nearly the same as on Education.

In the autumn of 2032, there occurred one of the periodic global financial crises. Heightened tensions in the seas around China and the closer integration of Russian & Chinese interests caused uncertainty in the financial markets. Oil prices increased as it became obvious that the developed countries' reliance on fossil fuels for energy was not going to diminish any time soon, despite the public pledges on reducing carbon emissions.

Interest rates rose across Europe and the sovereign wealth funds of Norway, The Arab World and other oil economies got more circumspect where they would place their funds. The main credit reference agencies had previously downgraded UK debt to A+, now they reduced it further to A, which denoted a higher risk of default and so UK borrowing costs increased.

The effect of having to pay more on existing debt and far more on new debt blew a hole in the country's budget finances. Parliament was recalled the day after Boxing Day and the Chancellor came to the House of Commons with a revised Budget that didn't say 'austerity' but screamed it out loud. The Chancellor was unable to increase tax receipts because he had pulled all of those levers in his last two budgets. The result was to look for reductions in expenditure. The two largest departments for spending were health (NHS) and welfare. This was a real problem for the Second Coalition as it was left of centre and the last thing it wanted to do was make the poor pay more or receive less.

The Chancellor decided to go for the slow pain option. Benefits were frozen at their present rates, public sector wage increases were pegged at 1% and all existing income tax bands were not to be increased until the end of the Parliament. Public sector recruitment was frozen. After the Budget, £1 dropped below parity with $ & Euro.

Predictably the financial announcement pleased nobody and the coalition's popularity in the country collapsed. The political parties involved in the coalition found that they were all tarred with the same brush. The respect for the first coalition parties had not returned and in this environment there was only one party that had grown in popularity, the National Endeavour Party. Too late, the Green Party exited the coalition but it made no real difference to the governing group, or sinking ship as it became affectionately known. Winter was coming in every sense of the words.

Funding for the main political parties collapsed and even the trade unions were reticent at providing the Labour Party with funds. Against this trend National Endeavour was attracting money from single donors (bankers/Hedge Fund Managers - large & small) and corporate donors (companies, partnerships, entrepreneurs). National Endeavour fund raising dinners became the hottest tickets in the major cities in which they were held. The party still maintained a small corporate office in Didcot with students, mostly from the Oxford colleges helping out as unpaid interns. The party refused donations from foreign companies unless they were UK publicly quoted on the London Stock Exchange. Julie had achieved celebrity status and was a particular favourite for donations with rock musicians, footballers, actors and golfers. All donations were recorded in the appropriate registers and made public on the party website in real time.

The next election would be held latest in 2034, but the state of the political parties, their unpopularity with the public and the economic climate, meant that all parties had started to plan for an earlier date. Julie asked Grace, her Chief of Staff, to arrange a closed conference that would have all of its sitting MPs and prospective Parliamentary candidates to look at the election strategy and prioritise policies.

During this meeting, those attending concluded that the only way to push through the policies that the country needed would be if a very large majority was won at the General Election. Julie looked around the hall and saw that the selection of candidates had gone very well. The total represented the sex and diversity of the population. There were an equal number of men and women, 316 of each. 10% of the total were black and/or Asian. Each was tasked with setting up the party infrastructure in their designated constituencies. They were provided with a briefcase, a laptop computer, a mobile phone to be used for party work only and some branded memorabilia.

The meeting was held against a background of increasing influence both inside and outside Parliament with Party membership growing exponentially.

Chapter 7

Grey Matters

After being attacked and nearly killed, the Labour Party MP for South Manchester resigned her seat from her hospital bed. Another MP, this time a Conservative, who had been suffering a long illness died in his sleep the day after the Manchester incident. A further two by-elections were called as their constituency MPs threw in the towel.

These four by-elections were moved to take place on Thursday, 13th November. Julie had been planning for these events for some time. The headhunters had come up with six potential candidates, all fitting the required profiles. Julie interviewed them in a hotel in north London and made her selection. She was particularly keen that they understood the terms for being a member of her party. Top of the list of requirements was loyalty and an ability to keep confidential information (no leaking) to themselves. All of the candidates had previous senior management experience and showed a background of administrative capability. The party had little money so the candidates were shown the parliamentary rules for elections and told to go out and make their marks. At these by-elections, the candidates used the videos of Julie and were supplemented by her appearance in large concert halls, proving the success of these presentations. The day of the by-elections came and Julie's four candidates romped home overturning significant Labour and Conservative majorities. The newly elected MPs gave rousing speeches at the counts and emphasised the ongoing ideas of this new party. The key message as always was "If you want it fixed, then supporting the National Endeavour Party will achieve it."

A week after these constituency by-elections took place Edward Grey, a loyal Conservative MP and a Junior Minister in the first coalition, crossed the House of Commons and joined Julie Carter's National Endeavour Party. Edward was sporting a deeply bruised left eye and refused to answer any questions about it. The Tory leadership was incensed at his disloyalty and unkindly briefed heavily against him. He later issued a statement that read "I have been a loyal supporter of the Conservative Party for more years than I care to remember. I have always believed that centrist market capitalism was the best form of government and in my time as a MP, the party has achieved much. However, I now see that the old mistakes are being repeated and both coalitions have been bereft of ideas. Neither the Conservative Party or the Labour Party have any solutions to the current problems, at best just kicking the cans down the road hoping that something turns up. I was very moved by Julie Carter's maiden speech earlier in the year because what she said was true and I was ashamed. It seems to me that only the National Endeavour Party has any realisation of the scale of the problems that face us and I want to help my country by supporting their aims." He wasn't the last defection from the Conservatives that year.

Whatever the Conservative Party could do to Edward Grey it was nothing compared with what his wife Estelle wanted to do to him when he announced his intentions to her the night before. This is her story.

❋ ❋ ❋

"I am Estelle Grey. Appropriately, I was born on Lady Day, 25 March 1981 as Estelle Watkins. From an early age, I knew that I was meant for the better things in life. My father, Joseph Watkins, was from a good working class family and had started as a clerk at Barings Bank in London. He had gone to evening classes and within a few years he passed his final examinations and became an Associate, later Fellow, of the Chartered Institute of Bankers. He met my mother, Audrey Duffield, at the bank's Christmas party, only recently being aware of her position in the Secretariat on the management floor and they started going out together with a shared love of the cinema. My father's career at the bank followed a good, but not spectacular, upward trajectory after being appointed Fellow of his professional body. In 1977, my parents were married in St. Nicholas's church in the pretty village of Godstone in Surrey. They bought a small semi-detached house in the same village as it had a good railway link into London Waterloo. My brother, John, was born in 1979 and I came along two years later. Mummy left the bank to have John and me and never returned to work. Daddy's career at the bank now provided them with sufficient income and after a few years they moved to a detached house in a nicer part of the village. My brother & I had idyllic childhoods. Mummy was at home so able to ferry us to school and the after school clubs like my ballet classes and John's Scouts.

"On my tenth birthday, I was given a small horse as a present, the most fabulous present ever. He was chestnut brown and called Hector. From that day I always had a horse. I just loved riding through the village on a Sunday morning looking down and receiving admiring glances. From my height I could watch the dog walkers, often bending down with their little plastic bags to pick up the dog's doodoos. My horse deposited large amounts of manure on the streets and bridleway. I left it there for the gardeners. Up there on my horse, I felt like a queen.

"My brother and I were sent to fee paying day schools even though the cost strained the family finances, of which I was unaware at the time. The family had to forego holidays for all of the years that the school fees were paid. John was a good student but I was brilliant. I didn't worry about being a day pupil while most of my friends were boarders. It meant that after school and at weekends I could be with my horse in the stables. My brother left school at sixteen to do a carpenter/joiner apprenticeship, I did my A-levels, getting good grades and applied to go to university. My degree from Bath University in business studies led me in to the accounting profession. Three years later after completing my final exams with distinction I was a Certified Accountant in a well-regarded big four accounting firm. My fellow accountants came from similar family backgrounds, all with professional parents. My best friend at the firm suggested that I join the local Conservative Party Association and I thought, "Why not?"

"My future husband, Edward Grey was the son of Harold, a prominent Conservative Party activist and election agent for his local constituency in south-west London. During his formative years, Edward met with prominent party members and even one Cabinet Minister, although the one without a portfolio. It wasn't until he had turned sixteen that he really knew what that meant. After getting a good maths degree from Durham University he was recruited as a trainee at the Unilever head office in London and looked destined for a fast-track management career in soap products. His father Harold enrolled him as a Conservative Party member and so it was that at an annual conference in Brighton in 2003 that we met.

"I first saw Edward standing at the bar of The Ship Inn in Brighton during a lunch break from the Conference agenda and I liked what I saw. There were not that many young people at the conference so he stood out a bit. I estimated that the average age of the delegates at that conference was well over fifty. In 2003, the Conservatives were in opposition and the Labour government were doing such a good job that it looked like staying that way for at least ten years more. The conference was downbeat with a little more time for social gatherings than was usual. Edward was talking to his local MP, Sue Knott, and I decided that this young man, with the right direction, could be going places. I had a gin and tonic in my left hand and stood a short distance away summing him up. I could see that he was well connected, handsome and sporting a very expensive suit and Oxford brogues. A little later, I sidled up to him as he was ordering a drink."

"Nice suit," I said.

"Are you an expert in men's tailoring?" he enquired with a smile.

"I'm an expert in men's tailors. My father has a suit from the same tailor in London. As you went for your wallet I recognised the label."

"I could have borrowed it from a friend," he doubtfully suggested.

"Only if your friend had your exact measurements as it fits you pretty well."

"Can I get you a drink, while we are both here, younger than anyone else and nothing else to do?" he asked.

"Another gin and tonic please. Any gin is fine." I then gave him my name.

"I'm Ted, but my mum calls me Edward."

"Edward is posher so I'll stick with Edward and your mum. Is she here?"

"She never comes to any political meetings but my Dad is here somewhere."

"And this is how my romance with Edward started. A pick-up in a bar in the days before Tinder and late night Internet chat ups. Within a year we were engaged and a further two years later we married. It was the grandest wedding that my village had seen in a long time. Among the guests were some prominent Members of Parliament and two Cabinet Ministers.

"Edward was now getting his career going forward at Unilever and we were becoming a fashionable couple in Conservative Party circles. At one of the constituency meetings, the election agent of the sitting MP approached us discreetly and enquired whether Edward or I had ever considered a career in politics. Before Edward had time to answer I said, "Oh yes, that is certainly his plan."

"The Agent told us that he would have a word with Conservative Central Office to enquire whether a constituency might be on the horizon. And so it happened that my Edward, resplendent in dark suit and blue tie turned out as the prospective Conservative Party candidate for a solid Labour constituency in Nottinghamshire in a by-election following the death of the sitting MP. He didn't win but with my help he performed well and reduced the Labour Party majority by 48%.

"As time passed we remained childless but that didn't bother us as we had full lives with careers and politics. A man from central office thought that Edward had a good chance of being elected in a marginal constituency for the 2019 General Election. We were ecstatic to be chosen for the safe seat of Brentwood in Essex and my husband was duly elected. This was where I wanted to be, socially at the heart of a constituency, where we now had a nice house. I managed the social and charitable work and Edward was soon a Parliamentary Private Secretary to a Cabinet Minister. This was an important rung on the ladder, but as the years went by he didn't progress to a higher office. My mother proved the saying that "Behind every successful man is an astonished mother-in-law." She always thought that I could have done better and whatever Edward did achieve she put down to luck.

"In 2032, Edward had been a Member of Parliament for over 12 years when he came home really excited after hearing Julie Carter's maiden speech in the House of Commons. My husband was not a man to show his feelings, but he was very affected, not so much by what she had said, although he believed that the admonishments were deserved, but by her presence in the Chamber.

"He brought home a copy of the speech from the Commons Secretariat and spent some hours studying its contents. He later admitted that the speech had had a profound effect on him. I read it and I thought that the little upstart should learn some manners.

"Over the next few months, Edward became quieter than normal and withdrawn. "What's going on?" I asked one Sunday morning over breakfast. "Have you got another woman, or man?

"Edward looked across the table at me over his glasses."

"Even for you that was a cheap shot. I think that I've got a crisis of confidence and I'm suffering from imposter syndrome. Ever since I heard this new independent MP deliver her maiden speech I've realised that every word of it was true and that we are basically hopeless, in government, opposition or Coalition. In fact, this Coalition doesn't have a clue on how to fix all of the things that are obviously wrong and broken. Every day I go to the Whips Office and we spend all of our time thinking of opposing the coalition's awful ideas without doing anything to make life better for anyone. I've decided to cross the floor of the House and join Julie Carter's party, National Endeavour."

"You will do nothing of the sort," I shouted. "Pretty soon you will be up for a knighthood and I shall by Lady Grey. I order you not to spoil it for me."

"I don't care about a knighthood, I came into Parliament to do some good and at the moment I'm not doing anything like that."

"You went into Parliament because I willed it. I knew that you wouldn't get high office. You're not bright enough for that, but you are loyal and that gets you the Knighthood. All the things I've done to support you, listening to your dreadful colleagues going on and on endlessly about boring stuff and their petty lives. We shall have to leave the Conservative Association and all of our friends will shun us. I'm a member of the committee and I'm in charge of arranging this year's annual party. You thoughtless bastard. After all that I have done for you I deserve to be Lady Grey."

"It was after what Edward said next that I hit him in the face."

"Lady Grey? That's a cup of tea isn't it?"

"That night we slept in different rooms, which frankly was less of a disappointment as sleeping in the same room had often turned out to be."

"The next day he went and crossed the House. Bloody selfish bastard."

"Later in the day, I sat with a very large gin and mused. In the final analysis every woman will be disappointed with her man."

❀ ❀ ❀

The coalition was fracturing and in a move to shore up the situation, the parties agreed to reshuffle the jobs and replace all the older Cabinet Members with youthful replacements. The displaced older and experienced politicians didn't enjoy being shoved to one side to allow the new cohort take their places. Many of them retreated to the backbenches and tea rooms to bitch about their bad luck. There were a few that could see this as the act of a ship fatally holed below the waterline and so now was the time to jump ship to a safer berth. By the end of 2032, less than one year after National Endeavour was formed, the party had grown to 19 Members of Parliament, now the fifth largest party.

Chapter 8

2033, The Year of Chaos & What led to it

The gestation of the truly dreadful year of 2033 started fourteen years earlier in 2019 with the Conservatives under Boris Johnson winning with a large majority in the House of Commons. Then came Covid, 'Partygate' and the lies and obfuscations so Boris reluctantly had to go. His replacement, Liz Truss, launched arguably the right growth policy but spectacularly in the wrong way and so after 49 days, she went as well. Rishi Sunak, an honourable and decent man, took over and despite trying to persuade the electorate to look to the future with him, everybody felt that the Conservatives had had their chance and it was time for a change.

In 2024, taxation was at its highest level since 1945 but nothing improved. "Where does the money go?" was a frequently asked question. Nothing worked well if at all. The NHS was in crisis again. The doctors were on strike…again. The rivers and lakes were full of raw sewage, power cuts were frequent and every day another town had to exist on bottled water due to pollution. The roads were gridlocked due to emergency repairs, the potholes devoured your car as they were so large and deep. The train schedules were reduced but that didn't matter as due to strikes, the trains failed to appear. Rishi's government was trying to hold his party together at the expense of the country and the people noticed. The Conservatives had it in their power to pass any law, do what had to be done, sort problems and people out, but their timidity always got in the way of the hard choice and difficult solution. This is the punishment for a split party.

When going to work fell out of fashion, the country had too many people unemployed and early retired. After Covid lockdowns, a lot of people liked the idea of working from home and then staying at home and not working at all. Mental health became the go to reason for the doctor providing a sick note or "Get out of work free card" as it became to be known. No growth, a stagnating economy, nothing working properly and a government more interested in its party than the country. And so the inevitable happened. The Conservatives went to the Polls and were heavily defeated. The scale of the defeat surprised many.

The Labour Party won the General Election of 2024 with a large majority because the country wanted a change. Labour soon realised what the Conservatives had known, but were reluctant to divulge. The country was a bastion of freedom, enjoying great culture and sporting prowess but was economically, technologically and socially a total basket case. A country that was on the United Nations Security Council, a prominent member of NATO, a member of the G7 and the birthplace of modern democracy now was unable to look after its economy and population. Labour ministers inspected the books, read the confidential papers, quickly called in experts and concluded that without serious and sustained remedial action the country was in irreversible decline.

Drastic measures were needed but the government feared that they would prove so unpopular that riots could break out in the streets and the whole governing structure might come tumbling down. The new government decided to do the only thing possible and that was as little as they could get away with, just tinkering at some edges. Better to have a slow decline than a disintegration of the fabric of the nation. A small group around the Prime Minister argued for a move to a socialist state, taxing the rich even more although the top 5% already paid more than 60% of the revenue. Prime Minister Starmer was aware that more personal taxes might lead to a flight of capital. Another small group argued for the destruction of the welfare state by reducing state benefits to force people back into work. "If only we could get some growth in the economy", they argued. Despite some logic to this, for some people the whole reason for electing a Labour government was to preserve the welfare structures, so dismantling them would be the greatest betrayal and would prove existential for the party. The sensible policy of limiting the winter fuel allowance to pensioners on pension credit was seized upon as an attack on all pensioners, some of those unhappy even from the governing party.

The ongoing war in Ukraine was costing money the country couldn't afford. The defence budget was pledged to increase to 2.5% of GDP but achieving that was costly. The meeting lasted three hours and there were still no economic ideas for the King's Speech due in Parliament the following week. The one thing that was decided was to make a big noise on housing. It was a good smoke and mirrors job. Building lots of houses takes a long time. The planning rules slowed everything and there wasn't a pool of labour or brownfield sites that didn't require expensive remedial work before a spade could go into the ground. To those who knew a bit about housing supply, the 1.5 million of new builds in five years already looked a tall order.

Nothing could get better quickly because there was no money. A £22bn black hole was identified and looked like a bitter legacy left by the Conservatives. For five years the country limped along with the same problems and the same lack of action to find solutions. The Labour majority meant that there was no early election so it was not until 2029, with the country obviously in further decline, that the election was called at the latest opportunity. The election date was set for 21st June.

The electorate was aware that a radical change was needed but the nature of British politics, first past the post, meant that all the divisions were obvious. Predictably, there was no overall majority for any party. There were 650 elected MPs but only 638 would vote in the Commons. The other 12 were Sinn Fein (8) and the Speaker (1) & Deputy Speakers (3).

Labour won 284 seats, the Conservatives 178, Reform UK 71, Liberal Democrats 52, SNP 40, Plaid Cymru 3, DUP, SDLP, Sinn Fein & Alliance 18 & the Green Party 4. There then followed a period of uncertainty while both of the major parties tried to build a coalition to form a government. The political haggling to form the coalition led to a government of the lowest common denominator. First the Conservatives, not the largest party but one that could build a majority, had a try, but that didn't last more than a couple of years. In 2031, the coalition collapsed into acrimony and King William asked the Labour Party to form a new coalition government. This new party concoction had fewer ideas than the last one and suffered the same malady. Coalitions, without goodwill to make them work are doomed to fail. It was into this uncertain political landscape that in February 2032 Julie Carter was elected as Member for South Oxfordshire. Nobody was prepared for the *annus horibilis* of 2033.

Like all seismic or major changes to the status quo, it all started with a small, quite insignificant event in the big scheme of things. An example of this happened in a small town in Tunisia on 17 December 2010, when Mohamed Bouazizi set himself on fire because he had been (in his mind) persecuted by a female police officer. Mohamed operated a vegetable cart and it was confiscated by the woman. It was the last straw for him but the first straw in the wind for the Arab Spring that followed. His self-immolation led to the downfall of the President, who, after riots and scores of civilian deaths, fled the country. Across the Arab world, the citizens rose up to protest their living conditions.

In the United Kingdom at the beginning of 2033 the tinder was there and waiting for the spark. The year started with the NHS in crisis. A severe winter and a particularly virulent and deadly flu virus had put intolerable pressure on a system already crumbling under a demand that couldn't be delivered. The headlines told it all. In The Times, "Dead people in the corridors, ambulances and wards." "Patients abandoned to die in four NHS Trusts", screamed out from The Mirror. There were other headlines and none of them any better. The Secretary of State for Health was sacked as the government tried to deflect criticisms from its collective obvious inadequacies.

In February, unemployment in northern industrial areas rose following simultaneous closures of steelworks and car manufacturing plants. The effect on local communities was catastrophic and spending on welfare sharply increased, which meant more government borrowing. The financial markets got spooked and interest rates had to rise to stop the flight of capital from government securities.

Financial experts openly questioned whether the country would be able to service the National Debt in the future. Then a secondary bank collapsed under a weight of debt and poor investment management leading to rumours that one of the large clearing banks was in trouble. Even though the clearing bank wasn't mentioned, and anyway the rumour was unfounded, the effect was immediate. Queues formed outside all of the major banks and building societies as savers tried to withdraw their money. The Bank of England and the Treasury announced support for the banks and building societies and guaranteed savers' funds. This action had a slowing effect on the panic, but just as the situation eased, the stock market suffered its largest one day fall in its history. The largest holders of cash in the country were mattresses.

In March airline pilots went on strike followed swiftly by air traffic controllers. Airports were shut down and hundreds of thousands of holidays were cancelled and as a result, a major holiday package firm went into administration. In order to deflect the catastrophic situation at the airports, the Foreign Office expelled 10 Chinese and 6 Iranian diplomats allegedly for spying. The expected retaliation followed, but nobody cared other than for their cancelled holiday to Spain.

In April the steelworks in Port Talbot shut down its two arc furnaces to lockout the staff who had been conducting guerrilla strike activities. The owners had lost patience and closed down the plant. The union bitterly complained and threatened legal action, then agreed to suspend all action and to discipline the most militant shop stewards, but that wasn't sufficient. The management had had enough and the plant closed laying off over 3,000 staff. A major Japanese carmaker, which had recently agreed to use British steel rather than having it sent from Japan, suddenly discovered that no steel was available, so it suspended operations and mothballed the plant laying off over 5,000 employees.

In May police corruption and incompetence reared its head once again. A computer geek in his bedroom exposed activity by police on the Dark Web where officers assisted in a major welfare fraud. Many of the police, with the help of some colleagues, escaped to non-extradition jurisdictions. The County Council elections were held amidst great apathy for politics and there was a record low turnout.

In the first half of the year there were 6 by-elections and National Endeavour were successful in all of them. The party now had 25 MPs.

In June, all infrastructure projects were mothballed at a great cost in contracted monies and employment. The projects were cost updated and reassessed for value for money. The reviews found corruption and overpricing on a massive scale. The owners of Royal Mail decided that it could not operate as a going concern and sold it to another foreign parcels carrier, but before the end of the year the company collapsed into administration. There was no point in posting Christmas cards as they wouldn't be delivered.

It was a month for company collapses in a year of record company failures. OFWAT refused increased water charges for customers and enforced a no sewage discharge policy that resulted in two water companies going into administration. The government took them into public ownership and had to write off hundreds of millions owed to HMRC in tax and national insurance liabilities. They still had the problem of what to do with all that sewage.

In July, the Cabinet met for a brainstorming session and decided to invite National Endeavour into the coalition government. Julie declined the offer and saw it as a last act of desperation of a dying administration. She suggested that there should be a General Election, but the coalition was not falling for that one. It might be good for the country, but more importantly it would be very bad for the coalition partners.

On 28 July, Andrew, Duke of York died and a week later a modest funeral took place in St. George's Chapel, Windsor attended only by his ex-wife Sarah, his daughters and their families. There was little publicity of the ceremony and it was mostly ignored by the press and public.

In August the value of the pound declined further against the euro and the dollar making foreign holidays for many unaffordable. Interest rates rose again and a record number of borrowers were in difficulty paying their mortgages. While the rich took flight by investing in gold and silver, the ordinary working, or in many cases not working, man and woman had to adopt their own budget austerity measures. There was a steep rise in personal bankruptcies. Unemployment rose to 5.3% from a recent decade high of 4.4%. The month was so wet that farmers were unable to harvest the crops and they rotted in the fields. As their produce was wiped out, many farmers abandoned the land.

Also in August, King William V was involved in a horrific helicopter crash. He was the only survivor of the six on board but he sustained terrible, but not life ending, injuries. At the end of the month he decided that it would be in the country's best interests for him to abdicate in favour of his son George VII.

In September, summer came to an end, the most miserable on record with a record rainfall and strong winds throughout August. Just as schoolchildren were returning to school, the train drivers on the overground railways and London Underground decided to have a series of strikes about safeguarding ancient working practices. At a rural station in Surrey, two train drivers on a strikers' picket line were attacked by angry commuters and beaten to death with their placards. The continuous rain had caused the water systems to buckle under the relentless pressure on the system and in some areas the water was deemed to be undrinkable.

The Somerset Levels, one of the lowest and flattest areas in the country, was inundated with water and great flooding occurred. This area, known in ancient times as The Summerlands (from where the name Somerset is derived) had no way of discharging household sewage and the drinking water was contaminated. "Water, water everywhere nor any drop to drink", wrote Samuel Taylor Coleridge with some prescience.

In October, the poorly invested computer systems in government failed an important upgrade and as a result Universal Credit to most recipients was delayed or a lower amount than what was due, was paid. There was an immediate breakdown of law and order with shoplifting on a massive scale and at night many shops were looted and burned. In the face of this lawlessness, the police's softly, softly neighbourhood consulting approach completely disintegrated and there were recorded scenes of violence on and by the police. In the days of hand held mobile cameras and 24 hours news channels the footage was tough viewing. The Chief Constables deplored the footage of police beating up protesters, but in private they urged officers to give back as good as they got.

In November, the coalition looked like it was falling apart. The only party rising in popularity in the polls and in the country evidenced by the by-election wins was National Endeavour. With an election looming in 2034, many Members of Parliament were looking to their futures. National Endeavour was now receiving increasing interest from sitting MPs wanting to defect from their party to it. As the selection criteria was rigorous many of them were turned away, mostly because they refused to agree to the loyalty stipulations.

With so many MPs looking to jump ship and dusting off their CVs, the government became paralysed by inaction. The NHS standards had deteriorated so that assaults on hospital staff and in GPs surgeries increased alarmingly. A National Strike was looming as the unions united in their actions to gain control of the government agenda. The ports were at a standstill and the hint of food shortages led to panic buying and the food shelves being stripped of almost anything edible. Electricity was now being rationed as wind and solar power couldn't make up the shortfall of fossil fuel supplies to power stations. In some areas the National Grid was vandalised and the stealing of copper wire from railways and power generators led to rationing with some households only getting 12 hours power per day. Freezers couldn't preserve the food when the power was off and so the food situation became critical. Students, not wishing to be left out of the general chaos, occupied campus buildings and made ridiculous demands on international issues from a government that could not manage itself, let alone the actions of foreign powers.

Christmas was a miserable time except for the very well off middle classes and those even more fortunate. The army was called on to the streets at the end of the year and after the first confrontation with protesters, the soldiers mutinied and refused to fire live rounds into the protestors.

The United Kingdom was only united in that all parts of it were suffering similar problems and lacking solutions. Scotland's Hogmanay celebrations were the most muted in living memory amid heavy snow falling across the land. Wales & Northern Ireland, in the west, suffered continuous Atlantic storms and winds so strong that power lines were frequently down. The misery of sitting in the dark in a cold room in winter was compounded by the government increasing taxes on whisky, wine and beer in December to raise money.

Early in January 2034, King George VII stepped in and demanded that a general election be held as soon as could be managed or he would dissolve Parliament.

Chapter 9

General Election 2034

1st January to 22nd June 2034

One of King George's first acts in 2034 was to call in the coalition Labour Prime Minister Burnham and tell him that Parliament should be dissolved due to the dire state of the nation, in particular the constant rioting and protests. Burnham did not agree and was granted more time to put things right. The coronation date of 5th May was looming closer and the government had made no progress on quelling the unrest so at his weekly meeting with the King on 4th April Burnham agreed that an election should be held and asked the King to dissolve Parliament ahead of a planned election on 22nd June. The London Boroughs and Metropolitan Districts elections on 11th May would be unaffected.

King George's next major initiative was to hand back Buckingham Palace to the country and designate Clarence House as his London home. The palace was not owned by the Royal Family but it was occupied by the sovereign and held in trust by the Crown Estates. George also announced that it was his intention to renegotiate the cost of the Royal Family, the Civil List, with the incoming government with the objective of reducing the cost to the taxpayer.

The coronation of King George VII at Westminster Abbey on 5th May 2034 was a low key affair. His sister Charlotte and brother Louis were in attendance at the ceremony, alongside Catherine, the recently created Duchess of Windsor. William the ex-King, now the Duke of Windsor, was unable to attend because of his injuries sustained in the helicopter crash. The Duke and Duchess of Sussex attended with their children Archie and Lilibet. Anne, the recently widowed Princess

Royal and the Duke and Duchess of Edinburgh made up the royal wedding party accompanied by their children and grandchildren. As usual for this type of event there were representatives from foreign and Commonwealth countries and all sorts of guests who had been honoured for their services to their communities and members of the civil service. Sir David Beckham and Tom Cruise were in attendance.

The date of 22nd June had been selected as the date for the General Election to give all the political parties plenty of time to prepare and mount meaningful campaigns. Every media outlet agreed that this would be a very important election for the country, as they all were, really. Despite the governments' ministers working hard, the two coalitions did not resolve the crucial matters and the country was now looking for a decisive government, one that would resolve these critical issues, often described in the media as 'The Great Mess'. Some commentators referred to it less kindly and more graphically as 'We need somebody to get the country out of the shit'.

In normal times, the date chosen would have conflicted with some matches in the football World Cup. However, this year the competition was going to be held in Saudi Arabia. For obvious reasons it could not be held in the summer months, so it would be held in November.

Without any great enthusiasm and with very small battle chests of funds, all the political parties, except the National Endeavour Party, were struggling. No person of any calibre, or common sense, wanted to spend over two months campaigning among an electorate who despised them. National Endeavour had completed the headhunting process and would be fielding a full complement of very able candidates in England, Scotland & Wales. The group was unified by a message that loosely translated into "Vote for us because we can change things. We know the problems and we can fix them. Not talk, but do."

Julie recognised that she could not do everything and be everywhere but in order to ensure that her ideas came to fruition, in addition to Grace as her Chief of Staff, she would need two personal assistants who could maintain discretion and not leak her plans to the media. These people must be happy to be subordinate to her, competent, organised and above all loyal, especially during the tricky times ahead. On a Sunday in early May, in her front room sat Edward Grey, her first real believer. He had crossed the floor to her because he believed in what she had said in Parliament. He had sacrificed his own personal career and possibly his marriage to Estelle too. Alongside Edward on the sofa was Harry Armstrong, her constituency office manager. Julie presented them both with a paper titled "When we win by a very large majority".

"Are you so certain?" asked Harry.

"Oh yes, there is no other logical conclusion based on what we know and the polls tell us."

"But you and the party are not prepared for government. I've been an MP too and I don't know anything like enough of what will be needed. If you so firmly believe that National Endeavour will win a majority, we have made no plans for it. You haven't got a cabinet. We will have a Manifesto and that will contain a list of items that we want to achieve, but not how we will do it. The press will tear you apart."

Harry asked, "If we do win, what bad news will we get out early?"

"The country knows all the bad news and that is why they will vote for us."

Edward rather glumly said, "Julie, you have no experience of governing. You will have a senior team of newly elected politicians with no experience. The civil service will eat you alive."

Julie responded, "We've had our fill of experienced politicians and senior civil servants and the country is in this state because the experienced have messed up. We can't do worse and we won't."

It was in these moments that Julie's worth shone through. In this mood she could melt hearts with a simple phase. Any doubts that Edward and Harry had were now dispelled and they believed that everything under her leadership was possible.

Over the next few hours and many cups of tea they discussed the content of the party manifesto. They agreed upon a document that would bear its heart on its sleeve but not be a future hostage for their plans. The manifesto would be written by expert speechwriters but it would contain mainly Julie's thoughts and mission for government.

She had decided that the country should be managed like a successful business with a small corporate team. Pictures of the current cabinet table had shown it to be so congested that half of the attendees could not be seen or heard. If a cabinet meeting lasted three hours and was attended by thirty ministers, it would mean that, on average, they got six minutes each. Probably much less time with the Prime Minister hogging the microphone.

Julie had been recommended to read a management book by Tom Peters, an American guru on the subject of management and customer satisfaction. Peters had defined eight themes that would deliver excellence.

- A bias for action with active decision making, basically 'getting on with it'.

- Getting close to the customers' needs.

- Foster innovation and nurture 'champions'. He famously said that "a person who makes no mistakes makes nothing".

- Productivity and growth would happen if all employees were treated as a source of quality.

- Management had to be hands-on and value-driven. It was management's philosophy that guided everyday practice by showing continuous commitment.

- Successful businesses stayed with the business that they knew.

- Keep it simple with few staff and minimal headquarters staff.

- Keep it tight at the centre but allow autonomy at the business producing end.

She had read the book twice and studied these eight themes in depth. She liked the emphasis on the customer as the driving force. "Give the voter what they want without them having to pay too high a price and it works well", she thought. She also considered for some time the apparent conflicts of Urgent vs Important.

The modern thinking was that something was urgent if it had an imminent deadline and should be dealt with immediately, whereas an important matter may also have a deadline but it will be further out and manageable. Urgent matters needed solving quickly and would deliver a positive change for the people. Urgent matters would be the unemployed getting a job, housing the homeless, making sure that welfare benefits claimants get sufficient money, relieving child poverty and dealing with crime and anti-social behaviour that blights lives.

The Important matters she defined as those that made society better. These would include sorting out the prisons and the inmates, reducing the availability of harmful drugs, improving policing, making the NHS work better and making it easier to get around by car and public transport.

She had looked at these lists and realised that dealing with immigration was not really urgent or important. It was only a perception that it was both, because it had been used politically by all parties. She had to concentrate on those issues that had traction with voters and ordinary people. Most of them couldn't care about how Parliament worked, the suitability of the House of Lords or the relationships between the separate countries of the UK. These were only interesting to those in the Westminster bubble. She would deal with these matters quickly but not devote too much time to them.

She decided that what the country needed was a strong Executive Team led by her, a person of vision, who was prepared to make the tough decisions and see them through to successful conclusions. The structure would be a high level management team of Prime Minister (+ Downing Street Chief of Staff), Chief Whip (no portfolio but in charge of business progress), then five heads of departments. Each Head of Department would have a number of senior ministers (departmental heads). All of the five heads of department would have extensive senior management experience.

Julie announced that she would be releasing the National Endeavour Manifesto on Thursday, 1st June at a press conference. Copies would be circulated to accredited press agencies and all 632 chosen candidates on the day before, under strict embargo. This release would give journalists time to read it and prepare questions.

At the launch, Julie addressed an audience of the media and those constituency candidates able to attend. "Good morning everybody. The printed Manifesto in front of you is in two sections. The front section contains all of the waffle, attacks on other parties, particularly the present government, and motherhood statements about how wonderful we will be in government. This is not the important section. The second section is the best part as it contains our policies for a future government. We believe that if you do the right thing, you deserve things right. We've had levelling up lite and the rich got richer and the poor got nothing. When we write levelling up, we mean it. You have everything to gain if you work hard, pay your taxes, get on with your neighbours and live within the law. As you have had the document for a couple of hours, I will answer questions. In the interests of time, please just raise your hands and I will acknowledge you to put your question."

"What makes your party different from the other parties?"

"Everything in the country is broken, nothing works as it should and the country is in a mess because of decades of mismanagement. There is a real chance that under the weight of increasing debt and interest payments, we could be in a position when universal credit, pensions and public sector salaries may be delayed or not paid in full. Not accidentally as has happened recently, but as a matter of policy because the country has run out of money. We can do something about this before it happens and this Manifesto sets out how we can achieve it. I say to all voters that if you vote for our party and this Manifesto, I will guarantee that the changes and improvements contained in it will be implemented. This is a Manifesto for a national endeavour."

"What does National Endeavour really mean?"

"It means that we are all in this together so there are no free rides on the bus. It means that we look after the vulnerable, we make sure that nobody gets left behind but also that we all make a contribution according to our means and abilities. National Endeavour is not about money, it is about a shared purpose. If we get it right there will be enough money in the future for everyone's needs. We will not be able to continuously borrow money so we will have to fund day to day spending. National Endeavour means that if everyone pays the right amount of tax, eventually the rest of us will pay less. The penalties for tax evasion will be very significantly increased. For the most egregious cases we will be introducing long prison sentences. Taxes are too complicated so we will simplify them by reducing reliefs and allowances. National Endeavour is about public service too. If you have already done well then you should be prepared to give something back by helping your fellow citizens without always expecting to be paid."

"How will you get the unemployed into work when there isn't any work in the areas that the unemployed live?"

"We need to get the unemployed back to work because the unemployed are a wasted resource. We will set up UK plc to invest in and promote manufacturing in those areas of high unemployment. We will produce food and make goods that are currently imported. The unemployed will no longer be paid for being out of work. To earn the daily amount of benefit, the unemployed will be required to meet and carry out community work or be recruited into the armed forces or a National Guard. No work, no pay. Everybody, except the clearly unable, will be expected to be in work, in education, in training or doing community work. We shall not permit our key industries to be bought by investors or companies from abroad, which will then control the workforce.

"How are you going to help families who rely on benefits?"

"All children should have the support of both parents. Absent fathers will make a financial payment for their children. The benefits system is rife with fraud so we will introduce ways to eradicate fraud. Where fraudsters are caught the penalties will be severe. All children should also have a proper place to live, preferably with a garden in which to play. We have too many children living in temporary accommodation. We will support mothers to return to the workforce."

"How are you going to fix the housing crisis?"

"Housing is not a business or an investment opportunity. Housing is a basic human need and we should treat it like that. In this country we have a housing crisis and we all know what it is. Housing is in short supply and far too expensive to buy or rent. We have enough housing units for everybody, yet we have nearly 2 million adults living with parents, in sub-standard accommodation, bed and breakfast local authority placements and on sofas with friends and family. Demand from young people and families to buy their own house or apartment outstrips the supply, even it were affordable. For most people under thirty, owning their own home is an impossible dream. We are going to make it possible. We go even further. During the term of the next Parliament, if we are the majority party, we guarantee to provide the long term momentum to solve the housing crisis. We want to make sure that every adult at or over the age of twenty-five can be provided a chance for a home, either buying or renting. If you are single it will be a one bedroom flat or house. If you are a couple, it will be two bedroom apartment or house. Families should be able to have at least a three bedroom house with a garden. Obviously larger families will have their needs considered too.

"In a country where we have an acute housing shortage, it seems perverse to have so many houses lying empty. These properties need to be rented out or sold and this applies to local authorities which have many empty units. To give councils the money to refurbish where necessary, two new Council Tax Bands will be introduced for properties valued at over £1m and £2m. Properties still empty four months after the election will be subject to a 100% Council Tax levy until they are occupied. This levy will double if the property is still empty after 1 year and each year after that. If a property is empty and the owner cannot be contacted or does not engage with the local authority by paying the

Council Tax in full then a compulsory purchase order will be granted at 50% of the open market value.

"We also believe that it is a stain on our society that people can own a second home that largely remains empty while others do not have anywhere to live. We think that no greater than 10% of all of the residential units in any parish, village, town or city should be owned as a second home or a property let. When that limit is reached, legislation will demand that when the house or apartment is sold it will only be to a person wishing to live in it as their main residence. We will require local authorities to progressively increase the council tax on second homes and holiday lettings to provide funds to build new social housing units. We will acquire brownfield sites by compulsory purchase and where necessary land for housing from farmers and other owners at agricultural prices so lowering the price of each unit substantially. We will introduce a moratorium on evictions from rented properties for 6 months after the election, except for proven anti-social behaviour. Tenby in Wales, Oxfordshire and the West Country counties have tried similar levies on second homes and let properties, but in the main they failed to have a sufficient impact due to too many exemptions. We will have no exemptions.

"We have to build more houses and apartments. If the large housebuilders do not buy into our plans, our new company, UK plc will persuade insurance companies, building societies and banks to become developers and investors. All land with planning approvals that have not commenced to be developed within two years will be subject to a new tax. We will completely overhaul the planning system so that it works for the public good. There will be a sixty days service standard approval of plans for residential housing or improvements properly submitted or the project will be automatically referred to the Housing Minister for approval. The rights of Nimbys, environmentalists and any type of activist to delay or defeat sensible applications will be removed."

"Don't you think that you will meet tremendous resistance, particularly from second home owners?"

"Until we have housed everybody and given those who wish to buy, a chance to do so, then it is clearly unfair that people own a home that they can only spend at most, half of their time in it. We say things that people know are true and it is true that there are some properties that are rarely occupied in places where there is an acute housing shortage."

"Won't you be challenged in the Courts, particularly on compulsory purchases?"

"The Courts enforce the laws that Parliament passes. We will pass the necessary and specific laws so that the Courts will not be hearing cases that are unlawful and against Parliament's wishes."

"How would you settle the latest round of strikes by Resident Doctors?"

"The doctors on the picket lines no longer enjoy the support of the public. Strikes are not compatible with a national endeavour. All disputes will be settled by compulsory mediation. We need more doctors and nurses, so we will create additional training and educational places. Once trained, we need these people to work in hospitals and GP surgeries full time for a good part of their working lives. We will scrap all tuition fees for these professions, providing that they work for an agreed period full time for the NHS. National Endeavour means that we all put our country first. We will have as a priority the resolution of the care homes supply problems and their maximum cost to individuals. We will remove bed blocking in hospitals by creating more care home places and by ensuring that they are sufficiently staffed."

"Are you going to liberalise drug taking?"

"The war on drugs is lost. Addicts need treatment and access to clean drugs sold in controlled conditions. Social drug taking fuels crime so possession of these drugs will result in much higher fines relating to the criminal's means and there will be community punishments. The unregistered sale and distribution of drugs will attract very severe financial penalties and sentences in the harshest prison regimes."

"Will there be help for farmers?"

"We will have to grow more of our own food and give help to our farmers to do it. We will subsidise the cost of fertilizer and give grants to build massive greenhouses in the best locations. We will scrap inheritance tax on family farms."

"How will you help improve education standards?"

"We need to train and retain more teachers and we need to pay them with attractive salaries so that they stay in the profession. We fail our young people if we do not educate them sufficiently to cope with adulthood. Truancy will have zero tolerance so pupils will either go to their school or to a secure unit. Parents have an obligation to their children to get them to attend school and they will be punished if their children do not attend. Disruptive children in schools will be removed and placed in secure units. All university graduates achieving a 2.1 degree or better should be able to pursue a career based on their degree, unless of course the degree has very limited job opportunities. We will bring an end to home schooling as it takes place in an unregulated way."

"Will you be meeting the country's climate change targets?"

"As soon as we are able, we will move to 100% non-fossil fuel power generation. We will encourage more wind farms, solar and hydro-electric power and start constructing small nuclear powered generators. There will be a scrappage scheme to take diesel vehicles and old petrol models off the road. We will have a regulator with increased powers in every utility company. The CEO of utility companies and the Directors will have a personal financial and criminal liability for their company's performance."

"Is levelling up a dead end idea?"

"Levelling Up has been the most abused phrase in politics for years because no government has understood it or meant it. We mean it. There will be improved rail and roads infrastructure connecting Liverpool to Hull and Newcastle to Carlisle. The Oxford to Cambridge Arc with a road link will be completed. We see no reason why the nation's government ministries should be concentrated in London. If the country's regions were more equally prosperous it would aid social and employment mobility. The best paid jobs should be spread more evenly throughout the country."

"Are you going to be tough on crime?"

"When we are all trying harder and making sacrifices, we should not suffer from criminal activity. We will have a zero tolerance to crime. Justice must be quick and a deterrent. We will have more courts and judges and penalties will be enforced. We will be introducing a plea bargaining arrangement so that justice is quicker in return for lighter sentences. Fines will be paid one way or another, if necessarily by parents of underage offenders. Community service sentences will be served. We will have less people in prison so we will only lock up the most persistent and violent offenders. Prison will be drugs free and a place of work contributing to the national endeavour. Each of the forty-six police forces will be held accountable for their conviction rates. We need only violent and recidivist criminals in jail. There will be a lesser number of people serving short sentences and on remand. Having a passport and a driving licence are not a right but a privilege. Some sentences will remove the right to these documents for a period."

"Are you going to cut the defence budget to find money for other plans?"

"The Defence Budget will be 2.5% of GDP. We will institute an ethical foreign policy to oversee arms procurement and sales."

"Are you going to appoint a lot of people to the House of Lords to get your legislation through?"

"The House of Lords will be replaced by a Second Chamber of elected persons from the mayors of all cities and from the regions in the UK. At the same time we will discuss with the relevant elected bodies an increase in powers available to them. The House of Lords will not impede the will of the people. Everything that we are proposing to do is contained in the Manifesto."

"Can you solve the immigration issue?"

"Immigration to our country must be planned and meet our economic and social needs. National Endeavour's policy would be a mixture of reward and persuasion. Each asylum seeker who is able to work will be offered an incentive. They will be screened for their education, qualifications, experience, talent and willingness to work. If a qualified and experienced person is in this group, then they should be immediately offered temporary accommodation and employed in their qualified field of employment. If they were not especially qualified, then they would be persuaded to accept an offer of working in a care home, in the building trade or on the land. There will be work available picking crops in the new greenhouses that will be constructed on the Isle of Thanet, Essex & Lincolnshire. Any asylum seeker able to complete working in this way for two years would earn the right to stay. A further three years in paid employment and they would earn the right to bring over a wife and their children. A further five years in paid employment and they could bring over their parents and one sibling without spouse or children. If they choose not to accept this offer, or fail to fulfil the terms of any such contract, or be guilty of committing a crime during the probationary periods, then they would be sent to newly created facilities on one of the British Overseas Territories until they are voluntarily or forcefully deported back to their home country.

"Non-UK citizens would only be allowed into the UK with a Visa. Shipping companies and airlines will be fined heavily for allowing anyone to board a ship or flight without a valid visa, having checked its authenticity first. No unaccompanied minors even with a visa will be allowed entry. A new Border Force will carry out raids on business premises and multiple occupied properties and any person without the proper visa to stay and work in the UK will be detained and the business owner, company or landlord fined heavily. All students from abroad will need to renew their visa every year but at no cost. National Insurance numbers will not be given to asylum seekers until they have completed their planned period of work. All asylum seekers will have their personal identifiable characteristics and DNA recorded and each person will be issued with an Identity Card, an I.D.

"All employees and landlords will be required to inspect and record an I.D. showing a right to be able to work and live in UK. An agreement with France will be sought to set up safe routes in Calais where visas will be issued. In Calais, we will advertise that failed asylum seekers will be sent to a British Overseas Territory. By the time of the election there will still be at least 50,000 asylum seekers in hotels that the taxpayer is paying for or in camps with staff and food paid by you and me. We feed them, clothe them and pay to keep their accommodation clean and functioning. The annual cost is £5bn. In 2033, the UK repatriated twenty thousand but with net migration running at over 400,000 that means that the problem is getting larger by the day."

"How are you going to pay for your plans?"

"Solving what is wrong with the country will cost money. Some changes are urgent and costly, so we will increase revenues quickly by levying windfall taxes on excessive profits within thirty days of the election. We will end the practice of sending money earned in this country to outside jurisdictions and tax havens. National Endeavour means that all of us need to do something more as even the smallest additional contribution will get the motor of growth moving. The government will not have any money that is not provided by its people, so every penny spent must count. All governments spend money, lots of it. Some of it is essential, some is necessary, some of it is highly discretionary, a lot of it is contractual but a large amount is wasted. We will reduce discretionary spending, hunt out waste and limit all other spending until the economy improves. Immediately following the election all increases in pay to the public sector will be paid by reducing headcount. Members of Parliament will have their pay cut by 20% and all attendance payments to members of the House of Lords will be stopped. We will introduce import tariffs on certain luxury goods and goods from countries that are not friendly towards us."

After this final question, Julie Carter summed up her message to the media group. "Every incompetence, mismanagement or even just bad luck will not be tolerated. We don't have a solution now for everything, but the polls are showing that the voters are liking what we are saying.

We all live by the consequences of our choices. As a nation we have allowed for bad leaders to be chosen and for bad institutions to continue. Now is the time to break this cycle and change all of that.

"If the polls are right, National Endeavour will become the largest party after this election because we have the answers and the voters know it. So they will vote for us in very large numbers. We have set out our plans on everything that needs fixing. The other parties have adopted some of our ideas because they were good ones. However, the public are not stupid and they know that those parties, if elected, will be the same as they have always been. We will pursue our plans relentlessly and not allow the gainsayers to divert us from the path to achievement. There are fringe groups and destructive anarchists from all parties that will be swept aside. I state again that our goals are to remove all hindrances to making life better and that living in the UK will be more prosperous for everyone.

"It is a long held view in government and the highest levels of the civil service, but never articulated, that if you give the poor and manual working classes just enough money by way of social security and other benefits, that they will be kept in their place. This view was proved right in the small number of times that they did not get sufficient funds. Crime, burglary, shoplifting and robberies all increased. If a man or woman cannot feed the family they will take from somebody else what they need, irrespective of the consequences if caught.

"From the first day of the next Parliament, that I expect to lead, the balance will start to be redressed. Our country can be great again but we have to have this national endeavour, one that we all buy into and where the benefits are visible and tangible. My government will enable you, but it won't do it for you, but we won't hinder you either. The country is bankrupt in every way. Bankrupt because we can only spend to keep going by borrowing other people's money. Bankrupt of ideas, no vision, no energy and blaming it on everyone else except ourselves. In the future, we will all live by our efforts and be rewarded for them. We will reduce our carbon emissions in a planned and sensible way. If you want to trade with us then you must give us evidence that you are doing the same. This Manifesto invites everyone in the UK to come with me on a journey to a better place."

The press hacks renowned for their cynicism did the strangest thing. They all stood and applauded. A party leader had never before received a standing ovation let alone one as spontaneous, especially from a group as cynical as journalists. Julie went into the media group and shook hands with every one of them. Her constituency candidates cheered or sat in their seats awestruck. Now they knew what they had signed up to and they couldn't wait to get started. The event was taken up by all of the television news channels and appeared in full on YouTube.

Outside in the country, the main parties had stuck with their "Battle Buses" in party colours criss-crossing Britain in a frenzied attempt at harvesting their faithful and the great number of undecided voters. Their leaders were seen kissing babies, building walls, driving farm machinery and attending every type of school in each town and city.

National Endeavour's campaign would follow the same format that had been successful at all the by-elections over two years. Each prospective parliamentary candidate would have a laptop to show a prepared video featuring Julie Carter explaining her political philosophy, Manifesto and what National Endeavour would do in power. The candidate would have meetings in every village, town and city hall in their constituency. Word of mouth would ensure large attendances alongside local marketing with local press and radio. Julie would be the party's voice on the national stage. National Endeavour had no historic infrastructure to fight the election so proceeded without it. As the campaign progressed a large number of volunteers came out to help.

And that was how the election campaign was fought. Julie did not appear on TV programmes alongside other leaders and was called out as a coward. She did do one-on-one interviews with political journalists. Her face was on billboards everywhere with the simple message of "Vote for National Endeavour. We are on your side, we can fix it and you know it." Her party political broadcasts on the TV were widely viewed, even by those people who were not interested in politics. She proposed cross party agreements to resolve the NHS and care homes crisis. The NHS needed radical reform and it would be managed best if there were agreements between the parties. Other cross party subjects included a Federal United Kingdom, reform of the Second Chamber in Parliament and the introduction of identity cards. She made it clear that she wanted agreement but without it she would carry her plans through. The parties declined the offer to work with her and were damaged for it. The mood in the country was for a relentlessly focused leader.

Her final message was always "Please vote. It doesn't take long and I need you to help me, help you." The turnout on election night was high, because she had that effect on people of all ages.

Julie thought, "This election campaigning is exhausting. There are so many places to visit, so many things to say and so many opportunities to say the wrong thing and be blasted across all forms of media." Julie's party had one message and all candidates were asked to use it. The message was "Vote for National Endeavour and we will sort all of this mess out."

Opinion polls regularly gave the feedback that the message was getting through. As the day of the election got ever closer, the polls looked even better. On the eve of the election, Julie went to bed utterly shattered and soon fell into a deep sleep. She woke up with a start at 3.20am and was convinced that the same voice as before had spoken to her in her sleep. The voice had said "Now is the time. This is the way".

She awoke the next day at 8.30am totally refreshed and absolutely sure that she would win her own seat and that her party would win the most seats. What she was not sure about was whether all of her chosen team members would win their seats. If too many failed to do so, her planning would be put back by a week.

There was a clear advantage in being the government or one of the established opposition parties. The Shadow Cabinet positions were filled with politicians, who would probably be in the government front bench bar a mishap or two at the ballot box. Julie did not have the luxury of a team in place. In the month before the election, she had met the company of headhunters that had helped select all of the candidates. In the week before the election, she supplied them with a copy of her Management Structure Chart, with responsibilities clearly set out alongside a profile of the individual that she thought would succeed in the role, all twenty-nine of them. Julie had no previous experience of managing a company at any level let alone the management of a country. Her mantra had been the same all along when faced with what some thought were highly technical problems. She asked herself "What is your objective?" In the case of filling the role of the Chief Whip or Constable for example, what sort of person would do that job well? Her answer to herself was "a person with strong sense of loyalty, able to see through lies, smoke & mirrors, a fair judge of the situation, a person who could balance the cause and effect and a determination to set a good example personally and expect the same from colleagues." The headhunters used their database tools for all of the roles and out popped the names.

On the day of the election, by convention, the parties were not allowed to electioneer. It was supposed to be a day of reflection. Julie had asked Edward Grey to have a meeting of the twenty-nine selected by the headhunters in a hotel in Birmingham in the morning after they had all cast their constituency votes. The earliest time that they could all get to the venue was 1pm.

Julie addressed them all around a large conference table, while they were tucking into some sandwiches. "A momentous thing is going to happen today. I cannot guarantee that you will all win your seats, but I can predict that National Endeavour will be the largest party. You have all been selected by the headhunters as the best persons for the jobs in my government. In front of you is an envelope with the offer of a job in my administration. Let's hope that all of our elections go as we wish. In my favourite TV show "The West Wing" there is a moment when all of the senior team say one after another 'I serve at the pleasure of the President'. Is there anyone here who does not wish to serve at the pleasure of me, the next Prime Minister?" There was silence in the room, then they all stood up and clapped Julie Carter. None of them declined.

Julie carried on after they had all sat back down. "It is only in the last few days that I have had the belief that we will be forming a new government tomorrow. We have had precious little time to prepare for this. The note in your envelope sets out your job title and whether you are a member of the Executive Team. If you are, your ministerial responsibilities are also stated and you have the names of your Ministers. A formal structure chart makes it easier to follow. Edward Grey will be my Downing Street Chief of Staff. Grace and Harry will continue to manage my constituency obligations.

Every Monday starting at 8am at the same time, each Executive team person will each have ten minutes with me to discuss progress on plans agreed and new initiatives. If I am away, your meeting will be with Edward. Be very well prepared and submit papers ahead of that meeting. Papers are never more than two sides of A4. Remember, you can't sort out everything all at once and I don't expect you to. We need to get the ball rolling on all of the important matters, but make quick progress on the urgent stuff. Every Monday at 9am the Executive Team will meet for 1 hour to agree on the plans for the week, meet with the rest of you by appointment and discuss world issues. Between 10 and 10.30 I will meet with one or two of you in a room to see the regulators, select committee heads and heads of the civil service and police. Edward will arrange everything. Any questions? No? Good luck with your count and we will meet in Downing Street tomorrow.

Shell-shocked and smiling they all left and they were all elected.

Chapter 10

The Day & Night of Reckoning

22nd June & 23rd June 2034

In the days and weeks leading up to the General Election, it became clear that the electorate had had their fill of political incompetence. There were many instances of would-be politicians being verbally abused and pelted with eggs and tomatoes. Some of the more well-known figures had requested police protection while on the campaign trail. The public and the media suspected, but would never admit it, that what the country really needed was a benevolent dictator and the polls clearly showed that they saw in Julie Carter the person to fill that role. The two coalitions, like the two governments before them had policies that did not translate into action, so many words spoken, so many changes of directions and so little achieved. The people needed someone with the 'get on and sort it out' factor. Julie thought that from a zero base only two years earlier it was improbable that she could win a majority of the seats. The result was always more likely that it would be another coalition. She had thought for a while that National Endeavour would do well, but it was not realistic to think that they could win a majority outright. And yet the polls consistently showed that the other parties were haemorrhaging support to her party. Perhaps desperate times did call for desperate measures.

With the encouragement of her followers, she started to believe that it was possible. Harry Armstrong and Edward Grey persuaded her that if the unlikely did happen then she couldn't arrive at No. 10 Downing Street without any ideas on how to proceed. So, at the end of each campaigning day, Julie sat on her sofa with her laptop computer and worked out how best to get started from day one after the election. 'Hit the ground running' best described her plan. The way of government for two centuries had relied upon consult and choose the decision that was acceptable to the majority. Often it was the lowest common denominator decision. It was rarely the policy that the majority liked, more that the minority disliked. These ways had led the country to its current precipice. "A new way must be tried", she thought. She decided that the ends were always more important than the means. "I will go with my instincts. I will make mistakes". She recalled good old Tom Peters writing that if she made no mistakes then she would not have tried hard enough.

Over the weeks of campaigning, she had refined a list of personal priorities and now she studied it for the hundredth time.

- Change everything that will prevent us from carrying out our mission. If we have the parliamentary majority to change any law that we choose, then we should. Think BIG.

- Scrap all bodies and institutions that prevent us from carrying out our mission.

- Govern with a small effective management team, each member sworn to loyalty to her and discretion. History had shown that split parties always fail.

- Identify quick "wins" that immediately make a difference for the voters and raise money for expenditure. Get the urgent stuff done quickly and plan the important stuff over time.

- Contain capital to prevent flight from UK.

- Plan everything from Day 1 to Day 100 (the First 100 Days).

- Try to reach a consensus with the other political parties prior to taking on the big decisions.

Edward Grey had asked her "What was the significance of the first 100 days? Isn't it something made up by the press that has achieved some benchmark significance?"

Julie replied, "I studied this for my degree course. The first 100 days of a new administration has become an important benchmark of progress. The early days of Franklin Roosevelt's first US presidential term from March to June 1933 saw a flurry of laws passed by Congress which became known as 'The New Deal'. In this 100 days, Congress passed seventy-seven laws, a lot of them directed towards reviving the US economy through many public works projects. I think that the first 100 days is a time for courage, boldness and determination. The public will be on our side having given us a massive vote of confidence and the press will give us the benefit of the doubt. We must have all of our plans made, our vision of what progress and success looks like and we must not be swayed from our purpose. We will not put up with our people or others saying that an idea has been tried before and failed, or we don't do things like that, or it won't work. To get the best from this 100 days we need the right people in the right jobs knowing what is expected of them and getting on with it. At a senior level we must be in peak management mode, guiding and persuading but not micro-managing. In my mind I have started the planning for all of this already. In these folders, I think that I have it all scoped out."

"My goodness, you have been busy," said Edward looking at the six differently coloured folders on the floor. What the colours denoted, he didn't have a clue, but knowing Julie it wouldn't be long before he found out.

After all of the campaigning, at last 22nd June, the day of the election had arrived. The Polling Stations opened at 7am and from the start attendance was brisk. After voting, she met Edward in London and they took the train to Birmingham. After the meeting with her prospective team, they both returned to London. Edward went to Brentwood to prepare for his count and Julie returned home to spend some time with her son. Jamie opened the door for her and gave her a big hug. "My friends at school have said that today is big. Why's that?"

"Because today I will find out if all that I've done over the last six weeks will mean something. I've not been at home much and for that I'm truly sorry." Because she couldn't leave the house due to the cameras and journalists parked outside, they did a jigsaw puzzle together.

The polls closed at 10pm and the Exit Polls were broadcast. The headline was that National Endeavour would win 440 seats and have a majority of 190. Compilers had asked 20,000 voters to complete replica ballot papers in over 130 constituencies and this data produced a very reliable Exit Poll. A mass invasion of the South Oxfordshire constituency now took place when editors despatched journalists and film crews to Didcot to be on hand for Julie's count and reaction.

Julie Carter looked at the Exit Poll results on the TV screen and burst into tears. She was suddenly overwhelmed by what had happened. The best analysts in the media had predicted that the National Endeavour Party would have a good night, but nothing on the scale of this.

As soon as the election was called Julie had had a premonition that she would win with a majority. She had campaigned well, dealt competently with the media and had not been outwitted by all sorts of dark arts put in her way by the other parties. Her meeting earlier in the day with thirty prospective ministers and Edward Grey was surreal because not a single result had been declared, but it had to take place. Her party was going to be represented in Parliament and she needed people in their places. If the Exit Poll results turned out to be accurate, National Endeavour would have a large majority and a mandate to make all of the necessary difficult decisions and changes.

She dried her eyes and danced a small jig around the room with Jamie and her mum then said, "Oh my God. What have I done?" She then went upstairs and sat on her bed and took a moment to reflect on what was going to happen next. She changed into her new suit and white blouse and looked in the mirror. She smiled as she remembered a scene from the film 'Midnight Cowboy'. John Voigt had looked in the mirror just like she was doing and said "Where's that Joe Buck?" It was the moment that Joe gained the confidence to go out and make a name for himself.

"Where's that Julie Carter?" she said to the mirror. "Now is my time."

She went back downstairs and then as the clamour outside rose to a crescendo, she said, "They've found us and life will never be the same again." Her mother and Jamie looked at her and both laughed out loud. Harry Armstrong fought his way through the crowd and banged on the door. Julie looked through the spyhole and quickly let him in. "I've come to take you to the count if we can get past this lot. I've called for some police to help clear the way and ensure your safety. I've also booked Margaret and Jamie into a hotel in London." He turned to Margaret and said, "You better get a bag packed for you and Jamie." He turned to Julie and said, "You will need a bag too. A car will arrive shortly to take us to the count. If the exit poll is correct, we will have to go to London too. Grace and I have made all of the arrangements."

"You are a star Harry." Julie looked at Harry, her mum and Jamie and said, "I can do this."

In unison, spookily, they said, "We know you can."

The first national result came in at 11.15pm from the constituency of Houghton & Sunderland in the north-east of England and it was a National Endeavour gain from the Labour Party.

Julie's count for South Oxfordshire was underway in a large industrial unit on the Milton Park Business Campus. She had done everything that was needed and now the fate of the election outcome was in the hands of the electorate. A cheer went up as she entered the hall and a small crowd had gathered outside to wish her luck. Twenty hours after she had cast her vote, at 3.15am the result was that she had been re-elected with a much increased majority. In her victory speech she thanked all of the staff involved in the count, the Returning Officer, her fellow candidates and her team of workers in her constituency. A local reporter asked her to comment on the Exit Poll. "There are so many results to come in, I think I will wait for the picture to be clearer before I make any comments or announcements."

A slow trickle of results gathered momentum until at 5.05am, National Endeavour passed the magic threshold of 326 seats that guaranteed that it would be the largest party and would be forming the next government. Julie, in a quiet room in the hall of her count, sitting with Harry Armstrong agreed with his suggestion that they should go to London to get some sleep. She wanted to be refreshed and in place for all the arrangements that she knew would take place later in the morning. She did a short interview with a BBC Political Correspondent before leaving, openly admitting to the famous now phrase of "feeling the hand of history on her shoulder."

In the UK in living memory there had not been a politician like Julie Carter. After the votes had been counted, all the experts announced that it was the result that they had predicted for some time. They all pretended that they had seen it coming, but they were shocked by the scale of the majority. Julie had thoroughly trained all of the candidates in her party but it was her own personality that was the game changer. She crossed all boundaries and dismantled loyalties. No seat was safe after she had visited it. Her appeal was more than charisma, although she had that in a plentiful supply. She told the truth in a language that everybody understood. She told them that she was the only person who had the solutions and could make the change happen. She would often say "If you do the right thing then it will always turn out right."

When all of the results had been declared, slightly delayed by two recounts, the parties had the following seats:

National Endeavour	398
Labour	80
Conservatives	55
Liberal Democrats	41
Reform UK	41
Sinn Fein	9
SNP	9
Plaid Cymru	4
Green Party	4
DUP	6

UUP	1
SDLP	1
Alliance of NI	1

National Endeavour had an overall majority of 146, less than the Exit Poll had predicted. The overall turnout was 72% and the party had recorded a 50.42% of the votes cast. In England, Scotland and Wales, National Endeavour had taken seats from all of the political parties. Unquestionably, the party had the support of the majority of the people. What was the party going to do with it?

Chapter 11

JC as PM

23rd June 2034 – The First Day

Julie, Harry Armstrong, her constituency office manager and Grace Kilbey, her Chief of Staff as leader of the party, travelled by car to a London Hotel. Harry had already checked them in online and after getting the keys they went to their rooms. The time was 6.30am and Julie had to be up and ready for the most important day of her political life at noon. She mustn't keep the King waiting.

Burnham, the outgoing Labour Prime Minister of the coalition government had retained his seat in Bolton. He was in 10 Downing Street early, having travelled there from his count on the first train to London. By 10.30am he had said goodbye to all of his staff and accompanied by his wife he got into the ministerial car for the last time. The journey to Clarence House was short and transport had been arranged to take them home after tending his resignation to the King. At 11.30am King George had wished farewell to the one now ex-Prime Minister after receiving his resignation. He would have a little time to prepare for his meeting with Julie Carter, who protocol insisted, was to be invited to form the next government. The King, standing six feet tall in his Oxford brogues and wearing a tweed jacket and dark trousers asked his personal assistant to make some unusual arrangements. At noon, Julie dressed again in her dark suit but with a clean white blouse, was shown in to the room set aside for state matters by the King's uniformed equerry and personal assistant. This was when the ceremonial 'kissing of hands' took place but was in fact just a handshake. She went forward and bowed to this athletic looking man of twenty years of age. Julie expected the meeting to be over in a few short minutes after the exchange of pleasantries.

"Please take a seat", George said indicating a Louis XV chair to her left. "Can I get you some tea?"

"Just a glass of water please your majesty."

"No majesty stuff please, it makes me feel old and uncomfortable. For protocol, "Sir" is fine. I'm soon to be 21 and a good deal in age and experience, junior to you." Very quickly, a tray arrived with two glasses containing ice and a slice of lemon and a small bottle of water for each. They both helped themselves and the assistant withdrew to a discreet distance.

The King started the conversation with, "My family has had a few difficult years recently. My grandfather, Charles was a well-loved king but did not get the chance to serve as long as he would have wished. My father William had this terrible accident and for some time my mother has not had the best of health. I have had little time to work out what sort of monarch I want to be, but I am certain that I want a break with the past. I want my time as King to be remembered for repositioning the Royal Family into a new modern British society. I am fully aware that to most people, particularly the young, I am seen as an irrelevance. To others, particularly the older generation, who still fondly remember my great grandmother Queen Elizabeth, the monarchy is still a comfort in these changing times. With your help, may I call you Julie, I want to dispose of the Parliamentary roles and concentrate on the pageantry as this is what brings the tourists in and helps the charities and military organisations. These activities seem to resonate more for me than sitting in Parliament with a large crown on my head reading out a lot of words that are not mine and with which I am probably not in agreement. All this Black Rod nonsense and rituals that date back to 1640's are not anything to do with the lives of my people. I would like my first King's Speech in Parliament to be my last and not be asked to give Royal Assent to Acts of Parliament in the future. What do you say?"

"I agree that ordinary people care little about the Parliamentary stuff. The fact that most of it emanates from the time of the English Civil War means nothing to young people, migrants and those disinterested in the history of the late Middle Ages. What people do like, and are proud of, is the pageantry stuff that you mentioned. You don't need to be a monarchist to enjoy The Changing of The Guard, you and your family's attendance at Royal Ascot and the Christmas Message. Tourists particularly like to see Buckingham Palace, Trooping the Colour, a procession down The Mall and the Guards at Horse Guards Parade.

"The monarchy also carries out some important functions that mean a lot to the citizens. A card to a centenarian on their 100 years birthday is highly prized as is a congratulations card on 60 years of marriage. The attendance at D-Day and other significant military celebrations show a respect for what your ancestors' citizens gave in the past. The late Duke of Edinburgh instituted the Duke of Edinburgh Awards Scheme and the current Duke has given it his support.

"The funeral arrangements and the lying-in state in London of your grandfather King Charles III were attended and marked by a significant number of people. The same is true for coronations and weddings of members of your family. Many charities have benefitted from their connection to a member of the Royal Family. It is a proud moment for a firm to be recognised as a supplier to a particular family member and enables them to display a coat of arms on their vehicles and stationery.

"An important role for the monarchy and the country's foreign relationships is the meeting, greeting and hosting of state functions for foreign heads of state and dignitaries. Commonwealth countries and countries that we have good relationships in trade, defence and humanitarian concerns welcome a state visit from a monarch who can trace their lineage over a thousand years and by connection to all the royal houses of Europe."

The King was clearly moved at this respect shown to his family. "All of my advisers tell me that the country is ready for you to lead them as Prime Minister because you have articulated policies that will get us out of the mess in which we find ourselves. Clearly this conversation must remain private. You now know my wishes and intentions and I'm sure that you will keep them between ourselves. Now I formally invite you to form the next government. Normally, I believe, there is a weekly audience on a Wednesday for us to discuss matters of state. In this new environment, I think that monthly might be more appropriate and a bit more social. We will meet again at my first and last State Opening of Parliament."

Julie rose, took a last sip of the water, bowed her head and King George offered her his hand. The assistant appeared from the shadows and offered to escort Julie through a discreet exit door to a waiting ministerial car. She had arrived by taxi but hadn't considered how she would leave. She thought, "I guess this is what is known as a seamless transfer of power." She stopped on the way and took advantage of the toilet, not because she particularly needed to, but she just wanted to see what it was like. "Impressive", she mumbled as she left.

While Julie was returning to Downing Street in a large black ministerial car, accompanied by some fearsome looking people, she took in the atmosphere of the moment. She knew that she would be expected to make a speech from the lectern outside 10 Downing Street. Her army of speechwriters, under direction, had produced prose to fit the occasion perfectly. Harry Armstrong had arranged for all of Julie's staff, supporters and successful candidates in London constituencies to form a guard of honour outside No. 10. In pride of place stood Julie's mum Margaret and son Jamie, waving a union jack flag.

The car drew up and a large security officer, a firearm discreetly tucked into his trouser belt, and with a wire sticking out of his ear got out and opened the door for her. As her left foot appeared, a crescendo of noise and applause greeted her. The street was lit up with the flashing of camera bulbs. She seemed so small alongside the large black bullet-proofed car and the two security guards. She raised her hand and waved, then approached the line of well-wishers. She walked slowly along shaking hands, some giving her a hug or a kiss or both. So many people to thank and enjoy the moment. She noticed Harry placing a folder on the lectern. She passed the black doors of No. 10 and No. 11 to get to her friends and family at the other end of the street. She paused to give her mother a long and special hug and then bent down not very much to smother Jamie with a hug and kisses. "He's shot up a bit during this campaign. He's going to be a big lad," she thought among the mayhem. She was overcome with the emotion of the moment. Hugging Jamie allowed her to regain her composure. After a few more hands to shake, she made her way to the lectern passing Edward and Estelle Grey on the way. Estelle, in a rare moment of humility, turned to Edward and whispered in his ear, "I'm sorry, you were right."

Julie opened the folder on the lectern and looked down at the prepared speech. She looked up at the gathered press, adjusted the microphone and closed the folder. She looked around and spread her arms wide then said to the country beyond the lights and cameras, "National Endeavour has asked for your trust and support, because we think we know how to make life better for every one of you. It is now up to us to prove that your judgement was right. Our work starts today and there are some difficult decisions to take. Not everyone will like all of them. All that we can guarantee is that every decision will be for the best of the majority. National Endeavour will ask you to give up some things. I am going to ask you out there in the country to give up some of your freedoms because they will hinder our progress. I am often asked, 'why does everything take so long'? It does, doesn't it and that is why nothing gets done. We will speed things up so you may be asked to give up some of your rights to disagree, but it will be for the general good. My fellow parliamentarians will be asked to give up their rights to delay and obfuscate but they will be asked to contribute to the forming of the big solutions. Without these sacrifices, there will be no changes for the better and no improvements. We have tried that way for the last 24 years. Now we will try something different. We will try my way.

"We may also ask you to give up some time, some money if you can afford it and for those who can give it, help and compassion. Together we will make life better for everybody, but there can be no free rides on this bus. If you need care and attention, you will get it. The work starts today to bring the United Kingdom forward into a modern era of market capitalism and social support, with respect for our planet and environment. Please be kind to each other, pay your taxes, don't commit crimes and love the children and your neighbour. Thank you all."

Applause started as a ripple from the sides and soon spread to all parts of the street. Holding Jamie's hand on one side and her mother's hand on the other, Julie Carter or JC as her friends now affectionately addressed her, entered the black door of 10 Downing Street to be greeted by the staff and civil servants inside.

She was introduced to them all in turn as granny took Jamie into a room for some orange juice and a biscuit. Sir Simon Thornley, the Cabinet Secretary and Senior Civil Servant showed Julie around the ground floor, pointing out the facilities and important rooms. She stepped into the Cabinet Room and let out a nearly silent whistle. "So this is where it happens?" she gasped to nobody in particular. Sir Simon asked Julie if she were hungry as it was now lunchtime. What a 24 hours it had been. It was only about eight hours previously that she knew that she had the party with largest number of seats and here she was in 10 Downing Street, having recently met the King!

Sandwiches and water were brought as she went through the security procedures to complete the transfer of power. She signed the protocols, permissions and authorisations to accept the seals of office, the nuclear codes and other top secret paraphernalia. Then came the phone calls from the President of the United States ("wow, it's Clooney!"), the Presidents of France and the EU (gosh!), the Chancellor of Germany and the leader of Russia (didn't expect that one) all congratulating her and looking forward to meeting her at the next G7 Conference. President Feckoff of Russia had arrived back at the top table following the peace accord with Ukraine in 2026 and the death of Vladimir Putin in 2030, although relationships with the West were still a little strained.

She sat alone in the Cabinet Room getting her thoughts together. For some weeks, she had believed, without any doubt that this day would come so she had prepared for it. It was time well spent. Her first job was to appoint her Chief of Staff, modelled on the position in the United States White House to be her gatekeeper. This was the most crucial role because through this person all information would flow to her and all of her instructions would flow the other way. She finished her sandwich and went to the door and in the corridor she saw Edward and Estelle Grey. "Edward," she called across the hall. "Can I have a word please?"

Edward looked up and without a second glance at Estelle, he crossed the hall and went with Julie into the Cabinet Room.

"Edward," said Julie. "I want you to be my Chief of Staff. The role used to be Cabinet Office Minister. Since you crossed the floor, the first one brave enough to join me, I have come to rely upon your loyalty and wise advice. Chief of Staff will mean that nobody, I stress nobody, gets in to see me without you advising me beforehand and I agree to it. Everyone will have to pass by you in your office before getting in to see me. I will meet with any of my Ministers by an appointment with you, but I don't want people popping in for a chat. Also, if I want to see someone, I will ask you to arrange it. You will have staff including someone who keeps our diaries so I don't miss anything important. Everywhere I go, you will accompany me. Estelle is well capable of carrying out your constituency duties. What do you say?"

Edward was beside himself with gratitude. "Thank you JC. I will not let you down."

"I know you won't, so your first jobs are to get me an office with a phone link direct to you then you let Sir Simon Thornley know what your position and responsibilities are. He will feel a bit side-lined so be gentle with him."

"On my way" and within half an hour Julie was in a private office ready to confirm to the nation the appointments to her new management team, which historically was called The Cabinet, but this one would be very different. She had prepared an envelope with the names of all of the ministers that she was going to appoint and asked Harry earlier in the day to give it to Edward Grey, while she was meeting with the King. Edward saw alongside the list of names, all of the positions that they would be appointed to and an instruction to get them all on their way to 10 Downing Street. He had seen them all at the meeting the day before in the Birmingham hotel but he didn't know what their positions would be. All of the persons on the list had been successful in being elected. She tapped the intercom on the phone and Edward answered. "Yes ma'am."

"Can you please get me Andrea Patel?"

In no time Andrea was sitting opposite Julie with Edward in a chair in the next office with the door between them open. "Edward is my Chief of Staff. You can have access to me if you speak with him. I am available at any time. Before yesterday I had studied your CV and background and I also have a report from the headhunters that selected you for your constituency. On all fronts you did really well. You were elected by a good majority and you followed the directions from central office to the letter. You were the Finance Director at a major investment bank and you are a qualified certified accountant. You were seconded to the Treasury for two years and you have attended Harvard Business School after a First Class Honours Degree from Oxford. We are having a different type of organisation to take our plans forward. I am effectively a Chief Executive Officer and as you discovered yesterday, I want to appoint you to the position of Finance Director, others will call it Chancellor of the Exchequer. You will report directly to me, one of only six direct reports plus Edward. You are at the top table of the management structure. Your direct reports will be the ministers set out on the chart given to you yesterday. All of your direct reports have been carefully selected for their roles in the departments indicated. I do the appointments but if they don't come up to scratch or you make a good case for their removal then you will be given permission to dis-appoint them and recommend a replacement. Your departmental responsibilities, in addition to being the government's Finance Director, are Energy, Levelling Up, Business and Trade & Welfare. Each of these Ministers will report directly to you on a brief agreed between us. In addition I will need you to recommend to me how we can raise substantial billions before our plans for growth kick in. My advice is to look at windfall taxes and trusts. Yesterday was a dress rehearsal. Today is the real thing. Are you willing to accept this appointment?"

Andrea was not fazed by the appointment or the role. She looked straight in to Julie's eyes and said, "Yes, Prime Minister. I will have some ideas on your desk before the day is out. Will I have access to the headhunters to get some background information on these Ministers?"

"Edward will make the arrangements for you. It is up to you to contact your ministers and get their agreement to serve. When you have done that, please let Edward know and he will make the announcements. Welcome to the Executive Team. I will make the announcement about your appointment. I suggest that you go to the Treasury and introduce yourself."

Edward showed Andrea out and went to release the name of the appointment to the media. When he returned he said, "Who's next?"

Hillary Armstrong-Lewis was shown in by Edward. She had an upright gait and was clearly a keep-fit enthusiast. She wore a dark blue trouser suit that shouted out 'power dressing'. There followed the same conversation that Julie had had with Andrea and her list of ministerial appointments. Hillary had a law degree from Cambridge, had trained as a barrister and took silk at a young age, in her thirties. She had been a member of the Bar Council and had acted as a prosecuting barrister at a major public inquiry.

The Justice Director, previously Lord Chancellor, had the brief for Courts, Prisons, security services and the Police. Julie said "We have forty-three police forces in England and Wales, along with the British Transport Police and the separate police forces in Scotland and Northern Ireland. I think that we can leave Scotland and Northern Ireland alone for now but please impress on the rest of them that their performance must improve along with what is going to happen in England and Wales. We have too many separate police forces and the British Transport Police is an anomaly. Please put forward recommendations to me on reducing this number, increasing crime detection rates and the introduction of anything that identifies criminals like facial recognition, automated number plate recognition and DNA sampling. We need a zero approach to crime and anti-social behaviour."

Hillary accepted the role and said "I understand what you need me to do."

Julie continued "We have too many people in prisons and they don't work. We need three types of prisons: rehabilitation, time serving and isolation. Sentences of less than twelve months and remanding some innocent to prison are a waste of time and money. We need community services that are carried out and fines that are paid. We have to use the latest technology to keep people under house curfew as it is so much cheaper than prison. We are not building any more prisons so you need to make recommendations on the three categories from the existing prison estate. Your most difficult task will be to get the judges to carry out sentencing according to the law, withstand frivolous and vexatious actions that stop us from achieving our programme and to judge in accordance with Parliament's wishes. Are you up to persuading them?"

"Absolutely", said Hillary. "Leave all of this to me."

Hillary Armstrong-Lewis as the new Justice Director called a meeting for the following day with 20 of the most senior judges, the Head of the Bar Council, The Chief Regulator of the Bar Standards Board, Chief Regulator of the Solicitors Regulation Authority and Head of The Law Society. She greeted them in her best court tone that befitted a Kings Counsel (KC), "As you know, we have a new government and a new Prime Minister. I have accepted the Cabinet position of Justice Director. It is as the new Justice Director with responsibility for the judiciary that I address you now.

"You are all aware that the country is sliding towards lawlessness and that a firm legal framework is essential for the incoming government to arrest that slide. The government will be passing a raft of laws and it will expect the judiciary to pass judgements on cases in accordance with those laws and keep to the sentencing guidelines. Maverick judges and judgements will not be tolerated and you can draw your own conclusions on what is meant by that. We will be changing the sentencing guidelines so that fewer criminals are sent to prison but recidivists and hardened and violent criminals get longer sentences."

She continued "Our aim is that all citizens pay their correct taxes, respect all of their fellow citizens and live within the law, including all of the new laws. If you have any reservations about what I have said, particularly enforcing the laws and abiding by the sentencing guidelines, please wait at the end of the meeting and we can talk about it."

Two judges took up the offer and met with Hillary separately. The first one sat down and said, "Madam, my name is Sir Anthony Pinder and I know the law because I have studied it and practised it for the whole of my adult life. From an early age I knew that I wanted to be involved with the law. I received a First Class Honours Degree in Law and Political History at Cambridge ensuring that I could have the pick of the Barrister Chambers in London. My pupillage was in the Chambers of Sir Desmond Hoare-Stevens in Middle Temple, specialising in criminal law, prosecution and defending. I took the Bar examination and after six months, at the earliest stage, I was called to the Bar and after a further six months under the supervision of Sir Desmond I was able to practise as a barrister, the youngest in London. I soon proved myself by prosecuting and defending some notorious persons in high profile cases. I don't need you to tell me how to be a judge and how to exercise my judgement. I will do as I think the case deserves even if that means ignoring the sentencing guidelines. You are not going to exert pressure on me to toe your party line. When I am the judge, in my court I decide on these matters. My last case is a good illustration of the point. A young illiterate nineteen year old, almost a child, from a disadvantaged background had broken into a widowed pensioner's flat, hit her a couple of times to shut her up from screaming and stole her wedding ring. Nothing of great value. The lad clearly needed to learn some manners and so I gave him a custodial sentence, suspended for two years. Quite appropriate, I thought, even though he should have been sent to prison according to the guidelines. The press didn't like it but I'm the judge so they have had to get on with it. A week after the sentencing I was called in for a chat with the Lord Chancellor. He was not pleased and said that the sentence given was against the government's policy for victims. I told him that I wasn't concerned with politics but with the law. I told him that the sentence was the appropriate one and before he criticised me the next time, he should spend a few days in court not Parliament. So I say to you that as a judge I will carry on as I have always done and dispense judgements in accordance with my experience and a lifetime of studying the law. You cannot take away the independence of judges that has been established for nearly a thousand years. I will pass judgements according to my knowledge and beliefs, one of which is a strong religious faith." Hillary thanked him for his contribution and asked him to go and think about what she had said at the meeting and encouraged him to fall in line with the new directions.

The second judge was seen soon afterwards. He said pretty much the same thing as the first judge with a short speech about his experience gained from lecturing in law at Oxford and a lifetime at the Bar as a KC and the Courts before being appointed by the Judicial Appointments Commission. Another thank you for his contribution. The day after the election, the Judicial Appointments Commission was asked to appoint eighteen new judges and interview them all closely beforehand. The two judges who had met with Hillary after the meeting received their Hearing List a few days later. The List was blank so they waited at home and occasionally in their Chambers for a notification as to what trials they would preside over. Neither of them were called to try another case. It wasn't long before the message of the new broom got through.

After Edward had shown Hillary out and advised the media of her appointment, Julie said "Tom Blandford, please." Tom had been a managing director of a haulage company before working in America as a vice president of a Silicon Valley company developing AI technology for trucking. He was an emeritus professor at University College London (UCL) and a visiting professor at Yale specialising in early years' education. For five years he had been a director of Freshfood, a large greenhouse company producing salad crops under glass in Kent. Julie went through the same procedures as for Andrea and Hillary. She offered Tom the role of Homeland Director. His responsibilities were for

Transport, Science & Technology, Education, Housing, Environment, Farming, Food, Fishing & Rural Affairs and climate change.

He was delighted to be offered such an important role and could see immediately those areas that would need briefs prepared to advance National Endeavour's plans. Julie stressed a couple of areas that interested her. "We need the railways to operate for travellers and freight. There are too many trucks on the road that could be moved by rail. Technology is the key to operating rail systems and not to be over dependent on drivers. In the short term, we may need to train more drivers and make working practices fit for 2034 and not be stuck in 1934. We must farm more land for arable crops and not increase red meat production. Fertilizer prices must be stabilized and in some cases subsidised. Our citizens deserve to have access to fish caught in our waters before the best is shipped to Europe. Importing fish from Vietnam and Bangladesh is against our climate change goals. Please work with Andrea Patel to come up with new fast rail lines in the north and a widening of the M62. I know that you have a passion for improving the education of children. Let me know how we can reduce truancy and bad behaviour in classes. I suspect that you will want more teachers, so do I. Wouldn't it be nice if every child was taught in a class of only twenty pupils or less? Housing is a big part of your responsibilities. I think that I have chosen just the person to get this moving. Let's not waste a day."

Tom got up to go with his pad of notes and thanked Julie for the opportunity. "I will make sure that in me, you chose well," he said.

"I already know that I did. You are the right person for this job." Tom left with a wave of his hand, which surprisingly had a small tattoo of a fish. "I must ask him about that one day," thought Julie. Edward released the details of his appointment to the media before Tom had even passed through the gates of Downing Street.

Every government needs its own internal person who ensures discipline and keeps the wheels of the party oiled. In the past it was the Chief Whip with a collection of Junior Whips. Julie had always thought that the name alone had unpleasant connotations. In her administration she preferred to call the person 'Constable'. She had been advised that the ideal person for this role would be the terrier from Hartlepool, Agnes Peters.

Agnes came pacing into the office in sensible shoes and shook Julie warmly and firmly by the hand. "I have a very special role for you Agnes, reporting directly to me." After the standard brief, Julie said "You will need to appoint the Leader of the Commons and the Leader of The Lords in accordance with the names on this paper. We have no Lords in our party so you will need to discuss how to effect this appointment with Edward Grey. He will get a recommended failed election candidate in and to his surprise he will be made a Lord.

"What I want you to do is maintain integrity and discipline amongst our new MPs. They shouldn't need much reminding because they were selected carefully from their backgrounds, but there will always be a couple who drink too much and are flexible with other people's personal boundaries. I want to know everything that is going on so at the end of every day, a brief report please, no more than one page of A4. You will also be overseeing, with the Leader of the Commons, the progress of our legislation. If you get wind of a disruptive blockage in the system that you can't get rid of, please let Edward Grey know or put it in your daily brief. We are going to have a heavy legislative programme and we want to get things done quickly."

Agnes stood straight and said, "JC thank you for this opportunity. We have so many new MPs that getting to know them all will be the top of my agenda." Agnes left and Julie ordered some tea. These appointments took time but they were so essential to get them done quickly so that the work could begin.

Next up was Dr. Indira Singh. Before the election she was a consultant with the NHS for over twenty years. She was the author of a number of pamphlets and articles about the integration of social care into the NHS and a book on the poor dental health of children. She was from a family of distinguished doctors, surgeons, pharmacists and dentists. She had undertook a business management course at Bath

University in a sabbatical year. Julie had had her eye on Indira from the very early days and asked the headhunters to persuade her to join National Endeavour. Indira sat and said, "I really admire what you are trying to do and I am delighted to be a small part of your plans."

"On the contrary," said Julie. "You are a very large part of my plans because you have, arguably, the toughest job in my team. As Health Director I need you to come up with plans for me that will combine the NHS with Social Care and have an integrated system. In addition you will be responsible for dentistry and work and pensions. The health of the nation and each individual will be in your hands. You will also oversee our plans for culture, media and sport. The health of the nation is measured in many ways and it is through culture and sport that we regenerate ourselves." Julie then gave the details as she had with the others. "No idea is off limits except throwing more money at the problems without measurable benefits and changes. Workers and retired people will have healthier lives if we have preventative medicine. All of science and technology will be at your fingertips but it is your brain and experience that will lead you to the right conclusions. Go for it Indira!"

After Indira had gone, Edward Grey came into the room. "How's it going JC?" he asked.

"We have so many talented individuals in our party. The money spent on those headhunters was worth every penny, even though we haven't got the final bill yet. The party has funds to cover it, so please see to it. All we have to do is manage these people, give them space and they will come up with some great ideas. They will make mistakes, but we'll deal with those. Our job will be to draft the laws that do what we mean them to. On that note, can you find out who were the six best legislators, politicians and civil servants, in the last government and have them seated in the large room later today?"

"Before or after dinner?"

"Before. I don't want to take up their evening."

The final member of the team was shown in by Edward. It was now 4pm and Julie had just finished a piece of cake and a cup of tea. She was looking forward to this meeting because this person was strong by name and strong by nature.

Ever since Brian Strong had been elected the Member of Parliament for West Byfleet in one of the first by-elections in 2032 he had proved a wonderful colleague. He had made sure that Julie was protected from the abusive members in the House and let it be known that he or she were not to be trifled with. He was a large man, a former first class rugby player and an Oxford Blue for rugby and rowing. He was in the unsuccessful Oxford crew for the Varsity Boat Race. He had already proved himself a valuable asset to the party as a mentor for many of the other candidates. He entered the room and they gave each other a warm hug. "Great to see you Brian as always."

Brian sat down opposite Julie in the chair offered and put his folder on the table. "As you know," Julie started, "I want you to be one of the team with the title of Borders & Security Director, essentially the Foreign Secretary. Yesterday you were given the list of your ministers for Defence, Overseas Development, our Ethical Foreign Policy, Commonwealth affairs which will include the Diplomatic Service, Immigration and for Wales, Scotland and Northern Ireland, but in a special way. This is a big job, do you think it's too big or can you handle it?"

"It is a big job. Won't the other UK countries feel a bit devalued by not having a Cabinet Minister?"

"Good question. I have developed some ideas on how the UK becomes a federal country with all of the four parts more devolved than they currently are. Tomorrow I shall be going to those countries and I will explain my thinking so that in the future they will require a lot less oversight. Of course, the toxic issue for you is immigration as nobody really understands how to deal with it. It's easy to say reduce it, particularly the illegal numbers crossing the Channel but so far nobody has come up with a solution. I think that during a weekend at

Chequers we will be able to develop some strong policies. Remember, I am always here and we will meet regularly to make sure that matters are moving along. Your background in Management Consulting and change management will stand you in good place to tackle the tasks ahead. You will enjoy your visits to France and Germany, because I know that you are fluent in both languages."

"You know a lot about me don't you?"

"I know a lot about all the people who are important to me. Have a busy day and we will meet up again in a couple of days when you will have formulated some ideas and had a meeting with your team."

After Brian had left, Edward came back into the room and Julie indicated a chair. "You have released the names and positions to the media. What was the reaction?"

"Surprise at the new management format, but many were intrigued by the idea of smaller government. Obviously much will depend on the effectiveness not only of the structure but also of the policies that come through. Is there something over which you will take responsibility?"

"The Constitutional issues. The federalising of the UK, the second chamber replacing the House of Lords and the changes to the monarchy in the Constitution as proposed by the King. I guess the big stuff as well. NATO, EU, UN, G7 are where the public expect me to be seen. Rubbing shoulders with other countries leaders is not my strong suit and it makes me uncomfortable."

"You'll have to get use to those. Not to be delegated, I guess."

"You're right of course. Have all mine, my mother Margaret's and Jamie's personal stuff been moved in to next door?"

"Still doing it now. They should be finished in half an hour."

"Where are we with Jamie's school trips?"

"All arranged, starting Monday. He won't want the police escort to the school gates so we will drop him, Doris and mum off around the corner and our chaps will keep a discreet distance. We've appointed a seriously competent female called Doris from the protection squad who, to the other kids, will look like an aunt. We've had words with the school and it's all been sorted. Same for collection in the evening."

"How is my mother with all of this?"

"She's fine. She's a lot more laid back about this than my mother would be."

"And how is Estelle?"

"Since the election result, you would think that I was God's gift to her. She has become so supportive and I know that she will be good with the Friday constituency work. By the way, how are you going to deal with yours?

"Harry Armstrong and Grace Kilbey will take good care of it."

Julie called it a day and went through the adjoining passageway into No. 11 and up the stairs to her new flat. Mum got up and put the kettle on and Julie sat down with Jamie. "I think you've met with Doris, she will be your special friend. If you need anything just ask her if we are not around. Tomorrow I am off to Scotland, Northern Ireland and Wales in a private plane. Do you want to come too?" she asked her mother & Jamie.

"Yes" they responded enthusiastically.

"All work for me, but you'll enjoy the trip."

Chapter 12

The Days leading up to the King's Speech

24th June – 4th July 2034

The United Kingdom was already a loose federation of countries with many powers devolved. The English question, sometimes also referred to as the West Lothian Question, concerned whether Scottish, Welsh & Northern Ireland members of Parliament should be able to vote on matters that only affect England, whereas the English MPs cannot vote on devolved powers to the other countries. It was an untidy situation, so Julie decided to make an early visit to the other UK countries to foster good relations.

The morning after accepting the position as Prime Minister, a car picked up Julie, her mum, Jamie & Edward Grey at 8am and drove them to Northolt, a private airport to the west of London for a flight to Edinburgh. Already on the plane were Brian Strong and Robert Hughes, his newly appointed Scotland Minister, Hywel Evans, the Welsh language speaking Wales Minister and Bridget Stimpson, Northern Ireland Minister. There were at least a dozen civil servants from the Scottish, Welsh & Northern Ireland Offices, ready to re-establish their working relationships under the new government and to support their minister. After a short speech on what she wanted to achieve from the trip, Julie spent some time with each one of the other passengers in turn. The plane landed at Edinburgh Airport and four large black cars transported those involved with this leg of the trip to the centre of the city. The Wales and Northern Ireland ministers and civil servants stayed on the plane and continued with their preparations. Julie's mum and Jamie were let out at the castle while the rest of them went down the "Royal Mile" to the Palace of Holyroodhouse opposite the now not so new Parliament building, showing early signs of wear.

The First Minister of Scotland, Douglas Murdoch, greeted them and introduced them to his small team. They divided into two groups. Brian Strong, Robert Hughes and the civil servants went to one room to deal with the day-to-day business and for Robert to become acquainted with his opposite number. Julie and Douglas went into a small room and helped themselves to coffee.

"Congratulations on your impressive election win, Prime Minister."

"Please call me Julie or JC in private and thank you."

"From basically a standing start, the learning curve must be very steep."

"It is, but I have a strong team to support me, as I guess so do you. We also have spent a good deal of time working out our objectives, strategies and plans covering all aspects of government. We know what the people expect of us and what they will do at the next election if we fail them. I came here today to meet with you in person and to try and establish a good working relationship. It is important that our ministers do the same. Primarily, I wish to get your considered opinion on some Constitutional proposals and whether you would like your devolved powers increased to other areas."

Douglas sat forward in his chair. "This is a big change of tone to what we have become used to from Westminster," he said. "What do you have in mind?"

"Currently your devolved powers are the economy, education, health, justice, rural affairs, housing, environment, equal opportunities, consumer advocacy and advice, transport and taxation. Under a federal system you would enjoy the protections of security, defence and MI5, MI6 and GCHQ. The UK government would represent Scotland in foreign and diplomatic affairs and the defence policy would cover us all. We would be integrated on cross border crime and have a shared immigration policy. I am offering you full fiscal independence so that all revenues from North Sea oil and gas and wind turbines, would be yours to keep, alongside any sum that we pay you for hydro-electric power. You can set your own benefits, control gambling, and have separate broadcasting powers and your own data protection and employment laws. You would cease receiving funding from the United Kingdom under the Barnett Formula. There would be very few 'Reserved Matters'. We would have the same currency, elections to a UK Parliament and rules on nationality. Your MPs in Parliament would only be allowed to vote on Federal legislation and Scottish issues, so removing the English Question. Clearly you need to have these proposals in writing so I have prepared this for you." Julie handed over a thin folder of papers. "In the King's Speech in Parliament on 5th July there will be a reference to 'Constitutional Reform' and this is what it means. Similar arrangements will be proposed for Wales and Northern Ireland, although for obvious reasons there are some sensitivities with the latter to address. Please keep this matter private before that date. Obviously your Parliament will wish to consider the implications and decide its outcome once the Bill is published. I am not offering independence for Scotland from the United Kingdom. I am offering independence for Scotland within the United Kingdom."

Douglas gave Julie a very nice bottle of Speyside Single Malt Whisky and Julie reciprocated with a bottle of Abingdon Gin. "This is made near my home," she mentioned with a chuckle. They went out together in the sunshine discussing a few minor items before the party was taken back to the airport, stopping to pick up Jamie and his gran on the way for the next stage of the itinerary to Northern Ireland. Lunch was served on board.

The plane landed at Belfast, George Best Airport, and similar disembarkations occurred with Jamie and his gran going to Titanic Belfast, the exhibition for the famous doomed liner. Julie met with the first and deputy first ministers as well as executive and opposition representatives at Stormont.

The welcome was warm and in the large cabinet room with a glass of fizzy water, Julie explained the Constitution plans and how they might affect Northern Ireland. The plans were not the same as for Scotland because the rarely said implication for the province was that it would one day become part of a united Ireland. The squaring of that circle was difficult but it needed to be addressed and Julie was going to offer to the politicians a way for it to be achieved. She started by offering Northern Ireland a place in a Federal United Kingdom with increased powers, initially not quite as wide as Scotland would enjoy, mainly because of the border with the Republic and EU. She reiterated the old offer that if the people of Northern Ireland, in a referendum, voted to unite the island of Ireland, the UK under her leadership would not stand in the way. This pleased the republicans in the room. She also put on the table a 'Hong Kong' solution of a lease from the UK that would expire in 99 years so that none of the people currently alive would be affected. This offer would not take precedent over any referendum before that lease expired. Any of these arrangements would of course require a trilateral agreement to include the Republic of Ireland. Again this was accepted with interest but with no commitment. The Protestant representatives sat in stony silence.

"I leave you with the pledge that nothing will be resolved without an agreement between all of the interested and affected parties. The initial steps will be slow and Bridget, my Northern Ireland Minister will be acting as a catalyst for your discussions. We welcome all elected representatives of your parties to Westminster to engage in any discussions on this issue. Clearly a Federal UK cannot exist fully without the acceptance and active participation of all parties, although we do recognise that the pace of change will be quicker for some."

On the plane to Cardiff, Julie sat thinking about the trip to Stormont. "So easy to cause upset by saying the wrong thing," she thought. "It was like walking on eggshells. The glares and nuanced expressions told all of their stories." Instinctively, if not geographically, she could see that it was inevitable that Ireland would be united one day in the future, but would it be in her lifetime? Could she be the person to bring this about without causing widespread civil unrest? "All parties, faiths and loyalties must be considered and respected. The Protestants must not feel that they are being sold down the river. The future could be very bright for all of the people," she concluded deep in thought.

The plane landed in Cardiff and she had talks with Gareth Griffiths, First Minister of Wales. She repeated the Scotland offer for Wales within a Federal UK. The Welsh Parliament, The Senedd Cymru, had floated the idea of an independent Wales but recognised that would be far into the future. What was being offered now was beyond their expectations.

Julie and the entourage returned to London pleased with the welcome that they had received in the three countries and confident that the constitutional changes discussed could be progressed.

While Julie was hopping between the UK countries, Andrea Patel, the newly appointed Finance Director was giving a presentation in the Treasury to financial journalists. Andrea had given a copy of the speech to Julie to read on the first leg of her journey to Edinburgh and Julie had telephoned her to agree the text without changing a word. Clearly, Andrea was an excellent choice.

Andrea stood upright at the lectern dressed in sober city dress and surveyed the room. She started by saying, "Good morning from the Treasury. My title is Finance Director although in the past you might have thought me as Chancellor of the Exchequer. We move in changed times. Today I'm going to make a few policy announcements and indicate the direction of travel that I will be taking in the months ahead. Around me in the room are my ministers. If you want some more information on a particular area, please seek them out at the end of the meeting."

Andrea put on her glasses and looked at the autocue, properly functioning with the first line at the ready. "Our mandate for change from the electorate is wide and comprehensive. We all know what the problems are and the electorate have chosen us to fix them and that is what we are going to do. The country needs financial stability and that is my absolute priority. I shall be introducing budgets that will work over time towards a balanced budget. The next full Budget will be on Wednesday, 18th October. As a country we must live within our means just the same as everybody in the country and in this room. When the finances allow, we will reduce the amount of debt and that will help us to reduce debt interest payments. So logically all expenditure from now will be met by having the income to pay for it.

"Growth in the economy is key to our plans, but growth alone will not solve our problems. If everybody paid the right amount of tax, then we would all pay a little less and our need to borrow would reduce. We shall be having a major crackdown on tax evasion with very severe penalties for those caught. I give notice to all tax and accountancy firms that from today, all schemes especially designed to avoid tax will need to be referred to HMRC before implementation, for a refusal to follow.

"At this moment, we cannot build enough houses to satisfy the demand from people to have a home, whereas there are a large number of empty properties that can be brought into occupation. I am announcing today that from 1st September all councils will introduce two new council tax bands above the top one to realise revenue from the more expensive properties. All of the money raised will be ring-fenced for the compulsory purchase of empty or abandoned properties and their refurbishment costs. Secondary legislation to allow this will be presented to Parliament on its first working day.

"It is unfair that during an acute housing shortage there are so many people owning second homes that are unoccupied for at least 50% of the time. In some holiday hotspots the purchase of second homes has distorted the market for local people. I am announcing today that also from 1st September all designated second homes, and you can only have one primary residence, will attract a 100% levy for council tax. It will be up to the individual to decide what their primary residence is. All of this money raised will be ring-fenced for empty properties too. In the future only 10% of any village or town will be available for second homes or holiday lets. Secondary legislation for this will be presented to Parliament on its first working day.

"It is also unfair that there are so many properties being bought up by prospective landlords for multiple lettings, which prices local people out of buying a home in which to live. A couple looking for a home cannot compete with a professional landlord who wishes to create multiple tenancies. I am announcing today that also from 1ˢᵗ September all properties let out will need to be registered with local authorities under a new property use designation. In the future only 10% of any village or town will be available for multiple let properties. Until the figure locally falls below 10%, no further permissions will be granted. To offset the increased local authority monitoring and enforcing costs, multi-let properties will have an annual wealth tax of 1% levied on the property owner from the next financial year. Secondary legislation for this will also be presented to Parliament on its first working day.

"We will establish UK plc with an initial seed funding investment of £5bn to enable it to act alone or participate with private companies to engage in new manufacturing capabilities. We will be promoting "Buy British" and expecting companies based in the UK to do so. All government contracts will stipulate a "Buy British" condition. There will be a lower number of trucks arriving from Europe with goods that we can easily manufacture ourselves and by doing so reduce carbon emissions. We will be in partnership with farmers to build enormous greenhouses in Essex, Isle of Thanet and Lincolnshire so that crops currently brought from countries with the same climate as ours, can now be grown in the UK. This and any other legislative matter raised today will be included in a Finance Bill laid before Parliament on its first working day.

"Even though the planning system was extensively reformed in 2025, vested interests have eroded the central theme that planning exists to help communities and is not a business prevention tool. We will give priority to housing and energy projects in the system to ensure they make swift progress including approval for small scale nuclear reactors. Decisions on large developments, defined as over 500 homes per site, will be taken nationally not locally. Priority for approval will be for companies investing with UK plc to generate jobs and growth in areas outside the south-east. Large developments will be expected to include infrastructure and reference shops, schools and amenities.

"There are too many people not working and if we could find them proper jobs they will grow the economy. We will tackle economic inactivity and get people back to work.

"To show that we are all in this National Endeavour together, I am announcing that all MPs salaries will be reduced by 20% from today. Also from today payments to Members of the House of Lords will cease as being in the Lords should be an honour enough. From today, all cafes, restaurants and bars in the Houses of Parliament will cease to be subsidised by the taxpayer.

"Today I am imposing a windfall tax on the excess profits of all banks, oil companies and utility companies, the funds to be used for the initial funding of UK plc. That is the end of this presentation. As you now have heard, we are resolved to put this country right and all of us will contribute towards it. I am sorry that there is no opportunity to ask questions of me today. I will be holding another press conference after the King's Speech."

25th June 2034

The morning after returning from her trip to Scotland, Wales and Northern Ireland, in the Downing Street Media Room, Julie announced to the media, "After the King's Speech on 5th July, the House of Commons will start fifty-seven days continuous session to consider and pass up to fifty Bills into law. After a brief summer recess, Parliament will use twenty-one days to pass all of the urgent legislation and make preparations for important legislation to follow. The twelve days from the election to the State opening of Parliament will be used to elect a new Speaker, swear in all MPs and lay statutory instruments to bring into effect secondary legislation. Those matters requiring primary legislation will be laid before Parliament in the week after it resumes.

The first two Bills of the Parliament will truncate and modernise the law making process and a third will establish a streamlined judiciary. We have set up a group of expert law drafters. They will ensure that a Bill is fit for purpose and once passed into law cannot be successfully challenged in the courts. We will do away with First Reading & Second

Reading by having the written Bill presented to Parliament. To reduce the paper trail, all Bills will be e-mailed to MPs at the beginning of the day that it is placed before Parliament. The Bill will be discussed and voted upon on that day. As we will have a very large majority, I expect that this will be a formality. The Bill will go to the Committee stage the next working day and it will have four days for amendments and suggestions. This process is open for all MPs to submit changes. The Bill then returns to the Executive Team who will seek guidance from the law making group, amend it and present it back to the Commons in its final form on the seventh sitting day. Voting will approve it and it will become law. We will adopt the process of Consult : Decide. This is our 'get on with it approach'."

Julie took a sip of water and ignored the raised hands of the media in the room. She continued, "The second Bill will be to reduce the powers of the House of Lords pending a new Constitution Act that will replace the Lords with a new Second Chamber and a law making scrutiny committee made up of law experts. The elections to this Second Chamber will take place in May 2035 alongside the Metropolitan Districts and District Councils elections. A new Constitution and a new Second Chamber were in our manifesto." There were a few gasps of 'crikey' and stronger Anglo-Saxon words from the hacks.

"We must ensure that all civil servants, from the most senior down, assist us with what we wish to achieve. If we come across individuals who just want to put problems in our way, then we must redeploy them. We will expect the judiciary to judge on the laws as they are. Some of the problems in the past have been that laws have been poorly drafted and smart barristers have been allowed to get their clients off from a charge on a technicality. We must ensure that the laws are clear in their intentions but also we do not want rogue judges following their own agenda. At an early stage we shall put the names of barristers forward for judicial appointments. These barristers will be singled out for their understanding of their responsibilities. Judges will still be tasked with discretion to impose punishments in accordance with the sentencing guidelines but they must not be sympathetic to nuances, which circumvent what the laws were expressly passed to address. We shall cease the right of Judicial Review and put an end to the endless rounds of appeals. The Court of Appeal will be merged with the Supreme Court to remove one stage of appeal that has now become pointless. When a judge settles a matter, it must be deemed to be settled. This Act will prevent special interest groups from interfering in the will of Parliament. These three Acts, when passed, will establish the primacy of Parliament. There will be difficult issues to be resolved and progress must not be hampered or delayed by judicial semantics.

"The only way to succeed is to try and we shall try anything to succeed in giving the people the society that they elected us to provide for them. As part of the debate on Constitutional matters we will confirm the arrangements for moving out of Parliament while it undergoes its much needed repair.

"We will be respecting our climate change commitments. By adopting 'Buy British' we will significantly reduce transport emissions. We will also look at where goods come from that we cannot supply ourselves and seek to reduce travel climate costs."

Julie took a few questions that didn't elicit anything new or revolutionary and retired to her room to prepare the King's Speech.

<u>26th June 2034</u>

The next day it was the turn of Indira Singh, the Health Director to present her plans to the media. She chose to do it in Westminster Hall, a large medieval great hall in the Houses of Parliament built in 1097. This massive hall was a bit draughty so she was pleased that she had on a thick sweater under her loose fitting blue jacket.

"Good morning. Today I will set out our plans ahead of the King's Speech to provide you with some information on improvements for the nation's health. Around me in the room are my ministers. If you want some more information on a particular area, please seek them out at the end of the meeting.

"The Health Budget will not be increased except for pay awards. All additional operational funding required will be met from existing budgets. We will undertake an equipment deficiency audit and supply to all hospital trusts the equipment that they require. Health cannot in future be denied by a lack of equipment or by the chance of where you live. We plan to integrate Social Care within the NHS. Where there is a lack of capacity of accommodation we will compulsorily acquire it. Where there is a lack of staff we will provide it. We will be offering asylum seekers and illegal immigrants with the required skills and commitment, a job in social care for a period of time for them to earn citizens' rights. We have started this screening and already the results are encouraging.

"Every dental practice will be required to provide 10% of their appointments to children seeking dental treatment paid for by the NHS. Children within a three mile radius of a practice will not be turned away unless the 10% capacity is reached.

"It is unhealthy not to have work if you are able to do it. We shall be working with doctors and health service professionals to define the level of work an individual can undertake. Doctors will be rewarded for every person that they examine and determine their ability describing the level of work that could be undertaken. We will cease paying for healthy people not to work. All workers will be subscribed into a work place pension.

"The health of the nation cannot be measured by machines and prescribed drugs alone. I shall be promoting the use of classes that provide healthy exercise and sports. All museums will charge a minimum of £5 entry fee that will be waived on production of a UK passport, driving licence or other approved identity card. Children and young people under the age of sixteen will be allowed free entry."

Later in the day, Tom Blandford, Homeland Director addressed the media from the media room in 10 Downing Street. Tom looked casual in his slacks and sports jacket but this hid his hard steely nature. Tom did things and was task orientated. A driven man.

"Good morning. Homeland Director I know sounds a bit American but just think of me as 'Home Secretary' until you get used to the new title. I have a wide range of responsibilities, quite different from previously, so I will try to give you some background on each. Around me in the room are my ministers. If you want some more information on a particular area, please seek them out at the end of the meeting.

"Over the past decade, getting around the UK has become a matter of endurance. There is no pleasure in going from A to B as I discovered on my way here today. The trains don't operate for the fare paying public, rural bus services have almost ceased to exist and the state of the roads are what you would expect in an underdeveloped country. Our first priority will be to sort out the trains. The establishment of Great British Railways a decade ago just brought together a Victorian infrastructure with ancient working practices by the unions. We will change all of this with the unions' assistance. We need more high speed rail, more fast motorways and more freight moved from road to rail. I have today commissioned feasibility studies into the provision of high speed rail services from Liverpool to Hull and from Newcastle to Carlisle.

"Some of the jewels in our nation's crown have been our inventions and developments using science and technology. We will be establishing a new enterprise, UK S&T plc that will have initially £3bn to invest alongside private sector interests in developing new Science and Technology industries.

"Education, education, education was a famous mantra in 1997. All of us in here in well paid jobs owe it all to the education that we received. We fail our young people if we do not provide them with an education that fits them for the world of work and opportunity. Truancy robs young people of the investment that they should be making in themselves. Fining or punishing parents in most cases will not result in getting their children back into their school. Persistent truants will be made wards of court and be taken into secure schools for their own good. When they commit to returning to school and not being disruptive in class, they will be returned home and have their phones returned.

"Much has been said by my colleague Andrea about funds for housing. During the term of this Parliament we will guarantee accommodation by either building it, acquiring empty properties or by assisting housing associations to provide social housing. We will establish a register of residential properties. The day after a Bill is passed into law, the purchase of a residential property will not be allowed to be completed by non-UK citizens or non-residents of the UK. We will purchase agricultural land for development at agricultural prices. Housing benefit tenants will be expected to make a small but increasing financial contribution for their accommodation, which will be partly reduced for tenants, who have not been investigated for anti-social behaviour.

"We will fix the cost of fertiliser for farmers and subsidise it to that price. We will discuss with the fishing industry increased quotas for fish caught and sold in the UK. The last remaining pub in a village will not be given alternate use permission, except for conversion into social housing when all possible business opportunities have failed.

"The Environment Agency will have a new Chief Executive and all of the directors of the utility companies will be tasked to improve the performance of their companies for the bill paying public, particularly those organisations involved in the water industry."

<u>27th June 2034</u>

Another day, another presentation by a member of the Executive team to the media. This time it was the turn of Hillary Armstrong-Lewis, Justice Director, who addressed the press from the media room in 10 Downing Street. Hillary was dressed for a day in court minus the wig. All black suit and white starched shirt.

"Good morning. Justice Director is the rebranding of The Lord Chancellor. I have a range of responsibilities previously associated with the Home Office. As my executive colleagues have mentioned in their presentations, I also have around me in the room my ministerial team. If you want some more information on a particular area, please seek them out at the end of the meeting.

"Justice delayed is justice denied. Denied to the victim and denied to the innocent person charged and also to the perpetrator. As a society we have forgotten the victim because when it isn't ourselves, remarkably we pass the sympathy to the accused. We need to use technology to stop crime from happening but when it does, to use that technology to catch the person or persons responsible. We have some no-go areas where the criminals act as their own enforcers and even give out summary punishments. We will bring all of these arrangements to an end.

"The police have been poorly led, poorly managed and we, the public, have used them too often as our punching bag. The police will be given the best facial recognition technology, automated number plate recognition and high quality CCTV in areas of high crime. DNA profiling will be available to catch criminals. Any person assaulting a police officer, prison officer or a hospital staff member will not only be fined a very large sum of money, but also receive a mandatory prison sentence. All demonstrations and protests will need to be notified to the police at least seven days ahead of the protest. We will adopt a zero tolerance approach to vandalism and graffiti. We will remove the defence of entrapment. In fact we will be using advanced techniques to entrap criminals. For too long the law has not been on the side of the victim. From today this has changed.

"We will be reducing the number of people in prison. First time non-violent offenders will go to rehabilitation units to assess their literacy skills and other behavioural problems. Recidivist offenders will go to jail and serve the whole of their sentences. There will be no time off for good behaviour but added time for bad behaviour. Violent criminals will go to USA style maximum security prisons. All prisoners will be expected to work during their sentence for the benefit of the nation. We will make extensive use of curfew and technology bracelets. The punishment for some offenders will be the removal of passports and driving licences.

"Fly tipping is a national disgrace. From today, council refuse tips will take all rubbish, private and commercial, except skips and receptacles over 1 cubic yard. Now there is no need to fly tip rubbish in the countryside. If you are caught, and we will catch you, we will impound your vehicle, fine you an eye-watering sum of money and require you to clean up someone else's fly-tipping mess.

"A new law of stealing from the public purse, benefit and tax fraud, will carry very severe sentences and very high fines. Benefit fraud, tax evasion, stealing power from utilities, driving without a licence, tax or insurance are not victimless crimes. Companies that fail to pay tax and national insurance to HMRC will have that liability fall on the directors individually and severally. The banks will be financially responsible for customer bank fraud because they have the systems to prevent it but up to now have not. Thank you for your attendance. Much of what I have outlined will be contained in the King's Speech in a few days' time."

Finally that afternoon it was the turn of Brian Strong, standing tall and upright at the lectern in the Ministry of Defence. He would not have looked out of place in combat fatigues. Today it was a smart blue suit and a purple tie. All of the presentations had a similar starting paragraph, because Julie Carter had sent around the opening lines. She had also had meetings with each of her Executive team so she knew what was going to be said. "What a great team," she thought. "All of them had got the feeling for the meetings right and the presentations were their words. The introductions and format were Julie's. "A few weeks and we won't need so much micro-managing," she thought.

"Good morning. Border & Security Director is the rebranding of The Foreign Secretary. I have a range of responsibilities. As my executive colleagues have mentioned in their presentations, around me in the room are my ministers. If you want some more information on a particular area, please seek them out at the end of the meeting.

"The defence of the realm and its citizens is the primary task of every government. We will ensure that defence spending is 2.5% of GDP but we will get better value for it. Defence procurement, often a synonym for wasting money, will be heavily scrutinised. We are forming an experienced team of procurement experts. We need to have professional armed forces supplied with the latest kit that technology can provide. The armed forces will integrate more closely with MI5, MI6 and GCHQ to provide internal security and external defence capability. We will form a National Guard to support the police when occasions warrant it. We have to provide our troops, sailors and airmen with accommodation that is of top quality for themselves and their families. Happy armed forces personnel are more effective than unhappy ones.

"We will devise and adopt an Ethical Foreign Policy. We will be friends with countries who are friendly towards us. Friendly countries don't send spies here or allow groups to hack into our public systems. Friendly countries do not have call centres that allow fraud to operate from their borders resulting in theft from our citizens. Friendly countries do not steal our patents or produce counterfeit goods to the detriment of our businesses. We will trade on equal terms with friendly countries. We will not send out diplomats to spy on other countries, that is all old James Bond hat. We have a large Overseas Development Fund that will only be offered to friendly countries. We will welcome students and immigration from friendly countries only.

"Our immigration policy will be based on demand for certain workers and they will be given work visas. After a number of years of working and paying taxes and not breaking the law, we will look sympathetically on the granting of a permanent right to stay. Family members up to four in number and up to the age of fifty-five will be allowed after an extended period of time. Failed asylum seekers, illegal immigrants not prepared to work and criminals from foreign countries will be deported back to their own countries. If their origin is uncertain or their country refuses to take them back, they will be sent to a holding facility on one of UK's Overseas Territories until they volunteer to return home or they show themselves to be rehabilitated. We will cease paying France money for failed attempts at stopping boats arriving in UK from across the channel. Owners of ships and aircraft arriving in the UK carrying people without the proper visa will be heavily fined and may lose their landing rights. Students will be issued with visas at no cost, but they will be for one year and renewable as they continue their course. Failure to return to their country when a visa is out of date will result in detention and expulsion and no right of return. Employing or renting a property to a person not eligible to be in the UK will be a criminal offence with very high penalties.

Thank you for attending today. Feel free to speak with my ministers."

<u>Wednesday, 28th June 2034</u>

Six days after the election, Parliament reconvened to elect the Speaker, swear in the new MPs, of which there were a great number, and give Julie her first opportunity to address the House of Commons as Prime Minister. MPs, led by the Father and Mother of the House, went to the House of Lords to receive a message from the monarch asking them to elect a Speaker. They returned to the House of Commons and began the process immediately. As Julie entered the Chamber all of the MPs, not just those from National Endeavour, rose and applauded. She had won the most seats by good electioneering and a total absence of unfounded criticism and invective against her opponents and their parties. For the election there had been an electoral pact between the Conservatives and Reform UK not to compete with each other for seats. After the election they had got together and agreed to merge the parties so forming the official opposition as Conservatives Reformed UK.

For Julie, the next few days in Parliament were taken up with getting the administrative stuff out of the way and holding her first Prime Minister's Questions. The questions were light hearted as the real business only got under way after the King's Speech, George VII's big state occasion.

The days between the election and the State Opening of Parliament had been used well. All of the ground rules had been established. The new government's programme was out there in the public domain. As expected, there had been howls of anguish from second home owners and specific interest groups that have seen their activities in the firing line. Predictably the right wing press saw the government's programme as an assault on the entrepreneurship and directors ability to manage their businesses. The left wing press saw liberty curtailed and the freedom of speech and action under threat. The legal profession members were not happy, but then they never were.

Secondary legislation was passed quickly giving effect to many changes. Councils had been given instructions on their refuse tips, council tax bands, holiday homes and lettings, second homes and empty properties. The Vale of White Horse District Council, the first to release information, had already identified 124 empty properties, 43 of them privately owned with Council Tax in arrears.

Police forces, quickly off the mark and not wanting a threat of merging with their neighbouring force hanging over them, had suddenly started arresting shoplifters and drivers without insurance. Julie had always said "What gets measured, gets done."

In interviews, she countered all of the arguments against her programme by saying, "When you exercise your rights to freedom is it at the expense of mine? How many days a year do you use your second home? Is it a lesser number of days than this family who are homeless for 365 days? We can have everything we want as a country, if the better off pay the right amount of tax and the benefit thieves stop stealing from us. It isn't good for the country that people sit at home in idleness when the country looks untidy and dirty. All communities should take more responsibility for the jobs that aren't being done, like removing shrub and tree growth from road signs. I say to Parish Councils, if it makes it easier at a road junction to see the way forward, cut the grass verge, don't wait for the highways department to do it."

The first twelve days had passed by and tomorrow was the big day, the State opening of Parliament. The King had received the written speech, which he would read out. His first and last time. The UK would be a very different place eighty-seven days after it.

Chapter 13

The King's Speech

5th July 2034

The day of the State Opening of Parliament arrived and the Yeoman of The Guard did what their regiment had done since 5th November 1605. They checked the cellars of the Houses of Parliament looking for a modern day Guy Fawkes and the gunpowder equivalent. Outside in Parliament Square, twelve protesters were arrested when their banners were deemed too inflammatory. The police had received prior intelligence that the demonstrators were intent on disrupting the proceedings and spoiling one of the country's spectacular shows of pageantry, beamed around the world. It was royal pageantry to some people, historical flippancy to others but to most people in the country, it was a ritual that had nothing to do with them and was a colossal waste of time, money and effort. Little did they know that the new King agreed with them and that he had already decided that after today, royal pageantry would have nothing to do with what went on in Parliament.

King George VII set off from Clarence House in the Diamond Jubilee State Coach, a carriage looking medieval but actually built in 2010. The coach was pulled by six white horses and attended by footmen in fancy dress. At the same time, thirty-six Household Cavalry Guards were positioning themselves on the King's Staircase in the Palace of Westminster. The large monarch's crown, the Cap of Maintenance and the Sword of State were delivered to the Crown Jeweller and taken to the Robing Room. The crown, weighing over 1kg, was festooned with two hundred and seventy diamonds and precious stones. At its pinnacle was the St. Edward's Sapphire, thought to have been in the ring worn by St. Edward the Confessor. Other notable stones were the Black Prince Ruby from 1397 and the Stuart's Sapphire.

George arrived and went into the Robing Room to get dressed in the formal regalia. The crown was placed on his head all the time defying gravity. While he was getting robed, elsewhere, lots of state rituals were going on in the Houses of Lords and Commons. The Speaker had arrived in the Commons and taken the morning prayers, a surreal experience for the MPs of other faiths and none. In the Lords, there were diplomats in formal dress and the peers dressed in their red and ermine. A diplomat from a South American country looked at all these strangely dressed people and was barely able to contain a giggle. "What a way to run a country," he thought. There was more to come for him to snigger about, as more dignitaries with strange titles and job descriptions entered the House of Lords dressed in golden tunics.

At precisely 11.27am George, slender and tall, left the Robing Room dressed in the massive robes of state that King Edward VII, who was a very large man, had worn for his coronation in 1902. This was the cue for a person with the title of Black Rod to go to the House of Commons and rudely have the door slammed in her face. Black Rod then banged on the door and when it was opened, she summoned the MPs into the House of Lords Chamber. It was all a bit of a squeeze as 650 MPs politely nudged their way into a room occupied by diplomats and up to 600 peers in big fancy clothes. At 11.30am on the dot, George, seated on the throne, was handed the speech that he was to read by Hillary Armstrong-Lewis, Justice Director, and nominally the country's Lord Chancellor.

This speech had been written on vellum five days previously, a copy of which on paper, had been handed to George the day before so he knew what he had to say. He also knew his constitutional role and that the words would not be attributed to him.

Larry Taylor, a journalist with a right-wing daily newspaper, was sitting watching live coverage of the King on a TV in an ante room to the House of Lords, pen in hand, waiting to report in a thousand words a piece for tomorrow's edition. He started the piece with "Young King George, the seventh of his name, started slowly, but with a strong voice." "A punchy start," thought Larry.

George, seated on his gilded throne, looked around the chamber wondering where Sir David Beckham and Tom Cruise were seated. He looked down at the text and started, "My government will bring forward a Bill setting out a new national Constitution and Bill of Rights that will replace the House of Lords with a Second Chamber, its members elected from all cities, metropolitan boroughs and regions of the UK. At my request, my government will redefine the political role of the monarchy. The four countries of the UK will be encouraged to come together in a federal system." A gasp went around the Chamber and Larry added to it. One of the journalists in the room let out an expletive. More shocks were coming. "My government will take early steps to vacate the Palace of Westminster and to commence refurbishment of the buildings at the lowest cost to the taxpayer.

"My government will introduce legislation to truncate the law making process to enable Bills more speedily to be passed. Proposed laws will be scrutinised, but when they are passed, my government will require the judiciary to judge cases in accordance with the wishes of Parliament. My government will merge some layers of the justice system to remove unnecessary stages and complexity.

"My government will solve the housing crisis by whatever means it takes. There will be a major Housing Bill. There are sufficient housing units in the UK but they are not available or affordable to all of those in need. My government will pass legislation to remedy this, which will include major changes to the current planning laws and their application." Larry's daughter was still living at his home at the age of thirty with her partner and their two young children. "God, yes," he turned and shouted and pumped his fist before turning back to the TV in embarrassment.

"My government will have as a priority, stability in the nation's finances. During the life of this Parliament, the Revenue and

Expenditure Budget will come into balance so that borrowing to fund everyday expenditure ceases. Growth in the economy is fundamental to my government's plans.

"My government will give additional powers to HMRC in the Finance Bill. Unexplained wealth will be targeted and evading tax will carry very high penalties including imprisonment. Tax evasion loopholes will be closed and transactions in cash will be reduced." Larry was scribbling like crazy. Mostly these occasions were really boring but there was a lot of meat on the bone of this one.

"My government will establish UK plc to seed fund investment by, or jointly with, private companies in new manufacturing capabilities. Buying British goods and services will be promoted in every project.

"My government will introduce Welfare Reform so that people not working will only be paid their benefit payments if they contribute towards community work. All mental health claimants will be professionally assessed." "About time", thought Larry. "So many people swinging the lead with mental problems. Not easy to diagnose them." His mate Paul had been malingering and taking the mickey for years. "Not too ill to go down the pub and play darts, though." He knew from an assignment that there were some blokes who had never had a job. Whole families that had never worked.

"My government will introduce a Criminal Justice Bill removing entrapment as a defence. The police will get greater powers and reduced paperwork. Criminals will be able to plea bargain for shorter sentences. Sentenced time in prison will become time served with time added for bad behaviour." Larry had never been able to understand this 50% off from the sentence. "If a prisoner behaves badly, keep them in, that's what I say."

"My government will introduce legislation that will require all dental practices to treat children and young people up to the age of 16 with free NHS dental care.

"My government will ensure that all children receive an education and will be passing legislation to greatly reduce truancy from schools and bad behaviour by students in school.

"My government will give the police all the tools that they need to catch criminals. Police will serve the public better by being in the community and not in the police station doing paperwork.

"My government will be proposing a Bill to change how prisons are managed and what convicted persons will be expected to do while serving out their sentences.

"My government will set up UK S&T plc to invest in private companies for the advancement of Science and Technology.

"My government will scrap the TV licence fee after the current settlement runs out in three years' time and privatise the BBC.

"My government will introduce an immigration Bill and clear the backlog of asylum seekers.

"My government will respect and keep to its climate change commitments.

"My government will introduce an Ethical Foreign Policy."

The King paused and looked around at the assembled Lords and MPs crammed into the tiny chamber. "What a way to run the country," he thought echoing the diplomat's thoughts from earlier. "The sooner JC reforms this lot the better."

The King's Speech was completed in seventeen minutes. When it was all over, George returned to Clarence House, his new official residence in London.

Julie decided to hold a press conference outside 10 Downing Street using the new shorter lectern so she didn't need to stand on a small box to look over the top. The sun was out and everything was going according to plan. Julie thought, "The best thing about being Prime Minister is that you don't need to know more than everyone else about everything, because you have at your beck and call the country's best specialists, just waiting to be asked." So she had asked them and invited them into meetings, requested policy papers and had lunch and dinner with them. She had asked Edward Grey to have Chequers, her country residence, ready at short notice so that she could meet with the best brains.

She looked down at the prepared text from one of her preferred speechwriters. She had read it before coming out and thought, "This is pretty good, I must remember to thank him. Small appreciations go a long way."

She focused on the middle camera less than ten feet away and said, "Today King George VII, presided over the State Opening of Parliament. It is his expressed wish that his government adapts itself to the modern age and casts off all of the medieval customs and practices that mean nothing to most of our people. In future, Parliament will be opened by the Speaker in residence. Our King and his Royal Family members will continue to preside over the pageantry that makes London and the UK a popular destination for tourists. As you are aware, he has returned Buckingham Palace to the Crown Estates and after refurbishment it will be open daily to the public.

"We will soon be putting before Parliament the Bills, the content of which have been set out in the King's Speech and our Manifesto. We have an Executive Management Team of the highest calibre and they are working on your behalf to improve our society. National Endeavour means that we will be wanting all of our people to contribute to making our country a nicer and more prosperous place in which to live." Julie then spread her arms wide and continued, "You, the people, have given National Endeavour a mandate to clear up the faults in our society. For some it will mean paying the right amount of tax and for others, to support their estranged children financially. The criminal justice system will be updated to give those who have broken the law a second chance, but not endless chances. We will unashamedly be putting the care of our children at the forefront of our actions. We are also very aware of the country's climate change responsibilities, moving to a low or zero carbon based economy. We do not need to be reminded of this by shameless acts of vandalism, which will be harshly penalised. We are planning a new Constitution so that both legislative assemblies will be elected by the people for the people. Today is another day along our 100 days of planned progress, not words but actions too. Thank you." She brought her arms together across her chest as in supplication and bowed to the cameras and journalists.

She moved away from the lectern and went inside No. 10 to a ripple of applause, which she was told was not the usual practice from journalists.

Chapter 14

Important to Have a Good Constitution

July 2034

Now that the official State Opening of Parliament had taken place, it was up to Julie's team to put together the detailed legislation to get the Bills passed into law. Before she oversaw this, her first act was to give a knighthood to Edward Grey. Sir Edward thanked her and said "Estelle will be so pleased." She also made James Manvell, a first class candidate who had failed to get elected in an ultra-safe Labour seat, Lord Manvell of Bishops Cleve, who promptly took up the role of Leader of the House of Lords, reporting to Agnes Peters.

The first Bill set out the legislative process to decrease the time for a Bill to be passed. On the day after King George's State Address, the Bill was finalised and given to the legislation group for scrutiny and tidying up. The Bill did away with the First Reading & Second Reading by having the written Bill presented to Parliament by a relevant Minister, who would answer questions on it for up to two hours. It would then be voted upon on that day. After hearing MPs comments and suggestions, the legislation group, made up of law experts, experienced legislation writers and two of the most pedantic judges that Hillary Armstrong-Lewis could find and recommend, amended it and sent it to Agnes Peters in her role as Leader of The House of Commons.

The Bill was then considered at the Select Committee stage the next day. All of the important Select Committees were chaired by National Endeavour MPs so a timetable of four days was allowed for amendments and further suggestions. The Bill then returned with a couple of minor amendments to Julie, who incorporated the changes in agreement with the legislation group. This process ensured that the Bill, and all the other Bills processed in the same way, when enacted, would be very clear in their intentions and application. The Bill returned to the Commons in its final form on the seventh sitting day. It was passed and sent to the House of Lords for approval, after which it would return to the Commons to become law. The King had let it be known that he wanted the Royal Assent phase to be removed from the process, and this wish was incorporated in the Bill. This Bill would be his one and only Royal Assent. If the Lords proposed amendments they would either be approved or declined by a Commons vote. The Lords knew that they would not be allowed to vote against the legislation, only to amend it.

The Lords incorporated multiple amendments of the most trivial nature with the obvious tactic of delaying the legislation and to show that the Lords couldn't be treated with disdain. They particularly didn't like the removal of the Royal Assent citing 400 years of Parliamentary procedures and that it hadn't been specifically included in the government's Manifesto. Clearly, the Lords were miffed that their maximum daily attendance allowance of up to £468 per day had been abolished. They still received travel expenses, but not subsidised food and drink in the in-house restaurant and bar. They could also see that coming down the road was the replacement of their chamber with a second elected one and they would all be relieved of their duties. The local ermine sellers were already planning to move to other clothing lines.

There were 842 members of the House of Lords, the second largest legislative assembly after the National Congress of the Communist Party of China. The Lords comprised bishops, archbishops and life peers. Hereditary peers had been removed in 2026. 46 of the members were independent or non-affiliated, the remainder being members of political parties. National Endeavour now had one affiliated member so getting legislation through without the other political parties' support would prove difficult. Julie Carter knew that as the Bill, with a clause giving the right to remove Royal Assent from the procedure, had not been specifically included in her party's Manifesto so she could not invoke the Parliament Acts. The Manifesto had the following clause:

'We will bring forward a Bill to amend the procedures for passing legislation into laws at every current stage. The objective will be to speed up the process and prevent vexatious delay tactics.'

Julie called in Agnes Peters and the newly ennobled Lord James Manvell. She explained that she intended to invoke the Parliament Acts because as Royal Assent was not specifically in the Manifesto, the intention was there and it was the King driving the change. "I have commissioned a brief on these Acts with recommendations on the pathways that we should follow. I have been advised that the powers of the House of Lords are limited by both law and convention. The first Parliament Act of 1911 removed the House of Lords power to veto a Bill, except one to extend the lifetime of a Parliament. This was a sensible exclusion as we can all see that never ending parliaments would have ensued. The second Act of 1949 reduced the Lords delaying a Bill to one year, previously two. It also defined 'Money Bills' which the Lords cannot amend or delay by more than one month. Most other Commons Bills can be held up by the Lords if they disagree with them for about a year but ultimately the elected House of Commons can reintroduce them in the following session and pass them without the consent of the Lords. Only seven Bills have been passed using these powers in over 100 years so we are not expecting a prolonged fight on these. Apparently, we can use what is known as 'The Salisbury Convention' as this will ensure that we can get through Bills, without a majority in the Lords if the Bill is mentioned in our manifesto. Our final recourse, if all persuasion and common sense fails, is that National Endeavour will nominate 850 peers so that we will end up with a majority."

Agnes asked, "Where would we get 850 loyal supporters from?"

"We have 398 MPs, so we have 234 candidates loyal to us, who, like James here, failed to get elected. We also have 632 election agents so I make that 866."

James said, "A House of Lords with potentially 1700 members will be a little cramped. Even now with 300 in the Chamber it's pretty close to full."

Julie said, "It won't be for long, just until we abolish the place or move the Chamber over the road in Westminster, or Leeds," she added with a twinkle in her eyes.

"Leeds?" gasped Hugo. "I'm not sure that I know the quickest way to get there."

Agnes chipped in sarcastically, "Nor would most of them. They all knew where to sign in for their daily allowance before they headed to the exit. Good plan of yours that we put a stop to that. The feedback from our focus groups is that reducing MP's salaries and stopping the Lords' allowance were the most popular things that we have done so far."

"So," Julie said. "Can you both get round the tearooms and let them know that we mean business and any delaying tactics will bring the other decisions together sooner?"

Agnes and Lord Manvell did a good job because the Bill returned to the Lords within a week and it was approved. The Bill returned to the Commons and then Julie was off to Clarence House for the Royal Assent. King George welcomed her warmly and with a flourish of his pen, he rewrote Parliamentary procedures that had been stuck in the eighteenth century. On her way back to Downing Street, Julie thought "A modern monarch for our modern times."

Next on the Agenda was the Constitution Bill, a major piece of legislation. Now that the Lords had seen her determination, Julie didn't expect to encounter any problems. The Manifesto was quite specific on the matter.

"The House of Lords will be replaced by a Second Chamber of elected persons from all cities and regions in the UK. At the same time we will increase the powers available to the four nations with improvements to local democracy. The House of Lords will not impede the will of the people."

The first ever written Constitution Bill was in five parts. Julie had asked all of the legal and constitutional experts to put together the first draft. When the Bill was in a fairly finished form, her job would be to meet all of the interested and affected parties to gather some form of consensus.

The first part of the Constitution Bill addressed that the monarchy would cease to be involved in constitutional affairs. There would be no State Opening of Parliament, no accepting resignations of governments, or 'kissing of hands' to invite the forming of a new government, no Royal Assents, no regular meetings with the Prime Minister and no red boxes to peruse. All of this would be replaced by open access. The King, or Queen, could request an audience with the Prime Minister at any time and this meeting would take place within seven working days. This timescale took into account the Prime Minister's attendance at global meetings. Members of Parliament would no longer need to affirm their loyalty to the monarchy. The continued attendance of Sinn Fein MPs in Parliament was now assured.

The second part of the Bill addressed the creation of a Federal United Kingdom. This Bill could only be enacted with the approval of the Senedd Cymru of Wales, the Scottish Parliament and the Northern Ireland Assembly, so for each country it was a separate Bill, only to be joined with the others after it had been passed by some or all of the constituent countries. Each Bill would become law in its standalone form. When all of the elements were passed, a Bill would be enacted bringing all of the strands together. That way, delay on one Bill would not prevent enactment of another one. This process also enabled each of the countries of the federal country to make progress without being slowed by the others, who might wish to have more time. Julie envisaged a speedy resolution for Scotland and Wales, but Northern Ireland would take a little longer. The proposed arrangements for Scotland and Wales were agreed by the Executive Team and laid before Parliament at the same time as they were sent to Edinburgh and Cardiff. A free vote in Westminster on amendments and the main Bill would take place alongside other discussions. It was a messy arrangement with lots of iterations and strands to put together, but if a final version could be agreed, then it would be acceptable to all. The proposals for Northern Ireland were to advance in stages. The first proposal contained increased powers, particularly on tax revenues. The Irish Taoiseach had made a visit to Chequers with the public intention of greeting the new Prime Minister but also discuss the Northern Ireland proposals. "All to be handled very delicately," thought Julie.

The third part of the Bill set out the arrangements for meetings of Parliament, not diverging too much from what presently occurred. It defined a sitting Parliament as the place in which The Speaker convened the meeting. This nicely avoided describing The Palace of Westminster as the intention was to move out, so that the buildings could be refurbished. This proposal was contained in a separate Bill that was put before Parliament soon after the King's Speech. The House of Commons would meet in the Queen Elizabeth II Centre and the House of Lords and later the new Second Chamber would occupy the Methodist Central Hall, both in Westminster. A project would commence to assess the feasibility of moving Parliament to Leeds, York or another Northern city. The Palace of Westminster after refurbishment would become a Museum of The Nation and be opened in full to the public.

The fourth part of the Bill defined the Second Chamber that would replace the House of Lords after elections had taken place. The elected Mayor of every city and metropolitan borough would have a seat in this second chamber as would an elected representative from each county. Currently there were 76 cities in the United Kingdom, 55 in England, 7 in Wales, 8 in Scotland, and 6 in Northern Ireland. In addition, there were 36 Metropolitan Boroughs and 92 counties taking the total to 204.

The fifth part of the Bill recognised the Overseas Territories as separate from the UK. Each Territory had its own Constitution and its own Government and its own local laws. In the Bill, the status quo was proposed so that the UK Parliament would continue to have unlimited powers to legislate for the Territories. However, the territories privileged tax status for UK residents would be abolished. The Bill put into law that the main opposition party would be the party with the largest number of MPs after the governing party. The forming of coalition governments and coalition oppositions was recognised. Julie inserted a provision that would allow asylum seekers and persons failing to gain immigration approval to be removed to overseas territory facilities paid for by the UK government.

During the passage of this very large and complex Constitution Bill, Conservatives Reformed UK, the main Opposition Party in Parliament, made it known to the media that they were opposed to the moving out of Parliament despite a number of surveys suggesting it was the most cost effective solution.

Conservatives Reformed UK also used the Constitution Bill to attack secondary legislation that had become law. They were against the assault on second homes owners (partly because a lot of them had second or more homes), letting restrictions (again because a lot of them had properties let out) and the abolition of tax havens (unsurprisingly). The Constitution Bill passed into law despite some administrative opposition from the civil service and a couple of short filibusters in the Lords. Since the election, this was not the first time that departmental civil servants had been less than helpful to National Endeavour ministers. Julie decided to ask Sir Simon Thornley, Cabinet Secretary and Head of the Civil Service in for a chat over a cup of tea. Their meeting was in the Cabinet Room attended by Sir Edward, Chief of Staff & chief note taker.

"Good afternoon, Sir Simon. Thank you for setting aside some time in what must be a busy day for you."

"Not especially busy," said Sir Simon. "The usual issues to be resolved so that everything runs smoothly."

"Are things running smoothly? My ministers would like things to run a bit more smoothly as they are experiencing some barriers from your people on their road to progress."

"I'm sure that if the ministers kept to the codes of conduct and allowed matters to take their course, they would feel less worried about the time that certain matters take."

"Unfortunately for my ministers, time is not a luxury that I give them. They are tasked with getting things done and putting policy papers on my desk. If they are late or fail to do so I'm not a happy person. You want me to be a happy person don't you?"

"Perhaps you should adjust your definition of happiness," Sir Simon responded.

"I would find it easier adjusting your definition of happiness. What do you think?"

"Are you threatening me?" Sir Simon asked incredulously. "I think that you should respect my position. I was doing this job while you were still at school. The problem for my colleagues in the service is that your ministers have no experience of governing, they know nothing about how this country operates and they refuse to be guided. Your Ministers don't understand the word 'no'. In this country we have ways of doing things and the civil service are the best judges of what can and should be achieved. I have not had issues with any of your predecessors holding your Office."

"Answer me these questions, Sir Simon. Who do you work for and who do your civil servants work for?"

"We are employed by the government. We offer unbiased advice and assist ministers in their work so that they achieve the outcomes they seek."

"The country might pay your salaries, but I think that you work for me and my government. Civil servants are usually employed by 'Ministers of the Crown', so civil servants working in government departments are therefore employed by my ministers. I want you to do something for me. I would like you to meet with your most senior colleagues, possibly over a drink at your clubs, and let them know that until we resolve our little concerns about their loyalty and abilities to work at our pace, then there are no more knighthoods or other gongs. I also want a list on my desk by this time tomorrow of the names of any civil servants who think that they don't want to work for me and my ministers and that includes you."

"The list won't do you any good as you can't sack anyone."

"Oh dear, that is a silly thing to say because I can sack anyone, including you and I think that I will. Let's see how that works out for you shall we? In your resignation letter, please suggest three names of individuals that you think are capable of replacing you and working for me. I'm sure that your defenestration will encourage the others, don't you?"

"You've not heard the last of this. You have no idea what sort of trouble I can cause you."

"I have a very good idea and the answer is not much. Close the door as you leave."

Sir Simon stood outside the door in mild shock and couldn't immediately work out what had just happened. He was normally so strategic in this type of meeting. He was a good chess player and could see moves at least two ahead. At no time in this meeting did he see the outcome of him losing his job. How had he allowed himself to be manipulated like that, when it was he that normally controlled things? He thought, "Was it her intention to get rid of me from the start of the meeting and if it was, how come I didn't see it coming? Good Lord, there is an iron fist in her velvet glove."

After a very short recruitment process, Julian Hornsby was Sir Simon's replacement. The news of the sacking ricocheted around government departments and suddenly a new enthusiasm gripped the senior civil service people. If Sir Simon could get fired without warning and so quickly, then they had better watch out for themselves. The sacking of Sir Simon Thornley also registered with the other legislative public servants, the judges. The message was clear that the government expected the judiciary to judge on the laws as they had been passed. The new laws would be better drafted and free of some of the technicalities that some judges allowed to influence their judgements. New judges with this positive attitude would get the better cases and so it would be better to stay 'on side'. Judges were still allowed discretion to impose punishments in accordance with the sentencing guidelines.

A Bill was introduced that abolished Judicial Reviews and set out how the Court of Appeal would be merged with the Supreme Court. The aim was clear. When a judge settled a matter, it was accepted as settled and of course this went down well with them. Perversely it put more of a spotlight on their judgements because their mistakes became newsworthy. The Justice Minister and Attorney General were still able to step in on any clear miscarriages, because these cases were fast-tracked to the Supreme Court. The number of Supreme Court judges was increased to cope with the additional workload. The Bill's provisions prevented special interest groups from interfering in the will of Parliament and it did away with the need to wear wigs and starched shirts in court. The Opposition supported the government in the passing of this Bill and it became law in accordance with the new timetable.

Julie didn't like sacking Sir Simon Thornley but she knew early on that she had to do it *'pour encourager les autres'*, to encourage the others. She needed to sacrifice somebody important for the good of her government or she and her Ministers couldn't make the progress needed in the next 85 days. She asked Sir Edward Grey to sweeten Sir Simon's exit with the full monetary amounts due and a position on the Board of UK plc. In the years to come, Sir Simon became one of Julie's staunchest supporters and a close confidant.

At the end of another busy week, Julie spent the weekend at Chequers with her mum and Jamie. She used these weekends to meet experts over a drink, who universally liked having conversations in such nice surroundings. If they had spouses or partners, they were also invited. Getting an invitation was soon seen as a recognition of a person's value to the government. It was in the field of management that Julie sought the experts most frequently. She was smart but had not had the working experience of motivating teams. She was taught skills like transaction analysis, the dynamics of teams and how to get the best out of her direct reports. At the regular Monday meetings, all of her ministers became aware of a more competent senior manager taking shape.

Chapter 15

Prime Ministers' Questions (PMQs)

12th July 2034

Julie's first Prime Ministers Questions (PMQs) took place on the Wednesday after the King's Speech. This would be the first time that she would be questioned by fellow professional politicians, so she needed some training. She spent the morning of the day with her advisers preparing for all the traps designed to trip her up and make her look foolish in the media.

She also knew from her limited Parliamentary knowledge and experience that there was always a strong demand from MPs to ask a question. It offered them a chance to get national exposure on a question often important in their constituency. Since her election as an MP, she had tried on a number of occasions to ask a question by entering the ballot but she had not been chosen. After the ballot closed on the Thursday prior to the next PMQs, usually 15 MPs were selected at random in what was known as 'the shuffle'. Their names were printed on the order paper for the following PMQs so Julie's team knew from where the questions would come. This knowledge meant that her researchers would have a week to prise out of the questioners, what they intended to ask. Preparation for PMQs began straight after the successful MPs in the ballot were announced. Julie's Parliamentary Private Secretaries got straight onto the case.

From the information gleaned, civil servants in Downing Street prepared a briefing pack, which included background information and draft answers for each MP on the order paper. The answers were prepared by government departments. If her team couldn't find out what an MP would be asking, the pack would include answers on all likely questions. The briefing pack would also include detailed policy briefs, prepared over the course of the week.

In the past, Prime Ministers could have spent several hours a week preparing for PMQs. Julie just didn't have the time to do this, but she did believe in her power of memory and recall. She took the whole process seriously, but didn't waste time looking for jokes. She entered the House of Commons a little before noon and took her seat. It had become conventional for almost all MPs to ask the Prime Minister if she would list her official engagements for the day. Only the first MP on the order paper actually asked this question.

The first question was from the MP for Walsall, who was shown to be at the top of the order paper. "Could the Prime Minister list her official engagements for the day?" Julie replied, "I will have meetings with ministerial colleagues and others."

The MP for Walsall then asked a supplementary question. "Could the Prime Minister tell me how she intends to deal with the increase in shoplifting from the hard-working shopkeepers in my constituency?" Her advisers had predicted this one correctly as recent statistics had put Walsall near the top of the shoplifting league. "They have a league for shoplifters? Julie had asked.

"We have supplied the West Midlands Constabulary with the latest high definition facial recognition cameras. We have also entered a supply arrangement with CCTV providers so that cameras can be purchased and installed with a discount from the normal price. Shoplifting is not a victimless crime as your constituents are aware. The police have agreed to a zero tolerance to all crimes so hopefully, you will see a reduction in offences soon."

The Speaker, following the usual protocol now allowed a question from a backbencher of National Endeavour. "Can my honourable friend advise my constituents how she intends to increase the housing stock in my area on the lovely Dorset coast?"

"As my friend is aware, the councils in his constituency have identified 49 empty properties in the last week and have commenced actions to secure them or collect increased Council Tax. In addition, one town on that coast has been identified as having exceeded 10% of the total of residential properties being let out or as second homes. That means that any residential home now coming on the market can only be sold to a person wishing it to be their main residence and to live full time in the area. We estimate that the house price will be at least 15% more affordable for a local person."

After these couple of questions, Nigel Hunter, the Leader of Conservatives Reformed UK and the Official Opposition Leader, was called by the Speaker to pose his first question.

"Are you going to make it a feature of your Premiership that you sack competent servants of the country?"

Julie rose from the green leather bench and looked over the lectern, barely able to see her questioner, "We received a very much larger number of voters supporting our plans than you received, because they wanted us to clear up your mess and get things done. It is important that we work with civil servants who have the same objectives that we do."

Nigel then gave his second question, "As a short woman, does it give you pleasure to discipline tall strong men?" A gasp went around the Commons at the sheer impudence and not very well hidden insult in the question.

"That question is beneath you and will I suspect alienate a lot of your female MPs. Normally, I wouldn't give that sort of question the time that it doesn't deserve, but I am going to answer it. I know I have the body of a weak and feeble woman, but I have the heart and stomach of a king, and of a king of England too." The Commons on both sides broke out in great applause and her MPs behind her waved their order papers.

"The lady is no Queen Elizabeth I", was the sharp reply.

"And the man is no gentleman" replied Julie to more applause and shouting.

Nigel indicated that he would reserve his remaining four questions until later in the session. The Speaker, with a smile, called on Linda Morgan, the leader of the Liberal Democrats.

"May I congratulate the Prime Minister on her stunning election victory? In a few short weeks she has made some controversial decisions using her Parliamentary majority. Are we seeing a new dictator using absolute power, absolutely?"

Julie rose again and half-turned to Linda, "The Lady's Party was at the forefront of every argument and campaign to reduce this country to a nature loving and animal friendly place, while not seeming to worry too much about the ordinary lives that were being put to the end of a long queue of help. We have no shame in thinking that people come first. We were elected to improve living standards, house the homeless, feed the hungry and make sure that all children get the best chances in life. If it takes exercising authority and will, then we are ready to use them."

The Scottish Nationalist spokesman rose to his feet. "Instead of offering Scotland a light form of independence in a federal system, why don't you grant it full independence?"

"Because there is no majority in favour of independence. The referendum in 2014 declined to have it. The referendum in 2028 was a resounding refusal to have it. Now six years later, with your party only holding 9 seats out of a total of 57, which any mathematician would describe as 'a low percentage', I conclude that you are one of a few lone voices crying in the wilderness. However, a federal United Kingdom with Scotland having greater powers seems to attract approval."

Nigel Hunter had a further question, "The other House's attendance has plummeted since you stopped the daily allowance. Do you think that it can be an effective Second Chamber with so few peers turning up?"

Julie was waiting for this one. "The members of the other place still receive their travelling expenses, so if they want to support their country then there is no monetary reason for staying away. If any of

Milords are short of a few bob, I can always bung them a couple of quid." Laughter from the public gallery broke out.

The speaker then called the third name on the order paper, Sheila Smith, a Green Party MP from a constituency in Bristol. "Despite increased regulation and scrutiny of the water industry since 2025, nothing has improved markedly in the last 10 years. The rivers in my area still swim with sewage every time we have heavy rainfall. Why doesn't your government have plans to nationalise the water industry?"

"Since 2027, when Thames Water was rescued by the Labour government, all the remaining water companies have improved their performance. Many of them have spent considerable sums installing new storm drains and increasing the capacity of their sewage works. The Victorian system is gradually being brought into the modern day, but it is a slow and expensive process. We prefer that the independent regulator guides the companies through their long term plans. For our part, we will only get involved if the companies make poor decisions on executive bonuses and shareholder dividends. We have imposed a windfall tax on retained profits, essentially shareholders' funds, on the industry of £2bn and we will not hesitate to do the same again."

The Speaker looked at the order paper and saw that 'the shuffle' had not been kind to National Endeavour, so the next time that a government MP rose from their seat (known as 'bobbing") she was selected. Julie dealt with the sympathetic question easily.

Nigel Hunter, chastened by losing the vocal sparring earlier in the session kept his questions on government policies, which Julie was easily able to answer.

The session continued until the clock showed 12.30pm at which point the Speaker abruptly called "Order" and announced the next business. Julie rose from the bench and went into a Committee room for her next meeting.

"That all went pretty well", she thought.

The press loved the Queen Elizabeth I reference and in private from then on they referred to her as 'Queenie'. That evening, Jamie asked her, "Can we have a cat? The Downing Street cat died last year and during the turmoil, it was not replaced."

"Of course, we can. What will you call it?"

"If it's a male cat, Lionel. I hadn't thought of a name if it wasn't a male."

And it was male. The cat rescue charity delivered an almost entirely black cat to Jamie after a couple of days. He announced Lionel's arrival on his social media page with a playful picture.

Chapter 16

Shake Those Money Makers

19th July 2034 – The Finance Bill after The King's Speech

Under Julie Carter's guidance, the National Endeavour government was a model of efficient integration. At the Monday meetings, Julie was able to nuance the progress on all current issues ensuring that the urgent matters were dealt with quickly and the important matters were well planned. She had told them that they couldn't expect to do everything in the first few days so some of their plans would have to wait. She asked them all to come up with some 'quick wins' from each department as these would be eye catching in the press and the country. A good example was the previous announcement that entrance to museums and art galleries for British nationals and all children would be free, but non-national adults would pay £5.

The Executive Team were co-ordinating their plans with each other and their direct report Ministers across the ministerial divides. When appropriate, Ministers also consulted with the other political party's senior spokespeople. Consensus and amiable discussions were leading to easier outcomes and problems were being identified early in the process of law making. None of this had happened in the past. Policies that required funding were cleared with the Treasury early in the thinking. All of these processes were later recognised as a form of Matrix Management.

All of the Executive Team had given their input for the first major piece of financial legislation, that of the Finance Bill. A good example of cross divisional co-operation was for the introduction of Identity Cards. To make the cards effective, they had to contain vital and useful information, but must not be able to be forged or the information accessed by rogue persons. All governments were at the mercy of technology companies to fulfil their software needs. The team decided early on that the resistance to the cards could be assuaged if the technology, data capture and security was all kept under government control, a bit like banknote and coin production. UK S&T plc set up a subsidiary and attracted a lot of bright programmers signing them up into the Official Secrets Act regime. It was decided to produce the cards within GCHQ at Cheltenham, the highest security facility. The Justice Secretary would include within her legislative programme the penalties for attempted card fraud. Of all of the policies that could go wrong, the acceptance and issue of identity cards ranked very highly to cause National Endeavour the most grief. But the rewards for getting it right were huge.

Andrea Patel was putting the final touches to her Finance Bill. This was the Bill that cemented the plans across government, and referenced back to the King's Speech. Here was a primary building block for the administration as this legislation would get some money in quickly and enable some of the new initiatives to get started. Ideally, she would like to reduce some government expenditure, but it was too early to do it sensibly as she had no data. Civil service recruitment was frozen until a review of the numbers needed going forward could take place. Expenditure plans would have to see the light of day in the annual budget scheduled for 18th October. There could be some small reductions in the welfare budget over time, mostly by getting people off benefits and back to work. The levelling up ideas would mean that any gains there would be swallowed up by increasing fairness into some of the procedures and payments. The Budget in October would be the time to set out the long term financial strategies. This Finance Bill was going to plug some gaps and get some much needed money in.

Even before the Finance Bill, Andrea had already put before Parliament Statutory Instruments for the secondary legislation items. The King's Speech contained *"My government will give additional powers to HMRC in the Finance Bill. Unexplained wealth will be targeted and evading tax will carry very high penalties including imprisonment. Tax evasion loopholes will be closed. Transactions in cash will be reduced."*

The first clause in the Finance Bill was that in future the antiquated pre-election term "Bill of Aid & Supplies" would henceforth be known as "The Finance Bill". There then followed clauses containing the following provisions:

Set up funding for UK S&T plc.

UK S&T plc had already been set up as a company owned by the taxpayer and was recruiting a professional management with the objective of investing in science and technology projects in partnership with companies on a commercial basis. £3 billion pounds would be its initial funding. Projects already identified were the issuing and monitoring of Identity Cards and producing ankle and wrist bands for offenders that could not be tampered with as they must be removed in tandem.

Identity Cards.

Through UK S&T plc, all UK citizens will be issued with an identity card. It will not be a requirement to always have it on the person and available for inspection, although, much like a driving licence, it could be used to confirm identity in a number of circumstances. It will be mandatory to produce the card to obtain certain services. The card will securely contain biological information like DNA, a photograph with a retina scan, blood group, organ donor data, full name and NI number. In time the card could replace the driving licence. All persons in receipt of state benefits will be required to register for a card. Failure to attend for scanning at a confirmed date will result in benefits being delayed. All persons visiting GP surgeries will be required to register at the remotely staffed secure terminal. All persons employed directly or indirectly by the government will be registered at their workplace. The registering for a card will be a statutory requirement. Any person refusing will not have their driving licences and passports renewed until they were registered. The costs of the system were estimated at £3.5bn over the next three years with annual running costs of £500m.

Abolishing tax havens.

All UK territories will have the same tax status. Income earned in these historic tax havens will be counted as UK income for tax purposes. In these territories HMRC will have the powers to inspect all accounts and transactions owned and carried out by UK citizens. Unexplained wealth will be targeted. UK citizens registered as non-domiciled and living abroad for tax purposes will no longer be able to benefit from free NHS care. A Visa will be required to enter the UK at a cost of £100 and be valid for a maximum of 90 days in any one calendar year. Tourist visas would not be charged but limited to 45 days stay.

Preventing flight of capital.

With immediate effect citizens are restricted from sending in excess of £5,000 in one transaction and £10,000 in any one month abroad. Greater sums will require permission from HMRC and may be subject to investigation under unexplained wealth orders. All permissions granted will be subject to a capital wealth tax of 5% of the sum to be transferred. There would be no tax for small sums of less than £250 per month to families of taxpayers domiciled abroad.

Unpaid tax by companies.

Directors will be held jointly and severally financially liable for all unpaid income tax, Corporation Tax, VAT and national insurance contributions owed to HMRC. The practice of going bankrupt or into administration with limited liability for the directors from HMRC will be ended. Any statute of limitations on funds owed to HMRC is abolished.

Cash transactions.

All businesses that want to deal in cash must register with HMRC or else trade cashless. HMRC will instruct banks to refuse to accept cash receipts from businesses not registered with them for cash. This clause will end black market trading and prevent shops and businesses that only took cash, to avoid some taxes. All businesses trading in tax will be subject to increased scrutiny. Overseas money transactions will no longer be allowed in cash. Stealing goods to sell for cash and drug transactions in cash will be severely impacted by these provisions.

Recruit tax inspectors & Commissioners' Powers.

HMRC will recruit and train tax inspectors on salaries with bonuses based on the amounts of avoided or evaded tax that they recover. HMRC Commissioners will have increased powers of search and seizure without the need for judicial warrants. HMRC will have unlimited powers of search and seizure for the payment of tax owing. Seized goods will be sold and the funds used towards tax owed. Sentencing guidelines for tax evaders will be issued with increased prison penalties and fines.

Set up funding for UK plc.

UK plc has been set up as a company owned by the taxpayer and managed by a professional management for investing in projects and in partnership with companies on a commercial basis. £5bn pounds will be its initial funding. Projects will include the taking over of a car manufacturing plant put up for sale by South Korean owners to build cars under the reborn Wolseley brand. Investments will be made in partnerships to build large greenhouses to produce salad crops. Any company nationalised or taken into administration for the public good will be funded and managed by UK plc. UK plc will give extra aid to companies that supply house building products and companies setting up manufacturing in areas of high unemployment.

Tax on new Trusts.

With immediate effect all new trusts created will be required to pay 5% of the trust value in advance to HMRC for each of the first eight years. This will take away the advantage of removing money from estates to avoid inheritance tax.

Child Benefit.

To be payable for all children repealing the legislation passed in 2029.

Child Support Agency (CSA).

The CSA will have increased powers and access to DNA records to establish paternity. CSA will be able to deduct payments from the salaries and wages of absent fathers without challenge. 90% of the money collected will go to the guardian of the child. The remaining 10% will fund CSA on a non-profit basis.

Buying British manufactured goods.

There will be an obligation on government departments, UK plc and UK S&T plc supported or invested companies and businesses receiving government support and contracts to buy British manufactured goods.

Windfall taxes and Transfer of profits.

The Bank of England will stop paying interest to banks for money on deposit. Any UK company that reports excess profits will be scrutinised for a windfall tax. All technology based and other international companies will not be allowed to move profits abroad except with the approval of HMRC. The movement of profits to countries with lower corporation taxes will be subject to a levy equal to the saved amount.

Prison Building.

There will be no prisons built during the life of the Parliament. Money will be used to change prisons into categories for rehabilitation, time-serving and incarceration.

Small nuclear reactors.

Funding will be set aside for the commissioning and building of at least two small nuclear reactors in each year of the Parliament.

Money Laundering.

A new task force will be set up to confiscate sums that have been proven to have entered the system from illegal means. All high end properties purchased by individuals or companies based abroad in the last five years will be investigated and may be the subject of confiscation orders. The bar for mitigating unexplained wealth orders will be raised.

All property and sums relating to prohibited substances will be seized. There will be a presumption of guilt that will need to be disproved.

Bank fraud.

Banks will be financially responsible for fraud committed against their customers without limit. Banks will be quicker to delay or stop fraudulent transactions if they were to pay for them. Large sums over £10,000 entering accounts and promptly leaving will be subject to 72 hours delay until the banks have investigated them. Property transactions will be expected to receive a 24 hours service.

The Office for Budget Responsibility had viewed the proposals and were pleased to announce that the Bill contained nothing that was at variance with its intentions. The Institute of Financial Studies, always a serious commentator on government financial matters came out with "We are frankly astonished by the scope and detail in the Bill. There appear to be some grown-ups in the Treasury at last." The Managing Director of the International Monetary Fund was complimentary and described some of the provisions in the Bill as an example for other countries to follow.

The Finance Bill was presented to Parliament to widespread media acclaim. "They've hit the right nails on the head" was a glowing tribute from The Times Political Columnist. "Eat the Jammy Dodgers" was predictably the front page in The Mirror and The Sun, never a paper to disappoint, "Dads on the Run".

The scope of the Bill had something for everyone. The Mumsnet website liked it and the Unions really liked UK plc as they saw job creation and were already lobbying for new factories where their unemployed former members lived. The left wing socialist workers groupings were ecstatic about the tax dodgers finally being brought to the pay up counter.

The Conservatives Reformed UK opposition made it known in the media that they were opposed to the abolition of tax havens, but that just put the wrong message out there. After that blunder, they decided to be a bit more careful in the future about rowing against the tide of public opinion.

Surprisingly, the issue of identity cards only received positive responses. It had been a firmly held belief for decades, since the Second World War actually, that making Joe and Joan Public carry an identity card was a great infringement on their personal freedoms. Everyone knew that the data, apart from DNA was out there in many forms and the benefits were obvious. Even the civil liberties organisations were not fully criticising the cards. Most European democracies had some form of card so it was no big deal.

The purpose of the Bill was to remove some of the inequities in the system and to raise some much need revenue to progress the other plans. The Bill passed into law and the effect was immediate. The coupon on the next tranche of government debt was lower than the previous one indicating that the market viewed the plans as positive. The Bank of England at its next meeting received such a large amount of positive economic news that it reduced interest rates by 0.25%! On the negative side, the value of the £ rose a little against the Dollar and Euro, which for the government was not really what they wanted at this stage.

The government was happy to get such a large piece of legislation through the system with its reputation for 'getting on with it' enhanced. There was a belief that the country over time would be more equal with the wealthy paying a bit more. But not everyone was happy with the new laws, particularly those who had got away with it for so long. A good example of this is what happened to Stanley "Stan the Man" Mann, Master Criminal and all round scumbag.

Chapter 17

Roger the Dodgers

A sunny day in August 2034 – A day to enjoy your money

Stanley Mann sat in his very large Jacuzzi bathtub, the water bubbling up and over his hairy chest. His right hand rested on a gold plated handle to prevent himself from slipping under the water. He liked to relax this way at three o'clock every afternoon. "It's my thinking time", he told his staff "and I don't want to be disturbed." His left arm reached out sideways and his hand came into contact with the glass of champagne, cold and fizzing nicely. Unless George arrived soon, Stanley might have to pour himself a refill from the bottle resting in the ice bucket close by. "That would be annoying", he thought.

In the same room as the Jacuzzi, was the indoor pool. Small by Olympics standards but at 9m long and 4m wide, still a decent one. In the pool, completing her tenth length of the day was Heather, Stanley's latest girlfriend. A bit older than his usual preference but at twenty-four years old, she was in good shape. She used to have a job at his bar in town, pole-dancing for the punters. "Now she pole dances for me", he leered in thought. Stanley was twenty-seven years older than Heather, but when you've got money and the sort of muscle that he employed, getting a new young woman was never a problem. Heather liked to swim thirty lengths of the pool a day and Stanley had positioned himself to watch her do it. "Beautiful mover", he thought.

Another good reason to be in that position in the Jacuzzi was that it afforded him an uninterrupted view of his pride and joy at the far end of the room. There, in a glass case, his red Ferrari 296 GTB shone in all of its glory. It had twelve miles on the clock, the distance from the production line via a transporter to his house and the glass box. Stanley

190

reasoned that, as it was a work of art, it shouldn't be driven. The car was a present to himself on his fiftieth birthday.

It hadn't always been like this. He was raised, dragged up in truth, by a single mother and a collection of 'uncles', transient men, in a flat in a council block in Montpelier Road, Peckham, south London. When this road had been named, the council thought it should sound sophisticated along with a number of roads named with a French theme. The locals called it 'motpeelierr', so defeating that idea. He had learned from an early age to take care of himself, which meant some casual violence when it was necessary, usually while helping himself to other people's property. In the late 1990's, drugs started flooding his area and he was quick to notice how much drug dependency would reduce an addict's ability to make any choice, good or bad, before their next fix. He grasped that drugs was the business to get into and in his early teens he had started off in a small way selling pills and cannabis to his friends, family and acquaintances.

Policing around his mum's place was non-existent, pretty much a no-go zone. He and his drug dealing gang mates figured that the police were more concerned with the better off, who lived nearby in leafy Dulwich, and knew how to complain, than with the low-life in Peckham. Stanley started to drive at the age of sixteen, younger than the legal age, but nobody cared. The local area had four cars that didn't seem to be owned by anybody, so if you needed a drive, you took one and returned it when finished, keys in the ignition. Every now and again you put petrol in it, usually by driving away from the garage without paying for it. Nothing happened, so why stop doing it? He didn't have a licence and had never had one to this day. Now he had a chauffeur so he didn't need one. In all of his life, he had never had car insurance. If another car hit the one he was driving, he would drive away, often after punching the other driver's face a couple of times. If it was too damaged, he just ran off and left it. If he hit another car, same thing. Drive away or run away. There would always be another car to borrow or just steal one from Dulwich and drive it home and put new number plates on it.

Amazing how many people left their keys in the car, especially while they were filling up with petrol.

Stanley had had little education, mostly truanting from school from the age of ten. He was street smart so he knew the price of buying and selling drugs. The big game changer for him was when he switched from supplying recreational drugs to cocaine and heroin. A local dealer called Sammy took a liking to him and set him up with a good territory in Blackheath, a much posher area with very expensive houses. He never understood why people, who obviously had brains and were smart, would want to get hooked on his stuff, but to his pleasant surprise they did. The price was no problem for them, just the guarantee of a regular and discreet supply. And Stanley was very discreet, particularly when enjoying sex with a bored wife, who openly called him "my bit of rough". Stanley persuaded Sammy to improve the quality of the product by cutting it with more pleasant materials and then raised the price. Everything was going well. Sammy and Stanley were making a good steady income until Sammy got arrested. He had been careless and the police decided that they couldn't ignore his more blatant crimes so they raided his flat and they found a large stash of heroin. Sammy was banged to rights and got sent down for five years.

Stanley was sorry for Sammy, but not for long. He decided to become his own boss so he set about getting his own supply. The people dealing with Sammy were happy to supply him and before long Stanley had young runners working for him. Stanley, now known as 'Stan the Man', was making serious money and keeping it where he lived was not clever. There were so many crooks living in those streets! Stanley opened a safety deposit box in a bureau in Edgware Road in London, close by Marble Arch and soon had enough cash to buy his first property.

Stan took another sip of champagne and thought of that little studio flat in the Elephant & Castle. It was less than four miles from Peckham but a life experience so different. He could close his front door and not return home to find another strange man with his mother. He felt secure and at twenty years of age he had done well, so far. In those days he was out until the late hours, servicing his customers and team. The one big draw back to his new flat was that he no longer had access to the community car, so he bought a small motorbike. He still didn't bother with a licence, tax or insurance, but he reasoned correctly that these bikes were not a police priority. He looked over at Heather, who had finished her exercises in the pool.

He had a good daily routine. In the morning he did business. This entailed arranging deliveries of his substances from and to various locations and discussing the profits from his various ventures that included a night club in Shoreditch, a bar in Soho and two houses in Streatham occupied by some women of eastern European origin, who came to the UK for secretarial courses but were now prostitutes and occasionally unwilling stars in some porno movies. Every afternoon an armoured van containing cash arrived full of dirty notes that needed to be counted and then secured in the house safe ahead of a weekly transfer to one of his lock-ups. His property portfolio of six multi-let properties in Notting Hill and South Kensington needed little attention but turned a good income. He also owned three houses in the village close by in which his staff lived. After the morning's business, which today included sending someone to visit a late payer of one of his loans for some attitude correcting, he had a light lunch followed by a free afternoon to indulge himself in the pool area. He looked over at Heather, who was dressed in the smallest of bikinis, drying herself with a towel emblazoned with the Millwall F.C. logo.

He described himself as an entrepreneur, even though he would have had no chance of spelling it correctly. A Deputy-Commissioner of the Metropolitan Police described Stanley and the other gangland masters in London as scumbags, but for over twenty years the police had been unable to land a single prosecution on any of them. The special unit set up to deal with organised crime employed dozens of police, some quite senior, but no prosecution of 'Stan the Man' had ever been successful.

Stan stood at 5'7" in his bare feet, the same height as Tom Cruise but without Tom's charm, good looks and charisma and at thirteen stones, quite a lot stockier. Heather was taller, younger and slimmer and made a good fist of pretending to enjoy Stanley's afternoon sessions that he described as 'playing hide the sausage'. She preferred the luxury of Stanley's mansion in beautiful leafy Oxfordshire to the tawdry terraced house in east London that was her previous address. She could put up with ten minutes of sex with Stanley, then afterwards slip into the Jacuzzi to erase it from her memory.

George Offiah, Stanley's personal assistant, came into the pool room. "You're a bit slow with pouring the champers today, George," Stanley barked out. Heather tried not to look too pleased with the interruption. Now George was a big man, towering over Stanley at 6'4" and weighing the best part of 20 stones, most of it muscle as the bulging arms stretching the T-shirt confirmed. He looked like he could have gone eight rounds of boxing with a top heavyweight, which he once did. Unfortunately for George the bout was scheduled for ten rounds. George ended up face down on the canvass listening to the referee counting up to ten, one minute into round eight. After this bloody pounding and a small amount of reconstructive surgery on his face, George decided that his future lay in fighting weaker and smaller people, in what was described euphemistically as 'personal security services'. It was when he was a bouncer, ahem Customer Safety Officer, at The Lazy Octopus, a prestigious night club owned by Stanley Mann for the discerning culture lover; or a clip joint according to the police, that he was noticed by Stan.

"Boss", said George. "You have got to come and see this. The electronic security gates have failed and there are all sorts of vehicles coming up the drive."

Stan pulled on his towelling robe and looked out of the window, rubbing a little condensation away as he did so. "Fuck", he shouted at nobody in particular and headed quickly towards the open front door. He got halfway through "Who the fuck are you?" when a piece of paper and a warrant card was thrust into his face. "I am Chief Superintendent Paul Gibson of the Serious Crimes Unit at Scotland Yard working as a Commissioner for His Majesty's Revenue & Customs and this is one of the many warrants that I am going to show you over the next few hours. This warrant means that we are able to search these premises and any other premises that you lease, rent or own, solely or jointly or in partnership and any premises that are leased, rented or owned by a company or partnership, of which you may be a partner or a director. The scope of these searches will include all safety deposit boxes and storage units. You must supply to us the details of their locations, and give us all of the keys and passwords. All items valued at £20,000 or more will be documented and removed by us for you to claim at a later date."

Six large men dressed in blue uniforms pushed past Stanley and entered the house and sealed off any escape route. Chief Superintendent Gibson then presented Stanley with another piece of paper. "This Order compels all persons in the property now to surrender themselves and all personal communicating devices to my officers and move outside. They will all, including you, be interviewed under caution."

"I want to contact my brief," Stan demanded. "I want my lawyer, now."

Gibson then presented a third Order. "This Order allows you to provide the names of all of your legal representatives and details of how they might be contacted. We will make those contacts for you. How many persons are there in the house?"

Stanley hesitated a moment, the cogs of his brain whirring. "Eight, possibly, how the fuck should I know?"

Gibson turned to a female colleague, junior to him by the look of the lesser amount of gold braid on her jacket and said, "Do you want to take these two in to the large trailer and place them in separate interview units. You can start interviewing the big man. You know what information we are looking for. The other one will be interviewed when his lawyer arrives." Just as Stanley was being led away Gibson said, "You will be required later today to tell us the location of all safes, hidden compartments and any other secure parts of the house. There will be less damage if you give up this information as we do have sophisticated equipment to find them, but there will be much less damage to the decorations if you show us where they are and how to access them."

Gibson turned to another colleague, this time a tall male. "Go into the house and round up the other six people, or more if there are any, and take them to the large grey trailer, and put each one in a separate interview room. After that retrieve all of the mobile phones, tablets and laptops and any other computers that you can find anywhere on the property. Don't neglect the outbuildings."

"Yes, sir," was the quick response and the tall officer made lengthy strides up the stairs and disappeared. Moments later he reappeared saying that he would go and get a large trolley from one of the vehicles as there were a very large number of mobile phones.

An hour later, Stanley's solicitor, Julian Marshall, arrived breathless and already churning out the usual stuff about persecution of his client. He presented his card showing Marshall & Clayburne, solicitors and Commissioners for Oaths. Gibson drew him on one side. "Are you aware that in the last week Parliament passed Secondary Legislation concerning the roles and activities of HMRC and the new powers for its Commissioners? Me for instance. Also enacted was a regulation affecting the performance and obligation of solicitors and barristers acting in potential fraud cases involving tax evasion? I have a copy for you."

Julian took the paper and studied it. His eyes went to the part about legal persons hampering HMRC and subsequent penalties if tax evasion were proven. He had known his client Stanley Mann over many years and had successfully acted for him in all manner of dubious matters. He had no doubt that Stan had evaded vast amounts of tax on most of his ventures so for him and his firm this could spell real trouble. "I must act with caution", he thought. "Can I see my client now?" he asked. He was taken to the interview room in the grey trailer where Stanley was pacing and shouting obscenities at the walls.

In another room in the trailer, the first person to be interviewed was Rubina Stradio. Opposite her sat Helen Rose, a seasoned tax professional with a degree in law from Sheffield University and a reputation amongst her colleagues for being really tough. Helen had worked for HMRC all of her career, often frustrated by the department's lack of determination openly allowing tax evaders to run rings around the inspectors and getting away with keeping secret large sums. After the election of 2034, Helen sensed a change in the air, particularly with the recent law changes. The interview started with Helen asking Rubina to state her name and address into the recording device on the desk. Helen then asked "Are you employed by Mr. Mann or are you self-employed?"

"I work 10 years now as cook for Mr. Mann and his staff and his guests," Rubina said with some pride and a rich Spanish accent.

"How much are you paid?" asked Helen, pen poised in her left hand.

"Mr. Mann, he give £500 for me every week and £500 more for groceries in cash and if there is a big dinner or party, he gives me some more."

"Does he always pay you in cash?" Helen asked scribbling on her notepad.

"Always cash."

"Do you get a pay slip with the cash?"

"No. Just the cash. Always in old notes, never the new ones."

Helen looked into a folder and lent forward "I see that the last time that you paid tax and National Insurance was when you worked in a hotel in London over 10 years ago."

Rubina gave a small laugh. "That was long time gone. Mr Mann asked the dining manager, which chef had cooked his favourite meal and they told him it was me. That's when he offered me the job as his cook. He also allows me to live in one of his houses in the next village."

Helen was scribbling furiously on her notepad at this priceless information. "Thank you Rubina, you may go home. We will be in touch with you again. I think that you will find that you will be able to take tomorrow off from work."

Helen's next interview was with George, the imposing personal assistant.

"Please state your full name, home address and job title for the record." The red light on the machine blinked as it recorded George's information.

Helen then went through the same questions that she had asked Rubina. George thought that he was employed, received £1,000 in cash every Friday and had no pay slips. He knew nothing about income tax or national insurance.

Helen then interviewed the housekeeper, gardener, chauffeur and cleaning staff and they all gave the same answers. They all thought that they were employed, were paid in cash and received no pay slips. Heather, the girlfriend, was not employed, but she had a credit card that she could use without any questions asked, which she said was very nice. Helen thought "A bit better than nice, but nothing comes for free if it involves Stanley Mann."

The last person in the household to be interviewed was Georgina Moore. Helen gave her the usual instruction concerning the recording machine and then looked at Georgina in the eyes and said nothing for a minute. She was wondering whether to give her a formal caution of an impending arrest, but chose to hold back lest she demanded a lawyer, which would slow the progress of the interview.

"Georgina. How do you describe your role in the house?"

"I pay the hired help the amounts that Mr Mann instructs me should be paid."

"Do you keep a record of these transactions?"

"No."

"Where does the cash come from to make the weekly payments? What bank account do you draw the cash from?"

"Mr Mann gives me the cash from the safe in his bedroom."

"Why do you pay the hired help?"

"It's their wages. I am not a wages clerk or an accountant. I just hand over the cash in the amounts notified to me."

"Clever", thought Helen. "No chance of charging her with tax evasion matters."

"How do you get paid?"

"In cash, like all the others."

Armed with all of this information, Helen and Commissioner Gibson next wanted to interview Stanley Mann. He had been closeted with his solicitor Julian Marshall for over an hour. As they entered Julian rose and started protesting about the treatment of his client. Stanley sat there looking totally pissed off and said, "If you can't get them to get the fuck off of my property, you're in trouble, my friend."

Helen Rose and Paul Gibson sat down. Paul switched on the recording machine and with Stanley and Julian they went through the spoken formalities.

Helen opened the folder on the table and said, "Stanley Mann you are now going to be interviewed under caution."

"What would be the charge or charges?" Julian quickly asked.

"Tax evasion and defrauding the public purse for which, under the new legislation passed in the last week, the fines are unlimited and, in the worst cases, and you look like you might qualify for being one of those, a lengthy prison term may be imposed by the court."

Stanley whispered in Julian's ear "Get this over and done with because that's what I pay you for. Get the small fine done and let's get back to business."

"My client does not admit to any of the charges, whatever they might be, but if there are any he is prepared to make a small contribution and apologise."

Gibson said, "The new government has identified that there is a tax gap of £36bn being the difference with what is due and what is paid. It is tax evaders like your client who are responsible for a large part of this deficit. The days of cute deals and small fines are over. The government needs this money to fund the nation's recovery plans."

There was then a very loud banging on the door. Helen, slightly annoyed, got up from her chair, opened the door and said, "Yes."

"You have got to know about this ma'am. A large armoured van has just arrived and it is full of cash. We have impounded it and we have agents interviewing the driver. We have asked for an escort so we can take it to a secure unit for counting." Helen nodded in agreement.

Helen turned back into the room with a very large smile on her face. She addressed Stanley, "Let's start with the small things and work our way through all of your business interests until we get to the large and important matters, including the small Fort Knox van that has just arrived on wheels. Our team has a wide range of warrants and are accessing all of the storage units that we know about. We have also accessed your safety deposit boxes at four different facilities. At the end of this interview after you have been charged, you will provide me with the combination of the safe in your bedroom or we will remove it with a large mechanical tool extensively damaging the wall."

"Can she do that?" Stanley turned and asked Julian. Julian was reading a piece of paper that had been passed to him.

"Yes, she can. The warrants presented to you exercise all of the powers under the new laws. I urge you to answer all the questions truthfully as lying to a HMRC Commissioner is a separate and serious offence, carrying a frighteningly large fine."

Helen continued, "All of your staff are paid in cash. They believe that they are employed by you. You have failed to deduct tax and national insurance for which you are now liable to pay. We have calculated that the sum due is rounded down to £242,000 and with 100% penalty and interest over the periods of their employment, the sum due from you is £736,000 payable today. If you do not pay this amount today, you will be transferred to a remand prison until the sum is paid. From today Georgina Moore has been instructed to move all of your employees at the house, including herself, on to employee contracts.

"We have copies of all of your bank accounts, including those held by you under various aliases in Jersey, The Isle of Man and the Cayman Islands. In those accounts you have a total of £28m. The balances in these accounts will be frozen until you have proven that the money has been legitimately earned under an "Unexplained Wealth Order" that will be served on you later today.

"We now move on to your other business interests. You own two business premises and ten residential properties including the house, in which grounds we are parked. The other nine properties are let out to tenants and staff members. Any income from these properties have not been declared for tax purposes and a further assessment will be issued with 100% penalty plus interest payable on the date of issue. We have impounded all of the fleet of vehicles owned by you and your companies including the armoured vehicles.

"The two business premises are a night club called "The Lazy Octopus" and the four floors above it, and an office block in Harrow at which your companies are registered and based. The accounts for those companies will be re-audited and any discrepancies will be subject to further action and penalties. We have calculated that the rents received on your properties, allowing for three of your staff living rent free, is rounded down to £1.4m, so adding penalties and interest, we will require you to pay today £3.15m. You may ask your accountants to contact us and we will supply the calculations. We think that the sums demanded are at the lower end of any estimates on what is due to be paid. A full audit will be undertaken on all of your assets and a final demand will be issued and the sums deducted from your bank accounts.

"We now wish to deal with the companies, which have you registered as a director, sometimes the only director. You are registered at Companies House as a director of thirty-eight separate companies, four of which are dormant or not trading. All companies list their purpose as an exporting/importing business. Our investigations show that all of the companies have underreported their earnings and profits so there will be a Corporation Tax liability to be calculated for each entity. We have today taken in for questioning the finance directors of all of these companies and they are providing useful information for us. We put you on notice that charges of fraud will almost certainly be made against all of the directors, including you, and some of the companies will be wound up.

"Finally, for today, we come to what are known as "Unexplained "Wealth Orders". We believe that you have been involved in the purchase and supply of Class A drugs. We have found evidence of drugs and unregistered firearms being stored in the lock up at Arch 7, London Bridge. We will be issuing unexplained wealth orders for the remainder of your assets as it appears to us that you have never had legitimate employment."

Julian quickly chimed in "My client knows nothing about this unit or its contents. You have no proof that he has ever been there."

"That is correct", said Helen, "but Dave Harold, who was apprehended there has given us a detailed account of how the drugs come in to the unit, go out to your dealers, and how the funds end up in your client's bank. Dave, who said that you pay him in cash every week, also showed us a lock-up in Marylebone Road that is rented in one of your client's companies, of which he is the main shareholder. This secure lock-up contained £1.35m in cash, which has been seized until your client can account for how it was legitimately earned.

"The contents of the safety deposit boxes have also been seized and will only be returned to you once you have been able to provide receipts for the jewellery, details of when and where the gold coins were purchased, how you became to be in the possession of a painting stolen from The Dulwich Art Gallery and a pair of Glock 26 pistols, which will be the subject of separate charges.

"We will be seizing every item in the house with a value greater than £20,000. You will be given thirty days to prove that the items were bought with funds that had been subject to a declaration for taxing. The nice red Ferrari in the pool area has already been impounded."

Stanley exploded at this news. "You won't get away with any of this. I will get the most expensive barristers in London and get a judge to throw this lot out and you can all go and get fucked. Julian get yourself in front of Judge Jackson as he will put a stop to this."

"Judge Henry Jackson took early retirement yesterday, pending investigations into his past judgements and connections with organised crime." Julian reported hesitantly.

Commissioner Gibson said with unhidden pleasure, "I think that you will find that under this new government the laws and future verdicts by judges will reflect a new regime for HMRC to deal more firmly with people like you. The cases against you will not be strung out for months. There are special tribunals and courts ready to make sure that you pay the right amount of tax and stick to making any money legitimately."

Paul Gibson pressed a buzzer on the desk and in came Chief Inspector Moorhead from Scotland Yard and a dishevelled technology person carrying a computer. Gibson said, "First we will deal with the transfer of funds for the fines. You will be provided with a list and breakdown in case you wish to appeal them at a later date, but bear in mind, if appeals are lost they might garner further financial penalties for you."

Moorhead then stepped forward, gave the usual caution and read out the charges relating to drug supply, money laundering, unauthorised possession of firearms, defrauding the Exchequer and tax evasion. The transfer of sums was carried out with Stanley muttering all sorts of oaths under his breath. As he was led away Helen said, "We are issuing you with a Garnishee & Attachment Order which will freeze your assets until we recover all outstanding amounts due and any future identified liabilities."

The downfall of Stanley "Stan the Man" Mann and the total of his fines and penalties made headlines. Not often did the public see a gang leader and criminal mastermind get brought down so completely. The media relished his court appearances and subsequent imprisonment for fifteen years without parole by a judge refusing to be swayed by his expensive barrister's defence and later mitigation. In payment of the fines and unexplained wealth orders, HMRC confiscated most of his assets and seized all of his properties. Julie Carter's government was ecstatic that such a strong message had been sent out. She stood up in Parliament and warned the other gang leaders "We are coming for you and your ill-gotten gains. If everybody paid the right amount of tax, we would all pay less and the public services would have more money." HMRC saw an instant increase in tax receipts and responded to many requests from individuals for face to face interviews and tax audits. Following these meetings more tax was paid voluntarily as the evaders wished to avoid the punitive fines, criminal charges and prison sentencing. Some individuals known to the police, tried to leave the country with suitcases full of cash and valuables and were stopped at the airports and ferry terminals. Some held out hoping that they wouldn't be caught but every week there were reports in the media of more evaders brought low. The media frequently mentioned that it wasn't for all the crimes that Al Capone committed that he faced justice and went to prison. It was for tax evasion.

The Treasury revelled in a sharp increase in tax receipts. £6bn projected in the first year and increasing to £11bn in year 2. Another consequence of all of this publicity showing eye-watering fines was a sharp reduction in the black economy. All businesses accepting cash had to register with HMRC so payment for services in cash was almost eliminated. Estimates suggested that a further £2bn had been added to tax payments.

Next in the Treasury's sights was the money from lettings like Airbnb and companies based in low tax havens but carrying out business mainly in the UK.

On a date, only publicised afterwards, all safety deposit boxes were sealed by law and the owners had to apply to the Police or HMRC to have them opened and the contents inspected under supervision. Owners were advised that if no contact had been made before sixty days of an officially acknowledged notification, the boxes would be opened and the contents would become the property of the state. The result was that much of the contents were not claimed and the state took control and auctioned gold bars, diamonds, jewellery and expensive watches. After six months, Julie quoted to her team a line from the musical 'Evita'. "The money kept rolling in."

The Finance Act also contained important changes to the way absent fathers would be held responsible for their children. For some time, a DNA database had been held by the police with information taken from convicted criminals. There had been a previous judicial judgement that only allowed a convicted person's data to be stored. Those found to be innocent had their data removed. The gathering of information for the new identity cards would vastly increase this database. All immigrants who had entered the country illegally were now having their DNA information securely stored. The ultimate objective was for every citizen to be part of this database because the benefits were huge. Unfortunately, those groups trying to protect the freedom of the individual were not keen on this idea, although their arguments were obscure. The advantages of having this database were for the detection of criminals, the elimination of benefit fraud, familial matches for organ transplants and the tracking down of absent fathers, who had made no contribution for the upbringing of their children.

Even though the database was not complete, the police had been reluctant to allow the Child Support Agency (CSA) access to what was available. National Endeavour had no time for the police's preferences and passed laws that gave access to the CSA under secure supervision, which really meant seconding a few officers into that department. The effect of this change was immediate as Steve Bradley's story confirms.

Steve Bradley was proud of being a dad. He liked it that he was leaving something of himself for posterity. His son Oliver would turn out to be a good lad he was sure. Oliver's mum, Serena, was hard working and a good mother. Every time that he saw Ollie, which admittedly was not often, he was always pleased to see how well dressed he was. Steve liked to pop in with a present for the lad's birthday, when he remembered. The next one coming up would be Ollie's tenth. "Where did the years go", he thought.

Serena was always a bit of a pain when he visited, asking for money for shoes and the like. Her latest request was to help with her moving to a better flat. Steve didn't have much money to spare, what with his car drinking the petrol like it did. Still it was a lovely motor, if a bit on the big side. Steve was a fan of the Arsenal and season tickets had become so expensive, the cost rising every season. But you've got to have one haven't you? He liked to meet up with his mates before every home game, have a few beers before kick-off and when the result was good, which it often was, then they had a bit of a session after the game. Steve was approaching thirty-five, still lived with his mum, who was on her own since Steve's dad died a couple of years ago. He gave his mum a few quid when he could manage it. His job as a van driver paid better than the minimum wage so with no rent and mum doing the shopping and laundry, his outgoings weren't much.

Ollie wasn't Steve's only child. There was a daughter somewhere but he had lost touch with her over the years.

Steve's life was pretty settled. He drove the van from Monday to Friday with the weekend for football and clubbing. Most weekends he managed to get off with a woman for the night, or even a couple of weeks if he liked her. This coming Saturday the Gunners were playing away up north somewhere so he had arranged a second visit to the tattooist to give some colour to the Arsenal badge, presently just an outline on his left calf. At £100 per hour the tattooist was not cheap, but this girl Svetlana was an artist and it will look good when it was finished. Two hours a couple of weeks ago, two hours this Saturday and the last two hours in a couple of weeks. £600 well spent.

Steve looked at the time on his watch, a recent acquisition for £250. It was called 'Mission to Mars' and was red, the colours of the Arsenal. His lunch break was nearly over and after a few more deliveries it will be back to the depot to pick up his monthly wage slip, the money going directly into his bank account.

Deliveries done, Steve parked up the van and went into the office. Eileen, the wage clerk, didn't like his banter having complained about his lewd suggestions so he kept it strictly business. She passed the envelope and said "Bad luck. I see that they've caught up with you."

Steve had no idea what she meant. He tore open the envelope and looked at the net figure after deductions. "What the fuck is this?" he shouted out loud. His wage slip showed a new deduction for "Child Support" of £400. Steve was furious. He couldn't afford to lose £400. "I bet that bitch shopped me to the authorities. I'll have a word with her when I find out where she has moved to."

Eileen watched Steve with some pleasure as his emotions seemed unable to be contained. She said, "I hear that the recent DNA sampling has been matched with children, when their mothers are claiming Universal Credit and you got a match, obviously. I bet you hope that this is the only one, or you won't be getting much pay next month."

The £400 monthly deduction by the CSA resulted in Serena receiving £360 in addition to her Universal Credit. At a meeting with the Benefits Office Supervisor, Serena had been required to have Ollie's mouth swabbed to provide a DNA sample. If she had refused, she was told that her access to Universal Credit might be compromised. In any event, the prospect of getting more money without her benefits being reduced was enough of an incentive. She also took some pleasure with the thought that Ollie's dad was at last going to financially support his boy.

The difference that it made to her and Ollie's lives was significant. She had not wanted to supply Ollie's DNA but the offer of the money was too good to turn down. All around the country there was a similar tale. Some men discovered that their pay was affected and had to tell their wives why. The reluctance of mothers to supply their child's DNA soon dissipated as stories of significant payments made the headlines. The CSA was careful never to make the deductions so large that it removed the incentive to carry on working. When multiple children were involved, the sums were smaller for each but cumulatively large for the absent father.

Julie's team thought that this, in a small way, was a little progress in levelling up.

On 11th August, on her 50th day as Prime Minister, Sir Edward Grey passed her a "Congratulations" card. In it he had written, "You are now <u>not</u> the Prime Minister with the shortest term in office."

Chapter 18

Wheels Turning Slowly

18th – 30th September 2034 (100th Day)

Since the election, Members of Parliament had had to endure fifty-seven full days sitting and a relentless agenda of Bills and secondary legislation. The Finance Bill now passed had started to generate income and news on the latest discovered tax evader was hitting the newspapers daily. The Leader of the House of Commons announced that there would be a two weeks recess from Friday, September 1st. A huge sigh of relief and gratitude went through National Endeavour's ministers and all other party's politicians.

When Parliament resumed sitting on Monday, September 18th, there were only twelve days left to September 30th, the end of 100 days since the election. Franklin Roosevelt's "100 Days" had set the standard for governments getting things done. Any government that failed to make an impact in its first 100 days was considered a failure. 100 days can be a long time in anything or everything. Many marriages have lasted a lesser time. Kings and Queens have ruled for lesser days than this. Queen Jane ruled for only nine days. Liz Truss was Prime Minister for only 49 days. 100 days can seem like an eternity but flash by in no time at all. 100 days is a third of the time of a human pregnancy, whereas a mouse's gestation is only about 20 days. In 100 days a country could hold an Olympic Games or World Cup three times over. Napoleon returned from exile on Elba to Paris and less than 100 days later he was on a boat to another exile, this time on St. Helena, having lost the Battle of Waterloo.

Getting the streamlined procedures for passing legislation into law was the first important building block in place. Bringing the Lords onside meant that the easy sections of the Constitution Bill would now pass into law in the next week or so. Julie asked Sir Edward Grey to schedule meetings in Scotland, Wales and Northern Ireland so that progress could be made on the federal UK plans. Now that the proverbial 'cat was out of the bag', the media was demanding more knowledge of the plans and how they would be progressed. Before the publishing of the Constitution Bill, Scottish Nationalists, knowing little of what was proposed, were demanding full independence. Julie also asked Agnes Peters, with titular responsibility for both Houses of Parliament, to put forward the plans for the election of the Second Chamber. Those cities that wanted to have representation, but had not got an elected mayor, would be given this opportunity at the elections to be held in May 2035.

Moving both Houses of Commons and the Lords into effectively temporary accommodation was a big task and tenders went out for the job. Parliament would be in these buildings for many years, so the upgrades would not be cheap or quick. Alongside these costs, the original refurbishment surveys and plans for the Palace of Westminster were dusted off and new estimates for the work commissioned. The building had deteriorated over the years that the Parliamentarians couldn't make up their minds. The cost in 2024 was estimated between £7bn and £13bn for a full empty building and the work would take between twelve and twenty years. Ten years later, the costs were estimated between £10bn and £16bn with the same timescales. Julie's Executive Team at a scheduled meeting decided to take the most pessimistic projections and Andrea Patel in her first Budget in October would allow for £20bn spread over twenty years, £1bn per year.

Early on Monday, September 18th Julie held a meeting of the Executive Team in the Cabinet Room. They were joined by Mark Sutton, Housing Minister. Sir Edward Grey had prepared the Agenda under Julie's guidance. After the formalities of enquiring after each person's holidays, they sat down in their places with their papers, tea or coffee and for some a chocolate muffin.

The days were passing by in a flurry of activity, so at the same meeting, plans were drawn up for the next Bills in order of priority. Tax revenue had been prioritised, so the Finance Bill had been passed by Parliament before the recess.

Almost as important as the money was the Bill for Housing. If National Endeavour was going to be judged on anything, it would be whether it fulfilled its commitment to getting the homeless housed. A couple of quick wins were important. Some of the plans had already been put in place using secondary legislation. Introducing two new bands of Council Tax had been done as had the 100% levy on second homes, empty properties and holiday lettings. There were challenges in the Courts against these introductions, but the judges hearing the cases had thrown them out because the laws had been passed to allow for the changes. Local Authorities were delighted with the potential additional income, which in some districts was very significant. Some authorities were quicker than others to identify empty properties and letters were already speeding their way on the first steps to compulsory purchase. For every empty property brought into use, there was one less family on the housing list, or in bed and breakfast accommodation. Residents in towns and villages got caught up in the idea that empty was bad and were keen to email their housing departments with addresses.

The Housing Bill giving Local Authorities powers to compulsorily purchase land was primary legislation. The Bill also gave them powers to re-designate Green Belt land so that it could be developed for housing. Julie said "A separate Bill will be proposed if we decide to go ahead with new towns. We have someone coming later to talk to us about these towns."

Changes to the planning rules were difficult to negotiate. Having no planning restrictions would mean large and unplanned sites that might not solve the problems as intended but the too fussy planning restrictions had been a barrier to development.

Julie said, "In front of you is a paper, previously circulated, proposing a new National Planning Policy Framework, which includes top down targets for councils to meet the need for apartments, two bedroom houses and social housing. The Bill to introduce this will also cover the proposed compulsory purchase of land owned by the Church of England, Great British Railways, Ministry of Defence and the National Trust. You have all had a time to look through this. Are we agreed?" They were.

Julie continued, "In the past two decades, too many four and five bedroom executive homes have been built as developers made more money from them. What the country needs is a mix of apartments and one-bedroom houses for single occupants or a couple without children. Builders need persuading to build two-bedroom houses or apartments for a couple and a three bedroom house for a small family. Small gardens are still in demand for all sized houses. The most efficient way of housing people must be a terrace of properties but these have fallen out of favour.

"Also, too many estates have been built with no increase in the connectivity to major roads, so getting out of the estate in the morning can be a nightmare. Large estates have been constructed without schools for the children, communal play areas, GP surgeries, shops, pubs and bus connections. There is no profit incentive for the developers to provide these amenities. They've bought the land for such a large price that the only way to extract any profit is to build expensive houses or cram as many into an acre as possible. These are the excuses frequently given for the lack of amenities. I want to invite Sir Peter Jameson in to our meeting at this point. He is an expert on planning and new towns." Sir Edward got up and called Sir Peter in from an adjoining room.

Sir Peter took his seat after acknowledging Julie and her ministers. He started, "I have been asked to give you some information on the Town & Country Planning Act 1947 and the 1946 New Towns Act. After the Second World War, the incoming Labour Government needed to rehouse large numbers of people, particularly from the bombed out areas of east London. The solution was the 1946 Act which established an ambitious programme for building New Towns. It gave the government power to designate areas of land for new town development. A series of 'development corporations' set up under the Act were each responsible for one of the projected towns."

The Team then had a question and answer session. Julie thanked Sir Peter for his valuable contribution to their debate. After further discussion the team concluded that ambitious housing targets could not be met by piecemeal development and what was needed were new towns with infrastructure and amenities. There was an emphatic agreement, when Julie asked, "Shall we add the provision of New Towns into the Housing Bill?

Tom Blandford, the Homeland Director and Mark Sutton were tasked with coming up with twelve locations in the areas of greatest demand for housing. They agreed that none of the new towns could be inside the M25 motorway. The team did agree that within the M25 no land, except the land designated as a 'park', would now be categorised as 'Green Belt'.

In order to build houses at scale the shortage of tradespeople had to be met. There were not enough bricklayers, plumbers, carpenters and other housebuilding trades available in the areas likely to be chosen. Every asylum seeker was currently being screened and their skill set logged. Any potential immigrant with the skills required would be offered a fast track to the right to remain. It was also agreed that much of the materials and finished goods that went into new housebuilding could be manufactured in the UK without having to import them. UK plc was holding discussions with small manufacturing businesses to see whether they could scale up their production with inward investment for machinery.

"How are the people in UK plc getting on?" Julie asked.

Andrea Patel replied, "We have recruited a very good CEO, who was previously the Chief Operating Officer of a major logistics company. His main strength is getting projects started and completed on time and on budget. He is supported by a Finance Director who has moved over from the Treasury, which is good for us as it means we have our eyes on the money. The company has made its first investments. The first was in an upscaling of a sanitary goods company that will now be able to produce good quality toilets, basins and shower trays at volume.

The company is in the potteries so good employment for the people of Stoke and surrounding towns. The three very large greenhouses for sites in Essex, Kent and Lincolnshire have received fast track planning approvals and we expect the ground to be broken before the end of the month."

"Excellent", said Julie. "We need a member of our team as a non-executive alongside Sir Simon Thornley. Who do we have who is particularly good as seeing through the bullshit?

"Sounds like me doesn't it", Brian Strong said. "If you all agree, I'll touch base this afternoon with the CEO and Company Secretary." They all agreed.

During the discussions and presentations from the construction industry it became apparent that house developers could manipulate the supply of houses by not developing land that they already owned. Often these developers had obtained outline planning permissions but it was not in their commercial interests to flood the market too much as this would depress prices and mean that finished stock would remain unsold. A blunt instrument to persuade the developers to get started would be to withdraw the planning permissions granted if projects were not started within four years of planning approval being granted resulting in the land being compulsorily purchased at agricultural rates. The team agreed that in this case incentives would work better. Instead of developers deciding what units and how many should be built for a particular piece of land, UK plc would commission the builders to build to a defined number of units at a fixed price and UK plc would buy them all in stage payments so taking away the financial and interest rate risks. The idea could be scaled up if building societies, banks and insurance companies were to take the same development risks for a fixed return. The upside for the builders would be the guaranteed work, the removal of the development risks and a much larger business for the shareholders. The Team agreed that this was the model to be pursued for the new towns. However, the team didn't want to use UK plc money for New Town developments as it was supposed to be seed capital for manufacturing.

The Executive Team realised during this important first 100 days that much could be planned, but little action could be realised from a standing start. Planning approvals and getting Bills passed into law took time and the resources to start immediately on any project were just not available. Apart from illegal immigrants and asylum seekers, there was no ready supply of skilled labour doing nothing just waiting to be called upon. There was no stockpile of finished materials waiting to be purchased and moved onto site. There wasn't even a supply of bricks. The wheels of progress started slowly and gradually momentum would increase and results would start to appear, but that was all in the future. The Team were desperate to get on with plans that could happen straight away.

Fortunately for Julie's team, there were some areas that could be expedited and they honed in on them with a passion. The NHS desperately needed more doctors. Since 2029, the number of doctors joining the workforce each year had been more than double the number who left. In 2028, over 24,000 doctors joined and about 12,000 left. This growth in numbers was as a result of international medical graduates joining the UK medical profession. The UK trained about 12,000 doctors each year, a figure that had increased significantly over the last decade. The reason given for the modest number of medical students was that there were not enough teaching hospitals to train any more. Because senior doctors were working at full stretch, there was no provision for students to be trained in service. If the supply of international medical graduates dried up then the UK would have a serious shortage of doctors. The situation had to be remedied and so the team requested some more information. They were told that it took between six and eight years to fully train as a doctor and up to ten years to become a GP. Some medical schools offered accelerated programmes for the earlier time. Clearly, the situation could not be changed even during the life of the Parliament. Realising that some changes had to begin soon, even with a long dated time frame, the Executive Team agreed to double the number of medical school places by offering incentives. Incentives to the schools with more funding, paying doctor trainers more money and employing more doctor consultants for training in the work place. In order to make the training more attractive for the students, it was agreed that if they qualified and remained working full time in the NHS for ten years after qualification then all of their student debt would be written off with no payment made during the ten years period. These decisions would help the present and near future. It was agreed to fund the building of a brand new medical school facility in each of the four UK countries to offer two hundred and fifty new places per year in each, meaning that at the end of eight years, a further thousand new doctors would be qualified each year in addition to the existing schools. The ongoing screening of asylum seekers, it was hoped would disclose amongst them some persons qualified or part qualified in medicine either as a doctor, nurse or care home worker.

Another issue that could be addressed quickly was bed blocking by elderly patients too well to be in hospital but not with enough help at home to be discharged. A solution had been tried in 2026 but the solution had been done on the cheap so it hadn't really worked. The Care Sector had never been fully integrated into the NHS because most of the care homes were privately owned and no government wanted to get into the care home business. In the past, District Nurses carried out a worthy role, but there had for many years been a shortage of them. The lowly paid care workers could do a good job of helping, but were not trained to give any medical assistance and many of these elderly patients had complicated health needs. As each of the other UK countries had devolved powers to manage their own health systems, Julie's Executive team were only concerned with finding a solution for England.

Julie said "If they can't be discharged home and they are not ill enough to be in a medical bed why don't we create care bed wards within each hospital until they are ready to be fully discharged? The care given is much reduced and of lower qualification and medical staff are close by if needed. I bet each hospital trust has a redundant space for a dozen beds. I also bet that from the asylum seekers screening, we will find sufficient carers to carry out these important but low qualification roles." A murmur of approval went around the room. Sir Edward Grey was scribbling furiously in the corner knowing that he would be tasked with finding out which trusts could offer this solution.

Julie thought, "These meetings are exhausting. They are crammed into a busy calendar of not only domestic compulsory attendances like Parliament and diplomatic engagements, but there are also the international meetings." She shuddered at the thought that the next one she would be hosting. She had put together a good team of support workers and even as she sat there thinking, speeches were being written, cases packed and folders of information being prepared. She didn't see enough of Jamie and although there was a full time nanny and au pair helping out upstairs, she wondered about the physical cost of the burden of office. The meeting ended to be resumed the next day at 8am.

There's always another day and the next time they all met she knew that they had to come up with some ideas on how to reduce crime and take on the gangs.

The next morning, after they had all taken their seats and poured themselves a coffee, Julie said, "Today is our 100th day in power. Let's spend a couple of minutes and look back on what we have achieved in those days. It's pretty impressive in my view. Let's do more in the next 100 days."

Chapter 19

It's Criminal, It is

1ˢᵗ October to the Party Conference on 11ᵗʰ October 2034

The first item on the Team Meeting agenda was crime and the Criminal Justice Bill. Over the years, the pendulum of dealing with the rising crime rate had swung almost entirely into the wrong direction in favour of the criminal and away from the victims of crime. Detection and prosecution rates in some areas were so low that they were not measurable. Defence barristers were running rings around the Crown Prosecution Service and juries were prepared to find the thug, now dressed in a suit for the first time in their lives, innocent of every crime. Convictions for assaults and rapes of women were below 10% and that was of the cases prosecuted. The burden of evidence needed for a successful conviction was so great and witness tampering was a daily occurrence. The public had lost faith in the police to protect them and to catch any criminals. Shoplifting had made running a shop dangerous and unprofitable. Gangs openly paraded their bling jewellery and were driving luxury cars without a licence, tax or insurance. Middle classes gorged themselves on cocaine and purchased supplies not always clandestinely, from known criminals. In some estates, police dared not enter and there were regularly killings by knives and guns for drugs territories. Prosecutions for burglaries were at historic lows and convictions negligible. Even when there was a conviction there was a fine that wasn't paid or a community punishment not served. The prisons were full because the crime rate was at a record high and sentences were longer. It was against this background that Julie and her Executive Team tried to reset the dial.

The meeting with the police and crime commissioners and the passing of secondary legislation had produced some positive results.

The police were now on the front foot supported by better equipment and a lessening of paper work. The pursuit of non-crimes had been stopped and a new emphasis had been placed on ridding the cities of gangs. The justice system was now less pliable to barristers as the laws had been tightened up. Judges were handing down appropriate sentences and keeping within the guidelines. UK S&T plc had worked with a security company to develop curfew bracelets that had anti-tampering devices and these were keeping low grade offenders off the streets during the night time. The prison estate was being converted to three categories and the prison population was falling, so enabling the worst criminals to be incarcerated for longer. The first tax evaders had been jailed. One of them was a prominent financier and this had resulted in HMRC being inundated with requests for meetings and tax paying agreements.

"Let's start with the crimes," Julie said. "We have agreed that we don't want to lock people up in overcrowded prisons. The report in front of us reads that if we want to build a new prison it will cost £600,000 per cell and each prisoner that you put in that cell costs the taxpayer £50,000 per year. We lock up more people than any country in Europe so that isn't working well. We need a rethink on the whole way that we deal with crime and punishment."

Indira Singh, Health Director, said "Many of the prisoners shouldn't be in prison. They should be getting mental health treatments. Then there are the drug addicts who resort to crime to feed their habit. Perhaps we should decide why we lock some people up."

Hillary Armstrong-Lewis, Justice Director, said "Is prison a deterrent? It doesn't seem to be as so many come back to it a number of times. I wonder what would act as a deterrent."

"I think that we are all agreed that we should be locking up the guilty for crimes against the person. Victims of murder, rape, assaults, domestic violence, kidnapping and manslaughter are right to expect custodial sentences. In the King's Speech we heralded our intention of ceasing to let prisoners out after serving half of the sentence. I don't think that the public understand the logic behind that. Prisoners should serve their sentence and if they have been a difficult prisoner, then time should be added on to the sentence according to prescribed list."

"I suspect that all prison governors would say that there needs to be an incentive for prisoners to act reasonably and not assault their officers," said Brian Strong. "Do we want to introduce changes that will work or changes to satisfy the electorate? They might be different changes."

And so the discussion went on for two more hours. At the end of it Julie summed up what she thought that they might have agreed. "We want more prosecutions. The violent ones we want to lock up in maximum security jails and they serve their sentences in full. We segregate them into secure single cells to protect the prison staff and they have no privileges unless they earn them by contributing towards the smooth running of the prison. Drug addicts are to be incarcerated in hospital wings of prisons and taken through a process of getting clean. They are not released until they have beaten their addiction. We do not lock up non-violent criminals with sentences of less than twelve months. We remove their passports and driving licences and impound their vehicles for the period of their sentences. They wear wrist and ankle tags with 7pm to 7am curfews and an alcohol detector. If they break the curfew and take alcohol they get returned to a prison for the remainder of their sentence. The new technology tags will provide us with anti-tampering so that if both tags are not removed simultaneously a very loud alarm goes off and the local police station is alerted.

"Fines must be paid even when it means removing personal items of jewellery, phones, flat screen TVs, cars and motor cycles. Community service will be carried out or they will get the same time in a prison. Excepting with a doctor's note, there will be no excuses for missing community service appointments.

"Non-violent criminals serving sentences of greater than twelve months will on first sentencing get a rehabilitation prison place where the emphasis is on learning and not reoffending. Recidivists will be incarcerated far from their home base. Any prison governor who identifies a person who is exerting undue influence over other prisoners will remove that prisoner to a prison as far from their home as possible. The Crown Prosecution Service will set up a plea bargaining system that offers reduced sentences for early guilty admissions.

"The paperwork required to prosecute an individual must be greatly reduced to free up police time. The rules of evidence will be rewritten to enable cases to come to trial quicker. Non-violent offenders will not be remanded but have their passports withdrawn and have daily reporting to a police station with a curfew. Entrapment of criminals will no longer be a defence. Entrapment by police to clear up crime will be encouraged. Police forces with consistently poor detection rates may be amalgamated with their more successful neighbour. We have already put legislation in place that requires any organization wishing to protest must notify the police seven days before the event. The cost of policing the event will be paid by any or all of the organisations involved in the protest.

"Automatic number plate recognition cameras are to be rolled out throughout the country. Drivers without insurance, licence or tax will expect to have their car impounded. It will only be returned within thirty days after full payment of any fines. After thirty days the car will be sold or destroyed with all proceeds going to the police force. All drivers banned for more than twelve months will be required to take a driving test before getting their licence back.

"We will make funds available to install more and better CCTV at crime hotspots with remote recording to stop tampering. Facial recognition software is now being used and is giving positive results. Without an acceptable religious reason, it is now an arrestable offence to wear a face mask in public. Phew! I think that's everything," Julie said. "Did I miss anything?" No replies just nods.

"Right, Hillary. Please get your people to knock those matters not already legislated into a Bill and we will present it to Parliament next week. I will hold a press conference once it is published. I think that's all for today, see you all bright and early tomorrow morning at 9am. There is always more to do."

They met the next day for a meeting specifically to discuss some quick wins on crimes. Hillary Armstrong-Lewis had produced a discussion paper setting out how the police might be effective on those matters that affected the public most. Not always serious criminal activity, but more the anti-social behaviour that just wore people down.

"Hillary, please take us through your proposed Anti-Social Behaviour Bill."

Hillary pointed at a screen on the wall, where it displayed the areas the Bill was proposed to cover. "Anti-social behaviour is a hard nut to crack, because the perpetrators don't realise what they are doing and don't watch the news or read the papers to realise that they are the problem. I am proposing that initially they attend a face-to-face interview with the police where they are told what they must cease doing. If they persist and another complaint is made then punishments will include withdrawing their driving licenses and passports and in extreme cases the cancellations of their tenancies with six months' notice. They will be told that they are responsible for all children under the age of eighteen and those over this age will be subject to the same sanctions as their parents. The police have been tasked with identifying the persistent trouble makers, if necessary, by using entrapment. There will also be a designated telephone line in each area for anonymous tip offs. Barristers will not in future be obliged to represent any person that has had one or more convictions. There will be no more legal aid for those persons either. All of this will be in the Bill. We expect howls of protest from bleeding hearts and left wing lawyers, but if they want to act for these people then they are free to do so, but not with taxpayers' money.

"We have a problem in all parts of the drug chain. We can't stop the drugs coming in, although we think that we know where they are coming from. There are just too many points of entry. The best chance we have of stopping the supply is to confiscate the drugs after they have arrived here. We shouldn't have a scattergun approach to this. Going after all drugs by all suppliers dilutes our effectiveness. I am proposing that we concentrate on Class A drugs, where most of the profit is. Our new rules on cash deposits will help a lot. The police know who the head of drug dealing gangs are but they always fail to gather the evidence needed."

"What about using disruption?" Brian Strong asked. Can we cut them off from their distribution networks?

"I was thinking along those lines," Hillary said. The police could pick them up if there was a new offence of drug association. If we extended the time held in custody to the same as for terrorist offences then we effectively put them out of the game for a week or longer. Then we do it again until they cry foul. We can introduce a 'reasonable suspect' clause in this specific offence, which will also require them to supply their phones and computers for inspection. We will employ advanced computer techniques for monitoring their movements."

"What about the low level pawns?" Agnes Peters asked.

"We will ask the police and drug units to have specific intelligence. All those under sixteen not in school should be treated as truants and placed in secure accommodation for a short time. Those minors over this age will need to be in education, employment or training or they will have unexplained wealth visits and seizures. I suspect that the greatest penalty would be the confiscation of their smart phone. Random testing in the workplace for cocaine use will be mandatory with work place sanctions. Testing for drugs will take place for all suspected offences. Any readings will render the person unfit to drive for six months and have night time home curfews.

"Illegal or falsification of a number plate will lead to the car impounded until a fine is paid and the proper plates added. Any car or motorbike that has been modified to create a noise nuisance will be impounded until the vehicle is put right at the holding facility. The theft of high end motor vehicles for export or parts has become a growing problem. Any country that accepts such vehicles or components will fall foul of our Ethical Foreign Policy. Dock managers will be given extra powers to delay ships and open containers if there is a reasonable suspicion that there are stolen vehicles inside. There will be an export ban on vehicle parts.

"All animal stealing, whether it is domestic or from a farm, will be an offence punishable by prison for every offence at one year per animal.

"The Bill will contain proposals for the formation of a National Guard. Young people would be trained and when called upon, help deal with disasters, civil unrest and major disruptions. Any person under the age of twenty-five and not in employment, education or training would be obliged to attend training for the National Guard overseen by professional soldiers. The troops would be region-based in the north, south, midlands, east, west, south-west and south-east. The National Guard would be a federal resource and units could be deployed anywhere in the United Kingdom."

Hillary drew her presentation to a close. "The Bill in draft will be with you in the next few days JC", she said.

"What about the Human Rights legislation?" asked Sir Edward Grey. "Judges and barristers will defeat most of what you propose by citing provisions in this Act."

Julie replied, "You are right. I have had discussions with a senior judge and the Act is a problem for us. We will suspend our membership, involvement or whatever, in the Act and its provisions until we have the situation under control. We will need to pass the necessary legislation as soon as possible. Does anyone think that we shouldn't?" They all agreed because the protection of an individual's human rights had gone way beyond its original intentions.

Julie asked for any other contradicting comments from around those present, but there were none. These were tough Bills and there would be many critics from the left wing press. The team hoped that the right wing press would balance it out. The country had voted National

Endeavour to sort things out and these Bills set out the tough choices and actions to be made and taken.

The police had always been resistant to change believing that in policing matters they knew best. Unlike in America, where Sheriffs were elected, in the UK, Chief Constables thought that they had to operate without interference. This was particularly true with the Commissioner of the Metropolitan Police in London. The paper highlighted knife crime, drug dealing, children aged between ten and sixteen not being in school but part of drug distribution gangs, no go areas for police in some areas and physical assaulting of residents of those estates. All cities had the same inner city problems. The team agreed that the police had to adopt a zero tolerance to crime. Julie decided that with Hillary and James Dunbar, the Police Minister, they would tackle the police head on. Hillary arranged a meeting of all of the Chief Constables, Police & Crime Commissioners and the Commissioner of the Metropolitan Police for the following day.

This was a meeting of just under a hundred people, so Julie held it in a large London hotel just off Grosvenor Square. Tea, coffee and water with an array of Danish Pastries were available ahead of the start time. Julie welcomed them by saying, "Good morning. With me today I have Hillary Armstrong-Lewis the Justice Director and James Dunbar the Minister for Police. I hope that you all have studied my government's announcements on a variety of subjects. The objective of this meeting is for you to hear how my government sees policing going forward and for me to tell you what we expect from our police. You will pleased to hear that we are very supportive of the police and that you are essential players in our plans to advance our agenda. You will be given a chance to ask questions at the end of this short presentation.

"I suppose the first thing that you all must know is that we are determined to have our plans succeed. We are not persuaded by arguments that try to convince us that something cannot be done. If that is what you wish to say then you must follow it up by telling me how what I want, can be done, albeit a little differently.

"The second thing that you must accept is that my Members of Parliament are not fans of community policing. This idea has failed to reduce crimes, catch perpetrators and convict criminals who are able to flaunt their activities and criminal proceeds with impunity. We've seen enough of policemen and policewomen dancing at the Notting Hill and other carnivals.

"What my government likes is no crime. We don't like anti-social behaviour, no-go areas and violent crimes especially against women and girls. We do like facial recognition technology, good quality CCTV, stop and search, DNA profiling, preventative policing, entrapment, plain clothes police in crime hotspots, ANPR cameras, testing of drivers for drugs and alcohol, removal of unregistered cars from estates and stopping people driving if they don't have a licence, insurance or road tax. We do not wish to persecute people sleeping rough, we have other ways of giving these people shelter. We want everyone to be treated the same and in accordance with the law. So if you want to be a traveller, that's fine by us but your vehicle must be taxed and insured and your children must receive some schooling.

"We have many databases and the police must have access to all of them. If Data Protection legislation is a problem for you in some areas, we will change it. All forces should share information and there are to be no fiefdoms. You must act as one police force not forty-odd different ones. You know, as do I, that a small number of people are responsible for a large proportion of crimes. We want you to sort these people out by either persuading them to change their habits or we will have them locked up in a faraway place. Now you all know what my government wants do you have any questions?

"If we go into an estate, we will be attacked and our cars set on fire. There is no way that you will stop this."

Julie replied, "I said at the beginning that we don't deal with negative solutions. What could you do to give me what I want?"

"We would have to arrest and remove all of the main troublemakers inside and outside the estate. Where would we lock them up and anyway their lawyers will have them out in no time?"

Hillary joined in, "You are in Gloucestershire, so with the co-operation of the man sitting next to you who is, I believe, from Durham, you take them to a secure unit in his patch for processing and vice versa. While they are away, you will get a warrant to search all of their premises and you will find something that will lead to a charge and probably a conviction. Search warrants will be easier to get. If you are unable to find something then their homes, will become uninhabitable due to some hazard and they will be offered housing away from the area. These are people who spend all of their day hassling other people so you will hassle them back."

"What about their lawyers and human rights?"

Julie said, "Where lawyers find loopholes, we will close them. We don't see the human rights legislation as a problem going forward. You will find out why that is soon enough. We will ensure that crime doesn't pay for lawyers or the criminals. We will cease paying legal aid for offenders with one or more previous convictions."

"This isn't why I came into policing. This is all a bit close to being unlawful."

Hillary again, "Nothing that you will be asked to do will be unlawful and I am disappointed that you have said so. The softly, softly approach to policing in some areas hasn't worked. There is an area in London where last month eight thousand crimes were committed and you didn't make a single arrest. Hooded youths on electric bikes are responsible for a crime wave. You stop them by forward planning and closing off their escape routes. If they fall off of their bike in the process of getting away from the police, I'm not very concerned. We need criminals riding on mopeds to find out that it can be dangerous for them."

"We are ourselves over-policed. There are too many rules about what we can and can't do. We need to have some of these shackles removed."

Julie replied, "We will restructure these organisations. I'm not in favour of the police policing themselves. We will replace some of the oversight with organisations with different objectives. We will remove many of the restrictions including the force you can use to arrest suspects. Known criminals need to be arrested one way or another. We are on your side, but we don't want officers going rogue and beating up members of the public so you sort out your officers and we will stand with you against frivolous claims.

"What about us being used as a target during large demonstrations?"

Julie took this one, "Organisers of all demonstrations have to give you seven days' notice. The organisers will in future be financially responsible for any damage caused. Seven days gives you sufficient time to check or install CCTV and face recognition cameras on the route. The sentencing guidelines will be certain so that judges will jail anyone found guilty of assaulting you. Demonstrators with their faces covered can be arrested for a breach of the peace, because you will have notified the organisers and public ahead of the march that face coverings are not allowed unless they are for religious purposes."

"We get a lot of flak from groups when we carry out stop and search, particularly on young men of colour."

Hillary had a particular passion about eradicating knife crime as her cousin had been attacked by a person with a knife only recently. "We have to get knives and guns off the street. We can use airport scanning machines for the public to walk through in sensitive areas, but that is no substitute for a personal search. If you are looking for a knife or gun, don't prolong it with a search for carrying drugs. I'm not here to do your job. My purpose today is to tell you what my government expects."

Julie added, "We are looking into reducing the number of police forces by mergers so my advice to you is to get your arrests up and crime rates down or you may be one of the forces merged with another."

The Commissioner of the Metropolitan stood up and took a deep breath.

"Oh no", thought Julie. "We are going to have a Sir Simon Thornley moment here. I don't want to have another high profile sacking."

James Thursby, the most senior policeman in the UK, put down his spectacles and looked Julie directly in the eye and said "It's about time that we had politicians that will allow us to police as we should. In the last few years, governments have been more interested in how things look in the media than letting us do our jobs. We have let criminals outrun us in cars and motorbikes because we don't want them to crash and get hurt. We have had our fill of community policing. You give us the tools, give us the laws and all around this table will show you that we can do the job."

There was loud applause from the Chief Constables in agreement.

James continued, "We know who the criminals are but we have had the Crown Prosecution Service too timid in the face of clever lawyers for the defence. We could have prevented so many crimes but we were always charged with entrapment. We disagreed and said that it was just good police work. We are so pleased that the gloves are off. Zero tolerance to crime is what we wanted to hear. Thank you very much."

Julie rose, somewhat relieved, Thank you Mr. Thursby and all of you for coming. Please go out and make a difference."

And what a difference they made. Hardened criminals were hauled off the streets. Trouble makers on estates mysteriously ended up in police stations across the country while their flats and houses were emptied of contraband. In one house, eight young girls were released from sex slavery after being enticed to London from Bulgaria with offers of secretarial work. In another flat, a gun was discovered that was linked to two shootings in the capital. In every place the police found stolen watches, credit cards and smart phones. Facial recognition cameras started to show where some known and wanted criminals were hiding out and a large number of uninsured cars were taken from the streets every day. And best of all, Signor Alberto Dalboni, the well-known leader of a particularly unsavoury Albanian gang operating in

Soho, was arrested naked in his bath and deported back home before he had finished doing the belt of his trousers up.

Over the next two weeks, Parliament passed the Housing Bill, the Criminal Justice Bill, the Anti-Social Behaviour Bill and various bits of Secondary Legislation. Julie was setting a furious pace, but there was so much to do.

National Endeavour had never held a Party Conference before. This was an occasion when all eyes would be on Julie and her Team, so it must go without a hitch. Trevor Whitehouse, the Party Chairman, was in charge of all of the arrangements and soon after the election he had secured Brighton & Hove as the city for it.

Chapter 20

The Party Conference

11th – 13th October 2034

National Endeavour's first party conference since the election victory was going to be held in Brighton & Hove. Julie was not involved in the planning, preparations and arrangements as that was the job of the party chairman and his committee. All Julie had to do was show up at the allotted time and give her speech to the adoring masses. This time she decided to write the speech herself as it had to come from the heart.

October in Brighton was not the centre of the holiday season and the weather was expected to be autumnal. Nevertheless a trip to the seaside for Jamie was always an event, so Julie intended to spend a good deal of time with him and make it a mini-holiday. Inevitably, she would be pursued by the press so she made a deal with them. She would host a press meeting with them before the conference got fully under way and another after her speech on the last morning.

At the Executive Team meeting early in October, she announced that she would be going to Brighton by train from Victoria and if anyone wanted to share the reserved carriage then to let Sir Edward know. In the event, the whole carriage was booked to them, which was a great relief to the security detail. After arriving in Brighton, Julie, disguised in glasses and a large floppy hat, went with Jamie to the Toy Museum. He was enthralled by the exhibits and enjoyed talking with the curator, who only realised who they were, when he noticed two large men standing by the entrance door keeping everyone else out.

After the museum, a car took them to the Palace Pier for a bracing walk in the autumn sunshine. Julie declined to have her fortune told but they both had candy floss. Looking westwards from the pier they saw the rusting sad remnants of the West Pier. The pier was opened in 1866 but after it closed in 1975, disaster after disaster befell it. Major sections fell into the sea during a storm in 2002 and two separate fires in the following years left just the metalwork in the water. Another bit of the frame fell away in 2026. One day what remained was expected to disappear under the waves.

They returned to the seafront and a car took them to the Brighton Pavilion for a privately arranged tour. Jamie was enthralled by the eastern décor and the massive dining table. After a visit to the gift shop to buy a book on the building, the car took them to the Franklyn Hotel and the same suite that Winston Churchill regularly took in retirement on his painting expeditions.

As she had promised, she met with the press at the agreed time in the hotel's conference room. The question and answer session took about half an hour and was mostly to do with the government's financial plans and the Ethical Foreign Policy, which was now taking shape. The policy was covert in that there was no announcement to the world that "This is what it is", but more a change of emphasis towards those countries in an attempt to get some of them to behave better. A recent meeting with the Nigerian Ambassador impressed upon him the need to curtail all of the financial practices from his country that defraud the UK's citizens. A diplomat's job is to lie on behalf of his government and so he feigned innocence. A hint at repercussions for students and medical care by NHS seemed to get his attention and before the end of the month some arrests had been made in Lagos.

The great and the good of the party rolled up to Brighton in party mood. Party conferences were opportunities to meet with old friends, discuss party likes and dislikes, bitch about the leaders, have some drinks and enjoy some sex if you got lucky. Sir Edward and Lady Estelle Grey decided to visit the Ship Inn, where they had first met too many years ago to recall.

There were to be six main speeches in the main hall given by her five Executive Team members with Julie rounding up the proceedings on the last morning. In fringe meetings, the reporting ministers to the Team would give presentations and be in top listening mode. The agenda, like all party conferences, was manipulated for the benefit of the outside world, the press, TV and the party members in that order.

Hillary Armstrong-Lewis was first up with a good old law and order speech to get the conference going. "Julie and I have met with the police and we have all agreed that the forces return to catching criminals and stop with the community policing and policing by consent practices, which have resulted in too few crimes being solved. We have passed laws that have reduced the amount of paperwork required to charge a perpetrator and the Crown Prosecution Service has agreed to get more people charged and quicker. Human Rights laws have been derogated for a period and most of the Data Protection nonsense has been scrapped. Plea bargaining has become the norm for those wanting to plead guilty and get reduced sentences but not for violent crimes." A bout of loud applause came from the delegates in the room. Delegates of all parties like to hear a tough line on crime as it goes down well back in the constituencies.

Hillary continued, "More police are being recruited to crack down on local anti-social behaviour. Known foreign gangs have been targeted to disrupt their businesses. In the recent Criminal Justice Act there is a provision that makes all gang members liable for the actions of one of them. This has already meant that the leaders, who never got their hands dirty, are now in our sights. Proof of Wealth Orders are being used and these orders will allow confiscation of any goods that cannot be proved with documentary evidence to have been legitimately purchased." More applause.

"The removal of passports and driving licences has turned out to be a major deterrent for offenders. In most cases, a full driving test pass will be required before a new licence is issued. This is really something that criminals don't like as I suspect nor would we. Some accused have even been prepared to agree to a longer prison sentence in a plea bargain just so long as they didn't have to take a driving test again. Any person caught driving without a licence is banned from taking a test for two years." A few people stood and applauded this part of the speech.

"The first batch of Category 1 prisons have been adapted from open prisons. Category 2 prisons are being adapted from the better and newer prisons. The refurbishment of the prisons that will be Category 3 will take a little longer. Some very old prisons will close and the sites used for housing. All of these changes have been possible because we have got fewer prisoners locked up. The saving to the public purse has been considerable. I fully acknowledge that the Parole System has lost all credibility. There have been too many cases of dangerous criminals paroled only to swiftly commit a violent crime soon after. When prisoners serve their time they will be released. All prisoner releases will be overseen by a newly funded and integrated Probation Service. Finally on prisons, all prison officers caught bringing in mobile phones or drugs for prisoners will, if found guilty, be sentenced to up to three years and serve their time in a Category 3 prison. Thank you conference for your support. Members of the public recognise that not only are we the party of law and order but we take actions."

The conference audience rose to their feet and stood applauding for a little over three minutes. Next up was Andrea Patel fresh from the success of her Finance Act and soon to be broadcasting the annual budget to the nation. "Hello conference. Obviously I can't tell you what's in the Budget so you will have to wait but it's only a couple of weeks away. What I am going to talk to you about is welfare and identity cards and how these cards are a big deal and also a small deal. Firstly though a quick update on 'working for welfare'. We have now finalised the administration required to ensure that all those persons claiming unemployment benefit perform community tasks or they don't get paid. More announcements will be forthcoming in the Budget later this month. The roll out of identity cards is a big deal for us in charge of the nation's finances but a small deal for each individual citizen. Clearly, one of the benefits of having a large database of DNA samples is that criminals who have left DNA at the crime scene in current and importantly historic cases can be identified. The identity card will carry a photograph of the person and this would be an aid to facial recognition cameras. Photographs already appear on passports and driving licences. We have some young whizz kids at GCHQ working on these cards and the trial roll out to all asylum seekers and illegal immigrants has already started. The rest of the population will follow in phased stages.

"Absent fathers and mothers, who do not pay maintenance for their children, are being identified by DNA matching. Deductions from pay or Child Support Agency demands follow a positive identification. Failure to make payments will result in the suspension of driving licences and/or passports. DNA sampling will provide familial matches but these would only be disclosed by both parties requesting that it is done. 'Fishing' expeditions to trace any outstanding family members will not be allowed. The Identity Card will also allow for an intelligent chip to record a person's preferred old age treatment and, if required, a living Will.

"So these are all the reasons and benefits for them. We have the political will to issue them and we can sell it to the majority of people because, if you have nothing to hide then you have nothing to fear. Your ministers are aware of all of the issues and difficulties with human rights groups and anyone wanted to argue about personal freedoms being reduced. The fact that most countries in Europe have such cards may not cut much ice with many. We have spoken with the other party leaders and we believe that we have achieved a broad consensus on their introduction. The safeguards requested have been built into the system. Because we have a large majority and we think that these cards are a positive move with the technology available, we have decided that our party, National Endeavour, will accept all of the political downside for its introduction and give all the credit to our political opponents for being persuaded by us, which I have just done." A cautious murmur of agreement went around the hall. "Thank you for your attention. Don't forget to get into your finest clobber because tonight is our first day party night. Make sure that you are in good condition for tomorrow." Another standing ovation happened as is expected on these occasions.

Then a hug from the leader who suddenly appeared at the side of the stage. "Nicely done," said Julie. "A difficult sell, but you managed it well."

The next day, the papers majored in on the Identity Cards, even though it had been discussed politically many times since the King's Speech.

The following morning Tom Blandford looked out over the audience in the hall, many of whom seem to be the worse for wear. "Good morning. For those of you who have not had the pleasure of meeting me, I am Tom Blandford and today I'm here to talk about education. I am joined by Gillian Weston, the Education Minister. Our priorities in government are for the children, first, second and always. We have already set aside additional funds for education because this investment will produce a generation of highly educated children. The new syllabus will prepare them better for productive roles in industry and the public services. My own children, Louise age fourteen and George age twelve, I hope, will go to university, but if not then I would be very proud of them if they took up an apprenticeship. There is no point in leaving university with an unmarketable degree and a large student debt. In the run up to the election, our party, National Endeavour, promised to sort out education and we are doing it. We are a can do party not a can talk and do nothing party like the others." Huge round of applause.

"We believe that young people must be at the front, middle and centre of our policies and plans, so we have increased teacher's pay and created extra teacher training places. We also think that young adults deserve a future that does not mean living with their parents up to the age of forty. We have to give people choices. If you want to live on your own then there should be an opportunity to do so. Social housing is important for those who don't want to, or do not have the means to, own their home. There must be security of tenure in all rented property, but only for those who pay the rent on time and do not intimidate their neighbours. Our Prime Minister has a simple philosophy; obey the law, pay your taxes and look after your family and fellow citizens. We know that this was one of the first simple messages that gripped the public after decades of political failure." More applause despite many of them nursing a hangover.

There then followed a facilitated question and answer session on Tom and Gillian's responsibilities followed by a break for lunch….and more drinks.

The afternoon had two sessions. Brian Strong gave a hearty and funny presentation on what it was like being in charge of foreign affairs in a dysfunctional world. He brought the curtain down on the country's spying activities and declared James Bond a relic of the past.

Indira Singh's presentation on the NHS was a curate's egg, good in parts. The General Dental Council had accepted that all dentists must provide NHS dental care for children up to the age of sixteen. This announcement was treated with a standing ovation of two minutes because the delegates thought that this was a real achievement and unexpectedly quickly managed. Indira gave some good news on adult social care. Nearly all hospital trusts had identified a ward so that bed blocking elderly patients had been moved into a convalescing facility within the hospital grounds. This had freed up many beds in all areas and queues at A&E departments had reduced significantly. Another standing ovation.

Indira beamed out from the stage. She had been so fearful of standing up before such a large crowd, but now her confidence was in full flow. She settled herself before delivering the bad part and that was that waiting lists will be stubbornly difficult to reduce. It was a sad fact that it was not possible to deliver twenty-first century care in hospitals built in Victorian times. Over fifty trusts had identified a hospital needing to be replaced. Those to be prioritised would have land surrounding the existing sites so obviating the need to sort out land requisition. "We are on the case and you will see action soon," she said. "In the meantime, tonight we will have our gala cocktail reception paid for by the UK's largest pharmaceutical company. Enjoy yourselves." The delegates rose and applauded as Indira waved and left the stage on the arm of her husband.

The next morning a sense of anticipation gripped the delegates in the hall. All of the seats were filled thirty minutes before the scheduled start. There was room for all the elected members and the remaining hundred seats filled by lucky ticket holders in a ballot held the week before. The journalists were there and the TV cameras were primed and ready.

Julie walked out onto the stage to a standing ovation. This short woman, dressed in a black dress covering her knees, seemed so small on the massive stage. She walked to the front and raised her arms wide as though welcoming the delegates to her not very ample bosom. She stood like this and the applause continued for at least five minutes. One delegate fainted and had to have medical attention, others were openly weeping as they were caught up emotionally in the occasion. Julie, looked from side to side and from the front to the back of the hall taking in those she knew. She stretched her arms to the front and gradually lowered them resulting in the room volume being turned down until it stopped. She stood still as they all sat down and without notes, she started looking around all areas of the room again. She had a microphone discreetly attached to the neckline of her dress.

"Hello friends in the hall and in the country. I do like to be beside the seaside and Brighton is one of my favourite resorts. Since the election, this is my first opportunity in open forum to thank all of you for what we have achieved so far, but there is still so much to do. We will be judged by how we affect our constituents, not by anything we say, nor by blaming anyone else. My colleagues have in their speeches covered our progress in government. We have reduced crime by catching criminals and locking them up. Not rocket science is it? We have moved closer to a cashless society so that stealing is now not rewarded. Drugs are difficult to buy without cash so demand for them has fallen. Not by locking up drug takers or suppliers, but by cutting off their gang masters' ability to convert drug money into banked cash. The prison population is falling and the money saved is being used for prisoner support and rehabilitation.

"The ownership of safety deposit boxes is now only allowed if the contents are declared annually to the tax authorities. All overseas tax havens, for which our country was notorious, have been abolished and all the funds in accounts held in them has either been repatriated to the UK or if held abroad, are being declared. A number of unexplained wealth orders have been issued and funds confiscated that appear not to have been legitimately earned. The effect on the economy has been instant. Suddenly, the tax intake has increased by the equivalent of £15 billion per annum and growing. Ordinary people don't have offshore bank accounts, safety deposit boxes or unexplained wealth. What they now have is the benefit that will be derived from us getting a grip on this nonsense." Ecstatic hand clapping in the hall.

"Crime has reduced and the voters love it. Yet the largest area of crime not yet seeing a reduction, are the crimes against the person. We are on the case and we hope that the new identity cards with DNA embedded will prove a game changer. I know that some of you are still uneasy about the introduction of these cards. Trust me, the idea has many advantages and by this time next year, we will all wonder what the fuss was about. I have a driving licence, passport, prepaid bus pass and a bank card so why not have only one card that is the gateway to everything in the country. It will act as a free bus pass if you are entitled to one, an Oyster Card so ensuring that you will have access to the cheapest bus and rail fares for your journey, an access point for government payments, a driving licence and an employment record card. We expect that on the day that the increased roll out of the cards begin, the places of distribution will be overwhelmed. We also know that there are five million more national insurance numbers in circulation than will end up with cards. This will confirm our belief that there is benefit fraud on a massive scale perpetrated by people with more than one identity and multiple national insurance numbers. The estimated amount of benefit fraud is over £8bn but could be as high as £10bn per year. Every year. We can do an awful lot of good with £10bn. I don't know how many new hospitals and schools we can build with that money, but it will be a lot and I will probably find out. Your constituents will need to register for a card to continue to receive Universal Credit. We expect that the benefits system will see an immediate reduction in fraud. We will set aside quite a lot of this extra money to improve the lives of our severely disabled constituents. I want you all here to set an example and be among the first to register for the cards." The effect in the hall was an immediate response of prolonged applause until Julie's hands gently quietened them down again.

"The DNA information collected will almost immediately lead to a number of arrests of cold case criminals, who had thought that they had got away with their crimes. Those who refuse to apply for a card for fear of being held to account for an unprosecuted past crime will be quickly identified because after a short period their bank accounts will be frozen. When they can't make a rent or mortgage payment and their wages and salaries are held in limbo we expect their minds to be concentrated on getting a card. Without an identity card, there can be no passport so no travel with the family abroad. "Explain that to the family" is a message that will appear on billboard posters in every town.

"Every day an arrest of a prominent criminal happens to the delight of everyone. For too long the crime bosses have got away with flouting the law and using the proceeds of crime to avoid paying taxes and living the high life. The ordinary citizen wants them all to have a life the same as them. Remember, if we all pay the right amount of tax, not only would we all pay less, but there would be ample funds for improving public services. Who can argue with that? As we predicted, some members of the legal profession started earning huge fees from the wealthy wishing to avoid prosecution and seizure of their unexplained assets. Our response was simple. We have introduced legislation that requires all wealth to be proven. If you don't have or have never had legitimate employment, then it will be difficult to account for the Ferrari in the garage and the second home in Tuscany.

"Except for the property rental companies registered in the UK, all residential property in the country is now going to be owned by individuals only. It will soon be illegal to buy a residential property in the UK if you are not a British citizen. This is not a new idea. Other countries, like Thailand, have operated in this way for decades. Companies will be required to divest themselves of residential properties and overseas owners will have three years to sell their properties, many of them empty since being purchased decades ago, or become British citizens. National Endeavour's policy has always been clear that while a law abiding British citizen cannot own or even rent a property at a sustainable rent, then it is obscene to have hundreds of thousands of properties empty or rarely occupied. When National Endeavour came to power, the housing market in the UK was broken and now we are fixing it." More loud applause, some delegates standing to deliver it.

"I have been approached by the Green Party with an idea that I like. They are proposing that the polluter should pay for the effects of the pollution they create. Water companies should pay for sewage spillages, industrial plants should pay for contaminating discharges and shipping lines for discharges of oil in coastal waters. On a micro scale, fly tippers should pay for their mess to be cleaned up in addition to a punitive fine and vehicle seizure. Every fly tipper caught will be required to clean up three unauthorised dumps because the chances are that the one that they were caught for would not have been their first offence. Entrapment will be used widely to catch fly tippers. Over the next few months you will see these suggestions gaining a lot of traction and I thank the Greens for it.

"But that is the end of the advertisement for what we have done and it is a good start. I now want to touch your hearts and souls and try to explain what sort of country I want my son to grow up in. In the past, we have had great orators and they have all been remembered for a memorable phrase, sentence or idea. Martin Luther King had his dream, John Kennedy asked what people could do for their country and our own Winston Churchill asked, 'what sort of people do they think we are?'

"What sort of people are we, you and me? I am not worthy to join this group of great men but I want to spend some time sharing this with you. National Endeavour, our party, is not in politics to talk a good game. We are here to make things better for everybody no matter what your race, religion, colour or sexual orientation. We are a multi-racial cosmopolitan country and we are here for the able, differently able, the sick, the healthy and people of all ages, but mostly we are here for the children. All children deserve from birth to have equal opportunities to live, to grow and to develop into those people that we wish we were and what we want them to be.

"Forget the Brexit nonsense, historically we are a European nation with an islander's heritage and along with everybody on this planet, we are all children of the universe. We don't live in a perfect world. This is not Camelot where the sun shines in the day and it only rains at night. What do we want for our children, our parents and our grandchildren? When you boil it down, we don't ask for much do we? I like a warm shelter with affordable heat and clean water. I like a clean and comfortable bed and healthy food. These are our minimum requirements so we mustn't rest until everybody has at least these things. As an aside, I also think that everybody deserves to be loved by at least one other person.

"In 1859, Charles Dickens wrote, 'It was the best of times, it was the worst of times, it was the age of wisdom, it was the age of foolishness, it was the epoch of belief, it was the epoch of incredulity, it was the season of Light, it was the season of Darkness, it was the spring of hope, it was the winter of despair.' Not much has changed has it? This perfectly describes where we are in 2034.

"These are our best of times and our worst of times. We are the sixth biggest economy in the world but we fail to house our people and educate our children to cope with the world of work. We have so many public servants trying to do a good job but failing through bad management and organisation. We should regularly ask ourselves what it is that we want from our police and public servants. For many of us having the phones answered when we call would be nice. It is right that we hold the police to a high standard. We must demand honesty from our public servants and a duty of disclosure, not secrecy and obfuscation.

"There is no way of avoiding it, but the rich really do have responsibilities for the poor. This is not a new idea. Since the Norman Conquest, the poor and disadvantaged in a village were the responsibility of everyone. The richer villagers looked out for those in need because they believed that it was their duty to do so. I ask the wealthy, 'how much money do you really need?' We should not be revered for what we own but judged by what we do with it. Politicians cannot solve all of the problems all of the time so the better off should step up more and I will ask them to do it. I was asked by a person with £100m to leave to his children "Why should I stay in UK and pay half of it in inheritance tax?" I replied, "If your two children must have more than £25m each then you should go and take your money with you. Your family is not worthy of what we can offer you."

"We all have some personal responsibility to endure what life throws at us. It is not the role of government to featherbed citizens' lives. We should stop pretending to our children that life is always fun and that nothing bad will happen to them. Our parents knew differently, often through personal experience. There has to be dignity in work so that we can be respected for what we bring and contribute to an environment that helps us achieve our personal goals. We should only be limited by the extent of our imagination, but not our hopes. For our older people, we must ensure that they have dignity in their last years. Dignity at the end of life, dignity in death." The room was silent as these messages were taken in. A male delegate in the second row wiped away a tear with a tissue.

"We must celebrate our place in history and know our place in the world. We should accept our culpability in the slavery debate, but not be apologetic, as nobody in this room was alive at that time. We can look to the past with humility and sadness but work for the future with pride. Our country must lead on climate change but not be too far ahead of the pack. We can be the good guys but not the only good guys. We are developing our Ethical Foreign Policy. The way that we deal with other countries. We should not be ashamed to call countries out and stop doing business with them. If we can't import their goods we will have to do without them. We are a world class country and we must not let ourselves be negotiated down to mediocrity. We are a united kingdom and we celebrate all cultures and religions because we value what they bring to us all. As adults we should have developed respect for others, empathy for the less privileged and a discipline to our actions so that we don't adversely affect others. Too many political leaders have stood on stages like this one and made lofty demands for countries to change. We call for a ceasefire here, a lowering of carbon emissions there and demand that all countries be like we want them to be. We can only rise on to this moral high ground after we have put our own house in order and led by example.

"We demand not to be victims of crime. There is no future to a life on drugs and so we must help the weak to break free from them. Social drug taking is worse than addiction. It is not cool to indulge in social drugs when the price tag on others can be so high. None of us want to live in a nanny state because there is no fun in that. However, we must have laws to protect the young, the foolish and those that should know better so we are firmly against tobacco products and vaping. We are in favour of alcohol but not when the drinking of it is in excess so that drinkers lose all rational thoughts or good behaviour. Pubs are glorious places and we have lost so many. If you want to keep your local pub, go out and use it. Support it.

"Who and what are our national treasures? Where are our heroes? We need people to look up to, who set a good example, particularly to our children. When we find them they must know how important they are and not disappoint us. Who and where are our role models for the young? We need heroes who force us to look up to the heavens and not down to the ground.

"We enjoy so many freedoms but there is a price to pay for each of them. We need a free press but a responsible press. We have a right of freedom of speech but not if that freedom is exercised as a weapon against a minority or individual. We must develop the skills and talents of people who make things. Waste is a terrible thing and must be eliminated at every level.

"We must respect our farmers and fishermen more. They are out there in all weathers making sure that we have food on our tables. When we have our five vegetables a day and oily fish once a week minimum don't forget the people who are responsible for them. We must applaud our emergency workers, volunteers, charities and everyone who does something for little or no reward. Our high streets must be our market places for the meeting of people, exchanging information in friendship.

"At the beginning of my journey to here today, I was regularly asked, what does National Endeavour really mean? I think that it means that we all have to give something up in order to get something back, but not in equal measures. Those more capable will give more and those less capable will take away more until they themselves become more capable. We should all try to be less of a burden on the state, because the state is everybody else. We have standards and we do not lessen them for a short term advantage. We don't compromise our principles and we do not bend to the winds. We will not sacrifice our principles for money. I think that it is better to be poor with integrity than be a rich hypocrite. There will be a British Grand Prix next year. When I was told by the FIA that I must give a visa waiver to all of the personnel and drivers otherwise the race wouldn't go ahead. My answer was, that if this billionaires sport won't pay for the visas then they should go somewhere else. We will be seeing them next year. We have principles and we stick with them. That is who we are.

"I look out to you all and I am immensely proud of what you have helped us do. There is more, so much more to do but we have made a start. We needed your loyalty to fix things and you didn't let us down. Divided parties get nothing done except extinction at the polls and a quick route to the exit. Our recent historical examples show the truth in that. As a party, we now move to a bottom up approach and it is your chance to have a real and lasting impact. For the next year we want you to come up with the ideas to make things better. We need some new ideas. We will establish five policy committees with members of each elected and chaired by some of you.

"I send you all back home with a plea that you wear your hearts on your sleeves and do not be worried about the outcomes, if it was your intentions to do the right thing. Thank you for listening."

There was a ten minute standing ovation and it only stopped after, with a wave, the diminutive figure walked from the stage and gave a hug to Jamie, who was standing in the wings.

As one cynical journalist said to his wife later in the bar, "She had them all in the palm of her hand from the get-go. She has this way of making you believe her even though I know that most of it is just polish, smoke and mirrors. I think that as a Capricorn she is probably capable of following you into a revolving door and coming out in front of you."

Her speech featured heavily in all of the news channels and the main bulletins of the BBC. Even those people who had no interest in politics, couldn't turn from their screens the moment she started talking. Her personal popularity ratings broke all previous records.

Chapter 21

Budget Day

18th October 2034

At the pre-Budget Executive Team briefing on 1st October, the first item on the Agenda was the next Parliamentary set piece, the Budget on 18th October. "All under control", said Andrea Patel. She then went through her proposals line by line.

The first 100 days of National Endeavour's administration had passed and Parliament was in its usual frenzy of activity. Speeches were made and the Prime Minister and other ministers had stood at the Ballot Box and answered questions. The friendly questions were from National Endeavour's own MPs often primed by the Constable Agnes Peters or another Executive Team member. The unfriendly questions were from the members of other parties. The other parties' members opposed, made fools of themselves and each other and the whole machinery of government turned its cogs. To the ordinary voter it was just words and playground antics, but little had happened to improve their lives. The Budget was often seen as the instrument to do that. Except Julie Carter who continued to have a very high poll rating, politicians continued to be held in low esteem and the journalists covering Parliament, cynical to their cores, often barely hid their contempt. It was in this atmosphere that the first 100 days of Julie Carter's administration passed. Big and important Acts had become law, the monarchy under a new king had changed the Royal Family's optics and the air of optimism that had produced National Endeavour its victory was becoming a distant memory. What the country needed was a Budget that put a pound in a person's pocket, to paraphrase Harold Wilson.

Andrea Patel, the Finance Minister, still difficult for reporters not to say Chancellor of the Exchequer, had produced a Budget for Joe Public, Mrs Mopp and all the other seventy million plus citizens. At the fundamental level, her Budget would set out how money comes in to the government, mostly in taxation, and goes out in the departmental spending commitments. If more comes in than goes out then the budget is in surplus and Mr Micawber is a happy man.

On 18th October 2034, Andrea was photographed in Downing Street holding aloft the red box containing the Budget that in a short time she would present to the nation through the conduit of Parliament. Unusually, the contents hadn't been leaked to the press beforehand, so they were able to share the anticipation with the country at large. One of National Endeavour's founding principles was that the Executive Team and their Ministers could keep matters confidential. Governments had found themselves on the back foot in the news cycle when confidential plans had been leaked. The management of news and announcements was crucial to ensuring that the correct message was issued at the best time. Agnes Peters had set the tone from the start. She had jumped down hard on two newly elected members and reminded them of their oath of loyalty to the party and its leader.

When a political party is given a big majority in Parliament as was the case in 2019, 2024 & now in 2034 it shows that the voters demand change. The Conservatives in 2019 and Labour in 2024 had been too timid and unsure of themselves. One of the reasons for this reticence was that the members of their party were not fully loyal to the leaders, the ministers and sometimes to the Manifesto commitments on which they had so recently fought the election. In the end it was the internal bickering and in-fighting that stopped their progress and led to their inevitable defeat at the next election. Right from the outset, Julie had demanded loyalty and had made it a condition of a candidate's recruitment. This commitment to following the party line and unequivocally supporting the leader had ensured that all the Parliamentary hurdles had been overcome. She was effectively a collaborative dictator with a strong set of loyal followers adopting benevolent policies that the public wanted.

Andrea entered the House of Commons to warm shouts of encouragement. At the time set out on the day's agenda, the Speaker announced her. She stood at the Ballot Box and surveyed the members of the opposition in the seats facing her. There was a glass of mineral water, but not whisky as some of her predecessors had chosen. She was dressed in a white blouse and smart suit that screamed 'I mean business here today.'

She stood up, turned and looked at the Speaker and started, "Mr Speaker, I present to the House today National Endeavour's first Budget. This House has already passed a post-election Finance Act that enabled my government to start raising the considerable sums required to carry out our plans for renewal and to address the poor state of the country's finances. This is a Budget for growth because without it, nothing else succeeds. This is a Budget for the majority of hard working citizens and not for the wealthy, although it is a Budget for enterprise.

"We have set up UK plc and its activities are already reducing imports, relieving unemployment and lessening our carbon emissions. The economic and fiscal context that influences these measures are well known. For too long government was persuaded to borrow money because interest rates were low. When those interest rates increased it left the country with an unsustainable burden of debt and payments that have led to austerity in many areas. Interest rates are still too high so anybody with a mortgage is paying the price of previous indulgences. The country continues to import goods that we can make ourselves. These goods come with the additional burden of carbon emissions and from regimes that are not friendly towards us. We must wean ourselves from cheap goods from government subsidised economies and promote imports from developing countries so that they can also enjoy some growth. I expect all of the measures that this government has taken and will take, will over time lead to a balanced budget, lower interest rates and higher standards of living for all." Murmurs of approval were heard from behind Andrea and mutterings from the parties in front.

"I am going to raise the basic rate of income tax by 1p and National Insurance contributions by 1% for employers and employees. At the same time I am increasing all thresholds by £5,000. This means that a lot of the lowest paid will not pay any income tax at all." A murmuring around the room and a nod of agreement followed.

Andrea continued, "I am increasing the inheritance tax threshold for each individual to £2m so most estates will be taken out of paying this tax altogether. However, I am increasing the rate above £2m to 50% and above £4m to 60%. I am making this tax simpler by excluding jewellery and cars, which are always hidden or undervalued. I am scrapping the main home allowance and bequests in Wills to partners by named identification will be the same as for spouses." More agreement and even a few order papers raised and waved.

Andrea turned the page in the folder in front of her. "Tax is too complicated. It's no wonder that people don't remember to declare items. A normal person should not need to employ an accountant to fill in a form. After all, income is income no matter where it comes from. I am proposing that we scrap all of the allowances and reliefs. I am also scrapping stamp duty on all share transactions and property purchases. Instead of property purchase stamp duty there will be a Property Tax of 5%, paid at the time of a property purchase or transfer, on all transactions above £1 million.

"Capital Gains Tax receipts last year totalled just under £20bn. This tax would be simpler to understand and to collect if it was confined to property and other items with a higher starting threshold. I am proposing that the rate continues to be 40% but is only payable on gains on the sale of properties that are not the main residence; and on the main residence for a gain exceeding £500,000. This property gains tax will only apply to properties sold in excess of £750,000. On all other asset sales, the capital gains threshold is increased to £20,000 in any one year. This will take out the majority of people from this tax with smaller assets and only apply to the wealthy.

"We will introduce a sales tax on all internet sellers like Amazon and EBay. We will no longer allow profits to be moved between jurisdictions and to lower tax havens by prohibiting transfer taxes for brand renting for instance. Corporation Tax in UK is amongst the lowest and I am proposing to scrap all reliefs but introduce "Supply British" deductions. All goods made in the UK and used in the UK will benefit from a lower tax regime. The details of this tax will be available in the library this afternoon.

"When the UK moves to a federal country, the Barnett Formula will be withdrawn from those countries. When that happens, each part of the UK, with the possible exception at the moment of Northern Ireland would be self-funding.

"It is still in my plans that we produce a balanced budget in 2035/6. We can achieve this by reducing tax evasion even further, reducing benefit fraud and by increasing Corporation Tax. In the next Budget, I am expecting to have some scope with freezing the tax thresholds.

"The bank surcharge will be increased to 8% and the bank levy currently at 0.1% will be increased to 0.5%. The 'energy profits levy' will be reintroduced to tax the exceptional profits of oil and gas companies that have arisen from unexpectedly high oil and gas prices.

"I now move on to the government's spending plans. Planned departmental resource spending will grow by 1% a year on average for the life of this Parliament. Higher awards will lead to reduced headcounts. Welfare benefits and state pensions will increase by the amount of inflation at September this year. The investment in UK plc & UK S&T plc have been made in this fiscal year. A further £3bn will be invested in each company in the next fiscal year.

"I have included a long term recognition of £20bn to be spent over 20 years for refurbishment of the Palace of Westminster at £1bn per year. There will be the usual tariff increases on wine, excess sugar products, junk food, but not on beer and cider. Taxes on tobacco products and vaping will increase by 10% annually during the life of the Parliament.

"This is a Budget that protects ordinary working people from inflation that I expect to fall to 2% in the coming year. This budget takes more from the better off and is in line with our strategies and plans. The Budget next year, I am confident, will show that income and expenditure come into balance. If progress along that path stalls, I will come back to the House with restorative measures. I commend this Budget to the House."

All of the National Endeavour's MPs rose and showed their admiration for a good job done. The opposition MPs sat in silence, possibly believing that this Budget was politically very smart.

The Office for Budget Responsibility (OBR) published its response to the Budget. It said it expected inflation and interest rates to be lower over the coming years relative to its earlier forecast.

The OBR noted that the package of tax reductions was partially offset by other tax rises resulting in public debt falling as a share of GDP.

The leader of the opposition rose and said "This is a budget that will send the better off to far flung shores. There is no incentive any more to make money as her party will take it from you when you are alive and even more now when you are dead. She is more interested in scroungers than the entrepreneur that will create the growth and wealth that the country needs." This invective went on for another ten minutes but by then Julie had left the Chamber.

The director of the Institute for Fiscal Studies, welcomed the focus on making tax simpler. He said the Budget contained positive work incentives but was concerned that taxes were going to rise with the sole purpose of balancing a budget for which there was little purpose other than to satisfy a dogma.

Chapter 22

Verdine Watts goes to Prison

28th November 2034

The new prisons regime was gradually taking shape. Some of the open prisons had been converted to Category 1 establishments with some additional fencing so they were not 'open' anymore. The Category 2 prisons, currently being converted, were the low security prisons, which were those prisons that were deemed 'not maximum security'. The eight 'Maximum Security' prisons, among them Belmarsh, Long Lartin and Manchester (Strangeways) were being converted to single very secure cell operation. All of this work would take some years to complete but with a reducing prison population the work had become easier to accomplish and was self-financing. It was against this background that Verdine Watts appeared for his latest court attendance.

"The defendant will stand", shouted the Clerk of Southwark Crown Court and Verdine Watts, age twenty-one, rose with an air of defiance. His clothes looked three times too big for him. A sleeveless vest reached down to his knees and his jeans seemed perched on his backside, six inches below his Calvin Klein embossed underpants. His trainers had no laces and he didn't wear socks. He looked around the Court but saw nobody that he knew. He had been estranged from his many step-siblings and lone parent mother for years. He never knew his real father, just a motley collection of men that had come into his life and disappeared as soon as his mother was pregnant again.

Verdine was no stranger to the criminal justice system. He had been an active member of it since the age of eleven and it would have been earlier than that, had the age of culpability been lower. He had a long list of charges and convictions yet none of it had deterred his behaviour. He was an accomplished burglar, drug dealer in a small way and liked to carry a long knife at all times. His latest charges were for handling stolen goods, carrying a small amount of a Class A drug and in possession of a bladed weapon. Normally, these convictions would mean a fine that he wouldn't pay or a community service sentence that he wouldn't carry out. He had had four different probation officers, had only met two of them, and them only once each. He knew that the system was soft and couldn't cope with people like him. It was all a game really and he had been winning for ten years.

He had never had a job, preferring to earn money to fund his pleasant lifestyle with theft, muggings, handling stolen goods and frequently supplying drugs to his neighbours on the council estate in Lewisham, south London. He drove a car that was not registered in his name and not insured or taxed. He had never held a driving licence.

Now he stood next to his court appointed barrister, Charles Wood. Charles had put a pretty good case in mitigation. Poor boy from a zero income family, no schooling after the age of ten, illiterate and failed by all of the government departments and particularly social services. Verdine had been caught with a large knife, but Charles explained that Verdine had found it earlier in the day and was looking at selling it. The four small bags of cocaine were for his personal use and the car in which he was apprehended did not belong to him. The police had put forward a solid case and the jury had convicted Verdine on all counts.

The judge started the sentencing by saying "Verdine, you are not of a previous good character. You prefer to live outside the law and up until now this has been tolerated. You have been a low level nuisance and a drain on society. You have been a member of a local gang, but none of them are here today supporting you. In the past months, there have been new laws enacted to deal with recidivist criminals like you and you will be sentenced accordingly." Verdine, for the first time, started to take an interest in the proceedings. He whispered to his barrister "I always get off with probation, has anything changed?"

Charles Wood whispered "Yes, but shut up and listen."

The judge continued, "You are sentenced to two years in detention at a Category 1 prison where you will receive all of the help necessary for you to lead a good and economic life after your release. This prison specialises in rehabilitating the offender. I advise you to take full advantage of it as it will be your last chance to do so. There is no reduction in this sentence for good behaviour. You will serve the full term. Take him down."

Verdine shouted at the judge, "You fucking can't do this, I always get community service."

Two court officers led Verdine down to the cells and within ten minutes he was in a secure van taking him to prison. After a drive of just short of an hour, he arrived at HM Prison Dartford on the edge of the M25 motorway in Kent. He was escorted straight into the receiving area and asked to take a seat. The Registration Officer offered him a cold drink. "This is more like it", Verdine thought. "This place will be a doddle."

Verdine was soon joined by four other prisoners despatched from vans at about the same time. The Registration Officer, a tall man in sports jacket and light blue jeans seemed very friendly. "Welcome to this Category 1 prison. Under the new regulations you will be granted great freedoms and assistance to ensure that your time here is valuable to you and that when you leave, you will be in a position to be a good member of society. There are a few rules but you will not find these too restrictive. You cannot leave the premises for any reason and I will explain to you later what will happen if you succeed or even attempt it."

Verdine looked around the group. They all looked like himself. Colourful tattoos on their neck and wrists, floppy clothes and expensive trainers.

The presentation continued. "There is no smoking and vaping allowed on the premises. For the first two months of your stay you can visit a designated smoking area under supervision but no more than 5 times per day. Cigarettes and vapes will be provided but there is no brand choice. During this 2 months you will gradually or suddenly give up smoking and vaping under supervision and with medical help."

This did not go down well with any of the group as the mutterings showed. "Think of this as a boarding school, where you will receive lessons in all of the subjects necessary to equip you for the world of work outside. If you show an interest in apprenticeships in say, plumbing, car mechanics or carpentry, you will be placed with a company at the end of your sentence that will give you the necessary training and work experience to become fully qualified. At the end of your sentence, if you are homeless, you will be given a place to live, a job that suits your skills and some funds to help you in the early months. Any questions so far?"

"I'm not interested in any of this learning stuff. I'm just here to do my time and then get released, thanks anyway." The Officer studied the tall youth. "What's your name mister?"

"Lewis Stubbs."

"Well Lewis, what you are interested in doesn't count in here. This is a Category 1 prison. It is set up to give you all of the education and skills necessary to leave this place and not engage in crime again. We are interested in rehabilitation. While you are here you will receive medical and dental checks to give you a healthy body. You will partake in organised physical exercise. You will receive counselling and psychological assessments so that you will understand why you are here and why you do not want to commit crimes again. This is the only Category 1 prison that you will see the inside of. We will treat you with respect and we ask that you do the same with us. But make no mistake. You are in prison and you will follow the rules and you will engage in the process. You will be allowed to make phone calls to your friends and relatives, restricted to one call per day. Mobile phones are not permitted. If you are found with one, your time here will be at an end. Some prisoners think that they can access mobile phones, SIM cards, cigarettes and drugs like their mates did in previous prisons. Those times are in the past. There are no corrupt prison officers here.

The present fine body of men and women are very well paid with lots of valuable perks and they are closely monitored and physically scanned all hours of the day. Delivery drivers are scanned at the entrance and all loads go through airport type X-Ray machines. Nothing gets in here, so forget that as an idea.

"If any of you are reliant on drugs then you must let me know at the end of this presentation so that you can enter a programme of detoxification. There are no drugs given out except by a doctor's prescription and none of these will be recreational. We aim to get you drug free as soon as possible, regrettably with some discomfort to yourselves.

"You will be given a laptop computer in your room for your schoolwork, but it has a very limited Internet capability. There is wider Internet access in the classrooms. Any more questions?"

"If our time here is brought to an early end, where do we go?" a tall white boy with spots asked.

"You will go to a Category 2 prison. This prison is a very different place to this. Tomorrow you will be taking a visit to see a Category 2 prison so that you can appreciate the difference." Through the door at the far side of the room a prison officer entered and addressed the group.

"If you would all like to follow me, I will show you to your rooms and give you your clothes." "The clothes that you are wearing are of no use to you and will be destroyed. All jewellery will be safely secured until your release. You will be given new smart clothes when you leave us. It is now 3.30pm, so you will have time to make yourself a drink in your rooms. You will be collected at 6pm to be shown the assembly hall, refectory, the classroom for tomorrow's lessons, gymnasium and the swimming pool."

Verdine followed the officer and collected his clothes, changed into one of the three sets and said goodbye to his favourite pair of jeans, ripped at the knees. He took off his two necklaces, bracelet, watch and rings and placed them in a container with his name showing. Holding his two further sets of clothes he was shown to his room, a little smaller than he was used to but spotlessly clean. He had expected to share with at least one person, and in the worst places two or three others. This was a single room on the ground floor. He later found out that in the three floors, the building contained only single rooms. There was a bed, a desk with a laptop computer and a comfortable chair. A kettle was provided with a small stock of coffee, tea, sugar, sweeteners and pods of UHT milk. On the wall was a flat screen television and at the far end a window that overlooked a grassy lawn. By the window there was a door that led to a room with a shower, basin and a toilet. "I didn't think that prison would be like this", he thought. "This is better than some of the gaffs that I have had in the past."

His eyes looked at the walls. A couple of rural pictures not to his liking and at the end by the window, a large poster with instructions. He walked up to it and took in the contents.

This room is your responsibility. You will keep it clean, be given a hoover once per week and use it.

You will clean the bathroom after every use. You will be provided with clean towels every week. You can refill your soap, shampoo and shower gel dispensers daily from a supply in the refectory.

You will clean the cups after use. You can restock the tea and coffee making facilities daily from a supply in the refectory.

You will be charged for all breakages. If you vandalise the room in any way, you will be removed to a Category 2 prison.

You will not deface the walls by drawing on them or hanging any personal item either by pins or tape.

There is no smoking in the room at any time. A smoke detector is fitted in both rooms that are very sensitive.

The computer is for academic use. There is very limited Internet access and all browsing is monitored.

The television has all the main terrestrial channels. The service will shut down at 10.30pm.

Lights go out at 11pm.

Books are available from the library and a maximum of three are allowed in your room at any time.

There is a laundry basket in the corner. You may change your clothes every second day. You have been provided with three of each item. One you are wearing, one in the laundry and one in the wardrobe for next use. There is a pair of hotel type slippers and a bathrobe in the wardrobe. Laundry will be collected and returned while you are in class.

You will be woken by an alarm at 7am. You will gather in the refectory for breakfast between 8 and 8.30am.

Schooling will commence at 9.00am with an assembly in the main hall. Lessons will start at 9.20am and each will last 40 minutes in accordance with the timetable set out on the desk. At 10.40 there will be a refreshment break for 20 minutes. Lunch will be at 1pm in the refectory and lessons will recommence at 2.20pm until 4.30pm. Unless you have kitchen duties, from 4.30pm there will be free association in the large games room until dinner at 6.30pm or you may visit the gymnasium or pool. After dinner you will return to your rooms until lights out, to read, study or watch TV.

If you wish to report sick, please use the telephone on the wall or press the red emergency button. A nurse or doctor will attend you in your room.

You may make one call to a friend or relative each day. All calls are recorded and monitored.

There are no locks on the doors. All corridors are monitored by CCTV. If you try to leave the building without authority, you will be transferred immediately to a Category 2 prison.

There is a gymnasium available for your use daily and a swimming pool at the weekends. There will be organised sports games at the weekend. Please see the bulletin board in the refectory.

Verdine's first thoughts were on how to work the system. "What's all this schooling about?" he thought. "I'm not interested in that. If there are no locks, I could walk out and disappear. They won't be bothered looking for me and anyway, I know where to hide."

He looked at the timetable on the desk, affixed with blue tack.

Monday	*Arithmetic, Writing, Reading, Life skills, Kitchen or laundry*
Tuesday	*Managing your money, Charities, Reading, Sports, Kitchen or laundry*
Wednesday	*Writing, Internet shopping, Dealing with the doctor and dentist, Kitchen or laundry*
Thursday	*Arithmetic, Selling on the Internet, Avoiding scammers, Sports, Kitchen or laundry*
Friday	*Home DIY, Biology, Human interactions, Business studies, Kitchen or laundry*

"You have got to be kidding", he said out loud.

Verdine sat on the bed thinking about what had happened. He had been unlucky to be caught as so few criminals were. His barrister had told him that the burden of proof for his crimes had been lessened and circumstantial evidence was now allowed to convict. His past record could now also be used in his prosecution. "You are likely to be convicted" he told Verdine.

"Yeah, but nothing happens. I've been convicted a few times. I get fined, but I never pay it. I just tell them that I've got no money and they forget about it. Last time I got a hundred hours of community service. I showed up on the first day, pretended I didn't feel well and never showed up again. Nothing happens."

"There have been a lot of new laws and the mood has changed", said Charles, the barrister. "You won't be allowed to get away with anything from now on."

"We'll see," thought Verdine. And he did. Slammed up for the first time.

There was a knock on his room door. A prison officer that he had not seen before stood in the doorway. "It's six o'clock", he said. "Time for the tour".

Verdine stood up and moved out into the corridor. The officer knocked on four other doors and all five new inmates followed him down the hall and into a large room.

"This is the Assembly Room where we meet after breakfast every morning. There are up to six hundred inmates and we are nearly full so make sure that you arrive on time. In the country there are twenty Category 1 prisons meaning that any time we could have up to 12,000 of you being rehabilitated. Five of these prisons are for females. All of the prisons are conversions from disused army barracks, open prisons, closed down private schools after the labour government in 2025 imposed VAT and in two cases, holiday camps but with the funfairs removed." He chuckled at this little joke.

"You might think that the Category 1 prisons should be full to capacity, and occasionally this is true. As the new laws have been far less pleasant for criminals than has been the case in the past, petty crime has fallen. Your chance of being caught has been increased and remember, this is only for first attendees. If you get caught a second time and sent down, then you don't get to come here. Tomorrow, we will show you where you will go. Follow me as we move on to the gymnasium and swimming pool buildings."

The five entered the large indoor swimming pool and a couple of them uttered audible gasps. "When do we get to come in here?" Verdine asked.

"At weekends, thirty inmates per hour from seven in the morning to seven at night with obvious breaks for meals. You will be allocated a time and a day. You will be provided with new bathing trunks that you can take home at the end of your stay. If you are late you get less than the hour. If you don't want to come then there will be more room for the others."

The group moved to the building next door, the Gymnasium. It was fully fitted with all of the latest equipment. There were lots of machines in long rows. As it was approaching 6.30pm, those already in use were being vacated and wiped down.

"This is a free association area from 4.30pm on a first come basis, so if you are keen, then get down here early. There is a lot of equipment so it can accommodate up to a hundred of you at a time, which we have found is just about sufficient. Any questions?"

"What happens if you get to the gym and there are no machines available?"

The officer moved closer to the questioner's face and leant forward. "You wait your turn. This might be a difficult concept for some of you. Here we respect each other and that means we respect a person's space and choices. Right, let's get you back to your rooms to wash up and then I will take you down to the refectory for dinner."

The refectory was large enough to seat all the inmates in one sitting. Sixty tables of ten on each. Service was by queuing at a servery and choosing a tray, plastic cutlery and a paper serviette. The meals catered for vegetarians, of which there were few, and accommodated all common allergies. The daily menus provided two thousand calories and much attention was given by the resident chefs to providing a healthy diet. The cooking was carried out by employed cooks, but up to a hundred of the inmates were occupied in the kitchen as food preparers and on cleaning up duties. The utensils, especially the culinary knives were closely monitored. Verdine collected his main course and dessert then looked around for a seat. He got a nod that he would be welcomed to an empty place.

"Is this your first day? My name's Roland, what's yours?"

Hi Roland, I'm Verdine. Yeah, I just arrived today so it's all a bit new. How long have you been here?"

"Just over three months with another twenty-one to go. No time off for good behaviour, but no one messes around in here. Once you have seen the Category 2 prison, you wouldn't want to go there. Are you going there tomorrow?"

"I think so. I see on the timetable Kitchen or Laundry. Do I get allocated to one of those?"

Roland between mouthfuls of dinner said, "You will get a note in your room tomorrow telling you what one it is and when to report there. It is usually one period of forty minutes in the morning and one in the afternoon. The classes are always given a priority so if you need special lessons, they will happen instead of laundry or kitchen work."

A bell rang at 7.15pm and the inmates picked up their trays, deposited them on the racks provided and returned to their rooms. "See you again", said Roland over his shoulder. Verdine found his way back to his room and sat on his bed. He looked at the telephone on the wall. He was allowed one call per day so he thought "Let's do it. Who shall I call?"

On entry to the facility, he had to give up his mobile phone and was provided with a list of his preferred ten numbers from his call register. He was only allowed to call one of those numbers as he found out when his attempt to call another number was blocked. "The number you have called is not registered to you. Please select one that is."

He called his friend Dwayne. The number passed to voicemail so he hung up. He then thought to call his half-brother Patrick. "I'm sorry but you are only allowed one call per day and you have already made that call." Verdine thought "That's a bit unfair. It went to Dwayne's voicemail." Nothing he could do, so he returned the phone to its cradle and looked at the timetable again. "Two years of this is going to drive me insane." He rolled over on to his side and was soon asleep. It had been a long day.

The next day after breakfast, Verdine was asked to stay behind after assembly with the other four new inmates as they were having a visit to a nearby Class 2 Category prison. An officer escorted them to the gate where a minibus was waiting. The journey took just over an hour and as they approached it down a long avenue of trees, they could see the prison some way off in the distance. It was a large imposing place and as they got closer, they could see the high walls and fencing that provided three areas of no man's land between the walls and the road. At each fence there was a guardroom for the purpose of opening the gates. Two gates could not be open at the same time. The minibus pulled up at the first gate and the officer provided his credentials, which were electronically scanned and approved. The first gate closed behind them and the second gate opened. The minibus went through to the next two guardrooms and repeated the exercise. Finally, the minibus approached the main gate and before it all of the guards and inmates got out. "We will now pass through various scanners", the Officer in charge said. "If you have anything electronic or drugs hidden about your body, now would be your best time to declare it. These scanners and sniffer dogs are 100% effective." Blank looks all around.

The inmates passed through the gates and were met with a powerful smell of drains and bleach. The main building was on three floors, like a traditional prison with a central well and protective netting to catch any person falling by accident or design. The inmates were shown into a cell that had four beds in two bunks formation. A toilet was at the far end of the room, but offered no privacy. There was no TV, phone or access to the Internet.

"Let me tell you about this cell and the prison." The senior officer said. "This is where you end up if you fuck up your stay at Category 1, our current home from home. You will also get sent here if your sentence is over two years or if you are a repeat non-violent offender. As you can see, there are four inmates in here sharing everything. The one toilet is not ideal but you have to get used to it, as you are all in here for sixteen hours a day. The rest of the time you are working. Between shifts all meals are delivered to this room. There is a shower block for use once a week and the showers are supervised at all times. There is no education or rehabilitation. You work seven days a week in the laundry, kitchen, hospital or on a prison work detail. There is no day release, not even for a family funeral. Regrettably, there is violence between prisoners at the current rate of one death per week. It was worse last year at two a week on average. There is no exercise yard as all of the exercise you will need is in the work. There is no mixing with other prisoners outside your cellmates or workmates. We have no gang leaders here because as soon as they are identified, they are shipped out to a Category 3 prison.

There is no parole or time off of your sentence. There is no smoking permitted at all, so giving up is mandatory. If any violence is committed, all those involved are sent to a Category 3 prison. There is no right of appeal. The rooms and corridors are monitored for unauthorised phones and every day sniffer dogs are used to find drugs or other smoking paraphernalia. If you are caught with a phone, SIM card, tobacco or any drugs then you go to a Category 3 prison. You are allowed one phone call per week and one visit every month. Consider if you want to come here, consider it very long and hard. Any questions?"

"How many prisons like this are there?" asked Spencer, an intimidating person with both arms heavily tattooed.

"In the country we have twelve prisons like this, but once the works have been finished, there will be forty. They are mostly converted from medium secure prisons. Each prison holds up to six hundred inmates, a bit like the one you're in. The big difference is that people don't like coming here so the re-offending rate from Category 2 prisons is low. Also Category 1 prisoners like you, see this as a place to avoid at all costs, so again the numbers are declining. Where possible, we will reduce occupancy to three or even two per cell as the numbers of prisoners fall. The government's changes to the prison regimes have definitely led to lower numbers of people in prison. Before the government changed the laws and the justice system, the prison population was approaching 100,000 inmates. The latest monthly figures show that we have a little over 74,000 detainees in prison and a record low of 7,500 on remand, down from a historical norm of 16,000 before the changes. Remand prisoners now have to wait only twelve weeks before their cases are started in the courts or they are released with ankle and wrist tags and all sorts of curfews. Most remanded prisoners stay at home as going out is problematic with all of the restrictions. If they are not allowed to stay at home, they are housed in bail hostels. Take it from me chaps, you do not want to end up anywhere worse than where you are. Take advantage of all that it is on offer, because it only gets worse from there."

Out of curiosity, Verdine asked, "This looks terrible here, so how bad can a Category 3 prison be?"

The prison officer took a deep breath. "If you have ever seen a film or TV programme about an American high security jail then this is where we start from. Every prisoner has an individual cell with a toilet and a basin. There are no showers as full body washes take place using the basin and a flannel. There is one hour of exercise in a small yard by yourself and the remaining 23 hours is spent in the cell. Meals are given through a slot in the bars. Books are provided, but of course, there is no TV. Smoking and vaping are not allowed. The only connection with the other prisoners is by shouting from cell to cell. The whole point about Category 3 is to show the inmate that they are not welcome in society because their crimes have put them outside of it. It is basically a trash heap. Mental illness and self-harming are rampant with no real treatment. Life expectancy in Category 3 prisons is the same as street vagrants used to have before they were all rehoused, about forty-five years of age or twenty years in that lifestyle. You do all of your time and then you get out with no support. It sounds harsh but career criminals do not deserve resources. Most of them will have all their assets stripped from them, so they have nothing to come out to. The only salvation for them is to join an ex-offenders group that might provide support if they wish to live a law-abiding life.

"In the prison system there are just over a hundred whole life tariff prisoners. They are housed in a separate facility and nobody has been able to find out what it is like. The recent legal changes mean that the facility is not protected by Human Rights laws. Bet your bottom dollar, it's not good. Are we all done here?"

The five nodded and shuffled out. There was not much talking on the way back to their Category 1, as the morning was a bit of an eye-opener.

Verdine did his time and stayed out of trouble. He learnt to read better and write with joined up letters. He learnt how to do sums, as he called them. He learnt how to use a bank account, manage his finances and he even became competent at Internet banking. He exercised and became physically and mentally fit and from an anger management course, he learnt how to control his temper. He now knew how to look after himself properly and keep himself and his room clean and tidy. After twenty-four months the time came for him to be discharged.

The Senior Prison Officer dealt with the details. He opened the brown envelope and said, "Here is your jewellery." Verdine said, "No thanks", I've got past that stuff. Just my signet ring and the rest can be junked."

He looked good in his new clothes and he carried a small bag with a change of underwear and swimming trunks. A car was waiting to take him to a flat in a block in Woolwich. He was offered somewhere closer to his previous home but he wanted a clean break from his past. The following day he was going shopping for clothes with some of the £2,000 he had been given that had been deposited in his new bank account. In three days' time he was starting at a job in retail, just a short bus ride from his flat. All of the persons involved in his development; the prison staff; the probation officers and his new sympathetically inclined employer, willed him to succeed, turn his life around and stay out of trouble. The odds were stacked against him but he did not disappoint them.

Verdine Watts became an assistant manager of a man's clothes shop, he met a primary school teacher and after six months they started living together in his flat. Over the next five years, they had two children, one of each, and moved into a small house with a garden in Belvedere, less than four miles from his shop. Verdine without knowing it, or was it ever explicitly said, was one of many successful outcomes of the new regime.

Lewis Stubbs, who went into Category 1 on the same day as Verdine, went the other way and ended up in a Category 3 prison and at the age of 38, he hanged himself in his cell.

Chapter 23

Trains & Boats & Planes

6th November to 31st December 2034

Another Monday, another week and the pace of government was relentless. The next item for the Executive team was the Transport Bill. Tom Blandford in his new very smart dark suit and light blue tie stood up and shone the key points of his presentation onto the screen at the end wall. "The Transport Bill will bring together all of our proposals and clear the decks in one fell swoop. Tom liked to mix up the metaphors, doing it deliberately. He once inserted the names of all of the then current English cricket team into a speech.

"As the number of electric vehicles has risen so the take from Vehicle Excise Duty has fallen. The solution is to do away with the tax altogether and charge for use per mile. This proposal has a number of things about it that we like. It will almost certainly reduce the number of miles driven, which is good for reducing carbon emissions. Foreign vehicles using our roads will pay and the cost to some haulage companies might mean that they use the roads less and put containers on to the railways. After the Bill is passed and from 1st June next year, all new vehicles will be fitted with a tracking device. From 1st March, all vehicles having a service or MOT will have a device fitted. All foreign cars entering the UK will be required to have a device fitted before gaining entry. UK S&T plc has invested in the manufacturers of the device and they can get up to volume speedily. These devices will emit a warning if they are tampered with, removed or fail to operate. The vehicle will be rendered stationary within a mile of that happening. That just leaves recent new cars not yet three years old or having had no service since delivery. DVLA will request owners to have a device fitted as their tax would have become due. All devices fitted will be notified with their unique model number to DVLA and any vehicle not with a device will be notified on ANPR. A debit or credit card will collect the payments monthly.

The move from petrol and diesel to electric power has not gone quickly enough to satisfy our climate change targets. The Bill will include a scrappage scheme of all diesel vehicles and petrol vehicles over ten years old. Any vehicle over ten years old not scrapped in exchange for an electric vehicle will have double the road charge."

Tom took a breather before starting on his favourite subject, the trains.

"The ideal train system would be one that runs trains according to their scheduled times at an affordable ticket price, that is easy to comprehend, with clean safe trains and not a financial burden on the taxpayer. Trains should not be run for the benefit of the staff, but for the passengers, who pay highly for the use of them. What we have doesn't come close to this ideal. Since the incorporation of Great British Railways in 2025, the franchises lapsed and we have a nationalised system. As the previous governments have discovered, the train drivers are not interested in providing an efficient cost effective service, not even when being offered high sums of pay. They always manufacture a reason to accept the money but give little in return. Their fall-back position is always that we need the train drivers or there is no service. It is this paradigm that we need to break."

Hillary asked, "We have some underground lines that do not require drivers, although one sits in the cab. Why can't we do this everywhere?"

Tom replied, "We do have some lines. The work required to install the software and the trains across the whole network would be substantial and all the time the drivers would make sure that there were no trains. It takes about 2 years to fully train a driver and that requires on-the-job training with other drivers. Asylum seekers could be trained to drive trains or we could make all the drivers redundant and rehire them with new contracts."

Julie had been thinking about this problem many days that she had to get her train from Didcot to Reading to go to work. "Why don't we make the job so attractive that the drivers will go around the militants in the unions? All of you, tell me what you think of this.

"We pass a law that requires strike action to be supported by 51% of all of members, not just those who voted. Every strike will need a new ballot. We offer 100% job security for all those employed now and increase their wages by 20%. All of this depends on drivers signing a new contract that recognises that the railways will move to driverless operated trains and that minimum service levels of 80% are guaranteed. Sickness days can only be taken after a consultation with a doctor on call all the time. We also offer the same deal to signal operators. No other workers are able to shut the system down."

"The unions won't like it," said Tom. "It would kill their power, but the drivers and signalmen might go for it. Job security and a big pay rise. What's there not to like. I'm up for giving it a try. I will incorporate it into the Bill if we all think that it is a runner." They did.

"We will introduce HS3, Liverpool to Hull and HS4, Newcastle to Carlisle into the Bill, both routes driverless and hi-tech."

The Executive Team met again the next day and finalised their thoughts on the Welfare Bill. They then took the unusual steps of leaking the details to the press. Julie knew that it was crucial for growth to get the working age unemployed back to work. There were some areas where there were no jobs but her plans still meant that welfare mustn't be free when some towns needed cleaning up. The proposed changes to the welfare arrangements were met with mixed responses. The organisations representing the disabled were pleased that disabled benefits would not be reduced or taken away. There had been many attempts over the years to stop payments but on appeal 85% of those had been reinstated. There were not too many howls on behalf of the not-able unemployed but there were many from the able unemployed. The Welfare Bill was tied up with the difficult changes necessary to the way that the NHS operated.

The NHS had waiting lists for over seven million procedures and many of these people would like to work but couldn't. With their health conditions they were in the main unemployable. "Everything is connected," thought Julie. "We can't get Joe or Joan Public out to work until the NHS fixes his leg and her hip. NHS isn't fixing them because they are not a high enough priority even though they might have been waiting two years for their operations. We have to get the waiting lists down but every time we make progress the doctors, nurses or auxiliary staff come out on strike. The country just can't afford more pay at the levels demanded. The Public Sector Review Body had just published its recommendations for increasing nurses and auxiliary workers' pay and the award was 5.5% against an inflation rate expected to reduce to 2.1%. None of National Endeavour's budgeting had envisaged such a large award and the money wasn't there. So what to do? If you pay it, you have to borrow more when the plan is to borrow less or nothing. Or you don't pay it and there are strikes and unrest. So what to do?

At the meeting, Agnes Peters, the Constable, made a clear good point that everyone came round to. She said, "We stood for election and told everyone that unlike previous governments we had principles. We were not right wing or left wing, so we would do what is right. There is no question in my mind that we should pay the award in full because to do otherwise would show us to be unprincipled."

"Well done, Agnes", Julie said. "Yes we should", and everyone nodded in agreement. That decision, although nobody in the Cabinet Room knew it at the time, was the true marker of where National Endeavour stood.

All of the Bills were passed to the legislative committee and tidied up. They went through the Select Committees where a few amendments were proposed that improved the provisions and were accepted. After passing the House of Commons the Bills went to the House of Lords. As usual of late, the Lords was sitting with a rump of less than two hundred peers. Those attending either turned up to perform a civic duty or perhaps they had nowhere else to go. Anyway, the Bills passed and came into law.

After the election, Julie had accepted an invitation to go to Washington to address both houses of Congress. At the same visit, she would attend the 85th anniversary of NATO. She didn't feel comfortable on the world stage but reasoned that it came with the job. She was well briefed but changed the usual way that previous prime ministers had acted. She wasn't interested in the photo shoot, the ten minutes of time with other important figures. She drifted around the periphery and selected her meetings with a simple question for herself, "At this meeting is there a benefit for the ordinary UK person?" She met with the leaders of Spain and France to discuss disreputable time share operators, property taxes on foreign nationals and the easing of import tariffs on Scotch whisky and London Dry Gin. She enjoyed her meetings with the leaders from Scandinavia who impressed her with their social systems and health provisions.

On her return to the UK, she decided to sit down at Chequers over the weekend of 9th and 10th December with Sir Edward Grey and Brian Strong to sort out a statement on an Ethical Foreign Policy.

Chequers was always lovely at Christmas with a large Christmas tree and expensive looking decorations. The staff never knew when a foreign leader needed to be entertained at short notice so a festive readiness was in place. Julie had decided as a real treat for Jamie to stay at Chequers over Christmas.

Over two days, they all concluded that an Ethical Foreign Policy was not easy to construct and even more difficult to maintain. A decision not to supply arms to nations in conflict presupposes that you feel the same about both combatants. This view of equal treatment would not have held up well in 2022 when Russia attacked Ukraine. So many rounds of ammunition were supplied to Ukraine that UK stocks fell perilously low. They wrestled with the questions, "Is an Ethical Foreign Policy the same as an ethical immigration policy?" Should the UK stop students from Nigeria coming just because the government in Abuja didn't have the means or inclination to bring the fraud gangs to account? Or perhaps that should be the lever required. Just ask the UK pensioners scammed out of their life savings.

If the UK had an Ethical Foreign Policy at the time, would it have meant that when China annexed Taiwan, the UK should have ceased all imports from China? Would the excuse have been that the UK as a free trading island nation would be unwise to stop trading with the world's second largest economy?

After that horse had bolted it had proved difficult to get tough with the Chinese as the deed was now history and they weren't going to go back on it. Realpolitik determined that the best that could be done was a smoke and mirrors job. Allow the imports but by pretence, stop or delay them at the border. Inspect every container and every item before releasing them. Change the allowable specification of some items at short notice even as they are in transit. Ban some products outright like vapes, or do the French video recorder trick of passing all one type of goods through a single portal, for example on the Isle of Skye.

Is ethical in the eye of the beholder? In the 2020's, supporting Israel was ethical for Jews around the world irrespective of the severity of their actions in Gaza, Lebanon or the occupied West Bank. Since the establishment of the Republic of Palestine in 2027, had Israel acted ethically with their new neighbour? Having been dragged kicking and screaming to the two state solution, the Jewish state had destroyed their illegal settlements rather than hand them over to Palestinians who had spent the best part of eighty years in refugee camps. The Jewish diaspora in the US, UK and other countries, alongside Germany's continuing guilt complex over the Holocaust, had ensured that Israel continued to act with impunity. The mere accusation of antisemitism would send politicians and governments running for cover.

The UK's arms industry was a big employer and too important for the balance of payments to discard, yet has not the sale of arms into conflict zones and to rich middle-eastern countries ever been ethical? "If they don't buy from us, then they will buy from someone else" has always been a good economic excuse. The best thing about arms sales is that the goods quickly become obsolete. The life of a strategic weapon was, develop it, build it, test it, sell it and scrap it.

The small group finally agreed that they would put the following policy for the team to discuss.

"The UK will adopt an Ethical Foreign Policy. We will be friends with countries who are friendly towards us. Friendly countries don't send spies here or allow groups to hack into our public systems. Friendly countries do not have call centres that allow fraud to operate from their borders resulting in theft from our citizens. Friendly countries do not steal our patents or produce counterfeit goods to the detriment of our businesses. We will trade only with friendly countries. We will not send our diplomats to spy on other countries. We have a large Overseas Development Fund that will only be offered to friendly countries. We will welcome students and offer immigration visas to citizens from friendly countries only.

"We will build alliances with our closest neighbours in the European Union. We will join with these countries in developing science and technological advancements. We will continue with our membership of NATO. The countries of the Commonwealth of Nations is made up of friendly countries. Students from the Commonwealth are welcomed with visas for the duration of their courses. Immigration from these countries will be favourably considered if the individuals meet the financial and other threshold requirements.

"Diplomats and consulate staff from countries on the unfriendly register will be closely monitored and if their activities indicate forbidden activities, they will be required to return home.

"We want to be on friendly terms with all countries. The government of China does not always show a friendliness to us. They steal our patents and send spies to spy on us. They support countries like Russia who are unfriendly to other nations. They do not trust us or they would behave differently. There is less of a trade imbalance since the annexation of Taiwan, but it is hoped that relations will improve over time. At present there are selective tariffs on some goods made in China as the companies producing them receive large state subsidies.

"Our Climate Change commitments mean that we will seek to import goods from countries closer geographically to the UK. As an example, cotton towels should not be imported from China when they are of the same quality from Mediterranean countries. The shorter distances of the ships carrying these items means that the carbon emissions are lower.

Julie was pleased and said, "I think that will do very nicely. I'll get someone to tidy up the wording. Anyone for a gin and tonic?" she said as she headed out towards the sitting room containing the drinks trolley.

Parliament went into the festive recess, which allowed MPs to return to their constituencies and homes. No such privilege for Julie. The wheels of government were relentless and so many things to do. She took the opportunity to invite all of her Team and their ministers to a drinks party on the day before Christmas Eve.

Christmas Day with Jamie and her mum was as traditional as they could have. Julie invited the staff at Chequers to join them for dinner and they all sat round the television to watch King George's Christmas message. They then had a game of charades before settling down to watch a film. Julie fell asleep in the chair and was awoken at 10pm by her mother with the suggestion. "Time for bed?"

Boxing Day was a walk in the grounds, cold but dry with no sign of a white Christmas. The next day Jamie and his gran went back to London so that Jamie could go and see his school friends. Julie stayed and tried to switch off from work until New Year's Eve when the Greys were coming for drinks.

Chapter 24

See, Judge, Act, Control

January to August 2035

2034 was all go, go, and more go for the UK. An election, a new government, a new team running the country and a new determination to make things better. All that the National Endeavour Party wanted to achieve by the totemic 100 Days had been managed. The building blocks of the country's revival had been laid and now it was all down to managing progress. The Budget on 18th October had been warmly welcomed inside and outside Parliament as it contained pragmatic steps to digging the country out of the holes left by previous administrations. The discussions on a Federal UK had now deteriorated into a haggling exercise, mostly about money. Wales and Scotland wanted as close to independence as they could get but with an annual hand out of money from England. This saga looked like going on throughout 2035.

The football World Cup competition in Saudi Arabia had gone off without a hitch, if you call seven spectators dying from heat exhaustion not a hitch. England had lost in the final again to a rejuvenated Brazil side that had shown little good form until it mattered.

As the New Year was cheered in, the season of goodwill to all men had been misinterpreted by some of the world's leaders. The Chinese brutal annexation of Taiwan had not gone well and the government in Beijing was ramping up the military solution against the islanders. The free world's opinion was against China so in retaliation they increased their interference in western technology systems causing power and telecommunications shutdowns. Russia, successful in Ukraine and with a seasoned hard line successor to Putin, was loathe to accept some of the treaty terms. The unrest in the Middle East continued. The independent state of Palestine was being rebuilt, but with no help from Israel and sporadic terrorist attacks continued. Hungary's exit from the EU had been expected for some time but had still proved messy. Border controls had been reintroduced and a through path to EU countries for asylum seekers and refugees had been quickly established. Christmas for Julie had been a few days at Chequers to spend time with Jamie and her mum, and a few days alone to recharge her batteries until they returned for New Year's Eve. The weight of office was never far away as she was expected to respond to every crisis both home and abroad. She now relied on her team and in particular, Sir Edward Grey, who with Lady Estelle, joined her for New Year's drinks. On 2nd January, they all returned to Downing Street to prepare for 2035.

On Monday, 8th January Julie sat down with her team and what did they see? The first thing that they had to admit was that the supply of houses to meet their Manifesto pledge, was not going well. There had been good progress but not enough of it.

Empty properties were being acquired and refurbished by local authorities. After the election, there were over 275,000 empty properties in the UK and about 120,000 homeless families and single adults. The team knew that not all of the empty properties could be acquired as they were in the process of being prepared for sale or let. A good number were owned by local authorities and people now in residential care and the families had to wait for the inevitable outcome before being able to sell and divide any proceeds. Lending institutions had taken over twenty thousand properties in possession from mortgagors failing to make their payments. Many of these were in a poor state but buyers would be found. However, every empty property filled with a homeless family was good news for the family, good news for the local authority in not having to pay bed and breakfast costs and good news, particularly for the children of that family to have a permanent home.

2.1m households had more than one home. Despite previous attempts by some councils to drive holiday lets and second homes on to the market, the effect had been minimal. Many homeowners had high expectations of their worth, having bought them at the top of that market. The reality of having to sell into the local market had not sunk in yet. The annual effect of doubling the Council Tax had not yet bitten hard enough. The removal of exemptions had sent a chilling effect on some owners, who had bucked the previous tax rises by inventing a reason that the council had bought. A no exemptions policy gave rise to howls of protest but only the dimmest could not see the writing on the wall. "What is the point of sticking with a second home that might be used infrequently and paying over £10,000 a year council tax for it?" Cheaper to buy or rent a villa on a Caribbean island.

The team could see some success with increasing the pool of skilled labour. 947 asylum seekers in the system had building skills and 914 of them had accepted a job with the major housebuilding companies. The remaining 33 had been sent to an immigration centre outside Oxford pending removal. Within one month all 33 had changed their minds. UK plc had taken a major investment in two building supplies companies and already sites for new factories on the outskirts of Sheffield and Northampton had been identified.

All of the new town sites had been investigated and all but two had proved to be suitable, so two more were added. The New Towns Corporations had been established and compulsory purchase orders for the land had been submitted. The major housebuilders had not been wholly co-operative. These companies had paid a lot for their land banks and sizeable sums for planning permissions and they wanted to build their expensive and very profitable executive houses. The team decided on a path of least resistance as these companies were the only game in town to build the new towns. They allowed their existing planned schemes to blow through the system and only approved plans for smaller units in the next phase.

Having given themselves a notional score of eight out of ten for housing, they now reviewed the state of the NHS. In 2024, the newly appointed Labour Secretary of State for Health declared the NHS as "broken". Over the next 10 years, he and his successors, made gallant efforts to reform the system by 'papering over the cracks.' At the dawn of 2035, the team recognised that the basic problems still existed. Too much management, outdated technology, not enough doctors and nurses, an ageing population and doctors through their union, the BMA, telling Ministers and their own management what they were, or were not, going to do. The care home beds within the hospital initiative was a success, freeing up beds for accident and emergency admissions. The waiting lists remained stubbornly high because as soon as there was progress, a strike by doctors, nurses or auxiliary health service staff sent everything back. All of the additional medical student places had been taken up. The team decided that they had seen enough and judged it to be a time to act and get matters sorted once and for all.

The government declared the NHS a "National Emergency" and adopted all of the relevant powers. Parliament was recalled and the declaration adopted by National Endeavour's vast majority. The provisions agreed by Parliament were that industrial strikes by any union representing staff in the service were banned and if called, or wild strikes enacted, the union's funds would be sequestered. An expert panel was set up with representatives of the doctors, nurses and auxiliary staff and health experts. The panel would report to Parliament within three months on how to restructure hospital trusts on a single model to provide management and clinical synchronicity. It was expected that some trusts would be designated to carry out clinical excellence on defined procedures, even though it meant the end of the haphazard local services in those fields. A separate panel of technical and clinical experts would propose a definitive technology that would satisfy all managerial and clinical needs and provide a holistic service for patients and health professionals.

Health tourism, particularly from Commonwealth countries, who accessed NHS treatments and disappeared without paying would be ended. The team agreed that patients presenting for care at hospitals or GP surgeries would have their eligibility checked at the earliest moment. If they were not eligible for free care, then credit card details would be taken and a preliminary charge would be taken. The sum was yet to be agreed but would probably represent one day's hospital care as a minimum. Anybody refusing or unable to pay, would be directed to a local private hospital, where they had the expertise to collect payment ahead of treatment. The relatives or community group of any person presenting as an emergency and unable to sanction payment, would be required to pay.

Hillary Armstrong-Lewis, the Justice Director, reported on the reform of the prison estate. The team could see that the changes introduced since the election were already having a positive effect on prisoner numbers. The total of incarcerated prisoners had fallen from a peak of 89,567 to about 74,000 excluding those on remand and with a home curfew by the end of 2034. This fall in numbers was mostly due to improved and effective tagging of remand and short sentenced prisoners into home curfew. If tampering with the new tagging bands was tried, the sound emitted was excruciatingly painful to the ears of anyone close by. The police, arriving within twenty minutes, always found the offender begging to have the noise stopped. All other occupants of the property had already fled from it.

The crime figures made for pleasant reading. The judges had really bought into the project. Lesser numbers of real criminals were being let off on technicalities. Sentences were now served in full so prison was no longer viewed as a soft touch. Jailing of a few high profile tax evaders, one a baroness, led to HMRC having a bumper collection in the last quarter. Mandatory jail sentences for carrying knives and guns, an amnesty for three months up to Christmas and an increased stop and search campaign had resulted in a big drop in stabbings and murders, particularly in London.

The harassment of drug gangs and removing all no-go areas on estates had proved successful. Taking away known gang leaders to places that they or their families had never heard of had had a disruptive effect on their networks.

Improved facial recognition technology and higher definition CCTV had reduced cases of reported shoplifting by over 50%. The arresting of protesters wearing face coverings had reduced the violence and criminal damage. New powers that enabled the police and HMRC to confiscate smart phones, wide screen TVs, games consoles and cars to pay for fines had proved a game changer as had compulsory community service. Some towns had never looked so smart. Police had been very receptive at being allowed to do their jobs. Julie's team now wanted better results from the new and better Automated Number Plate Recognition (ANPR) cameras with the removal of uninsured vehicles from the road.

Andrea Patel, the Finance Director reported on the nation's finances. The 'drains up' audit, or as it was referred to, 'bring out your dead', had exposed hidden liabilities left by the last coalition government. The black hole was about £15bn, thankfully less than expected. National Endeavour's investments in UK plc & UK S&T had been met by the increased tax take and a reduction in benefit fraud. The Budget on 18th October introduced some tax increases and reductions in departmental budgets that indicated that the nation's finances would be balanced in fiscal year 2035/6.

The team noted that the response to the Ethical Foreign Policy had been favourable with special interest groups but not completely around the globe. The relations with the EU, with the exception of Hungary, were almost entirely unaffected and in some countries improved. Spain had toned down the rhetoric on Gibraltar and had indicated that it would like to talk about a Hong Kong lease solution for this UK overseas territory. Nigeria was not happy about having all of its visa applications deferred but had taken the hint and agreed to do something about the fraudulent gangs operating from within that country. Imports of crude oil had ceased from Iran, Qatar, Russia and Iraq, not that much had been from these countries recently.

The biggest confrontation had been with China. The massive trade imbalance in China's favour had reduced to zero following reports of the harsh treatment of the Taiwanese people following the annexation in 2027. The weaning of the British public from Chinese made goods had meant shortages in the shops of non-essential items. However, it is an ill wind that blows somebody some good so the large reduction in supply from China had been gratefully snapped up by other countries. The big losers were those reliant on the latest version of the I-Phone and anyone wanting a MG electric vehicle. It was not a complete ban but it did wake up alternative suppliers and the good prospect of making goods locally in UK. The Chinese had further made relations difficult by the violations of patents for the development of a laser guided drone destroyer.

Israel had complained about being penalised by the policy. Even though the two state solution had come into being by the Helsinki Accord in 2027 with the creation of the Republic of Palestine, difficulties still had not been resolved nearly eight years later over compensation for the loss by Israel of the illegal settlements on the West Bank.

The team agreed to act against Russia as it continually was slow to pay over reparations to Ukraine after the settlement of the war in 2028. The death of Vladimir Putin had made extracting this money less easy although international banks still held billions in Russian reserves. The regime in Russia had stepped up its covert activities and the UK had expelled 14 diplomats that were accused of spying. Russia had expelled a similar number reducing the consulate in Moscow to the Ambassador and his dog.

The raised tensions between India and Pakistan had led to an armed sales embargo to both countries. This gesture was harmful to UK manufacturers in the short and long term as both of these markets were unlikely to return. It also proved pointless as other arms manufacturers gleefully stepped into the void. Ethical was proving an expensive policy but the team decided that the principal trumped the money.

The team were shown pictures on the big screen in the room of greenhouse structures almost finished in Essex and progressing well in Kent and Lincolnshire funded by UK plc in partnership with fresh food growers. The first produce from these investments should be in the shops in July replacing imports from the Netherlands, Belgium and Spain. New sites had now been acquired on the east coast in Suffolk, Norfolk and in the Isle of Thanet in Kent. The completion of these sites would double the capacity in the summer of 2037 and make Britain self-sufficient in most salad crops.

Andrea Patel now moved on to her control over Great British Energy (GBE) and reported that solar and wind power generation when all of the installations under construction were complete would account for 70% of the country's power needs. On the days of nil sunshine, the new onshore wind farms would take up the slack. Contracts had been signed between GBE, EDF, Siemens and Rolls Royce to commence the building of three new small nuclear reactors at Dungeness, Sizewell and Workington. Planning permissions for the sites had been agreed at a meeting before Christmas around the Cabinet Table to get the 10 years build projects started. A further two sites were under consideration for starting in 2036 and two more in 2037.

The asylum backlog was now reported to be below 25,000 and the net immigration figure had fallen from a record of 700,000 to 305,000. The lower number was almost entirely made up of student visas, essential workers in the NHS, building trades and the hospitality sector.

The final item on the Agenda for this meeting was for the team to consider a qualitative question. Did the electorate feel better off after six months of the National Endeavour government? Any data, mostly from focus groups, suggested that financially nobody felt better off but the feel good index (whoever knew that there was one?) had risen due to the government's actions taken so far.

In February, Margaret Heywood, the Transport Minister, opened discussions with the trade unions with the following introduction. "Do we agree that the ideal train system would be one that runs according to the scheduled time at an affordable ticket price that was easy to comprehend, with clean safe trains and not a financial burden on the taxpayer?" The reply was a general nodding of agreement. She went on, "What we have doesn't come close to this ideal. Since the incorporation of Great British Railways in 2025, the franchises lapsed and we have a nationalised system. We believe that the train drivers are interested in providing an efficient cost effective service and want to be rewarded with high sums of pay and good working conditions." More nodding in silence.

"We have some underground lines that do not require drivers, although one sits in the cab. The Docklands Light Railway doesn't even have a cab occupant. We now have the technology to run all trains in this country without driver intervention. Our meeting today is to explain that these are our plans and while that transition is ongoing, we aim to assure you that all of your current members will be rewarded and protected in their employment. The work required to install the software in signalling and the trains across the whole network will be substantial and all the time the drivers will need to drive the trains."

The leader of the main train drivers union stood up and said "You have no chance of succeeding in this. There is not enough money that you can offer that will persuade our members out of their jobs. We are the guardians of safety on the trains"

"Our intention is that we do this by agreement. The technologically operated system will be safe and will ensure that we do not have cancellations, when drivers go sick at short notice or don't turn up for their shifts. The trains have become unreliable and persistent strike action over the last ten years has led to the public losing faith with using trains."

The general secretary of the other train driver's union stood and through clenched teeth said, "I am going from here and telling my members that we have a government intent on ruining the railways and making them all redundant."

"I am sorry that you have misrepresented what I have said. Since my government was elected we have shown determination to put things right. The Unions have ensured that the railways continue with old practises and treated any improvements for passengers as a threat to their jobs. This is not the case and so I will tell you what we are going to do. Today, we have placed a number of Bills and Statutory Instruments before Parliament and when, not if, they are passed the following laws will come into operation. In future, strike action by all and any railway staff will need to be supported by 51% of all of the Union's members, not just those who voted. Every strike day will need a new ballot. Over your heads, we will offer 100% job security until they retire, for all those train drivers and other staff employed on this date and we will increase their wages by 20%. We will be offering this pay and no redundancy deal to all staff and drivers, who sign a new contract that recognises, that the railways will move to driverless operated trains and that minimum service levels of 80% are guaranteed. All of the changes proposed to the Unions previously and rejected will be incorporated into the new contract. Sickness days can only be taken after a consultation with a doctor who will be on call all of the time. Any staff member or driver who does not wish to take up this offer of the new contract will be declared redundant on three months' notice. At any time during this notice period they will be able to sign the contract and the notice of redundancy will be rescinded."

There was uproar in the room. At one point it looked like there would be violence.

"We are not having this. These actions will destroy the unions and kill our power to negotiate for our members. We shall be contacting our lawyers. This is a blatant attack on the working man and woman."

"If we are attacking them it is with job security, a massive pay rise and a commitment to invest in the railways. What we are doing is bringing the railways into the modern age and providing a world class service to the fare paying traveller. We intend to be the managers and determiners of what trains run and when, and not you in this room. We will invest in new trains, new lines and new high speed services. We have today notified Parliament that we will build two new high speed lines, both routes driverless and hi-tech."

At this announcement, the Union Leaders picked up their bags and headed for the exit. One of them shouted over his shoulder "You won't do this. We will destroy the railways and you." On hearing this, the Minister smiled and ensured that this clip went to all news stations. The Bills before Parliament passed and the letters explaining the deal went out to all employees of Great British Railways the next day. The eventual take up of the new contract offer was 94% initially, rising to 98% after three months. The remaining 2% took redundancy or early retirement. There was a legal action launched by the three railway unions but it failed at the first hearing. After all, what have they tried to get their members for 100 years? Job security and good wages and conditions. What was there to fight against?

The big event in May were the elections for the newly formed Second Chamber, a body now named The Senate. All the elected Mayors were members as of right, until they were not mayors, and then their successors were. Each county and metropolitan borough elected a member and, as expected, National Endeavour scooped up over 75% of the seats. Julie's party now had a majority in both houses. The House of Lords held its last session and then went with barely a whimper closing down with over a thousand years of its life confined to the rubbish bin of history. Its members continued to call themselves Lords and Baronesses, presumably because it helped with restaurant and theatre bookings.

Early in July a fire in Durham Cathedral was wrongly reported on social media as having been started by a Muslim asylum seeker. Mosques were attacked by the far right and Muslims were beaten up in the streets. Civil unrest broke out across the nation's cities just like it did in 2024. Police cars and anything in the way were set alight and many officers were taken to hospital. Face coverings, which were banned, were back in force, although thousands seemed not to care about being recognised. On consecutive nights rioting took place in Leeds, Bradford, Leicester and Oxford before order returned just in time for the Notting Hill Carnival at the end of August to end in a bloodbath for the community police in attendance. Clearly the idea of the police bonding with ethnic minorities had failed and the public of all races and creeds demanded some strong professional police action. The police now used water cannon with a purple dye that was a permanent marker. The police rounded up anyone with this purple dye and charged them with affray and many with more serious offences.

Throughout the year, negotiations continued in private between The Scottish Parliament, The Welsh Senedd and the Northern Ireland Assembly with officials from the UK government on the federalisation of the United Kingdom. It soon became clear that the Northern Ireland part of the process would take longer as it contained far more sensitivities. The Scottish Parliament wanted all of the benefits but didn't want to give up the financial support that it received. National Endeavour gave notice that the Barnett Formula that determined the funding for the countries would cease at the end of fiscal year 2036/7. This decision galvanised the negotiations although at its announcement there was a good deal of bad feeling. "You are putting a gun against our heads by withdrawing this Formula," one of the Scottish delegates shouted. All was silence for a couple of weeks than the parties reconvened and, surprisingly, the Welsh delegates were the first to accept the conditions. The Scottish delegates agreed soon afterwards. They reasoned that full independence no longer motivated the Scottish or Welsh voters but fiscal autonomy without the obvious downsides of full independence worked for them. The Bills were presented simultaneously in the Westminster, Edinburgh and Cardiff Parliaments. The date for the Federal Democratic United Kingdom was set as January 1st 2038. With those two hurdles out of the way, discussions continued with the delegates from Northern Ireland, who suddenly became a little more enthusiastic.

Parliament took its normal summer recess and Julie was able to take a holiday with Jamie and his gran. They had been lent a villa by a prominent European politician on the island of Sardinia. The security services took a week installing all of the telecoms required to keep Julie in touch with events and her Ministers. The work of a Prime Minister was relentless and Julie was never able to really relax.

In late August, no sooner had she returned to Downing Street than she had to call the Executive Team together for a meeting on the failure to stem immigration from France in small boats and the slow progress in housebuilding. She, and everyone else, could see that these situations needed sorting out. The Team judged that there were systemic failures that needed to be addressed. Julie was also receiving sharp criticism that the levelling up ideals in the Manifesto had not seen the light of day. Two high speed rail lines that would take ten years to finish held no day to day relief for the unemployed and disabled poor now. These were clearly jam tomorrow projects. Julie received a report from the Child Poverty Action Group and was sad to see that there were some real pockets of deprivation in the country and anyone could see and judge that something had to be done and done quickly.

Chapter 25

Let Me Level with You

September to December 2035

Julie had three bits of grit worrying her oyster shell and she needed to turn them into pearls. She feared that all three had the potential to tarnish her government's successes. She now decided to push levelling up, housing and immigration to the forefront of matters to be sorted in the remainder of 2035. Everything else seemed to be either resolved, working towards a successful conclusion or scheduled into long term planning. These three difficult issues became her main focus.

She had quickly decided that there should be a Minister for Levelling Up. The term was first brought to prominence after the 2019 election by Boris Johnson, the Conservative Prime Minister. Boris had won a large majority in the Commons, possibly because of his personal charisma, possibly because he promised to "Get Brexit Done", but numerically because he had won historically loyal Labour Party seats in the north of England "the Red Wall". Armed with these new constituencies he proposed that they should benefit from the government's largesse that was normally given by the Conservatives to their constituencies in the south. In the next five years, the Conservative government appointed a Minister for Levelling Up but that was the extent of its achievements. HS2, the country's largest infrastructure project, was supposed to go from Birmingham to Leeds and other points north, but due to the appeasement of Tory MPs in the constituencies north of London to tunnel under the Chilterns, the money ran out and the line was curtailed in Birmingham. The Northern Powerhouse Project, originally a Conservative inspired idea, was progressively abandoned by them and it was left to the Labour Mayor for Manchester and other northern politicians and business people to carry that torch, which they did pretty well, despite the lack of funds.

After the election of 2024, when Labour returned with a large majority, hopes were resurrected that 'levelling up' would gain some traction and deliver meaningful benefits for the deprived counties. However, the term was dumped within a week of the election and disappeared from the political consciousness until National Endeavour resurrected it in 2034.

While campaigning for the election of 2034, Julie had visited a number of northern constituencies in support of National Endeavour candidates, where there was a high prospect of winning. She also visited the West Midlands, Wales, Cornwall and the East Midlands. In all of these places she noticed a cultural deficit. There were no theatres or if there were, they were run down and looked grim. The high streets had many empty shops. She was supplied with data showing that life expectancy in some areas was a few years less than the southern counties, where she lived. Over time, she came to the conclusion that London and the south-east had benefitted disproportionately from government support over many years. Compared with these areas, wages in the south were significantly higher, but greater in proportion than the cost of living and essential services. Basically, it was "Grim up North" and many other places too.

The next day she asked her team to suggest an eminent academic, who might help her in her deliberations. Sir Edward Grey recommended an old friend, Kenneth Clarkson, Professor of Philosophy at Jesus College, Cambridge and a supporter of National Endeavour. She arranged to meet him at the weekend in his college rooms. After receiving a cup of tea and getting settled she thanked him for meeting her at short notice. "When the call comes from someone so high, how could I possibly refuse," he said.

Julie took a deep breath and asked "Could you define what you think 'levelling up' means".

As she took a sip from her cup she noticed that he had closed his eyes. He remained silent and still for nearly three minutes. When he opened his eyes, he said "In its broadest terms, I think that it means that nobody gets left behind. Perhaps the term does not convey what it was meant to, and it should be replaced by 'social fairness'." He then thought again for another minute and said "Nothing is fair." Another pause of three minutes in silence and then he said "I prefer 'Moving up the Median', although I accept that it isn't very catchy."

Julie replied, "If you move people closer to a median, then the median rises and they are once again far from it. The median may always be out of reach. Could the definition be related to child poverty? We say that a child is in poverty when that child is growing up in a family with an income below 60% of the average. Over the years, the numbers of children defined as in poverty has fluctuated, because the average income has fluctuated. Some deprived areas of the country have better road systems, I suspect because the unemployed in those areas had government support for public works. The Arts get less support outside London, support meaning money essentially. We've seen the Arts in the provinces starved of cash but the Royal Opera House in London has received large grants despite opera being a minority entertainment."

Clarkson then asked, "What about social poverty. If a child cannot afford to go to the cinema with their friends is that poverty? Some families would say that not being able to have a week in Spain on holiday is an indicator of poverty. Is Shropshire poorer than Kent? It may be nicer to live in Shropshire. You may have a higher salary, but is that an indicator of a better quality of life? Does levelling up to London not mean the giving of more opportunity? If levelling up to Kensington in London is your aim then the rest of London will be in your sights. If levelling up to Tower Hamlets, a poor area of London, is your goal, then there are places in Cheshire that would not thank you very much."

Julie suddenly seemed to get it in her head what she was seeking. "Levelling Up is like a platypus. Difficult to describe but you know one when you see it. Levelling Up is not a philosophical concept, it is real and if you are on the wrong end of it, then you know it. Can education be the real leveller or must it be combined with opportunity? Thank you Kenneth. I'm now convinced, that it is not to do with the individual. Inherited wealth, privately funded education, the House of Lords, the old school tie are all contributors to individuals disparity, but levelling up is to do with communities, towns, cities and villages. We must deal with those places that are the left behind. Places, because that is where the left behind people are. They might suffer disadvantages due to their race, gender or even sexual orientation, but geography marks them out for poverty and exclusion."

Professor Clarkson nodded sagely. "Good luck with reversing four hundred years of reverse enlightenment with a single period of government. The recent trend is that the electorate doesn't give you a second chance to get it right first time." Julie thanked him for his time and left in her ministerial car, much to the amusement of the undergraduates when he returned to his rooms.

Julia had given Andrea Patel "Levelling Up" as part of her portfolio of responsibilities. She knew it was potentially a very difficult department with which to do something. Andrea chose as her Minister for Levelling up, Kenneth Lane, the MP for Hartlepool. This town would be a worthy recipient of levelling up attention and funds if there ever were to be some of either available.

The Conservatives Reformed UK Party in opposition had complained that the Finance Act was an exercise in levelling down. Julie and Andrea, over a cup of tea, joked that this analysis showed why they had never really got the concept. The opposition party had become too southern in its outlook to understand the potential of the other regions, which Julie and Andrea did. Andrea was born in Middlesbrough in the north-east, a large town of heavy industry that had more brownfield sites than anywhere else. The Sunderland car plant had for decades shown that quality products could be produced in this area. Andrea had also identified towns needing regeneration in Wales, Cornwall, West Midlands and Lincolnshire.

The Levelling Up discussion paper, prepared by Kenneth Lane for Andrea and Julie was exactly what they had hoped would come from their man in Hartlepool. Much of what could be achieved, could be carried out quickly and within existing legislation. As Julie had realised, it was all about geography. Forget the other external noise about education and opportunity, it was geography that really mattered and each town and city should take advantage of its geography above everything else. In some sense, the country should return to the industrial revolution, because that showed that growth and wealth could be achieved by taking advantage of a place's position in the landscape. Manchester and the north-west thrived because of the moisture assisting cotton spinning and manufacture. Rivers were a resource as was the closeness of ports with road and rail infrastructure.

UK plc would be asked to identify twelve towns for Levelling Up infrastructure. An abandoned car plant had already been selected for the relaunch of the Wolseley marque and production would begin soon as the workforce interviews had been completed and models designed. The twelve towns would encourage manufacturing sites with UK plc investments and grants. A return to heavy industries was not on the agenda. High technology manufacturing with low carbon energy was the ideal. Local authorities would give assistance on business rates during the start-up period. All of the towns would have an elected Mayor and that Mayor would be a member of the Senate, the second chamber. Mayors had a good reputation for getting things done.

The principal objectives of 'Levelling Up' were to generate employment and wealth in the chosen locality and to reduce the amount of finished goods entering the country that could be produced there. Companies throughout the UK would be discouraged from importing goods at miniscule marginal prices by taking into account transport costs and carbon emissions. Imported goods might have a carbon tariff, particularly if shipped over long distances and with their government's subsidies. Stainless steel would be encouraged to return and expand in Sheffield. Derby, which already had a fine reputation for providing trains, would receive inward investment to set up a new facility to provide the latest generation of battery powered units. All of the proposed new housing would require sanitary ware and the potteries around Stoke had already benefitted from UK plc investment. Large container ships from the Far East would attract high carbon tariffs to discourage cheaply imported and subsidised finished goods from unfairly competing with the British made equivalent.

One of the benefits of the UK not being in the EU and subject to their anti-competition rules, was that UK plc could initially subsidise the price of the finished goods to make them cost attractive until the companies achieved sustainable volumes. UK plc would audit all companies receiving a subsidy and encourage profitable working methods. All housebuilding companies would be encouraged, more than that, obligated, to use goods from UK manufacturing plants with specific targets rising to 75% of the total over time.

Levelling up for UK would not mean that third world countries were to be deprived of their exports. Specifically, identified good quality finished goods from these countries would be protected from tariffs and not form part of any percentage targets. The International Development budget would be realigned to assist poorer countries in setting up carbon free manufacturing. The existing number of eight Freeports would be increased where necessary.

In addition to the high speed train lines proposed to run from Liverpool to Hull via Manchester & Leeds, and from Newcastle to Carlisle, the Transport Act was amended to include improvements to the M60 and M62 motorways.

Andrea presented the discussion paper to the appropriate Select Committee. They responded with a welcome number of amendments that were incorporated into the text. The Levelling Up Bill and accompanying Statutory Instruments became law. UK plc now had some context with which to operate and was soon in discussions with the motor assembly businesses and glass makers. The Liberal Democrats and Labour Parties welcomed the protections and incentives offered to third world countries. It had often been highlighted that cotton towels imported from China came halfway across the world on ships when perfectly good items were available from Egypt and Turkey, much closer to home. UK plc's activities started to draw down some adverse comment from China, who saw its activities as harming their exports. Julie responded that the UK had been the first industrial nation and had produced manufactured goods of the highest quality for 250 years. Unfair competition and state subsidised industries had made commercial life difficult and unfair. It was now the Government's and UK plc's task to redress this imbalance.

Chapter 26

Why is it so Difficult to Build a House?

September to December 2035

Simultaneously with sorting out the grit of levelling up, National Endeavour had to wrestle with the boulder of the housing supply deficit. In the Manifesto, bold promises had been made regarding the homeless and so far the actions taken had only scratched the surface of the problem.

If supply was the answer then demand was the question. Demand was inexorably rising in the short, medium and long terms whereas the supply of housing was relatively fixed. Demand was determined by the birth rate, which helpfully was not rising and immigration, which increased demand annually. The supply was not helped with the elderly living longer, so housing was not being recycled sufficiently quickly. Additional pressures on housing resulted with a rising divorce and partner separation rate, which increased the demand for single person housing. As far back as 1990, a survey was carried out by a major building society that recognised a shortfall of supply within twenty-five years of 3.5 million units, one million of which would result from relationship breakdowns. Forty-five years later those grim predictions had proved realistic and made worse by an additional one million needed to cover immigration.

So where does the country build 4.5 million units of accommodation? The initiative of freeing up empty properties and a decrease in second home ownership were one off gains and didn't get to the heart of the numbers. Every year, net migration into the UK totalled about 300,000. So every year, a city the size of Leicester had to be built just to keep still and cover the net migration inflow.

The new towns proposed would over time reduce the numbers significantly. 12 new towns of 100,000 people would mean 50,000 units so that is six hundred thousand, over time. A long time, perhaps 20 years. Where will the other nearly four million units be built?

The Labour Party on entering government in 2024 promised 1.5 million homes over the life of the Parliament of five years. This was historically a very big deal. Not for sixty years had any government got close to 300,000 in any year. They of course failed because they didn't have the workforce, the materials, the land, the appropriate planning regime and the main housebuilders convinced about running very hard at no increase in their profits. The two coalitions that followed had other things on their minds, more important than providing secure homes for their citizens!

Now it was National Endeavour's turn to sip from the poisoned chalice. Julie sat down with a map of the UK and a wad of statistics on the table in front of her. Scotland and England were clearly bigger than Wales and Northern Ireland. Scotland appeared to be 2/3rds the size of England but England's population was above 60 million, about 10 times greater than Scotland. The population of Wales was about 3.5 million and Northern Ireland just over 2 million.

Less than 10% of England's land area was of developed use. Areas designated as Green Belt accounted for over 12% of the area of England and was protected against development. "That is rather a lot," Julie thought. The figures in the papers showed that England was made up of 72% farmland, 14.5% natural land, 9.5% built on, and 4% green urban like parks. Julie put her biro into her mouth and thought, "The problem isn't the land available. Compared with some countries, the UK is sparsely populated. Admittedly, much of Scotland cannot be developed and nor should it be. The UK had 15 National Parks and although there were housing units in them, future development was heavily restricted.

So if land availability is not the problem, what is? People want to live where the jobs are so that is why the south-east is so heavily built up. The new towns will have special manufacturing, scientific and assembly status to provide the jobs but where will other houses go? One of the documents reported that there were about 1,200 towns in the UK. Julie leapt at this information. "If each town could have 1,000 housing units that would mean 1.2 million in total. What about villages?" Another paper was unearthed from the folder. There were over 6,000 villages and small communities. "If every village could take 50 extra units that would be only 300,000 in total. Not enough," she thought. The numbers required are just so large. "This is a problem that has arisen over the last sixty years, we cannot hope to solve it in five," she concluded. "What did we promise in the Manifesto?" Julie looked it up.

During the life of the Parliament we will give the opportunity to buy or rent to everybody over the age of 25 and working at least 20 hours per week. If you are single this means a one bedroom flat or house; a couple will have a two bedroom flat or house; a family at least a 3 bedroom house. You will be expected to pay a mortgage or rent of 30% of your net income. We will reform the planning rules so that they serve us and not hinder us.

"Oh dear, that was a bit of a pledge wasn't it? What are we going to do?" she shouted out loud in the empty room. She rested her head on her arms and fell asleep. She awoke with a start and looked at her watch. It was 3.20pm. A voice had woken her and quite clearly it said, "To complete the puzzle you have to have all of the pieces in your possession." It was that same voice in her head from years back, heard quite clearly. But what were the pieces?

She picked up the phone on the desk and called Sir Edward Grey. "Get the team together as soon as you can, we have some things to do." Within an hour, they were all seated around the table. Julie set out the problem. "In our Manifesto, we promised that during the life of the Parliament we would give everybody over the age of 25 the opportunity to buy or rent somewhere to live. We were quite specific about the type of property depending on their family status. This was an unequivocal promise and we are one year into our term and we haven't done enough. So we have to take control, otherwise time will drift along and before we know it, we will have let our people down. Any ideas on what we should do?

Hillary was first to chip in. "We have the same restrictions that all other governments have faced to a greater or lesser degree. Shortages of labour and materials, too long to get planning agreed and housebuilders not wanting to swamp the demand with supply."

"Exactly so, Hillary," Julie said. "In a nutshell. We can get the land by compulsory purchase. The developers have land banks but it is not in their interests to increase their volumes. We can't force the developers to increase activity and there are no new players wanting to come in to the market with large volumes. The small housebuilders, of which there were a large number, capable of doing 10 units a year just about got wiped out many years ago with the planning frustrations. Any more ideas?"

Brian Strong was next to speak. "When I was doing a course at night school, I recall a lecture on post war Britain that described local authorities as the main developers. The councils had their own workforce and the social housing they provided was of a very good standard, often better than volume house building companies."

Julie said, "That is interesting isn't it? Housebuilders always complain about the cost of funding. They have large sums invested in sites before the sales deliver them the returns on their efforts. Is there a way that could bring the providers of finance into the activity, either solely or in partnership? UK plc has provided seed finance for the new towns. Is there a way of getting financial institutions to provide it for other sites?"

Andrea said, "I remember that an insurance company, Legal & General from memory, took on the role of developer. I am pretty sure that there was an estate in your constituency, or close to it, which was built by them."

Julie responded, "Yes there was. It was near Shrivenham and very well it turned out. Insurance companies have lots of reserves as do building societies. I wonder what it would take to get them interested.

We still have the issue of the labour. It takes four years to become a plumber and three years an electrician. Apprentices for carpenters and joiners and bricklayers are not being taken up by enough adults leaving education. What about the old temporary building society model?"

"What's that?" they all said in unison.

"I was reading about it last night. I know it sounds sad, but there was nothing on the telly and this book was on the shelf upstairs. Apparently the first building societies were temporary, meaning that after they had finished the development, they were wound up. Only later did they decide to export their expertise to help others and so became permanent. I remember many years ago, one was called Leeds Permanent. Anyway, these early societies were formed with the specific objective of building a small estate. A number of individuals, some, but not all of them, artisans purchased a plot of land and each of them gave some money every week and an agreed number of hours work. When the first house was finished, they had a ballot, an old name for a raffle, and the winner got the house. That wasn't the end of it for that person. They continued to pay the weekly sum and do the hours work until all of the houses were finished and every one had a place to live. Wasn't that a great idea?

Brian said "What's that got to do with our big problem JC?"

"Everything," Julie said. "Don't you see? We provide the land by compulsory purchase or the release of Ministry of Defence or Great British Railways land. Insurance companies, building societies and banks or pension funds provide the funding for the land and materials. We attract the mix of artisans and labourers to the project with the reward that at the end of the building, they all get a house. As a government, on the very large projects we put in the infrastructure, the building of a village hall and a sports field. The small developments of say twenty houses can be on brownfield and greenbelt sites, on the edge of towns and villages. I am sure that if the idea catches on there will be families and individuals keen to have a place to live, who will take up apprenticeships and if already a skilled builder, it will give them an opportunity to get on the housing ladder. We can also introduce factory-made pre-fabricated houses that will bring down construction times by over two months per unit. Every site will have a building inspector employed by the local council to keep an eye on things. When the houses are finished, the financial institutions grant the mortgage and get their money back. We will have a standard number of designs of houses and no planning permissions will need to be granted, or if they are, we will approve them in government. It will be like in the 1930's when "Metroland" was built." Julie took a deep breath and looked around the table.

Tom Blandford, Homeland Director was the first to speak. "Where on earth do you get these ideas from? It sounds brilliant. My brief calculations suggest that on its own it will not solve the supply side problem, but along with the other initiatives, it will make a dent in the shortfall. I see this as good for couples and families. What about the single person?"

"You are right, Tom," Julie said. "We have to build apartment blocks of single bedroom or two bedroom units. Ideally a maximum of three floors so they don't need lifts as they make the service charges much higher. The estimate for 2015, admittedly conceived in the 1990 report, was for 1 million units. If every town built five units of twenty-four apartments in the four years remaining of this Parliament, that would be nearly 300,000 units. It won't be the full Monty, but it will mean that the issue is resolved within a generation. Not bad as the problem has been three generations in the making. I am sure that we can persuade our financial institutions to seed fund the constructions for the building as long as they are built for sale so that they get their money back. Let's think of it as philanthropy at 2% or some other low interest figure."

The Executive Team signed off all of the proposals and were agreed to "Let's get on with this".

The heads of the financial institutions were invited into Downing Street to meet with Julie and the Team. Over coffee and biscuits, the schemes were explained to them. They, of course, wanted financial guarantees and a high rate of return. Some were mentioning at least 8% per annum for the facilities. The requirement for a security was in their DNA. Julie at one point said to the well suited crowd "What is the purpose of interest?"

"To reward us for the risks that were taking."

"But there is no financial risk to you as the government and local authorities are guaranteeing that you get your money back. The financial guarantee is your government standing behind the schemes."

"We lose the time value of the money. Inflation reduces the value."

"Inflation is currently at 2% so where do you get 8% from?"

"We have administrative expenses."

"Historically, management expenses have been costed at about 0.5%. How do you justify your wish for the higher rate?"

"We could lend it elsewhere for a higher return. We are not obliged to provide these funds."

"If we increased the sums that you are required to deposit at the Bank of England, you couldn't."

At this point the mood suddenly changed and a new enthusiasm spread through the room. Each institution agreed to second a senior executive to work with the government and local authorities. Within a month, the first self-building scheme on the outskirts of Milton Keynes was underway with 30 units on a three acre site. Wantage Town Council started the first of its small apartment blocks for single people or couples on an old disused retail site.

The ball was rolling at last and progress was swift as Tom Blandford and his Homeland Ministry now had some seriously gifted free consultants from city institutions to keep up the pressure. These people, task and objective orientated and all studying for business degrees, were better equipped than civil servants to get the job on the ground done.

Julie stood at her lectern outside 10 Downing Street and announced the programme. "During the life of one Parliament, these initiatives will not solve a housing crisis that has been 70 years in the making. If all future governments stay with these plans, we will solve the housing problem within a generation. That is a very big reward and we should grasp it with both hands."

The response from the press was positive. Headlines like "JC sorts it out again" from the Daily Mail, "Banks bullied into funding housing crisis" from the Financial Times and predictably from The Sun, "Small woman robs room full of men". Not quite true as over half of the financiers were women and the penny dropped with them the quicker.

Chapter 27

This Precious Stone

September to December 2035

Julie decided that she needed some time with Jamie, who was now thirteen and into his third year at the local secondary school in Westminster. Over dinner she had asked him about his schoolwork and he had said that the class had to study a Shakespeare play. "Why can't we do something modern? This chap Shakespeare has been dead for over four hundred years."

"This chap," said Julie "is the world's greatest playwright and people come from all over the globe to see his plays performed exactly how they were written. Which one are you doing?"

"It's called 'The Comedy of Errors' but I've not seen anything funny in it yet."

"You probably won't. Comedy has difficulty travelling across generations, let alone centuries. Stick with it and I'll get someone to see if it's being played in a theatre and we can go together."

After his dinner, Jamie went to his room and Julie thought about her time at school. She had studied Shakespeare's 'Richard II' for her GCSE in English Literature and had the great thrill of seeing it performed at Stratford-upon-Avon in the Royal Shakespeare Theatre. A particular passage had always stuck with her and she remembered it well. It was John of Gaunt's speech that started 'This royal throne of kings, this sceptred isle.' Julie liked the bit in the middle, 'This happy breed of men, this little world, this precious stone set in the silver sea'. Julie thought that this speech, written over four hundred years ago captured what it was to be British and live in the UK.

Julie mused "The United Kingdom is a very different place from the time of Elizabeth, the queen at the time. Great Britain was just taking its pre-eminent place in the world and would later build an empire on which the sun never set. Britain was now a multi-cultural society with some cities, like Leicester, majority populated by people who were not born, or their parents were not born, in the country. Nothing in politics or the electorate stirred divisions like the subject of immigration. Was net immigration too high? Were the people coming in the right persons for the jobs available? Are immigrants a drain on society or are they the engines of growth? The British people have an ambivalence to the subject except for the hard right brigade that come out into the streets every few years to protest about the lost England. National Endeavour came to power in 2034 with an immigration objective, set out in its election Manifesto." She knew it word for word.

Immigration

We will have the net levels of immigration that suits our economy at the time. If you are wanted here for your skills and endeavour then you will be given a visa. If you arrive here without a visa, you will be interviewed to investigate whether you have skills that the country wishes to employ. If you have these skills, you will be allowed to stay. If you do not have those skills, you will be sent to one of our overseas territories, where you will be able to contribute to their economy. All asylum seekers who have not yet been granted the right to stay in the country will be expected to work on supervised community or paid work projects until their cases are resolved. Asylum seekers will be offered citizenship after a proven record of paying taxes, sustained employment and not breaking any laws. Foreign students will be welcomed but not their dependents. Student visas will only be for the duration of their courses.

She thought that, so far, her government had followed this wording to the letter. Asylum seekers in the system and those arriving, who were assessed as likely to be given permission to stay were set to work in care homes, agriculture and any work that British people didn't like to do, or thought was beneath them. Immigration to fill the shortages of doctors and nurses continued as the country couldn't train sufficient of these medical staff to cover retirement, emigration and those leaving the professions.

Student numbers had dropped because of the restrictions and that had caused funding problems at some universities. The government had little sympathy for those institutions that had built their business on the constant flow of high fee paying students from abroad. It seemed to Ministers that university lecturers might work more hours and have less prestigious dining and wine cellars. All in all the first year of her government had seen real progress.

As she rested in the chair, her eyes lit upon a picture on the wall. "Could that be an original John Constable painting? Probably not", she thought. "Surely a copy. It would not be right to have an original in her living room above number 11 Downing Street. I'll ask someone tomorrow. Still it is a very good agricultural scene." Julie's mind turned to farming and all that her government had manged to achieve in such a short time.

The stabilising of the price of fertiliser had been a real help to farmers. The government also instituted bulk buying that eased the delivery price. A major potash mine in Yorkshire was now under investigation. John Trout, the appropriately named minister for fishing, farming and rural affairs, had mediated agreements between farmers and supermarkets to give the growers a better deal. The greenhouses in Kent, Essex and Lincolnshire were starting to produce real volumes of salad crops and fruit obviating the need for imports. More greenhouses would soon be constructed.

National Endeavour's farming objective was, that all arable land that could be used to produce food, should be farmed. If land was not easy to farm then it should be considered for orchards. Grants were given for the planting of cherry, plum, pear & apple orchards with nurseries providing the proper varieties after advice from the Royal Horticultural Society and Kew. Farmers had complained early on in the Parliament that they spent too much time on filling in forms. A study was funded at the Royal Agricultural University in Cirencester with the objective of reducing by 75% the amount of form filling that farmers were required to carry out. The remaining forms and information were put in to a software package that eliminated all duplication. The National Farmers Union was very pleased when the package was delivered two months ago.

UK plc assisted farmers with the purchase of farm machinery with reduced prices for bulk buying and subsidised loans. All planning restrictions to prevent farm shops, car parking, farm cafes and restaurants to sell UK produce on a farmer's land were relegated to the dustbin of history. Some of the asylum seekers and new immigrants who came to work on farms eventually decided to form a co-operative and purchased land for their own farms. Many of them had been farmers or worked on the land before coming to the UK. In a payback for all of this support for farmers, the government insisted on the prevention of run off from the land into rivers and water courses. The Environment Agency introduced tough new regulations and set up intensive water testing throughout the kingdom.

Her thoughts then turned from the land to the sea. More of John of Gaunt's speech came to her mind. *'This precious stone set in the silver sea, which serves it in the office of a wall, or as a moat defensive to a house, against the envy of less happier lands...'*

She reflected that much of the country's history had been determined because it was an island nation. Before becoming an MP she had been dismayed by the ever increasing price of fish. What was once a staple diet for the lower paid was now priced beyond their means. Not only had the price of fish risen but the portions had reduced. She remembered as a child her mother would buy whole fish but now it was sold in single fillets. She was aware that fish stocks in the North Sea had fallen due to over-fishing. She had asked John Trout about the extent of UK territorial waters. He had replied that since the late 20th century the "12 mile limit" had become almost universally accepted. The United Kingdom extended its territorial waters from three to twelve nautical miles in 1987. The Royal Navy regularly patrolled the limits but the real damage was done by vast trawlers outside the zone. She reached for her laptop and sent John Trout a memo. "Why is it that most of the shellfish caught in our waters is exported to France and Spain? What would be the effects on our fisherman if they had to make the fish available to UK markets first?"

This memo triggered another thought in her mind. The mind worked in this way. That's how it is easy to spend a few hours on YouTube and wonder at the end of it why you are watching someone knock down a tree when you started by looking at the scrapping of ocean liners.

Time for bed, but not before writing a note to raise at tomorrow's early Executive Team meeting.

The next day when they were all seated, they looked at the Agenda prepared by Sir Edward Grey. In it were all of the usual items that needed follow up reporting. They dealt with the timetable dated items or gave them fresh target dates. As usual, this was all very efficient and then they came to last two items on the Agenda 'Defending the Realm' and 'Britain for the British'.

Julie said, "As you all know, it is our turn to host the next NATO Conference. Here is a fact that everyone knows but nobody dares to say. Most money spent in our Defence Budget is wasted. Every penny spent on the army defending this country from outside powers is a waste of money. We have no external enemies, plenty of internal ones, I accept. It is true that over twelve years ago when we offered support for Ukraine, Vladimir Putin had been mightily pissed off, but there was no threat to us from the Russian state. The idea that Russia might invade us was and is ludicrous. The Russian Red Army would need to fight its way across most of mainland Europe before they got to Calais. They could sail their navy into the English Channel but it would quickly be blasted out of the water from land based rockets and missiles.

"It is true that China has been royally miffed by our Ethical Foreign Policy as it has curtailed the dumping of its exports into our markets. However, it is highly unlikely that the Chinese Red Army will sail across the world to attack us. Most, if not all, of the European monarchies are related to our own royal family, but as most families are aware, that doesn't mean much. Many countries still regard us as 'perfidious Albion.'

"The Royal Navy has a role policing the twelve mile limit of territorial waters. The Royal Air Force can be relied upon for a prestigious fly past and an occasional humanitarian job. We all know that while conflicts rage across the globe, they aren't going to affect our island perched on the edge of the continent.

"So why are we going to spend about £75bn on defence this year? What are we going to spend £75bn on? I know we have obligations as a member of NATO but does this membership gives us any protections greater than our geography does? Costa Rica stopped spending any money on defence and put all of the money into its education budget. As a consequence, its children are among the best educated in the world. Now that's radical thinking. A big discussion at another time."

"Julie leant forward on the table and with some glee said "I thought of this last night. There I was, admittedly with a small gin and tonic by my side, thinking about the painter John Constable, John of Gaunt's speech in Shakespeare's Richard II, our farms and island waters and thought how lucky we are to be British. We have peace, freedom of speech, free and fair elections and almost entirely a meritocracy which means that if you work hard, you will have a decent life. These are the reasons that so many people from other countries want to come here. We, as the government, are the custodians of all of this." The people sat around the table were taken by this address. A lump swelled in a throat and a tear formed in an eye. This was Julie at her best. She could articulate where it touched the feelings the deepest. Some people spoke through their mouths or their brains. She spoke from the heart and it had the effect of persuading everybody to her cause.

"I intend making it part of our mission for the remainder of this Parliament that we make sure that we keep everything that makes us proud of this land in our hands. In the past we have allowed national treasures to leave this island and people from other countries to acquire our essential national assets. We are a multicultural modern nation and we welcome people who want to work hard, pay their taxes, avoid criminality and bring up their children to respect all others. What I am going to propose is not in conflict with these ideals in any way.

"I was always told that when you buy your house or any valuable item that you 'secure the asset'. We have in the past been too ready to grant export licences to items that should not have been hidden away and are now wanted to be sold abroad. We must encourage the public display of important works of art and establish galleries in areas that have none at present.

"We have companies that produce iconic food and drinks that are a part of us. It was a huge mistake, and everyone knows it, to allow Cadbury's to be acquired by a foreign business. We should not allow Scottish whisky distilleries to be owned outside of Scotland. This is not 'little England or Scotland' raising its head. It is the preservation of national identity.

"Too much of our land and corporate and commercial assets are held by companies that are registered abroad. Many of these companies are in British Overseas Territories under a cloak of secrecy. The shareholders of these companies are far from transparent and I propose that we bring some clarity and order to the situation. We have to know who owns what, and what power they exercise over the decisions. I have asked Tom Blandford's housing minister, Mark Sutton, to prepare a Bill for us to consider. The provisions will be that all residential property will be required to be owned by a company registered in the UK or in individual names resident in the UK. All companies registered in the UK will have to show who owns the shareholdings and companies registered abroad will not be eligible. This provision will allow us to know who owns our housing and there will be no hiding behind shell companies and companies registered overseas. For the purpose of this Bill, British Overseas Territories will not be considered as part of the United Kingdom."

This last part of the proposed Bill drew a few intakes of breath. The feeling was that the civil liberties brigade will experience some shock at this quite punitive restriction.

Tom said, "After your call this morning, I got Mark started on it as a matter of urgency."

Julie continued, "There will be a National Property Ownership Register, which will contain details of all residential property owned by individuals or registered letting companies. These letting companies are to be UK registered and must constantly achieve 90% lettings so that units are not left empty. Empty units discovered to have no ownership will after investigation become the property of local authorities. Local authorities will be tasked to have no greater than 10% of empty properties at any time. Any empty properties owned by individuals living abroad for longer than three years are to be let by the local authority. Empty shops will be allowed to be converted into houses and flats. All brownfield land will be registered for development."

There was a sense in the room that all of this started to look a little too dictatorial. "Whatever happened to Magna Carta?" one of them murmured.

"Finally, I am aware that the main opposition party of Conservatives Reformed UK has made it known in the media that they are opposed to moving out of Parliament, the attack on second homes, partly because a lot of them had at least one, letting restrictions, again because a lot of them had properties let out and the abolition of tax havens. Straws in the wind. We press on with our reforms, because this is what the British public want."

"Not sure about that", said one of the team under their breath.

When the plans were announced, they caused a great stir. All sorts of groups bandied together and the labels 'fascist' and 'dictator' were applied more than once. However, over time the plans brought to light damaging information on how some companies had operated in the housing sector. The National Gallery discovered that a number of artworks, thought to be held in private hands in the UK, had over the years found themselves into private collections in the Middle East without authority. As each corporate misdemeanour came to light, Julie's stance was vindicated. The country had to wrestle with 'the ends justifying the means' and for some it was difficult. The Executive Team now realised that a benevolent dictator was not always benevolent. Julie said "The ends always justify the means."

Silently the others disagreed.

⁘❖⁘

Chapter 28

My Business and Our Trade

September to December 2035

In Julie's in-tray there sat a note stubbornly difficult to move but the cornerstone of National Endeavour's growth strategy. The note read 'Business and Trade – Internal consumption, imported goods, Ethical Foreign Policy and exports to friends and non-friends.'

Andrea Patel, the Finance Director, had the department in her brief and had appointed Francoise Heureuse as Minister for Business and Trade. Francoise was born in France but had become a British citizen after Brexit. At fifty-four years of age, she had unexpectedly won the strong Labour seat of Mapperley in Nottingham. Her background was in Management Consulting specialising in the imports and exports sectors. She was tri-lingual in French, English and Chinese, her degree subject from the Sorbonne in Paris. She was in a civil partnership with Chloe, a schoolteacher in a comprehensive school in Mansfield, Nottinghamshire.

Francoise's department worked closely with Kenneth Lane at Levelling Up as they had cross departmental interests in internal consumption. Her main focus was going to be on trade, in and out of the UK.

Through her job in Management Consulting with major clients, Francoise knew that the UK had a severe imbalance in its trading relationships. It was from the government's statistics, that she saw that UK companies had exported £950 billion in the year before the election and imported £1,050 billion, a negative balance of £100 billion. So Francoise, principally, had two areas to address. The need to increase the exports and to decrease the imports. Plans were already in place to increase the UK's manufacturing capacity and to promote a 'Buy British' habit. This should result in a reduction of imports of manufactured goods, especially from China and the Far East. Relationships with EU, fractured in 2016 by Brexit, had improved since 2024 by Sir Keir Starmer of the Labour administration, but there were still a few areas of tension, notably a permanent access to UK fishing grounds. A good trading relationship, with the exception of those fishing rights, now existed so it was important not to rock that boat. Francoise, with her European perspective was seen as a good fit to further improve relations with the EU.

Francoise's big problem was China. She knew that everything that she picked up was stamped "Made in China" on it somewhere. Even though trade had reduced as a result of the invasion of Taiwan and the Ethical Foreign Policy, nevertheless, massive ships full of containers filled with goods still arrived in the UK ports every day. A train left Beijing or somewhere else in China every week and ten days later it arrived in London. If the country were to reduce the amount of goods imported from China then the British consumer, shops and manufacturers had to be weaned off of Chinese made goods and it was Francoise's job to work out how this could happen.

The British consumer was the least of her three problems. Customers rarely went to a shop or bought online, specifically asking for Chinese made goods. Often the country of origin was discovered after the purchase.

The shop was the next least problem in this chain. The reason that the shop ordered directly or through a wholesaler, goods from China, was because the items wanted were freely available, in stock and able to be delivered, in quantity, and in the main the quality was good. Traditional products like, cutlery, previously made in Sheffield were now imported from China. Price competitiveness had long put away the British supplied knives and forks. In the run up to Christmas the number of toys arriving from China was truly phenomenal yet the UK once had a thriving toy industry.

Francoise, again through her work at senior company management levels, had recognised that the problem in Sheffield and other manufacturers was that, in the face of competition from China, they had given up the fight too easily. Markets in the UK might have disappeared because of a small price disparity, but there were a good many reasons why a consumer might want to buy British. It could be quality, the saving of British jobs, national loyalty and better business and marketing techniques. The public, and this was shown by the Green Party doing so well in the 2034 election, was now tuned into climate change and carbon emissions. More should have been made of the cost to the planet of massive ships crossing the globe and trains travelling ten thousand kilometres burning diesel or electricity to deliver something that could be made in South Wales for example.

Manufacturers were the largest problem, particularly assemblers. Britain had turned from being a maker of quality goods to an assembler of finished products made from parts from other countries. Many of these components were made in China. Apple made smart phones in China and Tesla made cars in China. Major international companies made their products in China or other far eastern countries and shipped the finished goods to the first world countries. Good luck with trying to order a smart phone that is not made in the far-east. Dyson, a British company to the core of its founder, Sir James Dyson, manufactured some of its products in Singapore. Francoise knew that the UK, and other countries in Western Europe, had become less concerned about exporting jobs than they should have been. Stating that the UK, as an island nation, was reliant on free trade was not an excuse for becoming an importer of other countries' wealth and an exporter of UK jobs.

So as 2035 was drawing to a close, what could Francoise recommend to Andrea and Julie that would start to make a difference? Her first thought was that the UK should get its house in order first. UK plc was in the process of setting up and investing in companies that could manufacture and supply goods to the UK market. Until these companies could get to scale both in the producing and supplying of the finished goods, continued financial assistance by UK plc was essential.

Her second thought turned to managing, a euphemistic term for creating, shortages. France had successfully carried out this behaviour for years. At one time VHS video recorders imported into France had to go through a small customs post that inspected every item in every box. If shops were not able to receive supplies of seasonal goods, like toys for Christmas, the likelihood is that the following year alternative suppliers might be sourced. Disrupting import supply lines, if done cleverly, could be less transparent than the imposition of tariffs.

The cars that the UK exported, mainly to Europe, were from Japanese and South Korean companies, assembled in the UK with parts coming in from those countries. High value medical equipment was a UK speciality and was worthy of being built upon. Having studied the data and figures it was time for Francoise to make her recommendations. Some, she could put in writing but others were politically sensitive so she opted for the personal meeting after producing a skeletal redacted report. Francoise was invited to make her presentations to the entire Executive Team. Julie and Andrea had a sneak preview and were delighted with what Francoise would present.

"Good morning everybody," Francoise started. "Today I will try and set out how we can improve our balance of trade, employ our Ethical Foreign Policy and increase the UK's manufacturing capacity. What we are good at is technical innovation. We make clinical instruments and high value items for the world. What we are less good at is heavy engineering and those industries that employ a great number of workers. Over the years, governments have allowed themselves to be persuaded by the green lobby and other climate change activists to adopt inconsistent and bizarre policies. Heavy industry producing lots of carbon is a bad thing for the climate for us, but is it alright if it is produced by another country, as though we inhabited different planets? We have pilloried South American countries for the destruction of forests yet all of Western Europe has been deforested over the centuries. My presentation proposes that we ignore these voices from the side and we concentrate on what works best for us and then we ameliorate the effect on the climate. This is not only logical but would also produce a better outcome for the planet.

"My first contention is that we produce for ourselves those items that are constantly in demand. At present our steel is produced by wholly owned southern Asian companies. With government financial assistance over the years, they have changed from blast to arc furnaces. They don't however, produce the steel that we regularly need, like railway tracks, so the country imports them. My recommendation is that we enter into negotiations to purchase the loss-making steelworks in Port Talbot in Wales and produce the steel that the country needs. The current owners would leap at the chance of selling it. It's not worth much." Nods of approval around the room.

"We were the pioneers of rail and underground railway travel. Everywhere around the globe that you see a steam train, it has a plaque that says that it was made in the UK. Now were are buying trains made by Canadian and Japanese companies. One of these companies may be in Derby, but a few years ago it would have closed without government financial help. The next time we should be an active participant in acquiring these facilities. If that is not possible, then UK plc should build its own state of the art facility.

"I accept that we cannot compete on world markets, nor do we have sufficient domestic demand, to build very large ships. Our expertise is in building small ships, ferries for our islands and submarines. We must concentrate on these.

"Regardless of what the green lobby says or the amount that they protest, it is a fact that in this country we have a demand for a particular type of coal and under our country, we have a supply of it. We require small amounts for our heritage steam trains and for our steel industry. If we do not dig out this specialist coal then we would have to import it. The carbon cost of importing this coal is much higher than producing it ourselves. It is a no brainer and we should ignore those critics who do not understand the issue.

"The NHS has a massive demand for pharmaceuticals and health products. Many of these products are in use regularly and demand is constant. The NHS must review every item that is imported and provide a list to NHS England. If demand merits it, then the item should be produced in the UK.

"The years after China annexed Taiwan, our trade with China was mostly unaffected. Since this government has introduced an Ethical Foreign Policy many goods are no longer available for import. Other European countries are now adopting similar policies and although the reversal of the annexation is not expected, the effect on the Chinese economy over time will be significant. Countries in Africa and Asia have benefitted from these policies and the importance of membership of the Commonwealth of Nations has been emphasised.

"To sum up. UK plc is playing an important role in persuading companies to position manufacturing facilities in deprived areas. Levelling up by job creation is noticeable. UK S&T plc is providing financial and management help to companies that allows them to increase capacity in the provision of health products. The UK must control essential industries like steel, railway stock, electrical cabling, brickmaking, sanitary ware, housebuilding supplies and glass. Imports of these items are unnecessary, wasteful and contribute to global carbon emissions. The new Wolseley factory will produce electric cars at a quality better than its competitors to capture a good part of the UK market. Thank you."

Francoise sat down to a small ripple of applause. That afternoon events would take the world into a new twist of fate. If you read the news every day, it seems like there is always something happening, but this is mostly not the case. Most days are light on news so the media continues with the stories that are on their last legs, promoting trivia concerning so-called celebrities and seeking a controversial comment from a politician, intended or otherwise.

When Prime Minister Harold Macmillan was asked 'what was the greatest challenge for a statesman?' he replied: "Events, dear boy, events". Events Happen. President John F Kennedy liked to say: "Good judgement is usually the result of experience. And experience is frequently the result of bad judgement".

The events of that afternoon were going to tax the Ethical Foreign Policy to its limits, bring into focus the UK's ability to mount an offence or defence of any kind and set the thinkers at the Foreign Office into overdrive to outguess each other.

At 3pm London time, major hostilities broke out between China and The Philippines over some disputed islands in the South China Sea. The US was sending an aircraft carrier group and ten thousand troops to the conflict. The United Nations Security Council went into emergency session and the Executive Team met with its military advisers.

It was a week before the Party Conference in Liverpool. When the date of the Conference arrived, all of the delegates arrived in a pessimistic mood. Julie tried to lift the spirits with listing all that the party had done during the year, but it seemed that everyone knew somebody from the Philippines.

⟡

Chapter 29

Events Dear Boy, Events

November 2035 and 2036

For many years, China had asserted that its claim to the Spratly Islands dated back centuries. More than that, the Chinese government had stated many times that almost the entire South China Sea, including all of the island groups, were within its sphere of influence. Those with old memories of Tibet and more recent memories of Taiwan knew well what this sphere of influence meant. The Chinese claims were disputed by The Philippines and Vietnamese governments.

The spark that set off the conflict seemed innocuous enough as these sparks generally are. A Philippine fishing vessel was told not very politely to go and fish somewhere else despite it having a long history of fishing in that area. When it was slow to move, the vessel was boarded. Luckily, or not, a Philippine navy frigate was in the area and decided to help its native fishing captain out. As it approached the Chinese vessel it was hit by a missile, which caused an explosion and the frigate sank in fifteen minutes with the loss of ninety-four lives. The Chinese ship picked up eighty-seven survivors and held them prisoner for infringing Chinese waters and 'aggression'.

In August 1951, a Mutual Defence Treaty (MDT) was signed between representatives of the Philippines and the United States. The overall accord contained eight articles and dictated that both nations would support each other if either the Philippines or the United States were to be attacked by an external party. The US bases on the Philippines were handed over in 1992 but the MDT provisions still stood. Neither the US or China wanted a major war over the Philippine frigate but some face-saving was necessary from the Chinese side. The United Nations

321

Security Council met and avoided blaming China as this would be a 'veto' incident. From the UK's point of view this was all happening in a part of the world far, far away, but as a close US ally, the country was brought onto the American side at the UN. The Ethical Foreign Policy demanded punitive action on the Chinese, so the regular train from Beijing was stopped due to 'technical reasons' that were never explained. The diplomacy dragged on during the remainder of 2035 with little evidence of the Chinese giving ground on any matter.

A breakthrough in the talks emerged in January, when the Chinese government saw the economic figures for the last quarter. Its exports had collapsed for the very busy European Christmas trading period and civil unrest broke out as company bankruptcies soared.

The whole situation was resolved with some compensation paid from China to the Philippines government in the form of debt cancellation, but there was no retraction of its South China Seas claims. The US replaced the frigate with one from its own navy that was due to be scrapped. Just as the dust settled on the sea skirmish another event happened that would send shockwaves throughout Europe.

The nuclear power station at Kursk in Russia, not far from the Ukraine border, had a meltdown in one of its generators reminiscent of what happened at Chernobyl in 1986. The Russian government knew that all countries had improved their monitoring of such events, so this time there was not a delay in getting the news out. In typical Russian fashion, the first instinct was to find someone else to blame. Initially it was sabotage by Ukraine, but very soon that was proved to be unlikely as their country was going to be the most heavily affected by the fallout. The truth was that it was an old facility, poorly maintained and should have been decommissioned years before. The effect on Western Europe was considerable. The air and large bodies of water were contaminated. The UK, fortunately, was little affected, but still needed to carry out constant and comprehensive testing that cost money, which the government had earmarked for other uses.

Julie had a good touch when it came to a crisis. She took to the lectern outside No. 10 Downing Street and explained the problem and how the government was on top of it. This approach of facing up to bad news had always calmed public anxiety and was liked by the media. However, her luck ran out in March when a big scandal arose and she caught the mood wrong. At a reception in the Indian Embassy Julie had spoken with a diplomat from South Korea and they had got on well. Julie didn't have many friends and Yin Lu was intelligent and bright, and before long they were enjoying a glass of wine in Julie's flat in Downing Street. The security services had cleared Yin Lu as being more of an academic than a diplomat. Her principal role was to advise the Korean government about trade with Western Europe. When MI5 carried out its regular sweep of all government offices and important buildings it discovered listening devices that Yin Lu had planted in Downing Street accommodation and some offices. As news of this major security lapse broke, Yin Lu was spirited away and resurfaced in China. She had been a Chinese spy and had infiltrated the South Korean government apparatus. Julie had questions to answer in Parliament and the press had a field day. In the short term, she was damaged politically for a lack of judgement, but for her personally, it was a sad episode. She now knew that she couldn't have friends like other people.

In April, Vladimir Feckoff, President of Russia, was taken seriously ill. In an unguarded remark, a NATO official was heard to remark, "Nothing trivial I hope." Well it turned out that it wasn't, because after two days, Vlad died. The illness and death were unexpected as up to then he gave the impression of being a very fit man. He was eighty-four years of age and had been the leader of Russia since Putin's death in 2030. His death was not announced immediately as the internal committee of government started jockeying for position.

At least they knew that Vlad was dead. When one of his predecessors, Leonid Brezhnev, leader of USSR, died on 10 November 1982, somebody asked, "Are you sure he's dead?" Poor Leonid had been under such strong medication for a long time that they had to take his pulse regularly.

On hearing of the death of a Turkish ambassador, Talleyrand, a French diplomat of the late eighteenth century, was supposed to have said: "I wonder what he meant by that?" On hearing about Feckoff's death, US President Clooney repeated the quote.

There was no natural successor to Vlad, because in Russia there never is, so Prime Minister Boris Dostoyevsky, a distant relative of the writer, took charge until the matter could be resolved. The papers were pretty much united on describing Vlad's legacy. His intentions of carrying out Putin's work of restoring the prestige of Russia and extending its boundaries was because both Vlads felt intensely the humiliation of the fall of the Soviet Union in 1991. Putin's military incursions were almost wholly disasters, particularly the invasion of Ukraine, which cost it plenty in lives and treasure for not much gain in territory. The war had also cost Russia its global influence and prestige. The irony for Putin was that the world, and especially Europe, up until his incursion into Ukraine was developing a good and profitable relationship for Russia, but he blew it. In his six years, new Vlad was unable to reverse the legacy left by Putin.

In May, a major disaster was averted in the middle of the Pacific Ocean when the massive cruise liner SS Orcades caught fire in the middle of the night and lost all power. The drifting ship was aflame amidships and the passengers were looking to the lifeboats. The ship was three days from any land except a few unpopulated atolls. The Captain of the Orcades, in a show of naval brilliance managed to berth the burning ship upright on a coral reef of one of the atolls giving sufficient time for all the passengers to be transported to safety. Ships were alerted and the first arrived within 24 hours. There were no fatalities, but the ship was a total loss. Over the years it became a popular tourist attraction, a burnt out ship on a reef gradually settling on its side. The disasters and events kept coming.

In June, a cargo aircraft flying on cooking oil fell out of the sky due to the product not being as refined as demanded. The crash, costing the lives of the crew and a lot of children's Christmas presents, put back the acceptance of such biodiverse fuels by a decade. The UK passed a law obliging commercial carriers to advise their crews and any passengers if the plane they were intending to travel in was powered by anything other than conventional fuel.

The Olympic Games was held in Oslo, much to the continued disappointment of India, who had looked the favourite to be awarded the games. The cool climate of Oslo was a welcome change from the heat of Western Europe, which had once again endured record high summer temperatures. Greece and Spain had both suffered temperatures of fifty degrees centigrade, and deaths from heatstroke, particularly amongst the elderly were at record levels. The UK, fast becoming a summer tourist hotspot due to climate change, was now a preferred destination for home holidays. The uplift in tourism helped the national finances and the English Tourist Board was heavily involved with improving standards in food and accommodation. The UK's performance at the Games was not spectacular but not too poor either, finishing sixth in the overall medals table with twenty-two Gold Medals.

Julie's government was basking in political good news with everything in the country looking rosy except the continuing unrest about immigration. She thought that it must be the weather and no football on the television that brings out the right wing protestors in July every year. It all started off with uninformed media postings concerning asylum seekers arriving on a boat then immediately jumping the housing queue, because they had more children than those waiting from UK born and bred backgrounds. The police had to come to the aid of a Muslim family in the West Midlands whose house was attacked by vandals with flares. Predictably, other cities quickly had their riots, as an excuse to assault the police and loot the local shops was too good to miss. To most commentators, this annual trouble was all quite baffling.

Sensible people no longer thought that immigration into the UK was an issue. Net migration numbers into the UK had fallen to manageable and necessary components. Students still came and paid high fees, but went home at the end of their courses or stayed on with work visas. The ability to bring over family members was restricted and only affected the older post-graduate students.

The country still needed doctors, nurses and care workers so family restrictions were kinder to this group. The sensitive group were still those economic migrants, who arrived by boat from across the Channel. The UK border presence in France had helped to create some order and many prospective migrants were brought across in official transport. But the boats kept coming full of failed visa applicants and this proved a challenge for the government. The numbers crossing were small but visual and there were right wing groups anxious to make every crossing an issue. There was no disincentive big enough to persuade a poor young person from a war ravaged country to not try the perilous journey to the UK, for him or her, the Promised Land.

The Executive Team met and proposed the usual actions, which had proven to work in the past. Quick justice and prison sentences to quell the enthusiasm of the rioters. The solution worked but it did not solve the root of the problem. Julie took the team by surprise by asking, "Why do we rescue people outside our territorial waters? We seem to be operating a taxi service that gets closer to France by the year. Why don't we position our rescue ships at the twelve miles limit and if they get that far then alright. If not then it is not our problem."

The other members of the team looked visibly shocked by this proposal. Even Brian Strong, the most right wing of the group let out a low pitched whistle.

Indira Singh, the Health Director, was the first to speak. "Will you let them drown if they are two metres away?"

"I'm only exploring all of the options," Julie said.

Brian then spoke. "The asylum base at St. Helena is now operational and so are the new agricultural units. All those that arrive here from France on the boats are screened on arrival and allocated to work related options. Many of them had already been screened out in Calais. Those without the skills that we require, who cannot be speedily repatriated, and I accept that most of those arriving on the boats have no papers so they can't be, are sent quickly to the island. This is not a problem for us but we do suffer from the adverse optics. Once on the island, we have staff contacting their countries of origin and a good number soon decide to go home."

Julie said, "Well I guess that is the best that we can do until either the French police improve their performance or we cut off the supply of the boats. Where do all of these inflatables come from?"

There was a general shrugging of shoulders. "Perhaps we should find out." Sir Edward scribbled himself a note.

At the next meeting, three days later, Julie started by saying, "On 1 January 2037, the new Federal United Kingdom comes into being. In December, the referendum in Northern Ireland with the single question of "Do you want Northern Ireland to join with the Republic of Ireland and become a single nation as the Republic of Ireland?" will be held. If the result is yes, then that change is planned to take place on 1 January 2038. We must be prepared for these two events. We will discuss the arrangements at our next meeting."

Later in the year, Julie's government announced that for fiscal year 2035/6 a balanced budget had been achieved. This meant that day to day expenditure was now less than income received. There were some celebrations at the Treasury as this had not been managed since 2000/1. It was a remarkable achievement because it was against a background of growth, now the highest in Europe, and not austerity. The government was spending on services and social benefits that seemed sensible and what the public wanted. Interest on the National Debt had fallen and the increased income was from income tax, national insurance and VAT receipts. More people were in work and they had more money to spend. Andrea Patel's face adorned an issue of The Economist. Julie Carter was awarded the accolade of 'Time Magazine's Person of The Year'.

In October, the National Endeavour Party Conference 2036 was held in Scarborough. After two years in power much had gone well, but problems with housing targets, the prison estate and immigration by small boats from France dominated the agenda. MPs, party agents and business donors all met in the late autumn sunshine for a party at the coast. But all was not sunshine and cream teas. A fringe meeting was entitled "Are we just 'lobby fodder'?" Attendance was limited to backbench MPs and when word of this got out, the hierarchy were not pleased. This was the first sign of cracks in showing disloyalty to the party. When notice of it came to Julie, she was intent on stamping down on the organisers.

"I thought that we had given them the mechanism to influence policy. We have even gone forward with their propositions."

So far the National Endeavour MPs had been well behaved. They had all kept on message, supported the Ministers and the Executive Team and developed into very good constituency MPs. The progress of the welfare changes through the Commons in 2035 had changed the landscape for a few and there were some rumblings of discontent, particularly among MPs representing areas of high unemployment. Their bottom-up policy forums, in all truth, had not gone well. As the original headhunters had predicted, all the best people were in the most senior roles.

The first signs of a rebellion of sorts was when two MPs voted against one of the clauses in the Welfare Bill concerning the freezing of benefits. Julie called in Agnes Peters, the Constable.

Julie asked Agnes "What action, if any, do you think that we should take?"

Agnes said, "Don't worry. It's just a few flexing their muscles hoping to get noticed when you next appoint ministers."

"At the end of this conference, I'm considering deselecting the leader of this group for disloyalty and a Minister for lack of progress, or incompetence, on the prisons matter."

Sir Edward, always a man with his ear to the ground, in private, counselled against it. "You are seen as too dictatorial. You have to lighten up and bend with the prevailing winds sometimes," he said.

The year finished with changes in Julie's personal life. She started a relationship with a newspaper journalist called Ralph Austin and was immediately accused by the papers that didn't employ him, of being less focused on her job and guilty of leaking confidential information.

The people of Northern Ireland narrowly voted to have fiscal independence by 51.3% to 48.7%. The Northern Ireland Executive saw this as a once in a generation vote and wanted to quickly move the country into the Federal system. It was agreed that this should take place on January 1st 2038 as much time was needed to make the necessary preparations.

In the USA, the whole year was taken up with the Presidential election. The election in November would, for a change, be between two candidates who had not held the office before. The Democratic and Republican Conventions in the summer decided upon Chuck Owens, The Governor of Arizona, and Sarah Saskowan, Senator from Pennsylvania. As usual a close contest was predicted, although Sarah for the Republican Party looked to everyone to have the edge and that was how it turned out.

Chapter 30

Santa Claus is Leaving Town

2036

It had now been nearly two years since the election and, financially, things had mostly gone well. Legislation had been passed to tighten up the tax laws and already major amounts were coming in from tax dodgers. But the sums were not enough. If all of the estimated tax shortfall were recovered it would contribute £40bn but not all of it could be had. Previous governments would have been ecstatic at getting £5bn and National Endeavour had already exceeded triple that sum. The estimate from tax evaders, mostly companies in the current fiscal year was £20bn, so excellent, but still some way to go.

Julie sat at home during the summer Parliamentary recess and pondered the very large elephant in the room. The cost of welfare. There was no hiding from it. If National Endeavour were to continue to balance the budget and improve public services then the welfare bill had to be cut, but how do you take money from the poorest? Since the COVID pandemic the welfare bill had gone out of control. People liked not working and were prepared to imagine all sorts of reasons why they shouldn't.

The benefits bill for 2035/36 was expected to be £440bn. In addition to that, the state pension bill was to be £180bn. There was not much that could be done to reduce state pension payments short of introducing euthanasia for the elderly, which would probably be unacceptable! The benefits bill accounted for 30% of total government expenditure and savings had to be made from it. But how?

Since the introduction of social security, Universal Credit, or any other name that has been used since 1946, the net of provision had been widened and extended by governments. What started off as a safety net had now become entitlement. The creators of the safety net never envisaged working families receiving financial support, the increase in the number of one parent families and the cradle to grave housing benefit support. The recognition of a disabled person's rights had led to benefits that had greatly improved their lives. Disabled people were encouraged to live as full a life as possible and were given financial assistance in a number of ways to make this possible. In return, disabled people had contributed to the economy. So where would it be humane for savings to be made?

Around the world, there were some countries that had no recognised benefits system or paid any unemployment benefit. As first world countries had got richer, there had been a wider recognition that a social welfare system could rebalance the inequity between the rich and the poor. The problem in the UK in 2036 was that there were too many people taking out of the system and not enough people putting into it. Something had to be done before the country started to borrow money to fund the system, beyond its ability to pay the interest, let alone the capital. This had been the perennial problem for governments and addressing it could no longer be resisted.

Julie decided to get her senior team together at Chequers to agree a policy going forward. She also invited the Director of the Institute of Fiscal Studies (IFS), two disability charity chief executives and a leading psychiatrist. The meeting took place in the lounge in an informal atmosphere. The plush surroundings were to be witness to some difficult decisions.

Julie opened the meeting as they all settled down with fresh coffee and tea. Sir Edward Grey sat discreetly on one side of Julie taking notes. "Thank you all for coming. The discussions at this meeting must be kept between ourselves as any publicity will only lead to unpleasant headlines and fierce lobbying by affected groups before any decisions are laid before Parliament. We all know what the issues are to be faced. We need to reduce the welfare bill by between 10% and 12.5%. Is that right Peter?"

Peter Bartholomew, head of the IFS, took some time to answer fully but initially said that any saving is always helpful but beware the consequences. "If the economy grows, then the % of the welfare bill compared with everything else will reduce. As growth will take some time to generate and is an uncertain future benefit, you would be prudent to limit the growth in the welfare bill at least in the short term."

Andrea Patel, Finance Director, said, "Unless we halt the growth in the welfare bill, we have no chance of realising our budget projections and getting the public service improvements. The welfare bill is at present increasing above inflation and outstripping any of the gains that we have made with the tax payments and windfall taxes. My choice would be to stop any increases in current payments until the end of the Parliament."

"The problem I see with that is that we enter the election in 2039 with a lot of disgruntled voters", Julie said. "However, the effect would be less negative if we could treat the payments to the disabled differently." Julie then turned to Cedric Smallbone, the psychiatrist and behavioural specialist. "Can there be a positive presentation that limits the adverse publicity?"

Cedric looked around the room and his eyes fixed on a portrait of Winston Churchill appropriately above the drinks trolley. "During the Second World War all of the news was bad. Churchill had to tell the people that everything would get worse and that great sacrifices had to be made. The people accepted it and even conjured up the terms "Dunkirk Spirit" and "Keep Calm & Carry On". Perhaps, if the messages were skilfully presented by someone with presence and the right amount of gravitas, then any bad news might be received with understanding. We know that the stages of delivering bad news are firstly to identify the problem and we all know what that is. Secondly, identify what you want out of it, which in this case is a reduction in the welfare bill. Thirdly to identify the audience and there are many audiences here. The disabled must quickly know that they are mostly unaffected, although perversely some might feel that a small sacrifice would make them feel better in these difficult times. The taxpayers might like the idea that their taxes are not going to people who they feel are the undeserving poor, but the main message is to the claimants that they will be getting less and many of them might have to go back to paid employment. This way you major in on the cohort that are more easily fixed and you get across key messages to the target group. I suspect that you would favour a Party Political Broadcast or an address to the nation as you have proved in the past to be very adept at winning people to your argument."

Julie said, "That's extraordinarily kind of you to say that. Thank you. What about this? The message that we want to get across is that the country can no longer afford the welfare bill to increase. If we want to maintain the value of benefits in future years, there must be some belt tightening now. We have been successful in reducing the amount evaded in tax and this success has made the steps that we are about to take less severe then they might have been. If we were able to remove benefit fraud from the system then the pegging of benefits at their current level would not need to be in place for too long. We should also highlight the positive effect that identity cards has had in reducing fraud."

There was a general nod of approval around the room.

Brian Strong chipped in, "I like the tone. The words perfectly give some context to what we are proposing yet at the same time holding out the prospect that in the future we will able to increase the benefits. Although you don't say so, the words gave me the feeling that you were sorry to announce it and that any measures would be until we get through the present difficulties."

Julie went on, "I should be giving some comfort to the disabled and I want to persuade people to go back to work. We also have to look at how we can reduce benefit fraud further, which last year cost us nearly £10bn."

Cedric came forth with some helpful suggestions. "Why not relate the amount of fraud to the sum not taken from the disabled? Also psychologically it would be handy to connect the payment for not working to actual work, particularly if it were community based."

Julie said, "As you all know, the gradual introduction of identity cards has ensured that those entitled to benefits are the ones receiving them. We know that there have been a great deal of negative reactions to these plans. All new Universal Credit claimants are now providing DNA samples of their children, which has received some adverse publicity from groups carping on about the freedom of the individual, but we are now capable of keeping this information secure, which has not been the case in the past.

"Index-linking the disabled benefits would be easily covered by a reduction of £2bn in benefits fraud. I hear extraordinary stories of people still having multiple national insurance numbers and having more than one Universal Credit payment. The largest benefit fraud in history managed to cream off over £50m in this way. I am also advised, and in my position I get a lot of this noise coming through, that there are people in local authority subsidised housing, who move out to live with a new partner and let out the flat or house for a large profit. A large profit because they don't pay anything for it. Housing benefit fraud is a real issue, apparently. How do we get people off of benefits and back to work?"

Sir Edward Grey said, "Can we tie the benefit received into an activity? At the least we might tidy up the country for the money we pay out."

"What a great idea", Julie said. "We could have a daily checking in and out for a community based work programme in exchange for 20% of the weekly benefit. It would cost money to supervise it and we would need to allow time off for job interviews. For many, the discipline of getting up and actually doing something would be good for them and hopefully inspire them to rejoin the workforce. It will also create some new jobs."

After more teas and coffees, the meeting concluded and they all went to their rooms to get ready for dinner. Sir Edward said, "I will get the first draft drawn up for you by tomorrow morning. I will get in touch with the media. We can have a lectern outside 10 Downing Street as these public declarations go down well."

Three days later, Julie stood outside 10 Downing Street surrounded by cameras and made an address to the nation. She read from an autocue but radiated confidence and a serious composure.

"Good morning to you all. I hope that my government has given you the confidence to make positive plans, fulfil some of your ambitions and provided an opportunity to help someone less fortunate along the way. We all live in difficult times and I know that 2036, better than the year before, has nevertheless had its ups and downs for many of you. We are building for the future but still hampered by the legacies of the past. We have been successful in getting the tax evaders to cough up what they should be paying, but there is still some way to go.

"I felt that it was time that we had a grown-up conversation about our country's money, because the finances are not in a good enough way to improve public services how we would like. National Endeavour inherited a budget deficit of over £100 billion pounds annually and this was increasing our borrowings and interest payments. The annual interest on our debts is so high that it is equivalent to the amount that we spend each year educating our children and young people. The country is at last living within its means just the same as you do, managing your household budget, but it is necessary to put some growth into the economy. We have started a very big stone rolling on this and it will gain momentum in the coming years. We have increased our income from taxes and we now look to reduce our outgoings. The largest amount that we spend is paid out on welfare payments and state pensions. We have no intention of making life more difficult for those of you who are currently finding their finances a bit strained, but we know that it is in our nature, the DNA of the country, that when faced with difficulties, we all want to take our turn to relieve the burden. Essentially, that is what National Endeavour truly means.

"We are not going to take welfare payments away from anyone, except those people that are involved in benefit fraud. We have introduced increased penalties for anyone convicted of this type of fraud, which means that we will recover all of the amount defrauded even if it takes a long time and the courts will impose community and custodial sentences, where they are deserved. We have employed more scrutineers to assess each welfare claim and so far, unfortunately for some claimants, this scrutiny has already shown positive results. We are legislating to give us better access to vital data held by third parties, like banks, so we can more proactively detect fraud. We are stepping up our actions to take down the organised criminal gangs targeting the welfare system and introducing eye-watering fines and prison sentences if we catch perpetrators. We have recently passed legislation that will allow us to cancel passports and driving licences as well as seize properties by forfeiture. Remember this. A fraudulent claim by one person reduces the benefits available to a needy and worthy claimant. As soon as an investigation commences into a fraudulent claim, all payments to that person will cease. Any person found guilty of making a fraudulent benefit claim will not have the rights to further benefits payments until after a ten years' period has elapsed. We will be introducing a cash reward scheme for anybody who provides information of benefit fraud that is subsequently proven. All information and subsequent awards will have the highest levels of anonymity.

"All new claimants for benefits and anyone having a review of their arrangements are now required to submit a DNA sample for holding in a secure place. This information may be used to detect fraud and for any other lawful purpose. Failure or refusal to give the sample will mean that benefits are suspended until compliance takes place. As you can tell, we are going to be relentless in our actions to ensure that the country can afford to give our citizens the support that they need.

"When we take into account the additional sums now received in taxes and the potential reduction in benefit fraud, we calculate that the sum we need to save on welfare is greatly reduced. We are not proposing a cut, but there will be a freezing of Universal Credit payments at their existing level for one year. Rents on residential properties to persons receiving housing benefit will also be frozen for the same period. Disabled welfare benefits will not be treated in this way as those payments will be inflation-proofed. There will be no cap on how many children qualify for Child Benefit.

"The number of people on housing benefit has had an adverse effect on all of us. Providing free housing throughout a person's life is unfair on all of you that pay rent or mortgage payments. We do understand that without housing benefit payments most people receiving this benefit would be potentially homeless. We are therefore going to introduce a number of changes. Firstly, everyone receiving housing benefit towards a property owned by a housing association or local authority will be required to be assessed in the property every three years. If anti-social behaviour is proven or obvious, then that tenancy will be terminated with six months' notice. Housing benefit will not be continued for households with working age adults and no family members under the age of eighteen. At the three year assessment, notice of this withdrawal will be notified in appropriate cases. Housing benefit for retired persons will be assessed against their retirement income but no person receiving only the basic state pension will be affected.

"We all know that work has positive psychological and physical advantages. The discipline of attending a place of work and enjoying the outcomes is good for an individual's physical and mental health. We therefore feel that it is the duty of government to provide an alternative to paid employment for everyone on Jobseeker's Allowance. Starting from 1st October, all persons on Jobseeker's Allowance, but excluding those on Jobseeker's Plus, will meet at 9.30 every morning for five days at the place advised to them and they will work on community projects. Failure to turn up on time or not at all means that 20% of the Jobseeker's allowance will be forfeited. Each day will finish at 4.30pm with a break for lunch of one hour. If a person fails to complete a full day, they will not be paid. Sickness will be counted as a day of absence unless a doctor's certificate is produced within ten days of any absence. The community projects will include, but not be limited to, picking up litter and removing graffiti. Tools and materials will be provided. A recruitment drive for these scrutineers in every local authority is being rolled out today, so if you want a job, make an application.

"The state pension has for many years been protected under what has become known as "the triple lock". The result is that a dwindling number of working people have had to support an ageing population with a benefit that is protected and always enhanced. We will cease this anomaly from 31st March next year and link all future state pension increases to the rate of inflation at 31st March and no other measure. This calculation will be easy to understand both by the young and old.

"These choices have been difficult to make. From the outset we have taken steps to show that we all have a part to play in the recovery of the nation's finances. Those with the larger houses and with second houses are paying more Council Tax. Disabled persons will continue to receive the current payments and an annual inflationary increase. State pensions will rise in accordance with inflation so that their value is preserved. Housing Benefit will be granted under the new rules. Universal Credit will be maintained at its current level and any effect will be ameliorated by the country moving to lower inflation levels.

"I promised you all that if you trusted me and voted for me that I would sort out this country. Your government of and by National Endeavour is making progress in a difficult set of situations. We have much more work to do but rest assured that we are capable of the task and determined to succeed for you.

"Finally we think that it is important to work if you are capable of it. Thank you for taking the time to listen to me today." Julie then smiled and half turned to the camera and the light behind her had the effect of causing the look of a halo.

The effect of this speech in the media was instantaneous. The main TV news channels had analysts working out the effects of the changes and all sorts of left-wing advocates suggesting that this heralded the end of the Welfare State. The most ridiculous headline was "Attlee Betrayed".

After a couple of days the angst subsided and a more measured view took over. The economists now took a softer line on the changes describing them as "generational". Others saw a rebalancing of a system bloated by handouts and dis-incentivising work and self-improvement. The church as usual missed the mood of the country completely and put forward bishops wringing their hands about child poverty and destitution. One said that the country was returning to the Charles Dickens era of poverty and deprivation. An opinion poll of 12,000 adults, a very large sample, was positive towards the changes. Housing Benefit had been exploited and tenants making their neighbour's lives a misery had too long gone without sanctions. A particularly odious couple and their feral children in Blackburn were evicted to the cheers of everyone in the street. A case of benefit fraud was widely publicised when it was reported that six families had claimed Universal Credit for the same child.

✹ ✹ ✹

Terry Brooks lived in Shotton Colliery in County Durham. The colliery, after which the village took its name, closed in 1972 with the loss of eight hundred jobs, but all this happened long before Terry was born in 1996. Easington District Council built new housing in the 1970s, pulling down most of the remaining pit houses in an attempt to improve the village and Terry's parents had moved into one of the brand new ones and stayed. Throughout most of the 1970s, work was done to remove the pit heap, which was at one time the largest in the country. So even though the village was picturesque in parts and not in others, it retained the look of a mining village and the attitudes of the people were ingrained. Terry's father didn't work, had never worked, giving the reason that he wouldn't commute to Durham where the jobs were, even though it was less than nine miles away and twenty minutes on the bus. "My father worked in this village and until there are jobs here, I'm not going anywhere."

Terry's mother hadn't worked after she married his dad and they were now in their sixties living on Universal Credit and receiving free housing, as they had from the day that they had moved in. They had only ever had a lifestyle of living on benefits and saw nothing wrong in it. They didn't need a car, didn't go on holidays and spent their enjoyable leisure time tending their small garden and an allotment over the stream at the end of their road. In their early years of marriage, they had four children, which increased their benefits considerably, but they were now all grown up and with the exception of Terry, they had all moved from the village.

Terry met Claire and soon she was expecting their first child. She moved in to Terry's bedroom in his parent's house and little Winston was born. Terry and Claire applied to the council for a house of their own, but they had insufficient "points" to merit an offer. They had two further children, which gave them sufficient points and they accepted the offer of a three bedroomed terrace house payable by housing benefit. Terry didn't work and Claire gave up her job in a shop in Durham when Winston was born. It looked to everyone that Terry and Claire would follow the example of his parents and spend a lifetime on benefits. Terry's life changed when the post arrived on a Tuesday morning in September. It looked official and after reading it he called out to Claire to come and see it. She read it and said "Is this a joke?"

"It looks official. It says that I've got to meet at the Peterlee Bus Station at 9.30am next Monday. It says that if I don't get there on time or not at all, I will lose 20% of my benefits. Is 20% a lot, I've no idea how much that is."

"We can't afford to lose any benefits as we need the money for our holiday in Benidorm," said Claire.

"It says that I've got to go every day except Saturday and Sunday. I'll have to get the bus. Hang on, I can't go on Monday, I'm meeting Bob to go fishing."

"Perhaps you can get a doctor's note so you don't need to go."

"It says here that if I can't go then you will have to take the doctor's note to Peterlee. I can't get a note by Monday. You go and explain. The kids will be at school."

So Claire took the bus less than four miles to Peterlee on a totally wasted journey. When she got there, she saw about forty people, mostly men, being called forward to a person with a clipboard. When Terry's name was read out, Claire stepped forward and said "He's not well, sorry."

The Supervisor said, "Tell him that we're sorry to hear that, but without a doctor's note, he will be recorded as not attending. Hope he feels well soon but he will need to get that note."

"So will he get paid for today?"

"No. Now excuse me, I've got others here to register."

Claire went home and later in the day they had a flaming row. His day's fishing had just cost them £120.

Terry went to Peterlee the next day and spent six hours collecting litter from the town centre. He went the following day, was given a bucket and scrubbing brush and then spent six hours cleaning graffiti from a pedestrian subway wall. After a couple of weeks of this, he signed up for a training scheme that ended up with him getting a job as a postman, which he really liked.

Chapter 31

Take Up Your Bed & Walk

Every government since the creation of the National Health Service (NHS) on 5th July 1948 had had problems with it. The UK was the first western country to offer free health care to all of its citizens. Initially the formation of the NHS was opposed by the British Medical Association (BMA), the body that represented doctors, as it was concerned that doctors employed in the NHS would have less income. Many local authorities and voluntary bodies, which ran hospitals, also objected as they would lose control over them. From day one there was a shortage of doctors and nurses. What did change was the way people paid for care. They ceased to pay for medical attention when they needed it, and paid instead, as taxpayers collectively. The NHS improved accessibility and distributed what there was, more fairly.

As technology advanced and care or cure for almost every disease and condition became possible, so the demand for the services increased. A person's health needs became more complex as their life expectancy increased. Cancer was rare when people died at a younger age. Dementia and Alzheimer's disease were not common when the average life expectancy was seventy. When the average rose to eighty-five, then a whole lot of conditions became evident and with medical advances, treatable. Hip and knee replacements became so common that when they lasted ten years, people discovered they needed more than one.

Birth problems that had previously meant that life was not sustainable, now offered hope of a limited life in time or ability, and what parent would decline the chance? Care became more expensive and more of it was demanded. The cost of the NHS to the country soared and had to be paid from general taxation.

When National Endeavour (NE) came to power in 2034, all of the same problems for England landed on its desk. There was a shortage of doctors, nurses and auxiliary staff. The gaps in staffing were filled by immigration, as not enough of the requirement was satisfied from home training. One of NE's early decisions was to increase the number of doctors and nurses in training.

Bed blocking by patients unable to be discharged back to their homes was a big issue and NE had introduced a limited scheme to move these patients to lower care units within hospitals. The way of solving the problem would be for an increase in District Nurses, but these numbers were going in the opposite direction as existing staff were leaving the workforce. Many years ago, local authorities had moved away from running their own care homes and now paid a fee to private facilities for those people that remained their responsibility. This limited integration of NHS and Social Care was not really the centre of a local authority's obligations and so it was not always done well. That is the nature of priorities. As the saying goes "When you are up to your arse in alligators, it's difficult to remember that you were there to clean the swamp."

So the problems in the NHS were historic and could be summed up as not enough staff, the cost of staff too high and the care provided was slow and deteriorating in quality. In a nutshell, too much was expected for too little investment. So what could National Endeavour do with this puzzle?

Julie got a group of people from all health disciplines, union representatives, members of all political parties, a couple of senior and experienced management consultants and senior staff from the Treasury together and locked them away in a hotel in Manchester for a week. She chose as the facilitator a previous Chair of the BBC, Dame Laura Cumming. Julie told them that, by the end of the week, she wanted some answers, recommendations and a road map to sort it out for the future. In her best schoolmarm voice she told them "I don't want excuses, or blaming where we are on what has gone before, or you telling me that you don't agree with each other and that it is all too difficult. You are the best people to come up with the recommendations to sort this out and nothing is off the table. Think tangentially, wisely and with a vision of what you want the service to look like in the next ten years. Do not be restricted in your thinking in any way by what is there or how much change will cost. Change comes about with pain initially, so do not fail to recommend things that are difficult. I can deal with getting difficult messages across and finding money so that is not your problem, it is mine."

At the end of the week, she sat down with her Executive Team and studied the report. The Executive Summary with recommendations were the pages that they were most interested in. The rest of the report was setting the scene, which she knew, outlining the issues which they all knew, all of the alternatives suggested and how agreement had been reached. The most satisfactory paragraph that Julie read at the start of the Executive Summary was that this was 'not a minority report'. "So they had all agreed, I didn't expect that."

The report had the following recommendations:

- Integrate NHS care with social care and cap the amount that an individual would pay for social care to a lifetime sum of £120,000. Anybody with assets over £30,000 would be required to make a contribution to their care until the sum reached £120,000 or their assets dropped below £30,000.

- Clinical doctors and nurses are either in the NHS or out of it. Doctors should be contracted to work at least 35 hours per week for the NHS with a salary comparable to that offered in France, Germany, Australia or New Zealand. Nurses employed by agencies will not be employed by the NHS. Nurses' salaries will be paid on scales comparable to doctors at 60% of the rate. These salaries will no longer be set by pay review bodies but by the market. Doctors and nurses may work in the private sector after they have given the NHS the contracted hours. Doctors and nurses can contract for a lower number of hours in NHS, but not to work the hours up to 35 per week in the private sector (in simple terms, your hours worked up to 35 hours are for the NHS).

- All NHS Trusts will be managed by a professional management team, which will include a doctor and a nurse elected by and from the clinical staff, a union representative for the auxiliary staff, a head of finance, a head of facilities for building maintenance, head of personnel and head of technology. They will elect a Chair/CEO annually.

- All NHS Trusts budgets will be set according to the previous years' service and measured outcomes.

- All GP surgeries and hospital trusts will work under a single integrated technology providing patient records in real time. Private hospitals will pay the NHS for access to the stored data.

- GPs and their surgeries will be paid for every service provided at a tariff or rate determined by the governing bodies of the countries of the UK.

- All non-clinical treatments can be offered for a fee, paid either by the recipient of the service or a charity, but will be after the first 35 hours worked.

- Dentists are either in the NHS or outside it. NHS dentists and their nurses will be paid the same as doctors and nurses in the NHS. Private dentists must reserve 10% of their appointments for children for an NHS check-up and subsequent treatment with payment at NHS rates.

- Hospices will become a part of the NHS.

- All of this is going to cost a lot of money (Treasury addendum).

Julie looked around the table and her question was on everyone's lips. "How much is a lot of money?" Fortunately sitting outside the room was the Treasury delegate to this meeting so she called him in.

"Good morning Mr Feldman. We will get quickly to the question. How much will this cost?"

"I've brought along some charts and spreadsheets for you."

"Not interested in charts and spreadsheets. How much Mr Feldman?"

"If your government adopted all of the recommendations from the next fiscal year, the cost of implementation would be £20 billion per year rising by 10% per annum if inflation remains below 5%. In order to balance the budget, you will need to find about £22bn in the next financial year."

"Thank you Mr Feldman, we think." Sir Edward Grey rose and escorted the Treasury man from the room.

"Two stages", said Julie. "Do we accept the report?" Nods of agreement around the room. "And where do we get £22bn from?"

Andrea Patel pointed at the big screen on the wall and flicked a switch. The screen illuminated with a page of figures. "Here's something I prepared earlier. About 17% of all government income is National Insurance Contributions (NIC) at about £200bn. In order to raise £25bn, about 12.5% of the current sum, we would need to increase NIC by 1% but also to increase the catchment by including everybody, including pensioners, without a salary cap. Pensioners' contributions will be based on their pensions, but not include the state pension. We would get this sum every year. Income tax raises £300bn so 2p on all rates would raise about the sum we want. As this is an employee benefit we could this time not add to employers' costs. With this money a 1p rise in income tax would be sufficient."

After a few questions and a lively discussion, Julie said, "Thank you Andrea. Are we all agreed?" More nods of approval.

Julie looked again at the screen. "If we say that it is an increase in National Insurance contributions the money will become part of general taxation and will be resisted. Shall we call it something else, a new tax, a hypothecation tax made up of 1p from NI employee contributions and 1p on all income tax rates?"

Tom Blandford asked, "What is hypothecation?"

Andrea Patel replied helpfully, "Think of it as ring fencing. The sums raised from a hypothecation tax is for a specific expenditure purpose. If we decide to go along this path, then it might be more readily accepted by the payers. Hypothecation is not very catchy so we will need a good name."

A break for coffee gave them all a chance to think of what to call it.

When they resumed their seats, Agnes was the first to speak. "Health and Social Care Tax?"

Others chipped in with "Cradle to Grave Tax", "NHS Tax" and many similar iterations all discarded. As a sign of desperation someone suggested "Lazarus Tax."

Julie met with the leaders of all of the political parties for the fifth and final time on this subject. She had consulted with them at every stage and when they had agreed to the initiatives, she asked them to contribute a name for the tax. The name adopted was "National Health & Social Revenue." She also met with the First Ministers of Wales and Scotland to share what England was proposing to do. They liked what they saw and didn't want their clinical staff moving into England for a better and more rewarded system. They adopted the same provisions and hypothecated tax.

National Endeavour put to Parliament these new proposals, which came forward in a new Health & Social Care Bill for England. Julie decided that the announcement should come from Andrea Patel on a budget update. As all of the political parties had been involved in the discussions and recommendations, there was little controversy in the announcement. Some MPs to the left of their party's views or generally outspoken on health matters, found something in the proposals that they didn't like. The implementation and ongoing costs looked to some as understated and so it proved to be. The eventual initial year's sum was closer to £30bn but that was covered by the hypothecated tax revenue and reduction in some care costs.

The charities supporting the hospices found other ways to carry on the support by providing improved facilities. The sum paid by government to hospices increased from £1.5bn to £5bn, but this additional sum was included in the budget.

The reaction from the press and media was generally positive. The lifetime cap was large but at least a cap was now in place. Predictably, the doctors' union, the nurses' union and the other unions representing auxiliary staff were not overwhelmingly supportive, even though their representatives had been in the room formulating the recommendations. Many items on charges and tariffs had to be resolved, but the new management structures started working well as they introduced a new collaborative approach. Most Trusts were now headed by a strategic manager which meant that planning was improved and more use was made of expensive assets like operating theatres and MRI machines.

The previously failed integrated technology systems showed where the pitfalls were. A couple of clever programmers using the latest AI systems produced a prototype that worked and was subsequently adopted.

Julie rose in Parliament during a PMQ session and adapted Winston Churchill's war quote for the NHS. She said, "No this is not the end of it. It is not even the beginning of the end, but it is perhaps the end of the beginning of at last getting to grips with this national obsession."

Chapter 32

Everyone Needs a Bit of Energy

2034-6

Andrea Patel, Finance Director also had responsibility for Energy. She had appointed Monica Flint, as Energy Minister, who had an impressive background in the industry. Monica had received a First Class degree from Brasenose College, Oxford then did a Masters at Massachusetts Institute of Technology. She joined BAE Systems as a graduate engineering manager and quickly progressed to heading major projects. She then took a senior executive position at BP, responsible for major gas and oil projects in the North Sea. She understood all aspects of oil and gas production, decommissioning of rigs and the new generation industries of solar and wind. At the age of fifty-five, she had no intention of entering politics until she heard Julie Carter speak at a meeting and almost evangelically she decided that she had to join her. She was a great choice for Energy Minister.

Soon after the election win in 2034, Andrea had asked her to prepare a discussion paper on how energy could contribute to the public good. Now that the Finance Act was in place, Andrea and Julie were looking to put "some flesh on these bones". Her first thoughts were that much of what could be achieved could be carried out within existing legislation. Monica produced a paper setting out the objectives, strategies and plans for Great British Energy (GBE), a state company that was set up in 2024, with particular emphasis on meeting climate change commitments. Andrea discussed the recommendations with Monica and after a bit of minor tweaking she sent it to Julie, who returned it with one annotation. "Agreed, let's get on with it but bring Parliament along with you."

GBE was one of the earliest initiatives of the new Labour administration in 2024. The idea was that GBE would team up with the Crown Estates to develop onshore and offshore windfarms. It was capitalised with £8.3bn. This sum was immediately criticised as being too small for its ambitions and close to £50bn was required. The objective of GBE was to decarbonise the country's electricity production by 2030. The target was missed in every year so that by 2034 electricity generation was still reliant upon fossil fuels. Coal had ceased producing electricity in 2024, but gas was still used when renewables failed.

The reason that the 2030 target was missed was because GBE wasn't quick enough to install the wind turbines and solar panels. The planning system was amended, but vested interests lobbied and alongside a lack of political bravery, it was still a barrier to progress. In any event, the target of nil carbon by 2030 was unrealistic with funding massively short of the required amount.

Carbon capture of thirty million tons by 2030 was also a target that was missed. The technology to do it was untried and as the project progressed, it became clear that there were unforeseen problems of storage and measuring.

Monica Flint inherited these twin failed targets with no attainable goals. UK couldn't rely on wind and solar to replace all fossil fuels as there were too many days when the sun didn't shine and the wind didn't blow. The square to this circle was always going to be nuclear power. Rolls Royce had been leading the development of Small Modular Reactors (SMR). The planning application for each reactor exceeded 200,000 pages and various objections, appeals to the Supreme Court, identification of a rare snail on the site, river water extraction and Uncle Tom Cobley not liking it, just delayed the starting date let alone the completion of one reactor. So in 2036 imports of gas from the North Sea and from abroad were still taking place.

The country needed energy security and if it could be cheap, then it would be the main driver of growth. Customers, particularly business customers, would be wanting a lower price for energy so taking advantage of more nuclear, wind and solar power. Reducing dependence on fossil fuels was not only beneficial for carbon emissions but also reduced the reliance on those countries supplying the products. Solar and wind, onshore and offshore, had proven themselves as cheaper energy providers. The reputation and experience of nuclear generation was not so positive. GBE in partnership with UK plc would need to have a long-term strategy and join with, and support companies, with sufficient technology experience to build small scale reactors. This was a real opportunity for large engineering companies exiting North Sea oil to have new industries and grow an international reputation.

Nuclear power offered a protection against 100% dependency on solar and wind as they were not weather dependent. The Scottish Parliament had been consulted about exporting energy from their hydro-electric plants and had considered this in light of the revenue possibilities when a Federal UK was to begin in 2037 or 2038. Scotland had indicated that it would not wish to have nuclear development due to the cost and much lower population.

Julie particularly liked the recommendation that people living near power generation should have a lower price for energy or in the case of nuclear, free power. Someone just needed to define 'near'.

In early 2035, Andrea and Monica decided that the discussion paper and recommendations should be presented to Parliament for comments through the Energy Select Committee. After a short period of discussions and a very small number of amendments, the recommendations in the paper were put into the Energy Bill and Statutory Instruments. Later in the year, the Bill and its provisions became law. Unusually for any legislation, the Energy Bill was supported by all of the opposition parties. The Green Party MPs, previously anti-nuclear, were particularly enthusiastic. The Scottish National Party (SNP) with their canny attitude to money, immediately saw that income from their extensive hydro-electric generating facilities could prove a big earner for Scotland, and even more so if in the future, Scotland was an independent country.

The press and political editors in the media were not wholly enthusiastic or complimentary. Large areas of land had already been given over to solar farms and there was little enthusiasm for more. A charm offensive was needed to show that it was not good arable or building land that would be used. Local planning departments were asked to favour projects that used sub-standard sites, for instance next to a sewage works or recycling plants.

Since the ban on onshore wind farms was lifted in 2025, it was difficult to have a trip in the country without seeing a wind turbine or ten. The battle against offshore wind had been lost many years ago, but it was the countryside being polluted that seemed to upset some groups keen to protect the rural landscape. For many years, electricity pylons had looked like armoured soldiers marching into the distance. The addition of wind turbines, sleek though they did look, brought out the protesters in droves. The press, always ready to jump on a populist bandwagon, came out forcefully against wind farms in places of real beauty.

Housebuilders were required to dispense with gas for energy completely. The existing housing stock was another very different matter. Without a massive subsidy, the cost to a householder of replacing their heating, hot water and cooking with electric was almost impossible for ordinary people to contemplate. It was estimated that the cost of conversion for the average size house of 100 square metres would be £10,000. Over a period, some of this sum would be saved as gas was starting to get progressively more expensive than electricity, perhaps as a way to encourage the changeover. Julie asked Monica and Andrea how the government might fund the conversions by recruiting specialist teams to make the changes and offering a 50% subsidy to the householder. Assuming 20m households at a cost of an average of £5,000 each, the total cost over a 20 year conversion period was estimated at £100 billion, or £5 billion per annum.

The subject that generated the most ire was the programme of small nuclear power stations. The spectres of Three Mile Island, Fukushima, Chernobyl and more recently Kursk haunted every discussion. The press argued that the UK was a small country with densely populated areas. The really suitable places for nuclear reactors were in Wales and Scotland, but neither of these two countries were enthusiastic. Besides, when a Federal UK came to pass, then these countries would have a chokehold on power and might charge English customers ever increasing amounts for it.

The offer of free power would prove attractive for some, but many others were afraid of emissions, seen and unseen. A strong lobbying group of mothers and pregnant women came out strongly against having them anywhere near them ignoring the fact that their unborn children would be teenagers before any power was generated. It was decided that the quickest way of resolving this issue of siting was to go back to the well one more time and site them alongside existing sites.

Time was of the essence, as it always was on large infrastructure projects, so all planning decisions were authorised to be taken centrally. The quickest win was for solar power so the Energy Minister asked for site proposals from all local authorities with installations, within ninety days. If farmers were reluctant to proceed, compulsory purchase orders were threatened. Solar panels were now being produced from a site in Lancashire with UK plc backing and as the tempo of the installations increased so did the size of the factory and the workforce. A second factory was being constructed in Cornwall to serve the south-west.

By the end of 2036, British Solar Energy plc was in full production and employing four thousand people in a joint venture involving UK plc. There were no planning delays and the farmers had enthusiastically given up their worst arable land areas. The first two thousand conversions to electricity from gas had taken place and three nuclear sites had had their first spades going into the ground.

Chapter 33

Education, Science, Technology and Climate Change

2036

At the 1996 Labour Party conference, the future Prime Minister, Tony Blair stated that his three top priorities on coming to office were "education, education, and education". St Ignatius Loyola, the founder of the Jesuit Brotherhood, said "Give me a child till he is seven years old and I will show you the man." To humanity's error, for most of history, adults had paid little attention to the under-sevens. National Endeavour from the beginning had planned to take a holistic approach to education. The additional costs for the plans were underwritten in full. Julie's answer was that "the education of our children is more important than anything else so we will find the money". And she did. The teaching unions had not seen anything like it. "The best way to ensure that we have enough teachers, is firstly to offer them support so that they don't leave the profession. We do this by paying them the right salaries and by improving their working conditions." The number of teacher training places at universities was doubled.

National Endeavour, under Julie's guidance and insistence, developed plans to educate a child from the moment that it was born until it reached full time employment. The parent of every child was offered a nursery place at a subsidised cost and for the really needy, free of charge. All children were required to be toilet trained by the age of three and if they were not, social services interventions were mandatory. Early years teaching started gently at three years of age so all children were enrolled at a registered nursery class. National Endeavour did not allow home schooling and all schools had to be registered with the local authority. Faith schools were to be rigorously inspected and shut down if they did not offer a balanced curriculum. There were initial protests but in all aspects the rights and benefits for the child overrode all other arguments.

The pay review body was instructed to revise the teachers' and head teachers' pay scales to a level that made the profession attractive to undergraduates. The pledge was given that the scales would be enhanced annually by inflation.

The other reason that teachers gave up the profession was a toxic working environment. The problems came at them from both ends. The schools were over regulated and inspections emphasised negative outcomes. The other end of the problem were the children and their parents. Disruptive children and aggressive parents had forced out good teachers and Julie decided that this had to be stopped. Before a child entered a school, at least one of its parents was interviewed by the Head Teacher. At the end of this meeting, the parent was required to sign a form of contract concerning their own behaviour and that of their child. It was made clear that truancy and bad behaviour would result in their child being moved from the school to a new secure facility. Threatening behaviour by the parent would be followed by a visit from the police.

The new regime would identify failing schools and put in a plan to help them to improve, whereas good schools would be left alone until the next inspection. All Head Teachers would be mentored and trained in management practices.

Gillian Weston, the Education Minister, put great store on children attending a primary school close to their home. If, in rural areas, that distance was considerable, then transport would be provided. Attendance at school was mandatory and there was never a good non-medical excuse for not attending. Special arrangements were made for disabled students, who would have the ability to learn without holding their classmates back. Special classes were made available in every school with trained teachers to develop disabled pupils to the best of their abilities. All of this cost money, but money was never a reason for not doing the right thing. National Endeavour's mantra of "Do the right thing and you will receive the right thing" was never truer.

The movement from primary to junior school was planned to be seamless. Additional school buildings were to be provided in those places that up until then had separate facilities in different locations. Secondary school education had the buildings and the staffing, but required top quality head teachers. These individuals, now well paid, were not to be motivated by personal aggrandisement, but almost entirely by the success of turning out well mannered, skilled and socially minded adults. At an early stage, staff were tasked with finding the individual's skills and interests that could be encouraged. This meant identifying the ambitions of pupils and helping them to an academic or a vocational future.

Arts and crafts were encouraged alongside mathematics and all the sciences. A supportive environment was essential to educate in healthy lifestyles and eating habits, alongside team and individual sports. All students would be taught personal financial management, cooking, personal hygiene and how to develop and sustain relationships. This curriculum was a radical departure emphasising the preparation for adulthood, the world of work and personal responsibility. There was less emphasis on religious studies, languages and history other than recent political events. Computers were used for early learning but it was later at secondary schools that the curriculum majored in computer science, and programming.

Julie believed that in the future the difference between citizens was not where they were born or who their parents were. The difference should be the quality of education that they had received. The balancing of the budget and the ceasing of borrowing money to fund daily activities meant that the amount of interest paid on the National Debt started to reduce comparatively as the economy grew. She also unashamedly raided the International Aid budget when she was short of money to invest in education. A lot of people didn't like it, but she explained that "Aid should be given abroad only when there is surplus above the needs of our children."

Julie went on: "Another thing that has concerned me is the number of school truants, out of work teenagers and gang members. These are often referred to as NEETS. Not in education, employment or training. We need to know who they are. Not the numbers of them, but their names and addresses. Our objective must be to get them back into schooling or training for a job. These individuals are responsible for an overwhelming amount of petty crime, drugs supply, shoplifting and anti-social behaviour."

Julie remembered her first day at Exeter University and how overwhelming it all was. She didn't know anybody and although she had attended an open day, she couldn't remember too much about the campus. The site was large with so many buildings. Fortunately a kindly person directed her to the new students' reception area. All of the registration and financial details had been prepared online weeks before but "Freshers' Week" was an important rite of passage. After a few weeks everything had formed into a routine and the serious business, for her at least, of studying began. Julie quickly formed the view that university education was not for everyone. Some of her fellow students were there for the socialising and others to pursue their interests irrespective of whether a job would follow. Marine archaeology could be fascinating, but job opportunities were hard to find. She had spent one afternoon in the university library asking herself whether this education was a means to an end or the end in itself. Was all this effort that she was putting in going to gain her lucrative employment? Could she become a professional student and stay in the university system for years doing Masters Degrees and Doctorates?

All these years later, she understood that she shouldn't allow her experiences to formulate government policy? Surely, the way to devise policy is to take advice from experience. She had worked out even before leaving Exeter just exactly what was needed to make the learning at university a better experience. Lectures in the halls were fine but she got the most from one on one tutoring with her professor.

Sadly, the occasions it was on offer were rare. Her annual student fee was £14,500 then, goodness knows what it is now. Even at £14,500 she thought it poor value for some of the course. The three years could have been crammed into two with little sacrificed. Foreign students were paying astronomical sums for the same course so she was sure that it was poorer value for them.

She acknowledged that advances had been made for the safety of female students with zero tolerance policies adopted to promote best behaviour. Universities were again encouraged to be spaces for all ideas to be readily explored and freedom of speech was essential in places of learning. The student drinking and soft drug culture of even twenty years ago was now considered old-fashioned and the individual was expected to show more responsibility. In the end, the more a student put in to studying, the better the degree that was awarded. Over the years, it became accepted that university courses were not for everyone and now there were many alternatives. Many of the smaller institutions had merged with larger ones as the financials at smaller scale were no longer sustainable.

An area that had not been explored fully was a place for learning's involvement directly into a local business. Sandwich courses had been around for many years, but Julie was thinking of something more expansive. Day release had been established for vocational learning but what about a day a week in industry for university students taking business and engineering degrees?

Apprenticeships had had a colourful history. At one time it was a non-academic's route to employment as an artisan. The nation's plumbers, electricians, bricklayers, carpenters and even barristers worked a time served period of instruction, before being recognised as fully qualified. There was respect given to a person who had 'got their papers' and, in the really old days, became a member of their Guild. Periods of low employment meant that jobs were easily available so why work on low apprentice pay for five years? Being a plumber was less glamourous than a computer programmer and who wanted to repair somebody's blocked toilet? At a time when the demand for qualified tradespeople was at its highest, the numbers entering and completing apprenticeships was at its lowest. Unfortunately for National Endeavour, a big spike in people taking up apprenticeships was only going to produce results in approximately four years' time. Ideally, what was required was a cohort who had nothing to do at the present, who were keen to improve their prospects in four years' time and were able to learn full time. Who were these people and where were they? They were in prisons. All that was required was to provide the training, the facilities, the jobs and an early release upon qualification.

On coming to power, National Endeavour had set up UK S&T plc as its company wishing to provide seed and development capital as an enabler for technology and pharmaceutical companies. Its record had proved impressive so far. By scrapping the space project, admittedly to the big disappointment of people in that sector, large sums had been released for other scientific ventures. UK pharmaceuticals and precision medical instruments were world-leading and some small companies spun from Oxford and Cambridge universities were achieving unicorn status (worth more than £1bn). The five new battery plants were in various stages of completion, the first two being operative in the coming months. The ghost of Brexit had been laid to rest as the UK and EU had embarked upon joint scientific programmes. An unforeseen bi-product of UK S&T plc was that it had started to make money from its investments in start-ups. All of this money was siphoned into the education budget.

National Endeavour was firmly of the view that Science and Technology could be used for good causes like finding cures for diseases, but it could also be developed to protect the state and its citizens. Abuses in social media and internet trolling had been able to flourish as users were able to hide behind Internet Protocol (IP) addresses and Virtual Private Networks (VPNs). GCHQ had been given a new role and tasked with ensuring that on the Internet and in social media there were no hiding places for trolls and abusers. It was astonishing how popular these jobs were when they were advertised. Young people, closeted in their often smelly rooms suddenly became interested in working in teams online and developing programmes and algorithms. Who would have guessed that being talented in your hobby would result in a lucrative career for the government? Their successes were quick and meaningful. Within a month a small group, still working separately from inside their smelly bedrooms, had managed to track and reverse hack Russian groups providing an insight in the new leader's private apartments. A North Korean group suddenly found that they were responsible for shutting down their own communications network leaving them vulnerable to citizens openly crossing the border into South Korea and some misfiring of their nuclear facility. A meltdown was only just avoided.

Julie had lost none of her skill in communicating the news of every win to the public and Parliament. National Endeavour's lead in the opinion polls had never been higher but she could not escape the elephant in the room.

The UK had missed its Climate Targets for 2030 along with all of the other nations that had signed up to the accords. The planet had warmed by 1.85 degrees by 2030 exceeding the target of 1.5 degrees. Countries had failed to cut emissions by 45% compared to 2010 levels. What had followed the announcement of these failures was a blame game directed at the biggest polluters. Excuses were available citing forest fires, deforestation for agriculture, extreme climate conditions, the continuing burning of fossil fuels and wars. As a result, warmer atmospheres were measurably happening, the oceans were becoming more acidic and there was more rain and higher sea levels.

The country had committed to reach net zero by 2050, meaning that the total greenhouse gas emissions would be equal or less than emissions removed from the atmosphere. These lofty ambitions had been accepted in the early part of the century as achievable, but now in 2036, the clock was fast ticking down. The ambition to achieve 100% power generation from non-fossil fuels by 2035 had been missed. Coal burning power stations had stopped producing electricity in 2024, but wind and solar on a bad day had to be supported by burning gas. The same problem existed and would do so until nuclear power could provide for the times when the sun didn't shine and the wind didn't blow. The petro-chemical industry was adapting at pace into other areas and developing new industries based on plastics. Oil refining still took place to produce specialist oil products and fuels for aircraft.

The problem was global and solutions were only achievable if action were taken by all countries, especially the biggest polluters. The optics were really important because the public would understand the costs and sacrifices if they could see clearly a concerted approach, but there wasn't one. Julie read the latest 'doom and gloom' paper on the subject prepared by all of the experts and the news was bad. If the UK committed to the effort and money to achieve its own targets then it would make no difference at all to the planet because the other countries would miss their targets. So what to do?

Julie was talking out loud to nobody else in the room, throwing her arms up in despair. "What can I do, we do, to make it work? Why should we commit to the massive expenditure and disruption involved, by for instance insisting on an accelerated programme for the removal of gas from heating, when it will make no global difference? Gone are the days when the international moral high ground and good manners mattered for anything. Do we have enough prestige left, so if we said we were doing it anyway, it would persuade others to follow? Doubtful. If we do nothing and fail to meet our targets, are we no better than the rest? Who are the rest? According to this paper, everybody. If this paper is correct and we collectively fail, what will the world look like and be like to live in in thirty years? We've already seen fifty degrees centigrade in Spain and Greece. How bad could it get there and here?"

The answer to that question was contained in the Executive Summary.

In the event of a failure by over 75% of the total of greenhouse emitters to achieve net zero by 2050, the effect on the UK climate would be for hotter summers, higher and prolonged periods of rainfall as there would be more Atlantic storms, colder winters and stronger winds. Sea levels will rise making some coastal towns uninhabitable and there will be pronounced coastal erosion. There will be more inshore flooding of towns by rivers without flood management and alleviation areas. A particular concern would be the area around the river Severn, the county of Essex, The Fens and Lincolnshire. In the future, the climate might be described as bordering on sub-tropical. Farmers would need to change the crops grown and consider moving from dairy to arable farming. The effect globally would be more pronounced. Large areas of sub-Saharan Africa would be uninhabitable as temperatures exceeded 50 degrees for long periods. Droughts would make farming impossible. Populations would need to migrate to less stressful climate areas, probably northern Europe. Sea levels would rise and obliterate some island countries like The Maldives, Tuvalu, Kiribati, Nauru and Vanuatu. The UN has signalled that rising sea levels would badly affect China, India, Bangladesh and The Netherlands.

"Phew and gosh", thought Julie. "We are sleepwalking into a world disaster, so what could it take to wake everybody up? A disaster of unimaginable proportions." She decided that raising international awareness would be her next big project. She closed the report and trooped gloomily off to bed. "I could do with a cuddle in bed after reading that." Unfortunately for her it was not a Ralph day.

⊰◈⊱

Chapter 34

Culture, Media & Sport

Now that progress had been made on all of the urgent and important objectives, Julie was being pressured to devote attention to the nation's spare time activities. This was not easy for her as she had never been a hobby or sports person. She had enjoyed watching the Wimbledon Tennis Championships on the TV while in her teens. This was a golden age for British and world tennis with Federer, Nadal & Djokovic winning everything that Britain's Andy Murray didn't. She remembered very fondly, Sir Andy ending the Wimbledon jinx going back to Fred Perry's 1936 success, by lifting the trophy in 2013, then again in 2016.

She had studied Shakespeare's plays at school with little intention of carrying on being interested in them after she had left. Like all teenagers, modern music played a big part as the wallpaper to her youth, but since becoming a single mum life had swept everything aside. She had occasionally gone to the theatre, watched a little television and having seen an opera in Verona, her abiding memory was great venue but the opera left her cold. She was therefore not a person to get enthused about the Arts.

Fortunately for the country, there was a person in the government in charge of this Ministry who had more enthusiasm than many people combined. Chloe Temple-Sykes had rowed in the Cambridge Eight, was a patron of English National Opera and on the Board of The British Museum. She knew everything about the Arts and more importantly, what was good and deserving of investment and promotion. In 2034/5, The UK government spent just over £5.6bn on Cultural Services, the broad name for spending on the Arts, recreation and tourism. Of this sum, the Arts Council distributed about £500m to over 1,000 organisations such as music venues, galleries, museums, arts centres and libraries. Chloe, with her bright violet hair and hands festooned with bling jewellery, reported to the Executive Team that she had enough money for a comprehensive programme of support and enrichment, but that it was not always spent in support of National Endeavour's objectives and philosophy. Since the election of 2034 and her appointment as Minister she had carried out a fundamental review of every penny spent and was now in a position to make recommendations for 2037/8.

Chloe pointed to her first slide on the wall. It contained the following sentence, 'There has been little levelling up going on to date.' The papers supporting the presentation had been circulated two days previously and contained statistics, pie charts and spreadsheets. She was now presenting the Executive summary and her recommendations.

"We need to devote funds to enriching people's lives, promoting healthy lifestyles, supporting our national treasures and providing seed capital for local initiatives. Too much money in the past has been given to London and South-East based institutions, often prestige projects for elite entertainment. Just as our overseas aid budget has often missed the mark and given funds to rich countries, so the funding of Culture, Media and Sport has given too freely in the wrong direction.

"My recommendations are that we stop giving money to organisations which are profligate, that are capable of earning their own money or which produce events and exhibitions that most people don't want to see. As an aside, I received the quarterly programme for The Oxford Playhouse yesterday. There was nothing in it that I would recommend anyone see. I agree that we must support new and aspiring playwrights, but not every play for the season. The balance must be struck by providing popular entertainment because that puts 'bums on seats'.

"Our introduction of free entry to museums on production of identification and charging for overseas visitors has worked well. It has been estimated that there are about 2,500 museums in the UK, of which 1,800 are accredited institutions. I recommend that we support regional amalgamation of the smaller museums and provide financial support for this.

"We have so many beautiful paintings that are languishing in storage and not on display. We will provide funds to move these and for them to be put on display in public spaces and regional galleries. Every gallery should have a masterpiece, a painting that draws an audience. Believe me, we have enough Constables, Turners and Lowrys to go round.

"Since the BBC lost the licence fee income, a change made by the Conservative-led coalition government in 2030, it has progressed well under its new self-funding model. It now makes programmes that are commercially interesting for overseas buyers and has adapted well to advertising and sponsorship income. Its radio output has moved a little mainstream from its lofty objectives of educating us all, but the changes are not a matter for us to have any concern about. Local radio is now fully commercialised and along with all media, it is not favoured by the younger listeners, who have their own channels of entertainment. The rise of podcasts on every subject by everyone who wants a voice has been remarkable. Print newspapers continue to operate mainly by subscription online. The vast amounts of paper that were once used are a distant memory. We have maintained the freedom of the press in these difficult times. All in all the British media is in a good place but we have to be vigilant that other regimes do not sneak their corrupt messages in under our radar.

"I now move on to sport and our financial support of it. We long ago saw the distinctions between supporting professional sport, amateur sport and healthy sports promotions. We will continue with funding our elite athletes alongside National Lottery money. Our main focus is on promoting participation as an aid to a healthy lifestyle. I recommend that we pay the initial one month's public gym membership every year for the first 1 million applicants.

"Professional football does not need our money but it does need our oversight. Every one of the 116 clubs in the Premier League down to the National League are community ventures foremost. The owners, managers, players and staff come and go but always the fans remain. We will have a junior minister responsible for ensuring that all clubs are managed sustainably and our aim is that all of the stadia are designated perpetual assets of community value. This means that permission will never be granted for them to be sold unless a replacement is already in place. It also means that the club and its stadium are linked and cannot be separated. The clubs can improve their grounds but they are effectively owned by a fan's trust, meaning that they sit on a balance sheet as 'nil value'. It also means that in the future, the value of these football grounds cannot be used as collateral for loans taken out by the club owners."

Chloe paused for a mouthful of water from a glass on the table. "Nearly finished," she said. "We thought that we had solved the issue of ticket touts long ago but technology allows some individuals and ticketing companies to hoover up tickets using computer bots. We can't prevent a person selling on their ticket if they discover that they can't attend the event. My focus is on the large scale purchasing of tickets that are then offered at highly inflated prices. I recommend that we pass a Bill to make the venue financially liable for the ticketing of the event. The rule will be that a maximum of four tickets can be purchased by any credit or debit card and confirmation will be sent to only one email address for each performance. For the venue it means a lot of manual interference, but they are selling expensive tickets so they can afford it. That's it, me done. All of the recommendations are in the paper."

Julie said, "Thank you Chloe. Any questions?"

There then followed a small number of questions and after them, Chloe's proposals were unanimously approved. A Culture, Media & Sports Bill was presented to Parliament and became law.

Imagine the surprise of the trustees of Gainsborough House Art Gallery when they were advised that a Gainsborough painting, previously languishing in a store room at the National Gallery in London, was heading their way.

Similar positive reactions bordering on ecstasy were heard from Kirkcudbright Galleries in Dumfries & Galloway, the Museum of Modern Art in Machynlleth, Powys, the Piers Arts Centre, in Stromness, Orkney and many others who all received masterpieces connected to their surroundings and histories. Viewing figures at these galleries increased as local people were intrigued to see the new arrivals.

The Oxford Playhouse, having been singled out for criticism, included an Alan Ayckbourn play in its next programme and sold out all of its seats for the first time in years. Who would have thought it?

Chapter 35

Richard Montgomery

2nd December 2036

At precisely 7.13am on Tuesday 2nd December 2036 a loud boom was heard at the BBC building in Central London just as they were in the middle of broadcasting the Today programme. News started coming through from forty miles away of a major disaster unfolding. The SS Richard Montgomery, a wrecked American Liberty cargo ship on the Nore Sandbank in the Thames Estuary near Sheerness, in Kent had finally carried out the threat that it had posed since 20th August 1944, when its cargo of over 1,400 tonnes of munitions ignited.

On that fateful day during the Second World War, the ship, moored and full of explosives, dragged its anchor and ran aground on the sandbank. When the tide went out the ship broke its back. Three days later the crew and a munitions company started to remove the hazardous cargo, but the ship's hull cracked open further and the bow end flooded. The salvage operation continued into September when the ship was finally abandoned. The vessel had broken in two in the middle, still with much of its dangerous cargo inside. The wreck had sunk to a depth of about fifty feet and leaning to starboard. At all states of the tide the three masts were clearly visible above the water. The wreck was constantly monitored and cordoned off from the busy Thames maritime traffic.

Julie was awoken by the dull sound of the blast. She turned her bedside lamp on and immediately called the emergency security number. "What was that noise?" she enquired. The reply was that information was still coming in but it was a major incident.

"Is it terrorist related?"

"No information yet on that ma'am."

Julie quickly got dressed and asked the senior night civil servant to rouse her Executive Team Members and the Joint Chiefs of Staff, Heads of MI5 and MI6 for a COBRA meeting. The wheels of government were now quickly turning and information was being fed to Julie along with her breakfast of toast and marmalade.

It was quickly established that the incident had occurred in the Thames Estuary off of a place called Sheerness. There was extensive damage in Sheerness and other towns around the estuary. There was no tidal threat to London but a quick thinking operative had caused the Thames Barrier to raise. As soon as he saw the bright flash down river, he activated it fearing a tidal surge inundating central London. Soon Julie received the news that the SS Richard Montgomery had exploded while work was being undertaken to remove its three masts.

When they were all gathered in the COBRA room, the group were addressed by Deputy Commissioner Jagger of the Metropolitan Police. "Just after 7am this morning, the almost fully sunken ship SS Richard Montgomery exploded killing all fourteen workers on the tender alongside as they were preparing for the day's work. The locality in and around Sheerness has been seriously damaged and a tsunami has caused damage in Southend, Canvey Island, Westcliff-on-Sea and Shoeburyness. In Sheerness, there are reports of fatalities from flying glass and a small residential building has collapsed. Three people are recorded to have died after having heart attacks. According to the latest information, debris and a 280 metres wide column of water were thrown over a mile and a half into the air, fortunately most, but not all of it, vertically. A five metre wave was generated which has caused extensive local flooding and damage. Damage has been caused to many boats moored on the river and at the port at Tilbury, one ship lost two containers into the river. No ships traversing the estuary were damaged in the incident. As you can imagine, updated reports are arriving all the time. Fortunately the gas terminals sited along this stretch of river were decommissioned some years ago."

"Thank you Commissioner," said Julie. "Anybody know why the explosives haven't been removed before now?"

Admiral Blackmore stood and said "One of the reasons was the unfortunate incident of a similar operation in 1967. A cargo ship carrying explosives that sank off Folkestone in 1946 was having works carried out ahead of a munitions removal when it exploded with a force equivalent to a medium power earthquake. There were no fatalities. There were a few injuries but this ship was about four miles from land and in deeper water. After this, dealing with the Montgomery was put into the "too difficult" box.

"Do we know yet what caused today's explosion?" Julie asked.

The Admiral rose again. "Since 2020 a plan had been formulated to remove the ship's three masts as they were placing a strain on the ship's weakening structure. The Ministry of Defence was keen to get the work done and contractors were sought to assist the navy specialists. Every time since then, as work was scheduled to start, situations arose to delay the plans. Later inspections showed that the masts had deteriorated and metal objects had been discovered around the wreck. An inspection of the wreck three years ago showed that it was on the point of collapse so it became urgent to make the wreck stable. The removal of the masts was the first step."

Information was now being relayed into the meeting from the emergency services, of whom there were many on site. The town of Sheerness was the worst affected. Almost every window and glass door had been shattered by the force of the blast. There were extensive reports of people injured from flying debris and glass imploding into homes. All phone and internet communications were down as their masts had been destroyed. There was some connectivity through satellites. In addition to the residential buildings, a large office block in the town was severely damaged and a retail park on the outskirts was largely destroyed. There were reports of looting and the police were taking firm action and arrests had been made. Had the explosion occurred even one hour later, the casualty numbers would have been alarmingly worse. Most of the residents were still in their beds.

Julie asked Andrea Patel if contingency funds were available for the worst damaged areas. "No problem with that Prime Minister, I'll get the Treasury working on a good response."

"Can we designate this a State of Emergency and get the newly formed National Guards into the affected towns to help clear the debris and clean up the worst damage?"

Tom Blandford said, "I will liaise with the others and co-ordinate a quick response."

"Very quickly please," said Julie. "I will be off to the area soon after this meeting. Sir Edward, please clear my diary."

"Yes, Prime Minister."

Later reports confirmed that due to the natural path of the river and its currents and tides, the tsunami of water mostly flooded areas designed to take tidal inundation.

Throughout the day the death toll rose. Julie's visit to the area was welcomed by the shocked residents. In Sheerness, she had never seen destruction like it. "This is what the East End of London must have looked like during the Blitz in the Second World War," she thought. Total devastation. She pledged to have a memorial erected in the town to the lives lost after the centre had been reconstructed. She also visited Southend, Westcliff and the other places affected by the large waves of water. On her journey back to London, she took a phone call from President Amal Clooney in Washington offering her condolences and some financial assistance, which was declined graciously. "Even though this ship was built in your country, we should have dealt with this years ago so this is down to us," she told her.

The final cost of not dealing with this ship and wishing the problem away was one hundred and twenty lives. The initial estimates for the damage was £800m and not all of it covered by insurance. The final sum spent from the contingency fund was £280m. The clear-up using asylum applicants, the newly formed Kent and Essex National Guards of thirty-two members from each, Category 2 prisoners from a local facility in Chatham and the out of work locals, took over a year. On the anniversary of the explosion, a Memorial Service was held in Rochester Cathedral. Unfortunately, as we shall discover, Julie Carter was unable to attend the ceremony.

The one benefit was that a ship that had proved a hazard for nearly a century was at last neutralised, opening discussions on the siting of a new airport for London. Up until that morning the airport was always a hostage to the fragility of the ship.

In the evening, before Julie sat down for dinner, she called Sir Edward Grey. "Good evening Edward. Who was Richard Montgomery?"

"I looked him up."

"Of course, you did."

"He was born on 2 December 1738 in Ireland and served in the British Army. He later became a Major General in the US Continental Army and fought for the US against the British in the American Revolutionary War."

"Thank you and good night."

"Good night Prime Minister."

Julie turned to Ralph and said "No two days are the same, except the nights are when I end up here with you at the end of them."

Chapter 36

Keep Your Friends Close

2037

What is a friend? The Concise Oxford Dictionary (not very concise as it contains nearly a quarter of a million words) defines a friend as 'one joined to another in intimacy and mutual benevolence independent of sexual or family love'. 'My wife is my best friend' cannot be correct according to this dictionary. Makes you wonder what intimacy can mean in the narrowest sense. Anyway, we all understand the 'mutual benevolence'.

How many friends *can* a Prime Minister have? How many friends *does* a Prime Minister have? Julie as a single parent had a few other mothers from Elm Park as friends, but since she moved to Didcot her life had been consumed by politics, first by getting elected as an MP then as a party leader and Prime Minister. Friendship is like a plant. If you neglect to nurture it, then it withers away. Julie, like all of us, would admit to being friendly with a lot of people but not many of them were friends. The modern idea of friendship is to count the followers on social media. If that were Julie's case she would in 2037 have over six million friends. As we get older, apart from our families, we would be lucky to have four real friends.

If a friend is someone who you can tell a secret and make them promise not to tell another and they keep that promise, then none of us have any friends. 'I only told my wife or husband.' 'I can keep a secret, it's the people that I tell that can't.'

Perhaps a friend is measured in support and help. A friend will lend you money when you are desperate, but that act of kindness will inevitably lead to the friendship's injury or end. The power dynamic

373

has changed and when someone says "forget it" then you both know that it cannot be and will not be.

A friend is someone who you can share a difficult moment and explain to them your diagnosis of a terminal illness. Such a disclosure is a terrible weight for a friend to bear. How does your friend respond to you when you tell them that you are going to die? How much sympathy is the right amount before it is overwhelming? Can your friend receiving this news keep pace with the change in your deteriorating condition? Do you catch a glimpse from your friend that looks like they think that your illness is transmittable? Do you expect a friend to stay by you until the end? Not everyone is born a natural carer.

Should a friend love you for who you are and not what you do, until what you are doing ruins the friendship? "I know that as a true friend you will understand and forgive me for sleeping with your daughter." I don't think so.

What about a friend with benefits in the common parlance? "Hi dear. I need to tell you something and as a friend I know that you will understand. At that Las Vegas conference that I attended, I slept with a local hooker and I think that I may have the clap." That's a tricky one and might slightly harm any friendship with benefits going forward, especially if you've had unprotected benefits sex with the friend before having your bits inspected at the clinic.

Friendship is never equal between friends. One person almost always wants to keep it going or nurture it more than the other. "I always call you and you never call me." "You want to go to places that are too expensive for me and I can't accept your offer of money again." "Your other friends don't like me." Friendship is competitive. "I share in your good fortune and I am so pleased that you have done so well." Gore Vidal nailed it well when he wrote, "Every time a friend succeeds, I die a little." A cynic's view of friendship is that "A friend in need is a pain in the arse, get rid of them."

When you are lonely, you will do anything, agree to anything and give everything to have someone to call a friend. In the Gospel of John,

15.13, the ultimate expression of friendship is "Greater love hath no man than this, that a man lay down his life for his friends." There are instances recorded of this sacrifice, but because it is so beautiful in a human way, it has been scarce. The awarding of a Victoria Cross or a George Cross often follows such a sacrifice.

Julie had no friends unless you call her lover a friend. The closest thing to a friendship that she did have was with Sir Edward Grey at work. He was the first person to believe in her but they could never get beyond the power dynamic. She was his boss. In the past, it was suggested that over 50% of marriages were between people who had met each other at work. Inviting a work colleague on a date now had the real jeopardy of getting you fired. Workplace banter is fraught with downside possibilities and must now be avoided at all costs. Sharing a joke with a work colleague can be very tricky and risky. A news channel reported that a person recently got fired for meeting someone online and it was later discovered that they worked for the same firm on different floors.

Julie had a brief friendship with Yin Lu, a Chinese lady, who later turned out to be a spy. Julie's position made her vulnerable to chancers. So it was with some surprise to everyone when she announced that she had a date with Ralph Austin, a journalist from The Sunday Times. She had met him when doing a one-to-one political piece and profile, and they hit it off. He asked for a follow up interview and then another. Before long they realised a mutual attraction and he was invited to Chequers and the flat above 11 Downing Street. Alarm bells were ringing throughout the communications directorate as journalists were notorious for not drawing lines of distinction between casual remarks off the record and printable quotes. This could not be a proper friendship or a developing relationship without the glare of the public spotlight. Julie trusted him to keep the wall between his job and their meetings but others did not. Paranoia was not very far away.

They decided early on that the relationship, as it now was, could not be kept a secret as it was newsworthy to all of the other media. Ralph decided to take a six months sabbatical from his job to write a book.

This seemed like a good compromise and it also enabled him to be the significant other at formal dinners and prime ministerial walkabouts.

Julie's mood had changed since meeting Ralph. She was now more relaxed and enjoyed sharing some matters with another person with a political mind. On two occasions he counselled her on the content of a statement, which turned out to be very good advice. He was particularly helpful as she prepared for the 2036 National Endeavour Party Conference. After the six month's sabbatical ended, Ralph resigned from his job and was successful at having his first novel accepted. How much the publishers took into account his ongoing relationship with the Prime Minister was open to scrutiny, but sometimes that's the way serendipity works. The book was a moderate success. It didn't earn him as much as his lost salary but he was encouraged to write a follow up. The publishers really wanted a novel about political intrigue but he resisted the obvious pitfall of that suggestion and wrote a novel set in the 19th century slums of London instead.

Ralph was 52 years old, divorced with two grown up boys, both at University, one in York and the other at Warwick. He had a flat in Clerkenwell, a gentrified district in central London. Ralph did have friends, four very close ones. Before meeting Julie he had been on holidays with them, on one occasion, all five of them on the same all male trip to Ibiza. They usually met every Friday at The Devonshire Arms close to the Postal Museum near his flat. After seeing Julie for nearly a year he suggested that she join them there one Friday.

Her security detail went ballistic at the idea. The stipulation of the pub being emptied was not practical nor was another idea that everyone in the pub had to be cleared by security beforehand. In October 2015, Prime Minister Cameron had popped in with the President Xi of China for a pint at a pub near Chequers. Just a casual pint with twenty agents from each side pretending to be locals.

Julie was adamant that she deserved to have a private life. After a security briefing, she later accepted that she couldn't, because public scrutiny couldn't be avoided. She settled on a compromise and Ralph invited his four friends for a weekend at Chequers, all of them staying over for one night so that Julie would get a chance to meet them properly.

So it was on a Saturday in September, a month before the 2036 Party Conference in Scarborough, when Ollie Shaw the architect, Julian Street the investment banker, Richard 'Robbo' Robinson the doctor and Arthur Evans the teacher, joined their mate Ralph in a large black car that made its way to Chequers, the Prime Minister's retreat in Buckinghamshire. The SUV carrying the friends was escorted from London by two police cars. "There's no cocktail bar in the car," said Julian. "What a disappointment."

"Look lads," said Ralph. "We are all on our best behaviour here. Arranging for you to meet Julie has not been easy and security will be massive. Do not drink too much, do not steal anything, even the monogrammed toilet roll, if it is. This is not a stag do, so be respectful of the staff and keep the language clean. Not too much Anglo-Saxon."

"We don't need lessons on being civilized," said Robbo. "I'm going to take some photos because my kids will not believe this trip. Will there be any other members of the Cabinet there?"

"Firstly, I have been warned that all mobile phones and cameras will be taken from you at the door and only returned for the journey home. The other guests will be Sir Edward and Lady Estelle Grey and a lot of big security blokes following your every move," said Ralph with a smile. "However, I am sure that you will have no complaints about the wine and I hear that the brandy on offer was once in the cellar of Emperor Napoleon III of France."

The cars arrived at Chequers and just as Ralph had said, the mobile phones were taken away and stored. While in the hands of security they were all accessed and their history and social contacts recorded. As a result of this, special security attention was given to Robbo without him noticing. After they had been directed to their rooms, freshened up and unpacked, they were all told to meet in the large drawing room at 5pm for drinks and introductions. They all arrived in good time and at 5.05pm, Julie entered and shook hands with each of them. Over drinks, she, accompanied by Ralph holding her right hand, spent a little time with each of them and asked about their families and general social habits.

Arthur later described this first meeting to his partner George. "When she came into the room, I was struck by how she looked. Not the way she dressed, not the way her hair was done, but the way she looked. There was a radiance about her face that you just don't see on the telly. I couldn't take my eyes from her. She glided in like she was on wheels and when she spoke to me, my mouth suddenly went dry and I was like a kid again. Her smile was the prettiest thing that I ever saw. It drew you in and her eyes sparkled. I can see why she commands attention. If this is not what I call charisma, then I don't know what is. At the point that she shook my hand, I would have shot myself in the face if she had asked me to."

"You're having me on", said George. "Anyone would think that you are on the turn."

"For me it wasn't a sexual longing that she inspired, but I'm not sure about the other three. Each of us in the car home seemed in a daze."

"So what happened after the introductions and you not shooting yourself," said George.

"We were poured drinks expertly by a butler type. I had a perfect gin and tonic in a large blue bowl glass. We were then joined by Sir Edward and Lady Estelle Grey. She liked being called Lady Estelle, but he was just a normal bloke really without any airs and graces. She had enough for both of them. We went into dinner and I sat next to Ralph on this round table and Julian sat opposite the Prime Minister. He couldn't take his eyes from her and hardly ate a thing. The meal was not a banquet, but modest with a starter of asparagus, main course of roast lamb and a sticky desert followed by cheese, which I didn't have as I was too full. The white wine was a Sancerre, the red wine a good Burgundy and the port, if you wanted it and you would have, was a 1977 vintage Sandeman. We then went back to the drawing room for brandy, which was just as Ralph said, unbelievably good. The Greys retired about 9.45pm and Julie went up at ten. Ralph slinked off just afterwards, which of course fooled no-one. A couple of large security guys came in about 10.30pm and suggested that it was time to retire. It's funny how a casual suggestion can be made with a hint of menace. Anyway, it had been a long day, so we went to our rooms. Julian was very quiet throughout the evening, but he did loosen up a bit after a couple of brandies. There's no doubt that meeting Julie had had a profound effect on him.

"The next morning we all met for breakfast at nine and after short goodbyes, we were reunited with our phones, I expect with some spy software that wasn't there before, and we sped off in the cars. Julie waved us away at the door her arm in Ralph's and I saw the Greys upstairs looking from the window."

"Did you see the way that Julian looked at Julie," said Estelle, while peering at the disappearing car. "I thought that he was about to have an accident in his trousers. I've not before seen a grown man dribble like he did at dinner when she spoke about her plans for the coming week. The red wine made a nasty stain on his dress shirt. Smitten is the word my mother would use in these circumstances."

"You're imagining it. Why does there always have to be a drama with you? They all seemed like perfectly normal professional chaps with impeccable manners. The port was good, wasn't it?"

"I didn't have any, but you had my share so that's alright isn't it? Julie was in good form. I've not seen her so animated for a while. Ralph is good for her. I wonder if it is serious and going somewhere. Who knows?"

"I've got a meeting with her downstairs at half-past ten so you will need to entertain Ralph. Does he ride horses? If not, there is a carriage. It's a nice day for a trip around the grounds."

Bang on the agreed time Sir Edward met with Julie in the drawing room and helped himself to a coffee from the stand on the sideboard. "The Party Conference?" he said.

Julie said, "Before we start on that, what did you think about Ralph's friends?"

"All nice chaps, but wasn't Julian a bit too smitten with you? He spent most of the evening with his mouth open."

"I don't usually have that effect on people, but it was noticeable wasn't it? Actually a bit creepy in a way. Enough of him, let's talk about Scarborough. This year it could be a big one. It's not the last one before the election if we go to the full term but it might be if we go to the polls earlier."

"Why would we go earlier?"

"Because we haven't succeeded building enough houses and that was our big Manifesto commitment and the Opposition will major on it as a failure and broken promise."

Sir Edward helped himself to another cup of coffee. "You've done everything else and the country is in great nick. Crime is down, unemployment is down, immigration is under control and the budget is balanced. The regions have benefitted from additional help and the federal system in Scotland and Wales is ready and we're all pretty sure that it will work well for them. You worry too much."

"I do but we need some real progress on housebuilding everywhere."

"Another good reason not to think of an early election. Take all the time that you need. The signs are that there will be a big increase in the numbers over the next eighteen months."

"I guess you're right", Julie said. "Ah, Estelle and Ralph have returned from their buggy ride. Let's have some fun before lunch as I have to return to London soon after. You can stay on if you want."

"Why not?" Sir Edward said. "I'm in Estelle's good books at the moment and I see advantage in that."

The next time that Julie met Ralph's friends, this time with their spouses and partners, was at Chequers on Boxing Day. They had a good lunch, played Christmas games, Jamie drank whisky and disappeared to his upstairs toilet and Margaret got the hump over something that

Julian said. She thought that it wasn't appropriate. Julie was a little concerned when it became obvious that Julian was flirting with her, his friend's partner. Friendship is tricky but love distorts everything.

Chapter 37

No Housing for All

1st January 2037 was a day for reflection in the Carter household. Julie was sitting in a comfortable armchair at Chequers opposite Ralph, who had spent the entire festive season with the family. He was now firmly ensconced as her other half, a situation that had been mutually agreed just before the annual conference of the party in 2036, held in Scarborough. He had given up his job as a journalist, an impossible job when you are dating the country's Prime Minister. He was now writing another book. Peter Cook, the brilliant comedian, once replied to a friend who said that he was writing a book: 'Nor am I'. Probably the funniest three words ever spoken.

Jamie was in his room with his new games console reflecting on how awful he had felt on the day after Boxing Day having sneaked a drink of whisky from one of the decanters in the drawing room. A rather large drink as it turned out and he had spent a good part of that afternoon with his head in the white toilet bowl upstairs.

Julie's mother Margaret had returned to her house in Didcot after a small difference of opinion with Julie about Ralph's friends, who had come up with their partners and spouses for Boxing Day. In particular Margaret thought that Julian had shown less respect to Julie than was appropriate and that the other men had drunk too much. "It's a good job that Ralph doesn't have to report to his previous paper what those louts were up to," she said in Ralph's hearing after they had all gone. Julie and her mother decided to spend New Year separately. A normal family Christmas then.

Julie was in a reflective mood, empty coffee cup on the table in front of her and rain beating on the windows preventing a walk in the grounds. The Party Conference had been a triumph, so different from the year before in Liverpool. She had strode up onto the stage and called out all of the party's successes for the year. This was not an occasion to be modest about her and their achievements. Almost uniquely for the party in power, for the third successive year their popularity in the polls had increased and everything was looking good. The party members had behaved well and most of the MPs had stayed out of the limelight for the wrong reasons. There was an occasional misstep with trust in an individual's competence and loyalty sadly misplaced. Some others had bloomed when given the oxygen of space and time and their good works had improved so many lives. Never was it truer than it was said that 'we all suffer the consequences of our choices'. The country had chosen National Endeavour, and Julie in particular, and she in turn had chosen her people and the policies and had seen the consequences of all that.

The biggest event of 2036 had been the catastrophe of the SS Richard Montgomery exploding its cargo of explosives in the Thames Estuary off Sheerness. The clean-up continued and the total cost of everything so far was now nearly a billion, money the country didn't have, but fortunately Lloyds of London did for most of it. Julie mused on that number, a billion. A number often bandied about as though it was not really significant. The country used to measure amounts in millions but due to inflation and larger more complex projects, the measurement was now in billions.

A billion was a large number. A million seconds was about twelve days, but a billion seconds is over thirty-one years. The National Debt is now measured in trillions. A trillion seconds is over thirty-one thousand years, three times the time of human's measured history.

"Easy for the mind to go off on a tangent", she thought sitting in her comfy chair watching the rivulets of water falling down the window in the corner of the room.

Julie poured herself another coffee from the jug on the table and looked at Ralph to see if he wanted more. He was asleep and snoring almost silently. "Poor Ralph," she thought with a smirk. "I've worn him out."

She brought the cup to her lips and mused, "It is right that we have elections every five years maximum. Governments run out of steam and everything needs refreshing. Back in 2034, we were shocked to win and the large majority meant that we could do what we wanted to do, and we did. From a standing start, we changed the country, mostly for the better. The annus horibilis of 2033 showed us what we had to do and we did it. Those first 100 days set the pace and we were relentless.

I suppose it is summed up by the first year being planning and doing the urgent stuff and clearing away the past. The second year is putting the strategies and detailed plans into action and sorting out the finances. We balanced the Budget by good housekeeping. Mr. Micawber at his best and the result is happiness. The third year is the fine tuning and keeping the plans on course and now as we enter the fourth year it will be steady as she goes and preparing for the next election. The process of government is actually very tedious and in a way processional.

The important stages are the beginning, when there is all the enthusiasm and passion for change and then at the end when it is time to reflect on the successes and failure. This is the essence. We all start with the vision and thoughts then end with the accomplishments for good or bad." She reflected on one decision that she would always be remembered for. She had found the £1 billion from somewhere to push through the Bill to extend the HS2 railway line from Euston to St. Pancras to connect seamlessly with the Eurostar service. 600m of railway line that, when finished, would allow passengers to travel from Manchester or Birmingham to Paris without changing trains. Her decision on levelling up had already secured the extension from Birmingham to Leeds and work on that would be starting soon. Infrastructure is what governments leave to the next generations. "Each government must leave something" was a mantra that she had always believed.

She closed her eyes in the memory of what had troubled her for too long now. She was pleased with everything and couldn't have wished for better with just one exception, and it might be that exception that could prove to be her undoing. She knew that on National Endeavour's biggest promise she had failed to deliver. Her government had not provided the housing that the manifesto had promised. Admittedly, they did bring a lot of empty properties back into use and in the process managed to house almost all of the homeless families and a great number of single people. She silently reminded herself, "We have provided the future possibility of local people in holiday hotspots being able to buy in their towns by introducing the cap of 10% on holiday lets and second homes. The very large increases in Council Tax have put a lot of properties on the market at prices coming down to the level affordable by local people. All of these measures were important but we did not address the large number of people, mostly younger, wishing to buy their own homes. Could we have done more and could we have been bolder?"

Julie was now in full thought mode and she picked up her phone to record the next bit for her New Year's address to the nation that she was scheduled to give the following week. "When we came into office, the estimated level of housing shortage was over 3 million units. The most that any government before us had managed to build was 300,000 units annually and that number for only a couple of years. At that sustained rate of building it would have taken us ten years and we are not yet fully three years in. Our problem was that we had a standing start. There was not enough land available, not enough qualified crafts people, a shortage of materials and we had to persuade all of the major housebuilders that our plans would be profitable for them.

"We have started on eight new towns with two more agreed. A further two are now planned. Next year some of the early apprentices will become fully qualified and be added to the workforce. The asylum pool did produce a lot of labourers and a significant number of trades people and their integration, often with supervision, was a good result. In the UK, we now make 40% of all goods that are used in houses, and this number will rise as new factories gear up their supply. We have a lesser number of trucks clogging our roads and our imports are much reduced. Unemployment is now down to 3.1% as the new jobs have been taken up by the long term unemployed and school leavers."

Julie reflected on what more could have been done and spoke into the recorder. "In 2034, we barely changed the numbers from the previous coalition and 180,000 houses were completed. In 2035 we got the wheels turning and upped the figure to 250,000, a good increase on the year before but not enough. The legal challenges to our land acquisition programme delayed us a little but the outcome was never in doubt. When our lawyers pointed out the deficiency in the law that would scupper our plans, we just passed a new law allowing our plans to progress. In 2036 we broke the 300,000 barrier for the first time, just. This year we expect to add 350,000 to the stock, mostly in affordable units, terraced houses and apartments for single and couples without families. We still have a long way to go and in this Parliament we will not have achieved our aim of giving everybody wanting a home their chance to take that first and important rung on the housing ladder. The best that we can do is ask the electorate for another term to finish the job."

Another sip of coffee. "My speechwriters won't like that. It is too apologetic and allows our critics to agree with us that we failed. In footballing terms, a bit of an own goal. On the other hand, our message is always that if you don't try, then you can't succeed. I guess we can use that old hackneyed phrase 'we have learned from our mistakes'. Our biggest mistake was looking too far into the skies and not seeing how far away the stars were. We were over-ambitious and allowed our dreams to interfere with our reality. I was always a dreamer and on that note, it is time for a walk." She finished her coffee and gave Ralph a smack on the shoulder. "The rain has stopped and we are going for a walk. This place is driving me stir crazy."

On the way out, she asked one of the security men to keep an eye on Jamie. The whisky bottle was now secured in the locked cabinet, although it would be ten years before he tried it again, and then he would hate it.

She and Ralph enjoyed their day and watched a film together in the evening: 'Fast & Furious 23.' They retired early but during the night, she woke with a start and looked at the clock. Oh no, it's 3.20am again. She instantly recalled the message, if that is what it was. "Julie, you did good, lots of it. Rest long and well". She smiled to herself and rested her head on the pillow and dropped off in no time.

Chapter 38

The Ghost of John Bellingham

15th October 2037

Everything in the garden was rosy, not literally because it was mid-October and the blooms were past their best. Julie was sitting in the Rose Garden of 10 Downing Street with a cup of coffee and wrapped up in a warm fleece. The party conference in Birmingham had been a triumph, both inside the hall and in the country at large. All of her team had performed at their peak and it reinforced to her what fine choices all of them had been from the start. Two of them, Hillary and Tom, had had their rocky moments at the beginning, but she had never thought of replacing them. Each had come to Chequers with their partners and children and over a quiet walk and talk in the grounds everything had been smoothed out. Julie was good at the pep talk, because she led by example and had perspective. She was an inspired problem solver. When presented with a tricky issue, she could quickly see the alternatives for resolution and she unfailingly chose the right one.

Her conference speech had been written by Sam Secombe, her main writer. He had a talent for conveying the nuances for which Julie had become notable. His first draft was near perfect and with a small number of humanity insertions, Julie had perfected it. The cadences with classical references and amusing anecdotes flowed seamlessly through the text until the climax was instantly followed by applause and a standing ovation. The main message was that of revitalising the project. "We are not running out of ideas, we are not running out of steam." She had news on a new impetus to housing, manufacturing and paying down the National Debt. "It was not for our grandchildren that we borrowed the money and spent it, so it is up to us to start paying it back and not leaving it for them." She liked that sentence and it drew a big round of applause. She had plans for decreasing truancy beyond what had already happened, increasing apprenticeships, and she told them that she had not forgotten her promise to university graduates, to get a job related to their degree, although that did mean restricting access to some courses. "There are only so many jobs for rare plant biologists." That one drew laughter in the hall. She spoke again that there was a need for more doctors and nurses trained in our hospitals and colleges.

The press didn't know how to be critical of something that was so measured, honest and inspiring. "She's done it again" was on the front page of The Sun. "Small in stature, large in heart, massive in delivery" boomed The Mail on page three. "The markets moved upwards after her every word" from The Financial Times. The latest polls showed National Endeavour heading for another landslide victory, and if the results were to follow the predictions, bigger than at the last election.

Throughout 2037, Ralph continued to be a great support and her love for him was growing. He had become firm friends with Jamie and the three of them together felt like a family. Ralph was a good role model and Jamie wanted to spend time with him. When Julie was busy, Ralph took Jamie to watch Oxford United as that was his local team. Her mother Margaret finally gave him her stamp of approval so in Julie's mind that squared the circle. He was kind and considerate and always looking to please her while accepting her role as Prime Minister took preference over their plans. After the conference Ralph had given her a gift of a painting, not an original but a fine print, that she proudly hung on the wall of her bedroom. It was called "Behold the White Horse" by Judi Jordan. When she saw it a phrase came to her mind, but she was unable to recall it.

Julie was content and started to see a life beyond politics. She occasionally met Ralph's friends as he remained close with them. At the last meeting, Julian announced that he was getting divorced and was looking for a new place to live. Julian started seeing more of Ralph and soon became a regular visitor. He also went with Ralph and Jamie to the football. The security detail tried to be as discreet as they could insisting that the trio went to a hospitality box at the stadium reserved for them. Julie realised that after leaving politics she would be unable to return to living at her mother's house in Didcot and she would need to find a property offering more privacy. She understood the need to have a home properly protected from nuisance callers and even those intent on doing her or her family members harm. She had asked a prestigious Oxfordshire estate agents to keep an eye open for a period house in grounds with a long drive. They had made a few suggestions but none of them proved suitable. All of her predecessors as Prime Ministers had managed a lucrative career in public speaking after their time in office. There was a ready market for the publishing of memoirs, so she was sure that she would be able to afford something appropriate but not too grand.

She sat back in her garden seat and took another sip of coffee. Who would have thought that the UK, the sick economy of Europe in 2034, could be so transformed by 2037? The UK was now the only major economy to be reducing its National Debt in absolute terms yet enjoying reducing taxation and improving public services. Scholars around the world were documenting the decisions taken and politicians of all parties were looking to emulate the success. In comparison with other European economies, the UK tax take was rising without raising taxes from the ordinary citizen and the welfare budget was falling even though the worthy poor were receiving more help. There was some talk gathering that Julie Carter might be nominated for the Nobel Prize in Economics.

What was that phrase that was in the back of her mind for that painting given to her by Ralph? She looked at it every day and was sure of an allegory attached to it. She must Google it or get someone to do it. Who was the classical scholar in her government? He or she would know what it was.

The thought went from her mind as she was summoned back from the garden for her latest meeting with Indira Singh and Chloe Temple-Sykes, the Minister for Culture Media and Sports.

"Good morning, Prime Minister" they said in unison as she entered the room.

"What can I help you with today?" Julie asked.

"We want to stop an important painting being lent abroad so we are planning to issue a notice prohibiting it. The painting is in The Walker Art Gallery in Liverpool and the Metropolitan Museum of Art in New York wants to show it alongside an Albrecht Durer woodcut."

"What's the painting called?" asked Julie.

"The Rider on the Red Horse by George Frederic Watts. It is an oil on canvas painted around 1882 and bequeathed to The Walker Gallery by James Smith in 1923. I've got a picture of it here."

Julie looked at the picture and went quiet for a moment. Something had just tweaked a nerve and a memory that she couldn't recall. It couldn't have been the painting as she had never heard of it or the Walker Gallery before. "Do what you think is right", she said and the meeting finished. "It must be something to do with horses," she thought. Perhaps subconsciously I think that I should get one."

She called in her diary secretary, Nancy Wilson. "What do I have planned for the rest of the day?"

"You are meeting King George at Clarence House after lunch at 2pm. You are then in the Commons for the passing of the latest Bill on land acquisitions and new towns, then there is a reception at the American Embassy for the new Ambassador to the UK. That starts at 5.30pm and should be finished by 7pm. Ralph is invited."

"Can you get a message to Ralph that it would be nice to travel together if he is free? Can you also find out if there is a private dining room available at Hathaways in Covent Garden?"

Half an hour later Nancy returned. "Ralph is free but just needs to know the dress code. He was meeting Julian later but he said that he can cancel if you like."

"Why not ask Julian if he wants to join us at the restaurant. He is in the middle of a messy divorce and might like some company and would be disappointed to be left on his own."

With the days arrangements sorted out, Julie went upstairs to get changed for her meeting with the King. On the drive to Clarence House, she wondered what George would like to discuss this afternoon. He had grown in his role and was a popular figurehead. Now that he had lost his ancient and bystander role in the governing procedures he had developed his interests along the lines of his grandfather, Charles. He was a keen conservationist and spoke freely in world forums on climate change and the need for establishing forests in Europe, including the UK. He had personally overseen the planting of 200,000 trees for each year of his reign.

The car drew up at Clarence House and George was there to meet her. "Good afternoon, Prime Minister."

"Good afternoon Your Majesty," Julie replied and they shook hands warmly.

Julie followed George through into the main drawing room and took up the offer of a cup of Earl Grey tea. On the wall opposite the Louis XV chair upon which she sat was a large painting of a man on a black horse carrying a balance scale. George saw that she was studying it. "Do you like it? It's supposed to symbolise famine but I can't see it. I think that it was bought as a sort of joke as it was hung in the dining room when I came to live here. I thought that it looked better in here and would make my dinner guests feel less uncomfortable. You look like you've seen a ghost. Is everything alright?"

"I seem to be haunted today by men on horses. Have you ever had a thought niggling at the back of your mind but you just can't seem to shake it off or remember what it was? Oh well, it can't be important, so what would you like to talk about?"

"No surprise it is forests. We continually beat up developing countries about tree felling yet they are only doing what the whole of Europe has done since the Middle Ages. I want to reverse the trend faster than is currently undertaken. I have persuaded the German Chancellor and the French President to devote 2%, just 2% of their National Parks to tree planting. Can we do the same?"

"I have no idea what that means, but I do have the people to find out. I probably couldn't promise to give up 2% of each park, but I feel confident that 2% of the total is not a big ask. Is there anything else on your wish list?"

"As a matter of fact there is. I would like to endow a college in Lancashire as part of Lancaster University. As you know, all reigning monarchs are also the Duke of Lancaster, so I think it's an appropriate place. I want to call it Duke's College and I want it to specialise in degrees associated with green energy. The funds will come from the Duchy of Cornwall."

"What a lovely idea. Let me know what help you need and I will get Gillian Weston, my Education Minister to contact your private secretary. Your biggest difficulties might be finding a suitable site and getting the planning permissions sorted out."

"The land is mine so that's done but help with planning would be much appreciated. Thank you Prime Minister." George stood and signalled that the meeting was at an end. On the way back to Downing Street, she thought how fortuitous it had been for her to have a monarch so switched on to the important matters of the realm.

She made a call from the car and asked Gillian Weston to contact the King's Private Secretary. "He will know what it's about and is expecting your call." As she entered 11 Downing Street and went upstairs to her flat, she saw on the bed her clothes laid out for the reception. Ralph was already there in the adjoining room sitting on the settee reading a magazine. They hugged and kissed. "How was the King?"

"Regal and serious," Julie replied while pulling off the small tie at the neck of her blouse. Conversations between the Prime Minister and the monarch were private and protocol maintained that the contents wouldn't be repeated. Ralph as an experienced journalist knew this so he didn't press for further information. "After I'm changed I'll be off to the Commons and will be back no later than five to spruce up. Please have your best bib and tucker on as this is a formal one."

"Who is the Ambassador, anyone famous? Could he or she be a movie star acquaintance of the last President's husband?"

"Sadly not. Her name is Joan Crawford, same as the famous actress, but apparently, that is where the similarity ends. She is a graduate of Harvard and before this appointment she was Ambassador to the United Nations. She met King George a couple of days ago so he won't be there, although he was invited. Don't be nervous thinking that we will be the most important people in the room. Haha."

She kissed his head as she passed the sofa and made her way downstairs to the waiting car. Next stop the House of Commons. The Bill on land acquisitions was needed as there had been a successful challenge in the High Court by the National Trust concerning an endowment of land that couldn't be compulsorily purchased under existing laws. The land was crucial for the new town adjacent to a Trust property in Staffordshire. The Bill passed and at the same time the Bill establishing the new town did also. All nicely wrapped up with National Endeavour's large majority pulling together without any rebellions. The Chamber of the House of Commons emptied even though business continued with a statement from Chloe, the Minister for Culture, Media and Sport.

Julie returned to Downing Street to get ready for the reception. The US Embassy had moved to Nine Elms from Grosvenor Square but she was headed to the Ambassador's official residence at Winfield House in Regents Park. She and Ralph arrived promptly at 5.30pm and were welcomed by Joan Crawford. They moved through to the main reception room and saw some familiar faces from her own diplomatic service. She sidled up to Brian Strong. "What's a nice man like you doing in a place like this?" she asked.

"I'm only nice in a place like this. They have good champagne and that helps."

She ignored this remark and addressed Mary, Brian's wife. "Hi Mary. This is Ralph. How do you live with Brian?"

"Hello Ralph. We have a big house and a very big garden. We rarely occupy the same space."

"You're right. I need a big house. The flat in London is cosy but not spacious."

Julie and Ralph mingled with the other guests and looked around the beautiful rooms. They both spotted Sir David Beckham and Tom Cruise talking to each other by the fireplace. They all congregated in a large showy room and after a brief welcoming speech of introduction by Joan Crawford, they were heading for the exit, shaking hands with a lot of people on the way.

"Where is Julian meeting us?" she asked.

"At the restaurant. Your diary secretary has asked Hathaways to show him into the private room to wait for us. Depending on the traffic, we should get there in ten minutes."

Julian was waiting outside when the two black cars pulled into Maiden Lane in Covent Garden. The security men got out, looked up and down the lane and then opened the rear doors. The group went up the stairs to the private room on the first floor. A not very plausible rumour had it, that this was a room that the deceased Prince Philip, Duke of Edinburgh, used to meet his mates and some of their lady friends on a regular basis. Naturally, the restaurant had always been discreet about this rumour. Julian and Ralph were relieved of their phones.

Julie, Ralph and Julian went into the room and security took its place outside the door. Every waiter was frisked on the way in. After they had ordered the food; Julie the fish of the day with salad and Ralph and Julian steaks with some good red wine; they were left alone. The wine arrived with the food looking to follow shortly afterwards.

Ralph got up and said, "I must go to the loo. The champagne from the reception really goes through me."

"It's the quantity that does that," laughed Julie.

The waiter entered as Ralph left and brought the fish cutlery for Julie and a steak knife for each of the men. He poured the water and left Julie and Julian alone in the room.

Julian stood up and approached Julie. "I've wanted to be alone with you for so long. I want you to know how much I think that I'm in love with you."

Julie was startled and said, "Don't be silly Julian. You know that I am with Ralph."

"Yes, but you don't love him. I left my wife because I wanted you. I have given up everything for you. Please come away with me. I've bought a boat and we can sail away together."

"Don't be ridiculous. I could never go anywhere with you."

Julie rose from her chair and turned towards the door. Above the door was a painting of a man on a pale horse and she remembered what had been worrying her all day about these figures on horses. According to the Revelation of St. John they were the Four Horsemen of the Apocalypse and she was looking at the last one. The steak knife plunged into her neck from behind and she called out "You are death" and she pointed upwards. The knife came out and plunged in again. Her screams alerted the men outside who burst into the room and wrestled a bloodied Julian to the ground.

A frantic scene followed with a fight between Julian and a guard who disarmed him with a blow to the face. The other guard was trying to stem the blood coming from the severed artery in Julie's neck while calling out to a returning Ralph. "My emergency alarm has called for the ambulance".

The medics arrived within ten minutes but by that time Julie was lifeless. They pronounced death and covered her body with the tablecloth.

Within minutes, the arms of state and the heavy hand of security took charge. The Executive Team were summoned to Downing Street. Maiden Lane was blocked off at both ends and all of the many restaurants and bars were emptied with as little fuss as possible. A large black van arrived with a doctor, nurse and a coffin that was moved up the stairs, a few minutes after Julian had descended in handcuffs attached to a large policeman in the opposite direction. Ralph was sitting in the room with Julie's body, silently weeping with his head in his hands. As the coffin entered, he was moved seamlessly to another room.

The police took charge of the crime scene and a forensic team worked diligently and with precision.

The emphasis now transferred to Downing Street where the Executive Team were being briefed on events. They were all in a state of shock and Sir Edward Grey had tears streaming down his cheeks. They were sitting in stunned silence. Andrea Patel was the first to speak. "We have to issue a Press Release. I will call in Robin, the senior press officer, he's just arrived."

Robin Sheriff came into the room and said "My God, what has happened? I have never seen such a group as unhappy as this." The news, as they had it, was told to him and he was sent away to quickly produce a statement for the Press. He came back ten minutes later and distributed a draft to each of them. It said, "Tonight at 8.15pm, in a restaurant in central London, Prime Minister Julie Carter was attacked by a friend and has died from her injuries. A man has been detained at the scene and is helping police with their enquiries. Further information will be released during the evening."

The news hit the press and television channels and all broadcasts were halted and replaced with news programming and sombre music. The phones into Downing Street were ringing off their hooks but remained unanswered.

"What do we do now?" asked Hillary Armstrong Lewis. "Is there a written procedure on what we do? Surely, there is a Contingency Plan."

Sir Edward Grey left the room and returned accompanied by a senior civil servant in Downing Street, Jeremy Forbes. "We do have a Contingency Plan. It was drawn up following the only other time that a Prime Minister of this country has been killed in office. It happened on

11th May 1812 when Spencer Perceval was shot dead in the lobby of the House of Commons by John Bellingham, a merchant from Liverpool. Bellingham was hanged in Newgate Prison a week later. This is going to be a long night and there is much to be arranged. The Civil Service will put forward a programme of events that should take place for your scrutiny. The only thing that you have to do in this room is to pick a temporary successor until your party agrees on a new leader."

Jeremy Forbes left the meeting and three of the team broke down and openly cried into their hands.

King George VII appeared on television during the 10pm news bulletin and declared a period of official mourning until Julie was laid to rest.

Chapter 39

The Aftermath

16th – 23rd October 2037

At just after midnight the coffin containing Julie Carter's body was received at the Royal London Hospital and the cause of death was confirmed. A Certificate was issued and later that day her remains were released to Skinner & Daughter, funeral directors in Whitechapel for the embalming of the body.

The news of Julie's murder travelled across the country like a thunderbolt. Everywhere there were sharp intakes of breath and hands across gaping mouths. It was as though the whole of the United Kingdom's heart missed a beat. People woke their friends and relatives and the phone networks almost collapsed under the weight of calls. The National Grid reached its capacity as televisions and radios were switched on quickly accompanied by kettles and coffee machines.

All night petrol stations, supermarkets, mini-markets and every type of convenience store were inundated with people buying flowers until the stocks ran out. Within an hour of the news of the murder being broadcast a carpet of flowers appeared in front of the Actor's Church, St. Paul's in Covent Garden. The Archbishops of Canterbury and York announced that books of condolences were now open, even at this time of the early morning, in all cathedrals and in a lot of Parish churches throughout the country. Every professional football team in England, Scotland, Wales and Northern Ireland immediately opened books of condolences and senior hardened players were pictured weeping in the club rooms.

Countries around the world went to bed or awoke hearing the news. Even countries not friendly disposed to the UK sent messages of condolences and their ambassadors, diplomats and citizens went to their main squares to lay flowers. The outpouring of grief for a remarkable woman, and the manner of her passing, affected every person who had heard of her and her work.

Julie's son Jamie and her mother Margaret were at the flat in Downing Street being consoled by professional counsellors. Inevitably, questions started to be asked about how the Prime Minister was left alone in a room with a man who turned out to be a homicidal maniac. The Head of Security resigned before noon the following day.

The Executive Team, still in shock and like a flock of sheep praying for the collie to come and give them direction, turned as one to Sir Edward Grey. Indira Singh was the first to speak. "What do we do?"

Sir Edward said, "We do what Julie has shown us. We take responsibility and we deal with this in a professional and compassionate way. We must first agree between us a temporary leader. The country is looking to us for guidance and decision."

Hillary leant forward in her chair and said, "My vote is for you Edward. You knew her better than all of us and so you will have a better idea what to do until we can make a rational decision at another time." The others quickly agreed and Sir Edward Grey became Acting Prime Minister.

"Our priorities must be to get through the next week and show the country and the world that we are able to carry on in adversity. Please get the person who arranged the late Queen Elizabeth's funeral to come and meet with us. We must prepare ourselves for a great outpouring of grief that will not be too different from when Diana, Princess of Wales passed. As soon as I am finished here, I will go and see the King at Clarence House and on my return I will address the media out front in the road. Please arrange for the lectern and for someone to prepare a short statement."

At 2am, Sir Edward Grey arranged for a message to be sent to King George requesting an audience, which was promptly granted. A black car sped him to Clarence House. The King opened the door to him in a silk dressing gown and clasped him warmly in a hug, tears falling down both of their faces.

"A dreadful, really dreadful thing to happen. How was she alone with this person?"

"A full enquiry is under way and all of these questions will be answered. In the meantime, the governing of the country must go on. Do we have your blessing for a lying in state in Westminster Hall or The Guildhall with a funeral at St. Paul's Cathedral?"

"Of course, you have it, whatever you decide. The Guildhall would be better for the service and is more accessible than Westminster Hall, but that's not for me to say. Wherever you choose, my brother, my sister and I will stand vigil for one hour at the coffin's side."

"Thank you sir," said Sir Edward. "That offer is very well received. She was such a remarkable woman."

"I know. The whole country knows. Please keep me informed of the arrangements. I have already asked for my diary to be cleared for the next week as I would suggest a period of mourning until after the interment."

At 3.15am, Sir Edward returned to Downing Street and on the way into No. 10 he was handed a statement by a sobbing member of staff. He read the contents, a little smudged by tears. He composed himself and went out to a full Downing Street, lit by photographers' lamps, the gathered press in total silence. He read out a short statement. "Tonight, the country has heard of the dreadful news that our beloved Prime Minister, Julie Carter, was stabbed to death allegedly by a friend of her partner. A man will appear in court later today charged with her murder. The country will take some time to cope with this tragic event and news of the necessary arrangements will be released over the next two days. Books of condolences have been opened throughout the country and already queues are forming to pay their respects. Our thoughts at this time must be with Julie Carter's son Jamie, her mother Margaret, her extended family and her friends. In truth, we all have been her friend." At this point, Sir Edward broke down in tears and weeping uncontrollably he went back through the black door.

In a police station in the West End of London Julian Street, accompanied by a duty solicitor, was charged with the murder of Julie Carter. He had offered no defence other than it was a crime of passion.

Edward William Fitzalan-Howard, 18th Duke of Norfolk and Earl Marshal was in charge of the arrangements for the funerals of the late Queen Elizabeth and King Charles as well as the coronations of Charles III, William V and George VII. At 10am the next morning the Duke, accompanied by his son the Earl of Arundel, met with Sir Edward Grey in 10 Downing Street.

They quickly agreed to the government's request to arrange the funeral of the Prime Minister. It was agreed that there would be a lying in state at The Guildhall before a Funeral Memorial Service in St Paul's Cathedral. Sir Edward Grey said that he needed to discuss the family arrangements with Jamie Carter and his grandmother, but he felt sure that they would want a local burial afterwards.

Sir Edward, not for the first time in the last ten hours, climbed the stairs of No. 11 Downing Street to talk to Jamie and Margaret Carter. He had first spoken briefly with them the night before and explained all that he knew, which was not much. Jamie had grown up and was now fifteen years old and was sitting quietly on the sofa holding his grandmother's hand. He was obviously a great comfort to her.

Sir Edward started awkwardly. "I'm sorry to intrude at this appalling time, but I have to agree some arrangements with both of you. The government is proposing that there will be a week of national mourning with a lying-in-state in the Main Hall of The Guildhall in Basinghall Street in the City of London. The Guildhall will give the public the opportunity to file past the coffin. The King has already volunteered to stand vigil with his brother and sister for one hour. I was wondering Jamie whether you would like to stand with them, one of you at each corner."

"I would like that very much. Let me know what I have to do and when."

"On Friday 23rd October there will be a Memorial funeral service in St Paul's Cathedral. Naturally, you will both be in the front row. We would expect the cathedral to be full with people from home and abroad. This is a very big occasion so if you want to invite your friends and family that knew your mother, please give me a list in the next couple of days. The question that I have to ask you both and I'm very sorry for it, but do you know where you want your mother to be buried?"

Margaret now spoke, tissue firmly grasped in hand. "Julie was not overtly religious but there is a local church that she would visit, not for religious purposes, but to see the grave of Agatha Christie. Growing up she was very fond of her books and it was nice that she lived and was buried in a church not too far away from our house. Can we make arrangements for a burial at St Mary's Church in Cholsey?"

"Yes of course," Edward said. "Please forgive me for leaving but I have so many matters to arrange."

Sir Edward came down the internal stairs and entered 10 Downing Street. The mood was sombre and many of the staff were clearly suffering from frequent tearful episodes. He sat at his desk and saw a number of yellow post-it notes with messages to call it seemed most of the world's leaders. He picked up the phone and said, "Please get me the President of the United States." He spoke briefly to President Saskowan, who sincerely offered her personal commiserations and that of her people. The next fifteen phone calls were all similar in nature and all of the messages, he could tell, were heartfelt.

He grabbed a sandwich and after eating it and a banana, his car took him on the short journey to Parliament, where he was to make a statement. He entered the temporary Commons Chamber and at 2pm, the Speaker read out a personal statement of commemoration but found it difficult to finish it through his tears. Sir Edward Grey rose and addressed a silent packed house.

"I stand here today as the Acting Prime Minister in the worst circumstances that any of us could wish. Our beloved Prime Minister was cruelly taken from us last night. There will be a great deal of time for every member of any party, who wishes to do so, to stand in this house and make a personal statement. After I have given you the practical arrangements I will make mine.

"The country will today start a period of mourning that will conclude with the Prime Minister's funeral. There will be a lying in state in the Grand Hall of the Guildhall from tomorrow at 10am and the public are invited to pay their respects and file past the coffin. A guard of honour will stand vigil for every hour and the Hall will not close. The funeral will take place on Friday 23rd October at noon in St Paul's Cathedral and the Archbishop of Canterbury will take the service. After the funeral, the coffin will be transported by road to Paddington Station for a short journey to Cholsey Station. The coffin will be taken for a private family burial to St Mary's Church in Cholsey. I would now like to make my own personal statement.

"I knew from the very first time this lady stood up to speak that she was a gifted person of great character. She had all of the best qualities to lead this nation. She was charismatic, but matched this with the understanding of what had to be done and why. She completely changed the nature of politics in this country, and by example, many countries around the world. She had vision, perception and understood how problems could be fixed. She was a new type of politician, neither left nor right but committed to the centre ground with common sense. She formed a party that within one Parliament became the governing party of this great nation. She was my friend and I respected her. She was my leader and I followed her. She was my example and I never questioned her judgement. She was a great lady and I shall miss her." With that Sir Edward dissolved into tears, sat down and had to be comforted.

The leaders of the opposition parties took their turns and each was heard in silence. After them, the MPs were called and the process went on deep into the afternoon and evening.

What about Ralph? An important person but with no status in the planning and without consideration. He was Julie's boyfriend but they had not shared a commitment. He may have lived on and off in the flat upstairs but he also had his own flat. He wasn't subject to security on his own as he was just a private citizen. He would be invited to the family funeral in Cholsey, but would then fade into the distance with the memories that had been, but not the future that he wanted. A year later he would write a best-selling book about his time with Julie Carter.

Julian Street appeared later in the afternoon at Marylebone Magistrates Court. He confirmed his name, that he had no official abode and was not asked to enter a plea. He was remanded in custody to appear again in a week's time. After another appearance he was remanded in custody and he was ordered to appear for the submission of a formal plea and trial at The Old Bailey in January. At every court appearance he was met with great hostility and crowds attacking the police vehicle. He was obviously the most hated person in the country and was held in solitary confinement on remand after being attacked on three consecutive days in prison.

The lying in state at the Guildhall was attended by great crowds, who queued for hours to file past the coffin. On Tuesday 20th October at 12 noon, King George VII arrived with a Guards escort and stood at the front left hand corner of the bier on which the coffin was placed. He was immediately joined by his sister Princess Charlotte, his brother Louis, Duke of Oxford and Jamie Carter at the front corner on the right. The four of them stood in silence for 1 hour as the crowds filed past. At 1pm, they were relieved by four members of the Irish Guards.

The government announced that on the day of the funeral all businesses would be closed.

At 8am, on Friday 23rd October the gates of the Guildhall were closed so that the final preparations for the funeral could take place. At St Paul's Cathedral, crowds were gathering and world leaders, diplomats, British politicians and the great and the good took their seats progressively as the minutes ticked by. At 11.30am a gun carriage carrying the coffin left the Guildhall in Basinghall Street and went slowly past crowds throwing flowers and on its way to St Pauls Cathedral arriving there at 11.45am. The procession was led on foot by Jamie, Sir Edward Grey, the six members of the Executive Team and a large contingent of Horse Cavalry and Guards in their bearskins. At the Cathedral, six guards carried the coffin inside and placed it on a bier.

The service was taken by the Archbishop of Canterbury with readings by King George, Sir Edward Grey, the First Ministers of Scotland and Wales and the Leader of the Northern Ireland Assembly. All of the past Prime Ministers stood solemnly together, witnessing the event that they all had secretly feared.

The coffin was later transported by car to Paddington Station and on to Cholsey. The private ceremony was attended by the family and Ralph, with a great number of police and the Oxfordshire National Guard keeping the large crowd beyond the church perimeter.

After a short procedural contest, National Endeavour elected Andrea Patel as the new party leader and Prime Minister and she carried on with the work started by Julie Carter. However, the party lost ground as the public no longer had a charismatic leader to look up to. Over time politics returned to the normal of too much talking and not enough doing.

Julian Street pleaded not guilty at his trial and brought forward the defence of a crime of passion accusing Julie of having led him on. The jury took 60 minutes to reach a guilty verdict on all counts and he was sentenced to life imprisonment with a minimum term of 40 years. The legal purists commented that there was no way that he could have had a fair trial. It was impossible to find twelve people for a jury that was impartial.

Four years after her assassination, a statue of Julie Carter was unveiled in Parliament Square. The Palace of Westminster never opened as a Parliament again but as The National Museum of The United Kingdom. The terrace by the Thames was named the Julie

Carter Terrace in honour of her. Work had already begun on a new Parliament building in York.

Politics like life, taxes, eating, drinking and breathing carried on. But they never saw the likes of a Julie Carter again.

The End

About the Author

My big passion is blues music and guitar based rock music in all of its forms. From an early age I was a follower of Bob Dylan.

I like to create stories that have twists in the plot and leave the reader with a challenge to work out the conclusion. Throughout the books there are references to rock music and other cultural points. I like a good laugh and I will drop in occasional jokes and amusing anecdotes. I like to educate so in my books I take historical material and weave it into a modern story.

My first novel "Death of a Pieman" introduced Detective Inspector Ted Stone, a barely competent policeman who solves murders with the aid of his psychologist wife.

The second novel is called "National Endeavour" and was written out of deep frustration with politicians of all parties. It proposes the need for a benevolent dictator who can and does solve all of the country's problems.

The third novel, currently being written, is about a murder that takes place on an ocean liner and is solved 56 years later. It is another Detective Inspector Ted Stone novel.